I0646484

"Sunshine is the best disinfectant."

**U.S. Supreme Court Justice
Louis Brandeis**

SWITZERLAND SECRECY LAW

THE SWISS FEDERAL ACT ON BANKS AND SAVINGS BANKS
SR 952.0

ARTICLE 47

1   Any person who intentionally commits any of the following acts shall be punished with imprisonment of up to three years or a fine:

     a.   discloses a secret that has been entrusted to them in their capacity as an officer, employee, agent, or liquidator of a bank or a person referred to in Article 1b, or as an officer or employee of an auditing company, or that they have become aware of in this capacity;

     b.   attempts to induce such a breach of professional secrecy;

     c.   discloses to other persons a secret disclosed to them under letter a or exploits it for themselves or another person.

1bis   Anyone who obtains a financial advantage for themselves or another person through an act under paragraph 1 letter a or c shall be punished with imprisonment of up to five years or a fine.

2   Anyone who acts negligently shall be punished with a fine of up to 250,000 Swiss francs.

UNITED STATES RICO LAW

18 U.S. CODE CHAPTER 96 PART I – RACKETEER INFLUENCED AND CORRUPT ORGANIZATIONS

§ 1962 - Prohibited activities

     (a)   It shall be unlawful for any person who has received any income derived, directly or indirectly, from a pattern of racketeering activity or through collection of an unlawful debt in which such person has participated as a principal within the meaning of section 2, title 18, United States Code, to use or invest, directly or indirectly, any part of such income, or the proceeds of such income, in acquisition of any interest in, or the establishment or operation of, any enterprise which is engaged in, or the activities of which affect, interstate or foreign commerce...

     (b)   It shall be unlawful for any person through a pattern of racketeering activity or through collection of an unlawful debt to acquire or maintain, directly or indirectly, any interest in or control of any enterprise which is engaged in, or the activities of which affect, interstate or foreign commerce.

     (c)   It shall be unlawful for any person employed by or associated with any enterprise engaged in, or the activities of which affect, interstate or foreign commerce, to conduct or participate, directly or indirectly, in the conduct of such enterprise's affairs through a pattern of racketeering activity or collection of unlawful debt.

     (d)   It shall be unlawful for any person to conspire to violate any of the provisions of subsection (a), (b), or (c) of this section.

THE CYBER SANCTION

NICHOLAS GRETENER

A
LawForce
NOVEL

qualitas
Qualitas Publishing

QUALITAS PUBLISHING

Copyright © 2026 by Nicholas Gretener

All rights reserved.

Part of the *LawForce* Series

Qualitas Publishing
195 Cardiff Drive N.W.
Calgary, Alberta, Canada
T2K 1S1

First mass-market edition: January, 2026

Qualitas Publishing Mass-Market
ISBN 10: 1-897093-16-0
ISBN 13: 978-1-897093-16-0

www.nicholasgretener.com

TO
REGULA RIVELLA
AND
WHISTLEBLOWERS
AROUND THE WORLD

THE CYBER SANCTION

1

BERNESE OBERLAND

SWITZERLAND

"Falling!" Shane yelled, hoping against hope that Sepp could hear him. *Damn!* His last ice screw was twenty feet below, which meant he was free-falling forty feet. It would be a severe jolt for Sepp, although he had a solid belay stance. Shane just prayed that the ice screw would hold—if not, he'd fall to the next level of protection: a somewhat shaky piton. And if that didn't hold...

His mental calculations were rudely interrupted as the rope snapped tight, and he found himself hanging upside down, staring into the abyss. It was a 3,000-foot drop, visible to any tourists watching from the Hotel Bellevue des Alpes terrace at Kleine Scheidegg.

The Eiger North Face loomed above them like the prow of a ship, a formidable black mass streaked with ribbons of old ice. They were two-thirds of the way up the classic Heckmair route, at the frozen Waterfall Chimney of the Ramp. In this narrowing rib where every movement was crucial, Shane's Terrordactyl ice axe slipped on the verglas, and he was plunged into the void.

The sound of his fall echoed through the amphitheater like the crack of a rifle shot. His shout, brief and swallowed by the wind, was followed by a sickening thud.

"Steve!" called Sepp. He was belaying from a patch of iron-grey limestone near the Death Bivouac, anchored in a shallow crack system with a set of cams and a driven piton. Hearing the scream, he braced himself just in time as the rope went taut. It jerked him six inches off his stance, but somehow he held on.

"Steve, you've got to dig in if you can. I can't hang on much longer."

Shane dangled, groaning. He managed to twist himself upright again, but his right arm hung at an unnatural angle—his shoulder was dislocated or worse.

"Talk to me, Steve!"

"Shoulder's... gone. I think it's ruptured. I can't use it," Shane gasped, his voice thin with shock.

They were in a tight spot—too high to retreat the way they had come, but not high enough to summit. Though they were more than halfway up, they still had to navigate the Traverse of the Gods, the White Spider Icefield, and the Exit Cracks—impossible terrain with only one functional arm. The wind was picking up; a change in the weather looked imminent. Storms brewed quickly on the Eiger.

Shane felt relieved when he heard Sepp agree. The shout came from above: "Okay. We're going down. You remember the tunnel window? Stollenloch. We'll go for that."

Shane nodded through clenched teeth. He knew the story—everyone who set foot on the Nordwand was aware of the door. It was a hole in the mountain, carved by engineers a century ago to dump the waste rock from the main tunnel excavation. For some, it was salvation; for others, a bitter retreat.

Sepp clipped into the system and began lowering Shane to a thin ledge, then rappelled down after him. When he reached Shane, he made his usual cryptic comment, typical of a Swiss mountain guide: "You outran your pro, my friend."

Shane shook his head. "I didn't have many options to place protection; that chimney was full of rotten rock."

Sepp just grunted as he rigged the next rappel. The cold bit deeper now, psychological as much as physical. They had hoped for a clean ascent; now, they were trying to survive.

The Eiger North Face—the Mordwand, or Murder Wall—had claimed over sixty lives since climbers first dared to attempt it in the 1930s. Rising over a mile high from base to summit, the wall was a patchwork of ice fields, shattered limestone, and hanging seracs. Legends were born and buried here.

In 1936, four climbers—Toni Kurz, Andreas Hinterstoisser, Willy Angerer, and Edi Rainer—attempted the first ascent. A storm trapped them, and one by one, they fell, froze, or were crushed. Kurz's final words, "Ich kann nicht mehr"—I can't go on—were spoken within sight of his rescuers, suspended from a rope, just an agonizing few feet too short.

Since then, the face had become a proving ground. Climbers from all over the world came to test themselves against the North Face. Some found glory; others found death. The mountain didn't care.

The descent began with a series of short rappels. The rope snagged frequently on the jagged rock. Sepp moved methodically, keeping tension on the rope as Shane, groaning with pain, anchored himself with one good arm. Blood had seeped through the torn sleeve of his jacket. He didn't want to think about nerve damage or internal bleeding.

Snow began to fall—not heavily, but enough to slick the rock and blur the ledges below. Visibility dropped. They had maybe three hours of daylight left.

"How close to the door?" Shane asked, his voice slurring slightly.

"Maybe 300 meters below. If we trend west to the edge of the Second Icefield, above the Rote Fluh, we should be able to rappel down and intersect the ledge that leads to it."

They angled across a tilted slab, making a sideways rappel across exposed terrain. Below them, the face plunged to the scree field, which had seen its share of bodies tumbling from above.

Shane could feel the mountain pressing in now. The Eiger wasn't just a climb—it was a character in its own right. A villain, sometimes. Indifferent, always.

By the time they reached the end of the long rappel down the Rote Fluh, Shane could barely move. Sepp slung an arm around him and half-dragged him across the narrow band of rock. One slip here could send them penduluming into the void. They didn't talk anymore. Every breath crystallized in the air. Every movement was focused on survival.

Finally, the ledge widened.

"There!" Sepp pointed.

Carved into the wall, half-hidden by a jutting rock buttress, was the Stollenloch—the legendary tunnel door. It was less dramatic than Shane had expected—just a black square set into the stone, like a forgotten cellar door. But to them, it represented everything. Sepp reached it first, dropping the coil of rope with shaking hands. He swung his axe and knocked on the metal hatch.

Nothing.

He knocked again, harder this time. Then once more. Finally, after several minutes that stretched like hours, there was a creak. A faint voice emerged. The door opened inward, revealing a worker in fluorescent gear, eyes wide. Sepp addressed the stunned man in his native Swiss German.

"Grüezi, chönd mir inne cho?" (Hi, can we come in?)

"Himmel, Herr Gott und Verdammt nomol. Ihr chömmed vo de Nordwand?" (Expletive and Expletive. You're coming from the North Face?)

"Jo, ich gseh Si sind au it Schul gange." (Yes, I see you went to school too.)

"We need help," Sepp said. "My friend is in bad shape."

The man stepped aside, already reaching for his radio. Warm, dry air spilled from the tunnel as Shane collapsed inside.

* * *

Later, wrapped in foil blankets and sipping from steaming mugs, they sat in the service tunnel. The air smelled of oil and electricity. A second technician from the Jungfrau Railway gently patted Shane's shoulder, wincing in sympathy.

"You're lucky. That storm up top has gotten worse. If you hadn't found the door..."

Shane nodded. "We knew about it. We planned for contingencies."

"Smart," the technician said. "Most people only think about going up. You boys thought about getting back down."

Through a grated window, Shane could see the wall outside, now obscured by driving snow. The Eiger had shut its teeth again. Suddenly, the loud ringtone of his phone—the theme song from *The Good, the Bad, and the Ugly*—jolted him. How had he gotten reception up here? He knew Swisscom boasted ninety-nine percent coverage nationwide, but up here? Even near the airy opening, it was hard to believe. He grabbed the phone.

"Shane."

"Mr. Shane, it's been a while. I trust you are staying out of trouble."

Shane smiled at the slight British accent. It had been a while. It was good to hear from Jonathan Hendrix again. With the creation of Law-Force, Hendrix was somewhat his boss, and it had been a few months since their last assignment.

"Well, trouble just found me, Jon. My shoulder's going to need a little TLC in the next few weeks. Nothing that affects my legal skills, though. Is there anything on the horizon?"

"I'm not sure, but I think we may have something. I need to talk to you in person as soon as possible. Where are you now?"

"In Switzerland, but I can be in D.C. in a week, if that works."

"Yes, take care of that shoulder. Get here as soon as you can. This thing is moving fast."

"Can you give me an idea of what it's about?"

"I'll fill you in when we meet. Let's just say your Swiss ancestry will come in handy. We're not dealing with oil this time, but good old cash and banks. Trouble is brewing in Beantown. See you soon."

Shane grunted at the flash of pain as he put the phone away. Sepp looked at him quizzically.

"Well, Sepp, old buddy, I think I'm done dragging your ass up mountains for a while. My real job needs me."

Sepp nodded. "Good for you and your family. Instead of climbing, maybe consider knitting as a hobby. You're no Spiderman."

* * *

Shane's evacuation came by cogwheel rail. The Jungfrau Railway, which burrowed through the Eiger to reach the summit station at Jung-fraujoch—the "Top of Europe"—had been a curiosity since its construction in the early twentieth century. While the train no longer stopped at Eigerwand—North Face—Station, it did stop at the large picture windows of Eismeer—Sea of Ice—Station inside the Mönch, wowing tourists with a view of the glacier usually reserved for experienced alpinists.

As the train rattled downward through the darkness, Shane reflected on those who'd come before him. Over the years, the Stollenloch and the railway line behind the face had played a crucial role in rescue attempts, with special trains delivering rescue teams to the little hole in the wall or climbers themselves collapsing in, relieved that, unlike any mountain anywhere else, there was this little wooden door in the wall that could lead them out of danger.

The names of climbers who had used the railway and the Stollenloch as an access/exit point or to save themselves or their friends were a who's who of mountaineering greats, including Chris Bonington, Don Whillans, Toni Hiebeler, and John Harlin. Even Clint Eastwood made his escape through the Stollenloch in *The Eiger Sanction*. Now, it was Shane's turn.

* * *

The next day, in his apartment at Chalet Bergkristall in Wengen, Shane's arm was in a sling. The doctors had said he suffered a low-grade rupture of the rotator cuff. Thankfully, no surgery was required, but recovery would still take time.

Val came over to refill his mug. They sat in silence, sipping coffee and staring at the wall of windows that looked toward the Jungfrau, the summit obscured by clouds.

"I still see it when I close my eyes," Shane said quietly. "That moment—the fall. The sound. I thought that was it."

Val nodded. "Well, you made it home, babe; that's what counts. I'm glad you're meeting with Jonathan again. LawForce may have its dangers, but I sure prefer that to losing you to a rock pile."

2

YANQI LAKE

CHINA

The drive to Yanqi Lake felt like a journey into another world. Leaving the hustle and bustle of Beijing behind, the road wound north through the emerald hills of Huairou, climbing gently past pine forests and terraced slopes. Security outposts began to appear miles before reaching the lake—plainclothes guards at rest stations, drone sensors cleverly concealed in roadside lamps, and silent police cruisers that seemed to materialize from nowhere.

Finally, the road crested a ridge, revealing the Yanqi Lake Hotel across the still, mirror-like waters. The hotel complex was on an island connected by a single causeway, with its architecture blending modern minimalism and imperial symbolism: curved roofs resembling dragon scales and mirrored glass reflecting the surrounding Yanshan Mountains. To the untrained eye, it appeared to be a luxurious eco-resort; for those in power, it was a fortress of steel.

The hotel's infrastructure was built to host the 2014 APEC Summit, and its origins were evident—conference halls with Faraday-shielded walls, subterranean communication suites, and an entire floor of guest villas reserved for high-level delegations. The People's Liberation Army (PLA) maintained a discreet perimeter security network, and the lake itself acted as a natural moat; only the causeway and a single helicopter pad provided access.

Inside, the corridors were lined with cameras disguised as calligraphy medallions and biometric locks programmed to shifting encryption protocols. The staff, selected from elite service academies, were vetted to military standards and trained in complete discretion.

Gao Feng felt a mix of nerves and intrigue. His eyes blinked rapidly, a nervous tic he'd had since childhood. He knew he was about to meet a high-ranking party official but had no idea who that might be. His stomach tightened with the weight of the unknown. This was no ordinary assignment.

As they pulled up to the hotel, two valets approached—one opening the rear door, while the other rendered a salute. Feng stepped out into the cool air, which carried a faint aroma of damp earth. He had been thoroughly briefed on the assignment—more than that, he had been sworn to secrecy.

He was led into a large conference room. In the center stood a small table with a steaming pot of tea and two glasses. Flanking the table were two high-backed chairs. It became apparent this was to be a one-on-one meeting.

After five minutes, Feng heard the door open and rose expectantly. Two guards flanked a tall, thin man who entered quietly. Feng gasped. It couldn't be. But it was—Chairman Liang Ze himself. Feng felt weak in the knees.

Chairman Liang moved with the compact, efficient gestures of someone accustomed to command. He wore a plain dark jacket with a closed collar, and his hair was trimmed short, the tiny flecks of silver at his temples discreetly signifying his age. He approached Feng with a brisk gait. When he reached the table, he signaled for the guards to step aside and gestured to one of the chairs. "Please, have a seat," he said.

"Thank you, Chairman." Feeling light-headed, Feng was relieved to sit down.

After pouring tea for both—*imagine that, the Chairman pouring him tea!*—Liang wasted no time. "You understand the terms? This is off the record and not to be shared. Not even the names of the meetings or the filenames of the minutes can be disclosed. If anything leaks or a single scrap is found on an open desk, you know what will happen."

Feng had been aware of the warning for years; the Party's rules were strict. "Yes," he replied, his voice steady despite his racing pulse.

Liang continued, "Only you and I know the full details of DragonBreath. We will meet here from time to time as needed. There will be no other contact or communication—I cannot risk it. I will share necessary details only with my inner circle, which you will join from time to time."

"Understood," Feng replied dutifully. Liang's expression seemed both softer and more complex than in the public portraits Feng had seen; he did not appear to be a tyrant but rather a keeper of burdens.

"What we are proposing is not an act of wanton aggression. It is a policy instrument. However, policy sometimes needs to be enforced with an iron fist."

Feng inclined his head, "You want Helvex to use its position to gain influence in the U.S. banking sector?"

Liang's hand made a slight motion, not a correction but an emphasis. "Influence, yes," he repeated. "But at the same time, strong measures need to be taken—measures as robust as necessary to achieve our goals. The West's financial system exists because many believe it will endure. Belief is fragile. Once it is shattered, the system will collapse. So yes, we will leverage our influence, but we will also employ more forceful measures. These measures may involve cyber attacks, financial manipulation, or even coercion. Do you understand?"

Feng understood. He realized he had been given significant latitude in accomplishing the mission, and achieving the goal took precedence over secondary concerns, such as moral constraints.

"You will use the channel we have established," Liang said, employing bureaucratic language that concealed numerous actionable meanings. "Helvex is ready. We hold its shares, indirectly, through Zhonghua Capital. The Swiss authorities made it difficult to acquire control and maintain a name that suggests Swiss ownership, but we worked around that with a suitably complex web of intermediary companies. The dragon has a long tail. Helvex's Swiss pedigree will work to our advantage. Specifically, Mr. Egli informs me that his latest hire, known as the Ghost, will be integral to the operation."

Feng remembered that the dossier he had studied contained the credentials of the Ghost, a mysterious figure known as the world's premier cybercriminal, renowned for his invisibility and effectiveness.

Liang watched him, his expression flat. "You must not be seen consulting with anyone. You must not have any rumors about ties to us. If this operation takes the shape of a ghost, it is for the safety of our people."

"What about the mechanics?" Feng asked, carefully probing a gap in the conversation. He knew better than to ask for diagrams or timelines; the Party's doctrine forbade sharing explicit operational details to avoid accountability beyond a small circle. But he needed to make the mission tangible enough to carry out.

Liang tapped his fingers on the wood, a soft metronome. "You will have all the mechanical support you need. Mr. Egli and the Ghost will ensure that. And let me be clear: there is no malicious intent in bringing down the decadent Western bankers and their corrupt system. We seek only to secure our supply chains, allow credit to flow without being beholden to arbitrary choke points, and enable our people to sleep without fearing foreign coercion. This is not about revenge or conquest; we seek only a proper equilibrium."

There was a moment of silence.

"You must understand that there are dangers," Liang said finally. "In particular, the potential for tracing matters back to the Motherland. That cannot happen."

"And if, despite our best efforts, it does?" Feng asked, not out of doubt but because it was important to voice the concern. The stakes were too high for ambiguity.

"You know the answer," Liang said. "The rules are clear."

The mention of consequences sent a chill down his spine. Feng's eyes blinked rapidly. He had faced threats before, in training rooms and whispered lectures. It was part of the life he had chosen; yet the scale of this assignment made the threat feel like a cold wind.

He took a breath. "I will do as ordered."

Before Feng left, Liang spoke in a low voice, a mix of admonition and blessing. "Remember," he said, "we are not architects of ruin. We are custodians of our people's future. If your conscience cannot bear that weight, step aside. But if you accept this responsibility, accept it fully. There will be no turning back."

Feng bowed, a small and private salute to a regime that demanded loyalty. He stepped into the night, feeling the cool air wash over him once again.

* * *

Back in the city, Feng slept poorly. The plan unfolded in his mind like a map with edges blurred by fog: clear goals, vague methods. Despite his nerves, he felt invigorated—finally, a chance to rectify a centuries-old wrong.

Yes, he reminded himself with growing anger, the Western financial markets, swollen with arrogance and dismissive of our ancient civilization, stand hollow at their core. Like a decayed tree in the forest, their collapse is not only inevitable; it is just.

3

GREENWICH
CONNECTICUT

UNITED STATES OF AMERICA

His lips curled into a slow, amused smile. BostonFirst was opening new accounts at a dizzying rate. *Floodgates* was operating beyond his wildest dreams. His malware program operated on a compounding basis; once a new account was created, it served as a platform for subsequent accounts, and so on. He laughed out loud when he read a piece in *The New York Times* about "Bubbles," a goldfish, having a line of credit. *Good for you, Bubbles. Buy a bigger tank.*

This was no mere hack; it marked the beginning of a systematic attack on a financial institution by a man who understood the economy as intimately as a surgeon understands the human body—knowing where to cut, where to apply pressure, and where to let things bleed out.

Jerome Nadler—better known in the right circles as the Ghost—was not someone you noticed at first glance. He was built for the shadows, for the digital underworld where power was measured not in muscles or money, but in lines of code and the ability to breach what others thought impenetrable.

At forty-two, he still carried the awkwardness of a teenager. His posture was slightly hunched from years spent bent over screens, and his complexion was pockmarked from the remnants of adolescent acne. He typically wore hoodies and T-shirts.

A toothpick hung from his lips, a nervous habit that replaced the cigarettes he had tried and failed to enjoy. His fingers—long and twitchy, occasionally marked by ragged nails from compulsive biting—moved with surgical precision over keyboards, dismantling firewalls, implanting silent code, and erasing digital footprints as if he had never been there.

Nadler worked remotely from his home in Greenwich, Connecticut—*because why would he waste time commuting when everything worth doing could be done on a keyboard?* His loft was an architect's dream, set on the top floor of a converted redbrick warehouse near Greenwich Avenue. The space merged industrial precision with understated luxury: steel beams left exposed but powder-coated matte black, floor-to-ceiling windows framing the soft shimmer of Long Island Sound, and white-oak floors polished to the hue of whiskey.

The main living area was minimalist, featuring a sculptural leather sofa, a wall-mounted screen larger than most paintings, and bookshelves filled with cybersecurity journals, graphic novels, and the occasional spy thriller. A glass-encased mezzanine served as his workspace—a command post of silent servers, angled monitors, and the sleek hum of cooling fans. To a casual visitor, it resembled a financier's digital trading suite; to Jerome, it was both his laboratory and his lair.

He felt comfortable mingling with the upper crust. Once a colonial harbor town, Greenwich had become one of the most coveted bedroom communities for New York's financial elite. Here, hedge-fund managers, lawyers, and technology executives could retreat to gated tranquility after days of corporate warfare in Manhattan.

Greenwich attracted people like Nadler not only for its exclusivity but also for its convenience. When he needed to be in the city, the Metro-North train could whisk him to Grand

Central in less than an hour, allowing him to transition from the pulse of Wall Street to the peace of coastal Connecticut before the market closed. The town's proximity to both New York City and the Atlantic offered the best of both worlds—close enough to power, yet far enough to breathe.

From his terrace, Nadler could watch the twilight settle over the Sound, the water reflecting the pale orange of the setting sun. For most, Greenwich was a refuge; for him, it was camouflage—a perfect vantage point for a ghost who navigated between the world of finance and the world of code.

After operating for a long time as an independent, the offer from his old London colleague, who had risen to the top at Helvex Financial, was too good to turn down. Not only did it pay exceptionally well, but the job was fun. As head of cybersecurity, Nadler didn't just defend digital walls; he broke through them with enthusiasm, monitoring all top-level U.S. government cyber activity, emails, data transfers, and cell phone communications.

He had felt a particular thrill when he intercepted a cell call from Jonathan Hendrix, the U.S. Attorney General, to Steve Shane, a lawyer who had won a landmark tort case in Texas.

Shane was climbing the Eiger North Face at the time of the call. Incredible. The situation reminded Nadler of Clint Eastwood's movie, *The Eiger Sanction*. In that film, Eastwood's job was to "sanction," or kill, an enemy agent. Similarly, Nadler's objective was to "sanction" the Western financial system.

Eastwood used bullets, or an alpine "mishap"; Nadler would use code. His would be a "Cyber Sanction." *Yeah, that sounded pretty cool.*

He looked back at the screens in front of him. "Dude, they're screwed," he muttered under his breath, watching BostonFirst's accounts skyrocket. At this rate, every person in the U.S. would soon have a BostonFirst account—a remarkable feat for a bank with no physical locations outside of New England.

Nadler had been a prodigy—a Cambridge prodigy, no less. Born and raised in London, he was one of those kids who hacked into government systems at thirteen, not for money or ideology, but to see if he could. The university recognized his potential and brought him in, refining his talents. However, academia was never enough for him; he craved power—the kind that came from dismantling a system with a few keystrokes.

And then came Jasmine Lin. *Damn Jasmine.*

He had trusted her, even admired her. He was drawn to her intellect and passion. Together, they built a startup meant to revolutionize digital security. But then she betrayed him, shut him out, and treated him like an afterthought—as if he were some socially awkward geek who wasn't worth her time.

Worse, she'd *laughed* at his advances. That had been the final insult and a betrayal he never forgot.

Nadler leaned back in his chair, the dim light from the screens flickering across his face. Somewhere nearby, in a marble-walled government office, Jasmine was watching this unfold with growing horror. He almost wished he could see her reaction in real time.

How fitting she was now at the U.S. Treasury, tasked explicitly with preventing the kind of mayhem he was about to unleash. It would be her worst-case scenario, unfolding like a slow-motion train wreck—one she was powerless to stop. That's what she got for dissing him.

Nadler tapped a key, switching feeds, and watched as the news cycle caught up. Talking heads were already speculating on the Boston-First scandal, discussing potential ripple effects and whether the Feds would step in. They'd try to plug the holes, issue calming statements, and reassure the public. But the damage was done. Trust had been broken, and once trust eroded in banking, nothing—not even an army of Treasury officials—could piece it back together again.

He chuckled, taking a slow sip of whiskey. The beauty of it all was that it looked like a natural scandal. And this was just the beginning. Bobbi Sullivan, that golden-haired self-made queen of ethical banking, must be staring at her screens right now, watching her empire burn and wondering where she went wrong. Nadler closed his laptop with a soft click.

She'd find out soon enough.

4

BOSTON MASSACHUSETTS

UNITED STATES OF AMERICA

Bobbi Sullivan had been staring at the email for an hour, and it still didn't make sense. The subject line was blunt, almost rude: "Formal Notice of Litigation: Helvex v. BostonFirst."

Her hand hovered over the mouse as if moving the cursor would change the words. Each time she reread the opening paragraph, her bewilderment grew. Helvex Financial of Zurich—her partner and supposed ally in the great transatlantic expansion—was suing BostonFirst. Not some boilerplate arbitration, nor a procedural squabble over contractual clauses, but a full-blown lawsuit. The claim? That BostonFirst employees had been stealing customer accounts from Helvex.

She leaned back in the leather chair that had belonged to her grandfather, rubbing her temples. Sunlight filtered through the high windows of her office at One Financial Center in downtown Boston, catching the grain of the old mahogany desk. This was not some fintech start-up scrambling for market share; this was BostonFirst—the oldest continuously operating financial institution in New England, a cornerstone of the city's prosperity.

Bobbi was a banker who never forgot where she came from. She was the kind of woman who commanded attention the moment she stepped into a room. At forty-five, she exuded the polished confidence of someone who had climbed the ladder from its lowest rungs. As the CEO of BostonFirst, a mid-sized, fast-growing institution, she had earned a reputation as both a sharp financial strategist and a leader who still believed in doing the right thing, even in an industry that time and again rewarded those who didn't.

Physically, Bobbi was striking. Her blonde hair, always well-kept but never over-styled, often found its way between her fingers as she thought—an absentminded habit she'd had since childhood. Her glasses—thin-framed and elegant—were perpetually in motion, cleaned and adjusted with restless precision, as if she were always preparing to see things just a bit clearer.

Despite her position, Bobbi never lost her common touch. She loved the unpretentious comfort of a good pub, where she'd be just as happy nursing a pint of Kilkenney Cream Ale with a plate of fish and chips as she would be celebrating the closing of a multimillion-dollar deal in a three-star Michelin restaurant. She understood people—their fears, their ambitions, their needs—and that's what made her a formidable leader. Employees respected her because she listened; rivals feared her because she saw two moves ahead.

Born and raised in a working-class neighborhood of Boston, Bobbi learned the value of a dollar. Her father, an Irish immigrant, taught her about grit and resilience, while her mother, a schoolteacher, instilled in her a love of learning. She worked her way up, first as a bank teller during college, then navigating the elite corridors of Harvard Business School, where she learned to maneuver through the high-stakes world of finance without losing her moral compass. BostonFirst was her legacy—a bank built on integrity, a rarity in an industry often mired in scandal.

When she closed her eyes, she could almost hear her great-grandfather's voice. In 1898,

Patrick Sullivan—an Irish immigrant with little more than ambition, stubborn pride, and a knack for numbers—had founded BostonFirst in a rented office above a shipping warehouse on the wharves. He catered to dockworkers, longshoremen, and immigrants whom Boston's Brahmin-controlled banks turned away. He had believed stubbornly in two principles: prudence in lending and loyalty to depositors. From that tiny seed, BostonFirst had grown into a regional powerhouse.

Her grandfather, Daniel Sullivan, expanded into commercial banking during the postwar boom, financing factories and suburban housing developments. Her father, Robert, guided BostonFirst through deregulation in the 1980s, steering it onto the stock market without ever surrendering family control. Through careful stock accumulation, trusts, and voting proxies, the Sullivan family still controlled fifty-five percent of the shares. Bobbi, Robert's only child, inherited not just the titles of Chairwoman and CEO, but also the family's stake—the lever of power that ensured BostonFirst would never fall into hostile hands.

For over a century, BostonFirst had weathered panics, depressions, bubbles, and crashes. Through it all, the bank's name was synonymous with stability. It was her pride, her burden, her inheritance.

And now, Helvex accused them of running a scam that would have embarrassed a fly-by-night payday lender.

The allegations outlined in Helvex's notice were surreal. According to the filing, employees at BostonFirst—including branch managers, loan officers, and even mid-level clerks—had been opening thousands of fraudulent accounts. They appeared to be incentivized by a bonus system based on the number of new accounts opened. Many of these accounts were linked to existing Helvex clients. Entire families had duplicate checking and savings accounts, as if financial doppelgängers had materialized out of thin air. Even pets—dogs and cats—allegedly held joint savings accounts, and a goldfish named Bubbles had a line of credit.

It was grotesque and absurd, reminiscent of the Wells Fargo scandal that had dominated headlines a decade earlier. However, unlike Wells Fargo, there had been no directive from BostonFirst's leadership, no company-wide incentive scheme that Bobbi was aware of. She would never have permitted such a thing. Risking the bank's reputation—the Sullivan name—for a few thousand new accounts was madness. Yet, the data was damning.

Helvex claimed that tens of millions of dollars in deposits had been siphoned from their records and into BostonFirst accounts through these fraudulent openings. Even more troubling, they alleged collusion between Boston-First staff and a web of shadowy intermediaries—brokers who recruited "clients" with cash incentives. It didn't add up.

She curled a coil of hair with her fingers, her mind racing. She knew her employees. They were ambitious, yes—sometimes too ambitious—but not reckless. Someone was orchestrating this. She couldn't help wondering if Helvex was playing a deeper game.

The irony stung. Just two years ago, Bobbi had celebrated the alliance as the crowning achievement of her career. BostonFirst, though venerable, had long been provincial, its reach constrained to New England and a few branches in New York and D.C. Helvex, by contrast, was a titan of private banking, with roots as deep as the Alps and clients spanning the globe.

Hans Egli, the urbane CEO of Helvex, had courted her relentlessly. He spoke of synergies, cross-Atlantic capital flows, and the merging of Boston's blue-blood prestige with Swiss discretion. It was seductive, almost romantic—the old Yankee institution joined with the old-world Swiss powerhouse, a financial marriage that would dominate the century ahead.

But marriage could turn sour. In the cold logic of global finance, partnership could shift to betrayal overnight. Had she been naïve? Was this lawsuit not merely a reaction to a scandal but a maneuver to wrest control?

Her fifty-five percent stake gave her some comfort, but reputations mattered. If the public came to believe that BostonFirst had been running a fraudulent scheme, shareholder lawsuits would pile up, regulators would swarm, and even family control might not save them.

She could not—would not—let that happen. It would be another long day. She hit the line to her secretary. The response was immediate. "Yes, Bobbi?"

"I'm afraid it's going to be another working lunch, Janice. Could you have some chowder sent over from Quincy Market? Order a quart for both of us and make sure they throw in plenty of those oyster crackers."

She heard a chuckle on the line. "You got it."

After reading the email one last time, she reached for the phone. For a moment, she hesitated. Hans Egli was not a man one called lightly. He prided himself on being deliberate, formal, and distant. Their past conversations had been cordial, even warm, but always with an undercurrent of calculation, as if he were measuring her with every word.

Still, she needed answers. She dialed the Zurich number, her pulse quickening as the international tones sounded. After several rings, a secretary answered and connected her. There was a brief pause, then his voice: smooth, precise, and accented.

"Bobbi. To what do I owe the pleasure?"

She forced a steady tone. "Hans, I've just received notice of your lawsuit. I need to understand what's happening."

A sigh, barely audible. "It is regrettable, I agree. But you must understand, we had no choice. The activity emanating from your bank is... troubling."

"Hans, I'm as baffled as you are. We have no policy—no incentive structure—that would drive this. I want to get to the bottom of it. But suing us—suing me—without even a call? That feels like an ambush."

His silence stretched. Bobbi took off her glasses and wiped them slowly with a cleaning cloth. She pictured him in his Zurich office, immaculate in his tailored suit, gazing out over the lake as he considered his response.

Finally, he spoke. "Ambush? No. Defense. We are under scrutiny already. FINMA is asking difficult questions. To protect Helvex, I must demonstrate distance. The narrative must be clear: the wrongdoing lies with Boston."

Bobbi's jaw tightened. She understood the deference to FINMA, the Swiss Financial Market Supervisory Authority. The U.S. did not have a financial regulator with such consolidated power. FINMA's comparable responsibilities in the U.S. were fragmented across various agencies, including the Securities and Exchange Commission (SEC) and the Office of the Comptroller of the Currency (OCC).

"And what if the wrongdoing lies elsewhere? What if we're both being played?"

Another pause. Longer this time. Then his tone shifted, a shade cooler. "That is a possibility, yes. But perception shapes reality. If I cannot contain the perception, reality may not matter."

She gripped the receiver. "Then we need to work together, Hans. Not against each other. If this is some scheme, someone wants us at each other's throats. We can't afford to give them that satisfaction."

His voice softened, almost wistful. "Perhaps. But alliances are built on trust, Bobbi. And trust, once shaken…" He let the sentence hang in the air like a guillotine blade.

When the line clicked dead, she sat frozen, staring at the phone.

Trust. That was the word. She had trusted Helvex, trusted Egli, trusted the idea that BostonFirst could leap from a regional player to a global force. And now that trust was unraveling.

She rose from her chair and walked to the window. Below, the bustle of Boston's financial district churned on, oblivious to the storm clouds gathering above their venerable bank. She thought of her great-grandfather, his calloused hands counting pennies behind a battered counter. What would he say now, seeing the house he had built threatened not by a run on the bank, not by reckless speculation, but by something murkier—a war of shadows and accounts that did not even exist?

She clenched her fists. Whoever was behind this, whatever game was being played, she would not let BostonFirst fall. Not on her watch.

And yet, the doubt lingered. Was the rot inside her own walls?

Or had she, in reaching across the Atlantic, invited in a serpent cloaked in Swiss silk?

5

CAMBRIDGE
MASSACHUSETTS

UNITED STATES OF AMERICA

The streetlights were flickering off as Bobbi, suitcase in tow, quietly slipped into a cab and told the driver a single word: "Cambridge."

She needed a few days away from the stress of Boston. The trip across the Charles River was a return, in geography and in time. She hadn't lived in Cambridge since the mid-nineties, when she was just another Harvard undergrad with sharp elbows and bigger dreams. Life since then had taken her to Wall Street, Washington, and finally to BostonFirst. Now, just as suddenly, life had brought her back to this riverside town—not as a triumphant daughter returning home, but as a woman seeking cover, answers, and maybe even salvation.

She checked into a small inn off Mount Auburn Street, which had no more than a dozen rooms—anonymous and quiet. From her window, she could see the roofs of Harvard Square bookstores, steam curling from the early-morning cafés, and students bent against the wind with their backpacks. It looked the same as it had when she was nineteen, except that she now carried the burden of headlines labeling her the architect of BostonFirst's disgrace.

The scandal had taken on absurd proportions, and the press feasted on it. Thousands of fraudulent accounts, employees chasing bonus quotas by signing up anyone and everyone. *The Boston Globe* even ran a story that had come from *The New York Times*, complete with a mocking sidebar about Bubbles, the pet goldfish assigned a checking account with a credit line. The satirical cartoon featuring a fishbowl full of money had gone viral.

But the lawsuit from Helvex was more serious. They claimed that hundreds, maybe even thousands, of their customers had suddenly appeared on BostonFirst's books. To Helvex, it was brazen poaching; to Bobbi, it smelled like something else entirely—an intrusion, a hack, a setup.

She needed someone who could see beyond the banking lawyers and regulators, someone who spoke the new language of cyber warfare. She thought of Jasmine Lin, a Chinese-American software engineer who co-founded a blockchain startup, then left the corporate tech world disillusioned by its greed. At thirty-eight, she now worked at the Department of the Treasury, heading a crypto-oversight unit. She had a dry sense of humor and an unshakable belief in the power of technology to create positive change. Bobbi remembered with a smile how, when stressed, Jasmine would bite her lower lip or crack her knuckles.

They had shared a cramped dorm suite during their sophomore year, mismatched in nearly every respect—Bobbi, a brash economics major from Boston, and Jasmine, a quiet computer science prodigy from Cupertino who preferred to code at night.

They had stayed loosely in touch with holiday cards and occasional LinkedIn updates. But Jasmine had taken a different path: earning a Ph.D. in applied mathematics, spending time in Silicon Valley, and now—Bobbi had read recently—a position at the U.S. Treasury, supervising digital currencies and blockchain regulation. While based in Washington, Bobbi knew Jasmine maintained her apartment in Cambridge.

Bobbi texted her the day before. "Will be in Cambridge tomorrow. You around? Need to talk. Urgent. Coffee?"

Jasmine replied within minutes: "Yes. Café Pamplona. See you at noon tomorrow."

* * *

Pamplona was still there, tucked underground off Brattle Street, just as it had been when they were undergrads. The entrance was easy to miss—a flight of narrow stairs leading down into a basement café with yellow walls and small wooden tables pressed together like puzzle pieces—a hangout for poets, chess players, and graduate students with more time than money.

Bobbi arrived early and chose a corner table. The room smelled of espresso and buttered croissants, while Spanish guitar music trickled from hidden speakers. Outside, traffic in Harvard Square pulsed with the sounds of buses, bicycles, and the constant shuffle of students.

When Jasmine appeared, Bobbi recognized her instantly despite the years. She was slighter than she remembered, her black hair pulled back in a loose bun, tortoiseshell glasses perched on her nose. But her eyes were the same—sharp, amused. She was wearing a navy trench coat and carrying no laptop, just a leather-bound notebook.

"Bobbi Sullivan," Jasmine said, pulling her into a quick embrace. "I saw you on TV last week. Not the best of circumstances."

Bobbi winced. "No, not the best. But you look great. Government service agrees with you."

"Depends on the day," Jasmine said with a small smile as she slipped into the chair opposite Bobbi. "But let's talk about you. If you wanted to get away from it all for a few days, I would have thought a trip to Martha's Vineyard would fit the bill. Why are you hiding out in Cambridge, of all places?"

"Because this is where I know who I can trust." Bobbi leaned forward. "I'm in trouble, Jas. You've seen the stories."

"Fraudulent accounts, whistleblowers, lawsuits from your Swiss partner. I'd say you're in more than trouble. You're in headline hell."

"It's not what it looks like," Bobbi said quickly. "We did have an incentive program, but it wasn't aggressive. I suppose some people abused it, but it can't explain this explosion of accounts. And this issue with Helvex? Customers showing up on our books who were theirs? I don't believe it was my people. I think Boston-First was hacked. Maybe even framed."

Jasmine bit her lip. "That's a serious accusation. If true, it could change the narrative. But you'd need proof. What does your IT security team say?"

"They say their logs show nothing unusual." Bobbi stirred her coffee, frustration creeping into her voice. "But I don't buy it. The volume, the precision—it's too clean. It's like someone wanted this mess to blow up exactly the way it did."

"And Helvex suing makes it even messier," Jasmine noted. "They appear to be the victim, while you look like the villain."

Bobbi paused for a minute before nodding. "Exactly why I need you. You understand the digital landscape. I don't. Treasury must have tools we can't even dream of."

Jasmine raised an eyebrow. "I can't conduct official investigations for a private bank. It's a conflict of interest, not to mention illegal. But—" She paused and lowered her voice. "I can take a personal, off-the-record look. I know some people who monitor account migration patterns. If there's a hidden hand behind this, there might be traces."

Bobbi felt the relief wash over her. "That's all I ask. I just need to know whether I'm crazy."

"You've never been crazy, Bobbi. Reckless, maybe. Ambitious as hell. But not crazy." Jasmine tapped her notebook. "Tell me everything. How did this start?"

Bobbi outlined the scandal: pressure campaigns to boost new account numbers, regional managers cutting corners, and the revelation that some employees had created accounts in the names of pets and even fictional characters.

The deeper cut came weeks later, when Helvex's lawyers sued, claiming their private banking customers—Swiss industrialists, Middle Eastern family offices, Hong Kong financiers—had appeared in BostonFirst's systems as if they had been spirited away.

"I don't know how Helvex reacted so fast," Bobbi said. "It's like they were tipped off."

"Or," Jasmine suggested, "like they already knew what was coming."

That thought hung between them. Bobbi glanced around the café, lowering her voice. Students hunched over laptops, a barista steamed milk, and two tourists squinted at a guidebook. Nobody was paying them any attention.

"You think Helvex could be in on it?" Bobbi asked.

"I think," Jasmine said carefully, "that in banking, allies are sometimes adversaries in disguise. Helvex is old money. Conservative. They would envy your aggressive growth. If someone wanted to cripple BostonFirst, this would be one way to do it."

Bobbi felt a chill. "So, I'm not paranoid."

"Not necessarily." Jasmine flipped her notebook open, jotting down shorthand notes. "Here's what I'll do. I'll reach out to a contact at FinCEN—the Financial Crimes Enforcement Network. They've been tracking cyber breaches and network vulnerabilities amid the rise in ransomware cases. If BostonFirst's systems were infiltrated, they may well be able to confirm that and identify the entry point. If they find evidence of synthetic KYC files, that might explain the surge in new accounts."

Bobbi blinked. "Synthetic KYC?"

"Know Your Customer data—fake IDs generated with enough realism to pass automated checks. Think deepfake meets banking compliance. If thousands of those hit your system at once, they'd look like legitimate customers—until someone digs deeper."

Bobbi exhaled slowly. "That's exactly what it feels like. Like ghosts filling up the ledgers."

Jasmine smiled faintly. "Ghosts always leave shadows. We have to find them."

They paused as the waiter delivered fresh coffees and a plate of cinnamon rolls. For a moment, the tension eased. Bobbi tore off a piece of pastry and remembered late nights cramming for exams in this same café, with Jasmine lecturing her on linear algebra while she tried to memorize Keynesian models.

"You always did have the answers," Bobbi said softly.

"No," Jasmine corrected, "I just knew where to look." She took a sip of her coffee. "Listen, Bobbi, you need to prepare yourself. Even if we prove you were hacked, regulators won't go easy on you. They'll say you failed to prevent it. Shareholders will still want blood."

"I know." Bobbi's brow furrowed. "But I can't just roll over. This is my bank. My people. If someone's using us as a pawn, I have to know."

Outside, church bells from Harvard Yard chimed noon. The café door opened, and a gust of autumn air swept in, carrying the scent of leaves and exhaust. Students jostled past, and the noise of the square swelled.

Jasmine closed her notebook. "Give me a few weeks. I'll dig quietly. If there's a trail, I'll find it."

Bobbi reached across the table, gripping her hand. "Thank you, Jas. I didn't know where else to turn."

"Don't thank me yet," Jasmine said. "Sometimes when you dig, you find things you'd rather not know."

6

WASHINGTON
DISTRICT OF COLUMBIA

UNITED STATES OF AMERICA

The office of the Attorney General of the United States, on an upper floor of the Robert F. Kennedy Department of Justice Building between Constitution and Pennsylvania avenues, was not the sterile, bureaucratic space that many visitors expected. Jonathan Hendrix had transformed it to resemble Winston Churchill's study at Chartwell Manor, a deliberate homage to his British upbringing and the man he considered his greatest political hero.

The walls were paneled in dark oak and lined with volumes of military history, leather-bound biographies, and meticulously stacked reports. A brass globe, worn at the edges from years of handling, stood beside the fireplace. An oil portrait of Churchill in a bowler hat dominated the wall behind Hendrix's desk. Heavy burgundy curtains framed the tall windows, allowing the faint glow of Washington's late-afternoon light to spill across the Persian rug.

Hendrix sat behind his desk, a cigar between his fingers. He reached for a glass of single malt and let the amber liquid slide down his throat. With his tall, lean physique, Hendrix cut an imposing figure. In a crisp white shirt and tailored navy-blue suit, he reminded people of President Obama. Rising to the highest law enforcement position in his adopted country required something extra, especially as a Black man. He spoke rarely without purpose, and when he did, he had a penchant for quoting Churchill.

Across from him sat Oliver "Ollie" Weston, his bright young African American deputy. With his wild dreadlocks, hiring Ollie was a calculated risk in the traditionally staid AG's office. Ollie's gangly physique reminded Hendrix of Kramer, the quirky character from the television series *Seinfeld*. But despite his clumsiness, Ollie possessed an exceptional legal mind. He had earned his reputation by recognizing patterns that others missed. He carried a yellow legal pad filled with notes, his pen tapping a quiet rhythm against the paper.

Hendrix broke the silence. "Oliver, this BostonFirst mess stinks to high heaven."

Ollie looked up from his notes. "The fraudulent accounts?"

"Yes," Hendrix replied, setting down the cigar. "The press paints it as another Wells Fargo situation—overzealous incentives, employees gaming the system. But the numbers…," he shook his head slowly, "the numbers don't add up. My sources tell me that a bank of that size doesn't have the personnel, the hours, or the sheer human capital to generate thousands of new accounts in such a short time. It's beyond improbable. It's impossible."

"You think they were hacked?" Ollie asked.

Hendrix took a sip of his whiskey. "I believe it's more than just sloppy compliance. I have sources in the Bureau who've hinted that what we're seeing is too systematic, too precise, and too overwhelming. If BostonFirst's systems were compromised, then this isn't merely a banking scandal—it's criminal. The bank could be a target."

The deputy nodded. "Helvex Financial is already suing. They claim BostonFirst poached their customers. They've brought in Claudine Dubois."

Hendrix arched an eyebrow. "Dubois? That Dubois?"

Ollie's lips tightened into a thin smile. "The very same. She's a world-renowned litigator.

Half of the major international arbitration cases in the last decade bear her fingerprints. She's elegant, ruthless, speaks four languages, and knows how to make juries swoon. If she's on Helvex's side, BostonFirst is in trouble."

Hendrix leaned back in his chair, glancing at the Churchill portrait as if seeking counsel. "Churchill once said, 'You cannot reason with a tiger when your head is in its mouth.' Dubois sounds like that tiger, with BostonFirst's head firmly between her jaws."

Ollie scribbled something on his pad. "That's why I think this might be a case for LawForce."

Hendrix tapped the armrest of his chair thoughtfully. LawForce was the brainchild of his tenure—a legal strike team that was fast, agile, and unencumbered by bureaucracy. It was created to operate where corporate power threatened the American system itself. It was his answer to the twenty-first-century battlefield, where the weapons were not tanks and bombs, but lawsuits, hacks, and economic sabotage.

"You may be right," Hendrix murmured. "BostonFirst is not just another regional bank. It's a key node in the national system."

Ollie nodded. "Then we should bring Steve Shane into this. He's the right person to lead the effort. You trust him."

"Indeed, I do," Hendrix said with a faint smile. Shane had been with LawForce since its inception, a man of quiet brilliance and unshakeable resolve. "I've already called him. He'll be here in a few days."

"Good," Ollie replied. He paused before adding, "And I have to mention something else. If we're looking at hacking, digital manipulation, and synthetic accounts, Treasury will have the right expertise. I've heard about someone there—Jasmine Lin. One of my old classmates swears that when it comes to cybercrime, she's the sharpest mind in Washington."

The name jogged Hendrix's memory. He had come across it in briefings and had even heard her testify before a Senate subcommittee. He tapped the cigar against his desk. "Jasmine Lin. Yes. If BostonFirst's books were infiltrated by hackers, she'd be the one to confirm it. Brief her on the issue, although if she's reading the papers, she'll likely be up to speed already. Tell her we need a report that covers everything and dissects this mess. And Oliver, use my name. I want this to be her top priority. Time is of the essence."

Ollie shifted in his chair, pen hovering over the pad. "Will do. So where does that leave us?"

Hendrix's gaze grew serious. "It leaves us at the beginning of something larger, I fear. A scandal like this, splashed across headlines, may seem like an isolated corporate disaster. But I've lived long enough to know when the ground trembles before an earthquake."

He rose and walked to the window. Outside, the Capitol dome glowed in the fading light. For a moment, the only sound was the ticking of the grandfather clock in the corner. "Thanks, Oliver. That's all for now."

Ollie jumped up and smashed his leg into the glass coffee table, nearly shattering it. Hendrix couldn't hide his smile as Ollie muttered something on his way out the door.

7

BOSTON
MASSACHUSETTS

UNITED STATES OF AMERICA

At forty-three, Claudine Dubois was the undisputed queen of Swiss financial litigation. A former politician turned private-sector powerhouse, she wielded influence exceeding that of many CEOs. Axos AG was her firm, not just in name but in reality. The partners answered to her, the associates feared her, and her clients—well, her clients didn't hire her; she hired them. She decided whether they were worthy of her time, and Helvex Financial was.

Born into Geneva's elite, Dubois mastered the art of power early on. She possessed the charm of a diplomat and the ruthlessness of a prosecutor. Her transition from Swiss federal politics to corporate law was seamless—she knew whom to call, which levers to pull, and how to make inconvenient regulations disappear.

Dubois dressed the part of Swiss legal royalty—sleek, custom-tailored power suits, cut to project dominance. Her jewelry was understated yet unmistakably expensive. No flashy logos, no ostentation—just the quiet confidence of someone who never needed to prove herself.

Her mannerisms were just as deliberate. She tapped her fingers lightly on the podium before delivering a verbal blow, and a quick, knowing wink accompanied her almost always favorable cross-examinations. In the rare moments when she felt the strain, she tugged at an earlobe—a tell she had never eradicated. She was charming but never warm, respected but never truly trusted. Dubois understood that sentimentality was a liability in the world of high finance.

* * *

Bobbi Sullivan sat stiff-backed at the defense table, her throat tight as she tried to appear composed. It was a losing battle. Watching Dubois work was like witnessing a virtuoso violinist perform—effortless, devastating, beautiful in a way that only intensified the humiliation.

The federal courtroom in Boston had become an arena. Every seat behind the bar was taken, reporters lined the gallery like vultures, and cameras waited outside the doors to capture any image of Bobbi that might suggest weakness. This wasn't just a lawsuit; it was theater, and Dubois was directing the show.

Helvex's suit against BostonFirst had shaken the financial world. Still, today's hearing was even more concerning: a bid for an injunction that would forbid BostonFirst from opening any new accounts until the trial. Bobbi understood precisely what that meant. A bank that couldn't take in new business might as well start writing its obituary.

She had warned her attorneys and tried to spur them into action, but it hadn't mattered. The team from Whitcomb & Peters was competent enough on paper—an old Boston white-shoe firm with mahogany-paneled offices and brass plaques still polished by hand. But competence was no match for Dubois. Bobbi tensed as Dubois glided to the podium, her voice steady, melodic, and cold.

"Your Honor," Dubois began, switching effortlessly between French-accented English and the language of law. "We are not merely here to discuss accounting irregularities. We are here to address theft—systematic, deliberate, corrosive theft. Thousands of customers. Accounts cultivated over decades of trust between Helvex and its clients. What did BostonFirst do? They siphoned them away with fraudulent inducements, fabricated paperwork, and even digital manipulation."

Her hand hovered in the air, as if she were plucking each offense out of the ether for the court to see.

"The evidence is staggering," she continued. "Not only do we have clients testifying that they never consented to opening new accounts with BostonFirst, but we also have documentation—digital trails and metadata—that show BostonFirst's systems were manipulated from within. This was not an accident; this was not a few rogue employees. This was systemic, institutionalized misconduct."

Bobbi's stomach tightened. She wanted to leap up and shout it wasn't true, that Boston-First was itself the victim of some malicious intrusion. But she had been advised to remain silent, to let her lawyers handle it. They were not handling it.

Whitcomb & Peters' lead attorney, Harold Wilkins, rose with a dry cough, clutching his papers as if they might fly away. "Your Honor, my client categorically denies any wrongdoing. BostonFirst has always operated in accordance with the letter and spirit of banking law. What we are witnessing here is an unfortunate conflation of clerical errors, overly aggressive sales tactics by a few employees, and an international partner attempting to shift blame for its own internal failings."

Dubois didn't flinch. Instead, she cocked her head, as though regarding an insect trapped in amber. When Wilkins sat down, sweat visibly staining his collar, she returned to the podium with a faint smile.

"Clerical errors do not create accounts for deceased individuals," she said smoothly. "Nor do clerical errors open accounts in the names of household pets. A goldfish, Your Honor, registered as a customer of BostonFirst. Forgive me if I do not believe that Bubbles arrived at the branch on her own to sign documents."

The gallery erupted in laughter. Even the usually implacable judge hid a smirk behind her hand. Bobbi felt the blood rush to her cheeks. It was over. The moment had slipped away. Dubois had won the room.

The rest was mere formality.

With surgical precision, Dubois presented her case. "We have met all the criteria for an injunction. We have demonstrated that we are likely to succeed on the merits. We have shown that Helvex will suffer irreparable harm without the injunction. The balance of hardships favors us, and it is clear that the injunction is in the public interest." Bobbi bit her lip as she felt the nails being pounded into the coffin—bang, bang, bang, bang.

For two more hours, Dubois dismantled every argument made by BostonFirst's lawyers. Each precedent they cited was met with a sharper, more relevant counter. Every appeal to fairness was confronted with cold facts. When Wilkins suggested that Helvex's clients had willingly transferred their accounts, Dubois produced affidavits from clients denying that they had ever signed such authorizations.

When she finally concluded, her voice rang with finality. "If BostonFirst is allowed to continue opening new accounts while this case proceeds, every day risks further erosion of trust in the banking system. The damage will not be confined to Helvex Financial; it will spread like contagion. That, Your Honor, is precisely why an injunction is not merely warranted—it is essential."

The judge's ruling came swiftly. The injunction was granted from the bench—highly unusual for a matter of this gravity. The speed of the decision underscored the imbalance in legal representation. Dubois had wiped the courtroom floor with BostonFirst's lawyers.

Bobbi sat frozen, her fingernails digging into her palms. The words seemed unreal, echoing in her mind like a death knell. BostonFirst was forbidden from opening new accounts, effective immediately.

Her attorneys shuffled papers, muttering platitudes about appeals and motions to reconsider, but their voices blurred together. All she could see was Dubois, gracefully packing her leather portfolio, exchanging polite nods with the judge, and exiting the courtroom as if she had merely finished a lunch engagement.

Outside, reporters swarmed. Bobbi barely registered their shouted questions as she was hustled into a waiting car. Inside the tinted sanctuary, she let her head fall back against the seat, eyes shut. The humiliation felt total.

She thought back to the years she had spent building BostonFirst from a regional player into a competitor. Every deal, every long night, and every speech meant to reassure investors and regulators that her bank was different—innovative, responsible, built on trust—now seemed meaningless. That trust had evaporated in a single hearing. And worst of all, she was certain it wasn't BostonFirst's fault.

But suspicion was not proof. And without evidence, she looked like every other CEO caught with her hand in the cookie jar, pleading ignorance while her company burned.

She could still hear Dubois's voice, smooth as silk and sharp as steel: "A goldfish, Your Honor." The laughter cut deeper than any legal argument. It turned BostonFirst into a punchline, and punchlines didn't survive long in global finance.

Bobbi opened her eyes, staring out at the gray blur of Boston streets. She pulled off her glasses and rubbed the bridge of her nose. For the first time in years, she felt small, outgunned, outmaneuvered, and alone.

But she was not finished.

Dubois had delivered a devastating blow, yes, but there had to be a way to fight back, to prove that BostonFirst was not the villain but the victim. Somewhere, in the tangled web of code, accounts, and metadata, was the truth.

8

WASHINGTON
DISTRICT OF COLUMBIA

UNITED STATES OF AMERICA

The historic U.S. Treasury Building, next to the White House, was one of the oldest federal buildings in the capital. Its grand neoclassical façade featured towering Ionic columns, embodying strength, stability, and the enduring authority of the nation's economic system.

Jasmine's office was two floors below ground level, in a maze of hallways that smelled faintly of ozone, aging wiring, and government coffee that had been brewing since dawn. Most visitors to the Treasury Department never saw this part of the building; it was a hidden area where the light was always artificial, the ceilings were too low, and the hum of servers competed with the buzzing fluorescent lights. For Jasmine, it felt like home.

At her desk—a steel rectangle with a multitude of sticky notes, two monitors, and the softly glowing tower of a custom-built machine—she was in her element. Although the government had issued her a laptop, she never used it for serious work; it was a crippled piece of hardware compared to the powerful workstation she kept locked behind multiple layers of biometric and cryptographic security.

Her office resembled a graduate student's bunker more than a Treasury suite. It was cluttered with mugs bearing half-faded conference logos, a bonsai tree that had stubbornly survived months of fluorescent neglect, and stacks of books on cybersecurity, blockchain networks, and financial forensics.

This environment was where she felt most like herself, hunched over the glow of code, tracing the invisible patterns of digital footprints left by adversaries skilled enough to avoid evident traces.

Today's task involved BostonFirst Bank. The fraudulent accounts scandal had dominated the headlines for weeks, and now the court's injunction meant BostonFirst could not sign up new clients until the trial.

And it wasn't just Bobby who needed her help. She had received a request for a report from the Attorney General himself, who wanted answers—and he wanted them fast. Now she wasn't just doing a friend a favor; she had a green light from the highest level. The pressure was on.

She knew Jonathan Hendrix only by reputation—a sharp, relentless figure with a penchant for quoting Churchill, known for tackling impossible challenges. When her boss at Treasury's cyber division informed her that the Attorney General wanted a forensic analysis of Boston-First's systems, Jasmine felt a thrill she hadn't experienced in months: the excitement of a challenge.

Her fingers hovered over the keyboard as lines of log data streamed across her screens. Bobbi had arranged for BostonFirst to hand over its server records, personnel rosters, activity logs, and system access credentials. To a casual observer, the logs appeared clean—far too clean.

That was the first red flag.

Real banks, even well-run ones, had noisy logs. Employees made mistakes, scripts crashed, and accounts were opened and closed for legitimate reasons. There should have been the digital equivalent of mud tracked across a carpet. Instead, BostonFirst's logs looked as though a team of janitors had meticulously scrubbed the data every night.

Jasmine frowned and leaned back in her chair, cracking her knuckles. The pattern was too neat. She reached for her mug, grimaced when she realized it contained yesterday's coffee reheated in the microwave, and pushed it aside. She activated one of her custom scripts—a "noise re-generator," as she called it—designed to detect mistakes that normal log-clearing efforts might miss.

The script processed the data, highlighting inconsistencies invisible to the naked eye: timestamps that didn't align perfectly, micro-delays in authentication records, and network packets that took slightly longer routes than they should have. Individually, none of these findings was remarkable, but together, they suggested one thing: Someone had tampered with the logs. Someone skilled.

Jasmine pulled up a heat map showing account creation over the past eighteen months. At first glance, the surge in activity resembled what BostonFirst's critics claimed: an overzealous sales staff exploiting incentive programs. However, the growth curve appeared unnatural—smoother than any human-driven scheme would be. Real account creation, she knew, was messy and driven by people, while this curve looked as if a machine had drawn it.

A chill crept down her spine. She accessed deeper metadata to trace the chain of command for account authorizations. Some accounts were linked to actual employees, but when she cross-checked those names against HR rosters, she discovered anomalies: employees who had left the bank months earlier, interns whose system credentials should have expired, and even a cleaning contractor who had never worked within the bank's IT systems. These accounts had been reactivated silently and invisibly, used as shells to authorize hundreds of fraudulent new accounts.

Jasmine leaned closer to the monitor, biting her lip. Whoever had executed this scheme wasn't just a bored teenager with a hoodie and a VPN. This was a professional. Someone who understood banking regulations, knew which logs to alter, and could make the fraud appear as an internal failure instead of an external attack. They had almost pulled it off—almost.

She zoomed in on the reactivated accounts. Most were wiped clean, their trails deleted. Yet, here and there, just faintly, she found tiny signatures: gaps of milliseconds in log files, mismatched time zones in packet headers, and routing nodes that hinted at paths through obscure servers in Eastern Europe and Southeast Asia.

But the pattern wasn't random. It was intentional—choreographed. And faintly, just faintly, it felt familiar.

By late evening, the fluorescent lights had shifted from a sterile white to the soft yellow glow of "night mode." The rest of her corridor was deserted. Jasmine stretched, her shoulders aching from hours hunched over her screens, and compiled her findings into a formal report.

Her writing was clinical and precise, but the conclusion carried weight:

> **Preliminary forensic analysis indicates that BostonFirst's account scandal was not the result of internal misconduct but rather an external intrusion. The intrusion was carried out by a highly sophisticated actor (APT-level) whose methods included log manipulation, unauthorized reactivation of dormant user accounts, and systemic obfuscation. Attribution remains inconclusive. Further investigation is warranted.**

She reread the draft, trimmed a few adjectives, and encrypted the file using Treasury's highest-level secure channel. Then she drafted a cover message for the Attorney General:

**Report attached. Recommend imme-
diate escalation. This intrusion is not
amateur. It carries the hallmarks of an
organized, well-resourced actor. Suggest urgent coordination with Justice,
Homeland Security, and the intelligence community.**

She hesitated over the "send" button, her
eyes flicking once more to the heat map on her
screen. The curve of account creation pulsed
like a living thing, smooth and inevitable. Whoever had created it was still out there, possibly
watching, and maybe already preparing their
next move.

Jasmine clicked "send." The message vanished into the encrypted pipeline, destined for
the Attorney General's desk. She leaned back,
exhaled slowly, and rubbed her temples.

For the first time all day, she allowed herself to acknowledge what her instincts had
been screaming since morning. Though the
traces were faint and ghostlike, she recognized
the rhythm of a hunter. It brought back distant
memories of a colleague with special abilities. It
couldn't be him. Could it?

9

ZURICH

SWITZERLAND

Hans Egli exuded the polished elegance of a man who never rushed, never raised his voice, and never felt the need to explain himself. At sixty-two, he carried himself with the effortless confidence of someone who had won the game before the other players even realized they were on the board.

Leaning back in his armchair, he looked out at Lake Zurich. The eastern side of the lake, Zurich's Goldküste—Goldcoast—lay before him, although his own estate was out of sight. It lay further down the lake, at the tip of the Goldcoast near Rapperswil. He was delighted to learn that his newest neighbor was none other than Switzerland's golden child, Roger Federer.

Egli had specifically chosen this location for Helvex's executive offices. He preferred being closer to the lake than to Paradeplatz. The view from his fifth-floor penthouse was spectacular—a calming antidote to the hectic pace of his office. The address, Bahnhofstrasse 1, reflected his view of where he belonged in the Zurich hierarchy. While most people see Bahnhofstrasse as running from the train station to the lake, the street numbering runs in the opposite direction.

Helvex's main offices were a stone's throw from Paradeplatz—the epicenter of Swiss banking—but the lake offered a different mood: serenity. Egli believed that power should feel inevitable; it should soothe, not roar.

His silver hair, always immaculately groomed, framed a face that still bore traces of the handsome man of his youth. Time had not diminished him; it had refined him. His steel-gray eyes missed nothing, and he dressed with precision—a tailored gray suit, a subtly patterned tie, and cufflinks that cost more than some men's annual salaries. He embodied the archetype of Swiss banking: composed, calculating, and shrouded in an aura of untouchable power.

Born in Uetikon, near Zurich, Egli had long outgrown his provincial roots. Oxford had given him polish; London's ruthless financial world had given him an edge. As he rose through the ranks at Helvex, he did not just ascend—he orchestrated his climb. Deals collapsed precisely when he chose, and rivals made fatal missteps that mysteriously benefited Helvex. He understood one immutable truth: power in banking was not about money; it was about control.

He tapped a silver spoon against a bone china cup and watched the ripple slide across the surface of his coffee. The morning briefing folder lay untouched on the glass-topped table. The paper inside contained a map he had long learned to read with the same fluency as a chessboard—names, positions, vulnerabilities, and lines of leverage.

A faint smile crossed his lips; it was not warm but precise. When someone earned his approval—an increasingly rare occurrence—he would feign doffing an invisible hat and murmur, "chapeau."

His thoughts turned to BostonFirst and his legal Doberman. Claudine Dubois had performed flawlessly in Boston. He had tasked her with the assignment, and she exceeded his expectations, turning a messy scandal into a surgical triumph. The injunction barring BostonFirst from onboarding new customers was a crippling first cut. It would not kill BostonFirst by itself, but it would starve them of oxygen. From there, the rest of the plan would unfold—slow, legal, and relentless.

Egli regarded Bobbi Sullivan with clinical detachment. She had been helpful for a time—aggressive, hungry, and a leader who could effectively carry Helvex's messaging into heartland America. However, usefulness has an expiration date. The BostonFirst officers' desire for global reach had made them vulnerable; their appetite for growth had been the lever he needed. They welcomed the EigerNet partnership with open arms, only too eager to sign the agreements.

EigerNet was a name that pleased him—a nod to the Eiger's forbidding North Face, suggesting mastery over what others deemed unconquerable. Helvex's fintech platform was marketed as revolutionary—a digital gateway for cross-border transactions that promised speed, transparency, and privacy. To the public, it represented innovation. To Helvex, it was a means of folding other institutions into an ecosystem supported by the bank's reach and the quiet weight of its balance sheet.

The mechanics had been elegantly crafted. Helvex funded BostonFirst's investment in EigerNet by selling Helvex Bonds—on terms favorable to Helvex, though appearing generous to BostonFirst. The bonds were non-negotiable regarding certain covenants that subtly tied BostonFirst's liquidity and compliance architectures into Helvex's systems. On paper, it was a partnership; in practice, it was a trap.

Egli stirred his coffee, contemplating his next steps. He thought of his colleague from the early days at Barclays Bank in London—a brilliant computer technician named Jerome Nadler, a true tech savant. Nadler had moved to the United States, working from the shadows and self-styling himself online as the Ghost. He was one of Egli's first hires after he became the CEO of Helvex. Egli was convinced that the future of banking lay in cyberspace.

Now, Nadler had once again proven his worth by executing the scheme to destabilize BostonFirst. Egli observed it unfold with the detached satisfaction of a strategist who had set the pieces in motion and was waiting for them to fall as intended.

The press had sensationalized the "goldfish" anecdote with the fervor of pack animals, leaving BostonFirst's reputation in shambles. Clients called in a panic, counterparties adjusted their exposures, and small cracks began to widen.

Egli picked up a red phone on his desk, a secure landline with a direct connection to Gao Feng.

"The sky is blue," said the voice on the other end, precise and low.

"And tomorrow it will be black." Egli chuckled at Feng's insistence on their password routine. Every day, he received a refreshed, encrypted password sent to his dedicated email account. Feng fancied himself as China's answer to James Bond.

"The injunction is in place," Egli said after the password exchange. "Madame Dubois performed admirably." He listened as Feng's reply drifted over him. "Good. The next stage will be completed in a few days. We will integrate the remaining compliance hooks in EigerNet." He paused, waiting for Feng's reaction.

"Yes. Proceed, over and out." Egli chuckled again. *Agent 007 was on the job!* He gently replaced the handset in its cradle and watched the boats drifting on the lake below.

A knock at the door interrupted his thoughts. Claudine Dubois entered without preamble, as she always did, and inclined her head in a brief greeting.

"Madame Dubois," Hans said, a hint of amusement in his tone. "Chapeau."

Dubois allowed herself a small smile. "Monsieur Egli," she replied. "The court found the law as we wrote it." Her English was crisp, with a Geneva cadence emphasizing both clarity and charm. "The injunction will limit their ability to grow. It is, as we discussed, the proper first wound."

"And Ms. Sullivan?" Hans asked.

"She will be rattled," Dubois responded. "Good CEOs can weather storms; poor CEOs drown while rowing in circles. Ms. Sullivan is competent but overly moralistic, which makes her brittle."

Egli nodded. "Good. Stage three is approaching. After that, the bonds will serve as a noose for stage four. Continue with quiet pressure for now."

Dubois inclined her head. "As you wish."

Once she left, Egli looked once more at the lake and then down at the file where the terms of the Helvex Bonds lay open before him. It was brilliant in its simplicity: generous advances, staggered covenants, and a default trigger that could be activated by a sharp decline in Boston-First's share price.

Egli closed the file and smiled. "You built up a very nice bank, Bobbi. Chapeau," he said aloud, as if she could hear him across the Atlantic. "But nothing is forever."

10

BAR C RANCH
TEXAS

UNITED STATES OF AMERICA

Shane settled into the comfortable embrace of the old sofa on his wraparound deck, taking a moment to appreciate the breath-taking panorama of the valley unfolding before him like a living painting. The Bar C, a sprawling ranch nestled in the heart of Hill Country near Austin, was nothing short of idyllic. Its pictur-esque landscapes were dotted with wildflowers and framed by distant hills, creating a sense of peace.

The evening sun painted the sky in shades of violet and amber, with shadows stretching across the fields where cattle grazed lazily. He could hear the faint rattle of cicadas in the live oaks and the occasional call of a hawk overhead. For Shane, the place was more than just land—it was a refuge.

Memories of Cutter Davis's tragic death in the Gulf of Mexico surfaced, unbidden and bittersweet. Cutter had been more than a client; he had been a friend. His death, like so many others in the battles of LawForce, had left a void.

It was Cutter's widow, Sarah, who ultimately encouraged Shane toward this new life. She found the ranch too remote and isolating to raise her two children alone. Selling it to Shane was bittersweet, but it provided her with stability, especially with the home in The Woodlands he had deeded to her as part of the deal. Shane had insisted that the Bar C's gates would always be open for Sarah, Becky, and Ben.

The ranch carried Cutter's spirit—his grit, his humor, and his sense of legacy. On evenings like this, Shane felt the quiet weight of that inheritance.

He turned his gaze toward the French doors leading inside. Through the glass, he saw Val moving about the kitchen with their five-year-old son, Cody, following her around. Valentina Lopez had once been his colleague—a fierce advocate with razor-sharp courtroom instincts and an unshakable loyalty to the LawForce team. Now, she was his wife, his anchor, and the mother of their son.

Their marriage had transformed what had once been professional respect into a deep partnership—one marked by both fire and tenderness.

Cody had changed everything. Life, once dominated by work, now revolved around family. The Bar C was the backdrop for this new chapter: rolling pastures, neighbors who came by with casseroles and stories, and a rhythm that balanced work and home.

Still, Shane was no stranger to balancing contradictions. He was a lawyer, a strategist, and, when needed, a soldier in the shadow war that had birthed LawForce. There were always new battles, and when they came, they rarely announced themselves with civility.

Tonight was proof. On the side table lay the padded envelope couriered under federal seal from the U.S. Treasury. Hendrix had called the other day to say he had asked Jasmine Lin, a top cyber expert at Treasury, to prepare a report on the BostonFirst events.

He slit the seal with his pocketknife, pulled out the bound pages, and settled in as twilight deepened around him. The first lines brought him back to the fight.

Preliminary forensic analysis indicates that BostonFirst's account scandal was not the result of internal misconduct but rather an external intrusion…

Shane exhaled slowly. So it wasn't just a scandal. It wasn't merely a case of corporate greed, as in the Wells Fargo situation. Boston-First had been set up.

He read further. Jasmine's style was precise, her phrasing clipped yet illuminating. She described backdoors in BostonFirst's systems, infiltrations that disguised themselves as ordinary user activity. Scripts had generated accounts so carefully coded that even seasoned auditors missed the patterns. The hackers had buried their signatures under layers of false timestamps, with IPs bouncing across servers in locations like Jakarta, Warsaw, and Buenos Aires—smoke and mirrors.

And yet, she had found them. Barely.

Shane admired her work. He had known of her by reputation even before Hendrix mentioned her. The woman had a gift for seeing order where others only saw noise. One paragraph caught his attention.

The intrusions exhibited a cadence— an almost imperceptible rhythm— that resembled operations I had encountered before. While I couldn't identify the signature with certainty, I knew it was not random. The style was distinct, as if the operator intended to leave the faintest watermark.

Shane leaned back and closed his eyes for a moment, absorbing the sounds of the night around him. In the pasture, the wind rustled as it swept through the grass in waves. Inside the house, Val was teaching Cody another of her card tricks, while Gus, their three-legged dog, scampered about, the noise drifting out to him.

His thoughts wandered to the other homes that now marked his life. In Wailea, the beachfront condo overlooked sands so golden they seemed to make time stand still. Maui provided pure release—days filled with surfing, sunsets with Val and Cody, and a culture of aloha that soothed the battle scars of a man who had endured too many wars. In Wengen, at Chalet Bergkristall, the Alps offered him clarity. The jagged peaks of the Eiger, Mönch, and Jungfrau, the silence of the snow, and the occasional ring of cowbells brought him closer to Cutter's spirit and the truths that come only from high places.

Yet, no matter how far he traveled—whether to Maui, the Alps, or Austin Hill Country—the fight always seemed to find him. And now, it was here again.

He flipped another page. Jasmine's recommendations were urgent yet practical: Boston-First needed to shut down outside access immediately, launch counter-forensics, and assume they were still under attack. She warned that the attackers would adapt quickly. This was not a simple smash-and-grab; it was a long-term destabilization effort.

After a lengthy pause, he picked up the phone and pressed the speed-dial button.

"Steven. I figured I'd be hearing from you. I take it you received that report."

"You bet. It arrived today. Hell of a report."

"Give me a minute." Shane heard some rustling, then Hendrix was back.

"I just wanted to grab my copy. Jasmine's findings are pretty conclusive. Whoever did this was good—better than good. They nearly obscured their trail completely."

"Nearly," Shane echoed, sensing the weight in Hendrix's voice.

"Yes, nearly. That 'nearly' is what makes Jasmine uneasy. She says the patterns—the rhythm of the intrusions—feel familiar to her, but she can't place them yet. It's as if the hacker left a very faint footprint."

Shane interjected, "I saw that too. It seems we have a phantom. And a bank caught in the midst of collapse, pinned against the wall by Helvex."

Hendrix continued, "If you've been following events, you'll see that BostonFirst just got their heads handed to them," Hendrix said flatly. "Claudine Dubois—ever heard of her?"

Shane recalled the name. "Only by reputation. Swiss litigation ace, former politician.

Likes to make her opponents look like amateurs."

"Exactly what she did," Hendrix replied. "A few days ago in federal court, she walked in and gutted BostonFirst's team. She secured an injunction barring them from opening new accounts until the trial. You know what that means."

Shane leaned back in his chair. "You bet. A bank that can't take on new business is a bank on life support. They'll suffocate before the trial begins."

"Correct," Hendrix replied. "And the spectacle made headlines around the world. Reporters practically salivated over it. BostonFirst—the plucky American regional climber—reduced to a punchline in a single afternoon."

Shane recalled a curious bit in one of the reports. "Wasn't there something about a goldfish?"

He heard the exasperation in Hendrix's voice. "Yes. A clip of it is all over the networks. They're looping it—Dubois telling the judge that a pet fish had an account. It's gone viral."

"Bad optics for BostonFirst," Shane said."

He heard Hendrix groan. "Optics don't concern me as much as the substance. This report now confirms it. They were the victims of sabotage."

"By whom?" Shane asked.

"I suspect Helvex may be involved."

"Involved, or the architect?" Shane asked.

"Too early to tell," Hendrix replied. "The first step is to secure the evidence. The second is to ensure Bobbi knows she's not crazy. That hack flowed through her bank like a virus through unvaccinated code."

Shane chuckled. "You always had a knack for metaphors."

"Can't help myself," Hendrix said. Get some rest at the ranch, Steven. We may need you soon. And give my best to Valentina and Cody."

"You bet. Good night, Jon."

* * *

Shane rubbed his jaw, his instincts echoing Hendrix's conclusion—the attackers weren't freelancers. This wasn't the work of a rogue coder in a darkened basement. Helvex's lawsuit, arriving in the midst of the artificial surge of accounts, couldn't just be coincidental.

He thought of Bobbi Sullivan. She was harsh and unyielding when necessary, but she had walked into a trap she couldn't see. How could she? The enemy wasn't just inside the bank; it was embedded in the code, the very bloodstream of the institution.

Shane stood and wandered out onto the deck, the report dangling in his hand. The night had taken hold over the valley, with stars blinking awake and scattered across the indigo canvas.

Val slid through the door behind him, Cody tugging on her arm. "You look like you're wrestling with that paper," she teased. He turned to her, instantly softening at the sight. "Maybe I am."

She moved closer, brushing her free hand against his arm. "Work?"

He nodded. "BostonFirst's troubles aren't what they seem. It's bigger—much bigger."

Val studied his face. "Then you'll handle it, like you always do."

Her faith was unshakeable. Cutter had seen it in him once, Hendrix saw it still, and Val—Val lived it. He kissed her forehead, then Cody's, inhaling the sweet, powdery scent of his son's hair. "We'll handle it," he said quietly.

"Come help me with Cody," she said. "You can finish this up later."

* * *

Shane sat on the edge of Cody's bed, the room softly lit by the amber glow of a nightlight shaped like a Texas star. From the small Bluetooth speaker on the dresser came the slow, wistful chords of Don Edwards's "Patanio, the Pride of the Plains." The ballad filled the room—the story of a dramatic ride on a horse named Patanio, who saves his rider from a Native American attack despite being badly wounded.

As Edwards's smooth baritone carried the melody, Shane felt the familiar pull of nostalgia. He loved cowboy songs when he was a boy— tales of courage, redemption, and the code of the open range. He took a long time to outgrow his cowboy phase; somehow, those prairie nomads held a special fascination for him. On nights like this, listening to the cicadas and watching the silhouettes of the cattle on the range, he almost wished he hadn't outgrown that phase.

Cody's eyes fluttered closed as the final refrain faded, the last line a whisper of wind across the plains. Shane smiled, tucking the blanket around his son. "Sleep well, partner," he murmured. "The world still needs good cowboys."

* * *

He stepped back onto the deck, closing the sliding door behind him. Plopping down on the sofa, he picked up the couriered file once more and reread Jasmine's cover memo.

Recommend immediate escalation… Suggest urgent coordination with Justice, Homeland Security, and the intelligence community.

He might be back in the saddle sooner than he thought.

11

GREENWICH
CONNECTICUT

UNITED STATES OF AMERICA

Nadler leaned back in his Aeron chair. To the casual observer, he might have appeared to be just another tech bro—slouched posture, hoodie thrown over a designer T-shirt, headphones dangling from his neck. However, his eyes revealed a different story: cold, calculating, predatory.

A ventilation system whispered overhead in his Greenwich loft, keeping the room cool despite the heat generated by the processor racks. The workspace was minimalist by design—no distractions, no personal photographs, no keepsakes. Nadler had long ago abandoned anchoring himself to people or places.

The only object with sentimental value was a framed clipping from the *Financial Times*, with a headline dated nearly fifteen years earlier: "Upstart Trader Expelled from City Firm Amid Allegations of Algorithmic Manipulation." His face had never appeared with the article, but he kept it as both a warning and a source of motivation. The expulsion that should have ruined him had instead become his liberation. From London, he'd vanished into the underworld of cyberfinance, where men like Hans Egli found him.

Now, working under Egli's patronage and Helvex's discreet protection, Nadler was orchestrating his strike against BostonFirst that would reverberate far beyond Wall Street.

The first act had been executed with precision. His malware had infiltrated BostonFirst's system and begun spawning accounts—tens of thousands of them, each with just enough variation to appear legitimate. The media had latched onto it precisely as he had predicted. Commentators framed BostonFirst as guilty of reckless, incentivizing fraud. Analysts muttered about "the next Wells Fargo." Congressional staffers leaked that hearings were being prepared. It was beautiful.

Yet, BostonFirst's stock still held firm. The public had not yet panicked. Investors were shaken but not fleeing. Depositors largely trusted that their balances were safe. Scandal alone wasn't enough. So now came phase two.

Nadler adjusted his glasses and opened a program coded with an interface only he understood. He had nicknamed it *Betinipftsa*, a meaningless string of letters that disguised its real function. To outsiders, it looked like just another entry in the endless parade of crypto apps or fintech startups. However, inside its architecture was a machine built to devour trust itself.

At its core was a whisper campaign. He had deployed bots across X, Telegram, Discord, Reddit, and even the darker corners of encrypted forums. Each bot had a distinct personality: a concerned mother in Minneapolis, a skeptical accountant in Boston, an ex–banker with a grudge. They communicated in slightly different tones, using regional slang and varied grammar to avoid the uniformity that made bot farms detectable. Their scripts were designed to converge, like tributaries flowing into a river, on one shared message:

BostonFirst is insolvent. Withdraw your money now before it's too late.

He typed in the seed phrase and pressed enter. The program sprang to life. Screens filled with cascading text as accounts logged in simultaneously, spreading a deceptive narrative into every corner of the digital space. Hashtags were readied to trend: #BostonFirstCollapse, #BankRun2024, #GetOutNow. Influencers, bribed through anonymous cryptocurrency payments, were scheduled to post cryptic memes within the next twenty-four hours. "Heard it from a friend inside: BostonFirst is done. Protect yourself."

The brilliance of the campaign lay in its self-sustaining nature. Once seeded, the rumor would take on a life of its own, mutating and amplifying, becoming truth simply because so many people repeated it. No regulator, no fact-checker, and no sober statement from Bobbi Sullivan could contain it.

Nadler smiled faintly; he wasn't finished. The second payload embedded in *Betinipftsa* was far more insidious. Hidden malware triggers would activate across BostonFirst's customer-facing platforms. Login pages would crash intermittently; balances would momentarily display as zero before correcting; transactions would stall in digital limbo. None of these glitches was catastrophic, but in a moment of panic, perception mattered more than reality.

The script was elegantly designed: errors would be staggered to create the impression of a systemic collapse. A customer trying to transfer $500 might receive a "service unavailable" notice. Another might see their account "locked for security reasons." A third could open their mobile app to a temporary blank screen. These issues were recoverable and reversible, but in the context of a viral rumor, the glitches would confirm the worst fears.

He watched his code propagate. After the launch, the bots would begin their whispers. Within a day, journalists would take notice. By the time regulators issued reassurances, the market would already be in motion. Depositors would rush to ATMs, draining them dry. Hedge funds would short the stock. Rivals would circle like sharks.

Stretching back from the console, he flicked open the blinds and gazed down Greenwich Avenue through the broad industrial windows. He observed the morning routine unfold—the espresso crowd at The Granola Bar and the parade of Porsches and Range Rovers heading toward the Merritt Parkway. It was a civilized façade, with wealth and calm cloaking the digital chaos he commanded from behind glass walls and glowing monitors.

With a grunt, Nadler slapped the blinds shut and turned back to the screens, chewing on his toothpick. He resumed coding, his fingers flying across the keyboard. BostonFirst was living on borrowed time. He thought of Bobbi Sullivan in Boston, still clinging to the illusion of control—believing the worst had passed, that the fraudulent account scandal was under control.

But soon, Bobbi's bank would become carrion, ripe for the picking by a vulture like Helvex. Nadler watched the humming servers, their blinking lights dancing like constellations. He had always admired constellations, not for their beauty, but for their inevitability. Stars burned, collapsed, died, and no prayer could alter their trajectory.

BostonFirst's trajectory was already determined. He closed his laptop, stood, and stretched, feeling the ache in his shoulders from hours hunched over the code. He crossed the loft to the small liquor cabinet, poured himself a measure of Lagavulin, and raised the glass in a mock salute to the silent machines.

12

BOSTON
MASSACHUSETTS
- - -
NEW YORK CITY
NEW YORK

UNITED STATES OF AMERICA

Bobbi jolted awake to the shrill chime of her phone. Blinking at the screen, she saw it was 1:50 a.m., and her COO, Linda Prescott, was calling.

"What is it?" Bobbi asked, her voice hoarse.

Linda's words came out in a rush. "It's the market, Bobbi. The stock... It's in free fall in Tokyo, Shanghai, and Hong Kong. My market alarm went off an hour ago. I'm in the office."

Bobbi sat upright, her mind scrambling to process the news. "How bad is it?"

"We're down sixty-eight percent already."

Her heart sank. "Get the executive team together. I'm on my way in. No comments to anyone for now. All external communications need to be vetted by me."

"Yes, of course. Is there anything else?"

"We need to consider talking to New York about suspending the stock at the start of trading."

"That's a tough decision. It would send a bad signal to the market, but I'm not sure things can get much worse. I've already contacted the New York Stock Exchange operations desk. They're monitoring the situation. We don't have to make that decision until nine a.m., a half-hour before the opening bell."

"Okay, hopefully we'll know more by then. See you soon."

Bobbi ended the call and sat frozen for a moment. The city outside her window was still asleep, unaware. But by the time Boston woke up, the entire financial world would be staring at her bank's potential collapse.

* * *

Within an hour, Bobbi was at Boston-First's headquarters. Usually, she felt a sense of pride as she walked through the doors, but today, all she felt was the cold, clammy grip of panic.

She pushed into the boardroom. Graphs and data points glowed on the giant screens, displaying jagged lines crashing downward. Voices overlapped as executives tried—and failed—to impose order. Linda Prescott pointed to a flashing red graph. "Overnight, we saw coordinated sell-offs in the eastern markets. Huge blocks of shares. It's a classic run on the bank. Social media is full of stories claiming we're insolvent. If this continues, they might be right. Our liquidity pools will dry up."

Bobbi scanned the room. Panic hung thick in the air. Her team—typically composed and confident—looked pale and desperate. A sick realization struck her: nobody had prepared for this, not on this scale.

The room erupted into bickering—what to tell regulators, whether to suspend trading, how to spin the potential collapse. Bobbi's stomach churned. She excused herself and stepped into the hallway.

Desperate to hold back tears, she reminded herself that she couldn't break down in front of her team. She was tough, the formidable Bobbi Sullivan. If she fell apart, they would know it was over. All this chaos stemmed from one colossal mistake.

When she partnered with Helvex on Eigernet, a small voice in her head had warned her that the offer was too good to be true. But her ambition had pushed her to move forward. *What a fool.* She felt her fingernails dig into the table as she steeled herself to think about the next steps. Jasmine would know what to do. She dialed her speed dial.

"Hey, Jas, I'm in trouble."

Jasmine's reply was instant and tense. "I know, we're following the events. We're waiting to see what happens at the open, but it doesn't look good."

"What do I do? Did you find out anything from your inquiries?"

"Yes, I was going to call you today. We noticed irregularities in your system and suspect that Helvex is the cause. However, at this stage, it's only a suspicion. We don't have enough evidence to act, so you'll have to try to manage the damage."

Bobbi inhaled sharply. She knew Jasmine was savvy about the financial markets.

"What do you think about a stop trade order for this morning?"

"It might buy you a few hours. Circuit breakers can stem panic, but not for long. The SEC won't freeze a stock unless there are questions about your assets. Unless you're prepared for that level of scrutiny, tread carefully."

Bobbi sighed. "Okay, thanks, Jas."

* * *

At 9:29 a.m., the trading floor of the New York Stock Exchange buzzed with tense anticipation. Traders huddled in small groups, their screens already glowing with red indicators. BostonFirst's ticker—BFB—blazed like a warning flare.

At 9:30 sharp, the opening bell clanged, echoing across the cavernous space. BFB opened at $52, but in mere seconds, the number plummeted. Screens flickered like lightning strikes:

$39.20

$27.15

$18.04

Traders shouted orders so quickly that their voices blended into a wall of noise. Phones rang, brokers yelled into headsets, and hands shot up, trying to catch bids that weren't there.

Then everything collapsed.

$7.88

$3.14

$0.92

In under ten minutes, BostonFirst had become a penny stock. The ticker streamed across every screen in the room, flashing in red. Brokers who had dealt with BostonFirst stock for decades looked stricken; some swore under their breath, while others laughed bitterly at the sheer violence of the collapse.

Anchors from CNBC and Bloomberg, seated above the floor, spoke in stunned tones. "We are witnessing one of the fastest collapses in American banking history," one anchor said, his voice trembling. "BostonFirst stock opened at fifty-two dollars a share and is now trading under a dollar. This is... this is unprecedented."

Reporters scrambled with microphones, jostling against the throng of traders. The bell had rung only minutes ago, yet the bloodletting was complete.

* * *

In the boardroom at BostonFirst, silence reigned. Screens lined the walls, each confirming the disaster. Linda Prescott's voice was barely audible. "We're at seventy-nine cents a share."

Bobbi sat motionless at the head of the table, her hands clasped so tightly that her knuckles turned white. She had envisioned worst-case scenarios before—regulatory probes, a scandal over Helvex, even a temporary liquidity crisis. But this? Seeing her bank, her family's legacy, obliterated in real time?

Her COO tried again. "Bobbi... the market has declared us insolvent. There's no confidence left. This is—"

"Stop," Bobbi interrupted, her voice firm despite the tightness in her throat. "Don't say it. We're not finished."

But deep down, she knew the truth: they were standing on the ashes of BostonFirst.

The phone buzzed again, twisting her stomach as she saw the caller ID: Bernie, her younger brother—a retired firefighter who had recently rolled his pension into BostonFirst stock.

"Oh God," she muttered, then answered.

"Hey, Sis," Bernie said, his voice breaking. "What the hell is going on? My 401(k) is being slaughtered. It's on every channel; even the morning shows are running it nonstop. My entire retirement is at stake, Bobbi. Everything."

She closed her eyes. "We're working on it. I can't say much, Berns, but we'll find out who's behind this."

"You gotta fix this. Please. It's my life savings."

"Yes, Berns, I know. BostonFirst is my baby. I'll do everything I can."

He hung up abruptly, and she knew he was holding back his rage. If this was her brother's reaction, what about the millions of other investors? These wasn't just numbers; these were lives.

13

BOSTON
MASSACHUSETTS

UNITED STATES OF AMERICA

The boardroom at BostonFirst's head-quarters felt unusually warm, the air heavy and still, as if the ventilation system had taken a break. Everyone inside sat in silence, waiting, staring at the door, pretending to shuffle papers that no longer mattered. The collapse of BostonFirst's stock a week ago had reduced the institution to a husk, and now they knew their predator "partner" had come to finish them off.

The double doors opened with a muted push, and Claudine Dubois walked in. She was alone and carried no bulky folders, no stacks of notes, none of the props that the Americans had littered across the long oak table. She had only a black Hermès briefcase, slim and sharp as a blade.

The BostonFirst legal team, four middle-aged men, stiffened. Bobbi, at the head of the table, remained stone-faced, but inside, her chest was tight, as though a fist had closed around her heart. She had been CEO of BostonFirst for nearly a decade, guiding the bank through various challenges, earning praise, and weathering storms. But she had never faced an adversary like Claudine Dubois.

Dubois set the briefcase down on the table with deliberate care, sat smoothly, and folded her hands. Then she smiled, a small, precise gesture that conveyed both amusement and inevitability.

"Let's not waste time, gentlemen," and with a nod to Bobbi, "Ms. Sullivan. You know why I'm here."

BostonFirst's lead corporate counsel, George Martin, cleared his throat. A veteran of Boston's legal elite, he wore the weariness of a man who had not slept in thirty-six hours. He adjusted his glasses, stared down at his papers, and forced out words he must have known were futile.

"The Helvex Loan—there are... ambiguities in the language," Martin said, his voice dry. "We have grounds for delay. Potentially for challenge."

Dubois tilted her head slightly, like a teacher watching a child struggle with a simple equation. She allowed a pause, then exhaled a soft laugh. Not mocking, not cruel—worse. Disappointed.

"No, you do not," she said, her voice even. "There are no ambiguities. The terms are crystal clear. When the stock dropped in value by more than seventy-five percent from the time the loan closed, Helvex's right to control was triggered. A right that was exercised through proper notice by my client two days ago."

From her briefcase, she withdrew a single sheet of paper and slid it across the table.

"This is a legal opinion from FINMA." Her manicured nail tapped it once, lightly but with finality. "The Swiss financial authority has reviewed the terms of the Helvex Loan and confirmed what we already knew—Helvex Financial is within its rights to demand immediate control."

The Americans leaned in. One of the younger associates squinted at the document as if he could conjure a flaw with willpower alone. A New York attorney with a Wall Street reputation whispered, "This... this is airtight."

Martin swallowed, his face pale. "We are not in Switzerland. We could petition a U.S. court—"

Dubois raised a single eyebrow, silencing him.

"You could," she conceded. "But you would lose. And while you delay, your institution bleeds out. Depositors will run. Regulators will intervene. You will not survive long enough for a judge to rule."

Bobbi had listened without speaking. Her eyes were locked on Dubois, studying every gesture, every word. What unnerved her was not arrogance; it was something colder: inevitability.

"There has to be an alternative," Bobbi said at last. Her voice was controlled, but the tremor beneath it betrayed her strain.

Dubois smiled gently, as though humoring her. "There is, Ms. Sullivan. You can refuse."

The lawyers stiffened, glancing amongst themselves as if a new possibility had been born.

"But then," Dubois said, leaning slightly forward, her voice dropping, "we liquidate the bank instead."

The words fell like a guillotine. No one spoke. Everyone knew what liquidation meant—asset atomization, depositors left scrambling, employees ruined. BostonFirst would cease to exist.

Dubois allowed the silence to stretch, savoring it. Then she lowered her voice again, making the moment intimate and personal. "Be pragmatic, Ms. Sullivan. Accept the offer. Walk away with whatever dignity you have left. And think of your employees. After all their years of service, you owe them some consideration."

Dubois opened her folder and slid a single sheet across the table toward Bobbi.

"The offer is generous: one dollar per share."

George Martin, desperate, seized on the numbers. "Generous? For a tier two bank with a storied pedigree?"

Dubois raised her hand, stopping him with the smallest gesture. Her eyes never left Bobbi. "Yesterday's news, Mr. Martin. This morning, your stock is trading at eighty cents. And it's falling. By tomorrow, it will be fifty. By next week—if BostonFirst still exists—twenty. One dollar is a premium of twenty-five percent. Consider it a gift, or my appreciation of American traditions."

The BostonFirst lawyers looked at her quizzically. Martin stuttered, "Traditions?"

Dubois gave him a wink, her tone suddenly playful. "I rather enjoy shopping at one of your famous institutions—Dollar General. Everything for one dollar. A wonderful concept: clean, efficient, universal."

The BostonFirst lawyers sat stone-faced. Bobbi felt heat rise to her face, the mockery as sharp as the terms themselves.

Dubois leaned back. "Helvex acquires all outstanding shares at one dollar, including your fifty-five percent controlling block, Ms. Sullivan. That block is the jewel. With it, the transfer is clean, swift, bloodless."

The lawyers scrambled for a last defense. "We have fiduciary duties to shareholders," Martin insisted.

"The SEC—" one of the New York attorneys began.

"Litigation—" another added, his voice rising with desperation.

Dubois let them finish, her expression patient. When they fell silent, she spoke with surgical calm.

"You speak of fiduciary duties, litigation, and regulators. But you forget one thing: time. Litigation requires years. Regulators require months. You have hours. Your stock price is collapsing as we sit here. Depositors whisper about insolvency. Even now, the Fed drafts contingency plans. Do you believe they will fight for you when Helvex offers immediate stability? The chance to keep this venerable bank afloat. To keep your thousands of employees on the payroll."

The silence that followed was suffocating; they all knew she was right.

Bobbi felt her pulse in her throat, in her temples, in the tips of her fingers. She thought of her great-grandfather in 1931, standing on the bank steps, handing out cash to panicked depositors and declaring that their money was safe. She thought of her father, of long board-room battles, and of the pride of carrying the family name into the twenty-first century. And now it ended here—at the hands of a Swiss law-yer with a single sheet of paper.

"Why?" Bobbi asked, her voice breaking. "Why destroy us?"

Dubois's gaze softened, but only slightly. "Because you allowed it. You invited Helvex into your house. You signed the papers. You took the money. Do not look to me for blame, Ms. Sullivan. Ambition blinded you. That blind-ness is yours, not mine."

The cruelty was sharper because it was true.

Dubois stood, gathering her papers. "I will expect signed agreements by the close of busi-ness today. There is no need for courts. No need for regulators. We are civilized people, after all."

She glanced around the room one last time, her expression almost gracious. "Bos-tonFirst now belongs to Helvex. Congratula-tions, Ms. Sullivan. You have just made his-tory." The double doors clicked shut behind her.

No one moved. Papers lay scattered like de-bris after a battle. The lawyers stared at the ta-ble, at their hands, anywhere but at Bobbi.

George Martin cleared his throat. "We could still... attempt—"

"Attempt what?" Bobbi snapped, her voice cracking like a whip. She turned on him, her eyes blazing. "Where were your *attempts* when these covenants were drafted? When we signed those bonds? You let this happen. Don't sit here now and give me scraps of false hope."

Martin shrank back.

Bobbi pushed herself to her feet and walked to the window. Boston sprawled below. People hurried to work, sipping coffee, nibbling on their Dunkin' donuts, reading newspapers, unaware that their bank, their deposits, their pensions were now in foreign hands. They would not like that. BostonFirst's branding relied heavily on Boston's rich history of producing Patriots, Founding Fathers, and Daughters of the American Revolution. What would the good people of Boston think of her now—*Bobbi Benedict Arnold?*

Her phone buzzed on the table. Bernie. Again. She couldn't bring herself to answer. She knew what he would ask. She had no answers.

By evening, the press release crossed the wires:

Helvex Buys BostonFirst at $1 Per Share

One line. Clinical. Sterile. Bloodless.

For Claudine Dubois, it was triumph. For Hans Egli, a strategy fulfilled. For Bobbi Sullivan, the end of a legacy.

14

YANQI LAKE

CHINA

The limousine rolled silently along the final stretch of the causeway to Yanqi Lake, its black-tinted windows reflecting the pale shimmer of dawn on the still waters. Inside the lead vehicle, Chairman Liang Ze sat in measured silence, dressed in his simple dark tunic—the same understated uniform he wore to every meeting. Across from him, Gao Feng, the director of Project DragonBreath, studied the landscape with a mixture of awe and nervous anticipation. Today was his first status report.

As they entered the compound, guards in dark uniforms snapped to attention. PLA officers discreetly flanked the entrance, their presence barely visible to the untrained eye. The hotel was sealed for official state use.

Stepping out into the crisp morning air, the Chairman paused to glance over the still waters. "Peaceful," he murmured. "But the most peaceful places often conceal the most turbulent plans."

Feng bowed slightly. "Indeed, Chairman. I take it as a good omen."

Liang's lips twitched faintly—the closest thing to a smile.

The private conference suite was minimalist yet immaculate, featuring lacquered wood panels and a single broad table overlooking the mountains. A pot of Longjing tea steamed quietly between them.

Without turning, Liang spoke. "For too long, Feng, our nation has stood in the shadow of others. The West basks in the light it stole from us centuries ago."

Feng nodded. "Yes, Chairman. Yet the tide begins to turn. The markets are growing restless. The West is consumed by its own greed."

Liang snorted. "Greed is their only faith. They worship profit and call it freedom. But Heaven's balance cannot remain so tilted forever."

Liang turned, his eyes gleaming. "Tell me, Feng, what is the true weapon of our age?"

Feng thought for a moment. "Not armies, Chairman. Not missiles. Money."

Liang nodded approvingly. "Exactly. Once, the sages said, 'He who controls the granaries controls the realm.' Today, the granary is the global ledger. The fields are digital. He who governs the flow of finance governs the fates of nations. So, Feng, tell me how DragonBreath is progressing."

Feng opened his tablet and began the presentation. A holographic map of the world shimmered above the table, the Atlantic glowing faintly.

"Project DragonBreath," he began, his tone confident yet deferential, "is entering stage five. The financial platform and cryptocurrency vectors are operational. As you have seen in the headlines, stage four—Helvex Financial's acquisition of BostonFirst—was completed successfully. The Western press calls it 'a bold merger.' They have no idea what it truly represents."

Liang nodded slowly. "I've read the reports. It's all over the Financial Times and The Wall Street Journal. They think it's a banking story. But this..."—he gestured toward the map— "this is far more."

"Yes, Chairman," Feng continued. "The acquisition gives us control of both the conduit and the instrument. BostonFirst provides direct access to Western liquidity systems, while

Helvex serves as our Swiss facade. Through these entities, we are already influencing global flows in digital currency markets."

The Chairman's expression softened with pride. "You've done well, Gao Feng. The capture of BostonFirst was elegant—truly a work of art in financial warfare. You've struck at the Western heart without firing a single shot."

Feng bowed deeply. "It is the fruit of your vision, Chairman. I merely executed your guidance."

For a moment, silence enveloped the room, broken only by the quiet whistle of the wind across the lake. Liang stood and paced slowly toward the window.

"Do you know, Feng," the Chairman said softly, "I studied here as a young man, at Tsinghua University, before I ever imagined the path I would take. We were told then that China's destiny was to catch up—to emulate the West. But now..." He turned, his eyes hardening. "Now it is they who will emulate us—or perish trying."

He walked back to the table and placed a hand on Feng's shoulder. "You have served your country well. If Project DragonBreath continues on this path, I will personally ensure that you are awarded the Order of the Republic."

Feng froze, stunned, eyes blinking rapidly. For a moment, he could only stare at the Chairman. "The Order of the Republic, sir? That is—"

"The highest honor we can give to a civilian," Liang finished for him. "And one rarely bestowed. But I reward loyalty and results. You have provided both."

Feng bowed deeply, emotion tightening his throat. "It would be the greatest honor of my life, Chairman. I will not fail you."

"I know you won't," Liang replied, returning to his seat. "Failure is a Western indulgence."

The meeting concluded as the sun reached its zenith. The two men stepped onto the terrace. Liang stood with his hands behind his back, the crisp air lifting the edges of his tunic. "When I look at this lake," he said, "I see China's reflection—calm, disciplined, patient. But beneath the surface, powerful currents move unseen. The world above believes the surface tells the entire story. That is their mistake."

Liang turned back toward the hotel, the sun catching the faint silver in his hair. "We will not destroy the West through bombs or bullets, Feng. We will undermine their confidence. Once it shatters, they will do our work for us."

Feng inclined his head. "It will be done, Chairman. The timeline remains on schedule."

"Good," Liang said. "Because history does not wait for those who hesitate."

15

WASHINGTON
DISTRICT OF COLUMBIA

UNITED STATES OF AMERICA

Hendrix sat alone in his office, the television glowing in the dim light. The rest of the building was quiet, filled only with the hum of the HVAC system and the occasional creak of pipes in the walls. He leaned forward in his chair, elbows resting on his desk, his eyes fixed on the screen.

The camera panned over the Senate Banking Committee chamber, and even through the television glass, Hendrix felt the weight of the atmosphere—grand, imposing, and unforgiving. The chamber was designed to intimidate, with a high ceiling lined with coffered oak and plaster panels, every line drawing the eye toward the seal of the United States that loomed above the dais. Heavy velvet drapes framed tall windows, allowing filtered sunlight to fall in shafts onto the polished marble floors. The long mahogany witness table gleamed under the glare of the television lights, reminiscent of an executioner's block awaiting its subject.

The senators were seated on the curved dais, arranged like black-robed judges. Their chairs elevated them above the witness table, forcing any testifier to look up at them. Ornamental brass lamps cast a harsh glow on papers, glasses of water, and the gavel that sat before Chairman Howard Kellerman.

Behind the dais, staffers leaned over stacks of binders, whispering and slipping notes onto their senators' desks. The gallery beyond was crowded with reporters, cameras, and curious onlookers, the air buzzing with expectation.

The clerk's monotone voice filled the chamber. "This committee will come to order."

The gavel cracked, its echo lingering in the air.

Hendrix adjusted the TV volume. He had attended hearings like this before and had even testified himself; he understood the palpable tension—the stage-like quality of it all, the lights hotter than necessary, the cameras focused on every gesture, every blink. A witness might enter believing in the strength of their facts, but the chamber was ultimately about theater, and survival meant performing better than the senators sitting across from you.

Today, the stage belonged to Bobbi Sullivan.

The camera cut to her at the witness table. She looked small in the cavernous room but was anything but fragile. Wearing a dark gray suit that fit her like armor, her hair pinned back tightly, she exhibited signs of exhaustion—dark smudges under her eyes and lips pressed tight—but her posture remained ramrod straight. Before her sat a microphone, a small placard with her name, and a glass pitcher of water.

Notably, the seat beside her was empty. No lawyer. No team of advisers whispering strategies. Just Bobbi, alone, facing the semicircle of senators.

Hendrix shook his head and muttered, "Damn fools left her to burn."

Chairman Kellerman, tall and hawk-faced, surveyed the room. His voice reverberated through the chamber. "This committee convenes today under extraordinary circumstances. BostonFirst Bank, a pillar of American finance for over a century, has been taken over by Helvex Financial of Switzerland after a catastrophic collapse in BostonFirst's stock value. Jobs, pensions, and savings have been lost, and confidence in our financial system has been shaken. The American people deserve answers."

He paused, letting his words resonate in the marble chamber. "Our sole witness this morning is Ms. Bobbi Sullivan, former Chief Executive Officer of BostonFirst."

A rustle of activity rippled through the gallery as dozens of camera shutters clicked in unison.

Kellerman continued, "Ms. Sullivan, BostonFirst collapsed in less than a week. Depositors panicked, your stock plummeted from fifty-two dollars to pennies, and Helvex Financial swooped in to purchase controlling shares at one dollar. How could you let this happen?"

Bobbi leaned toward the microphone. Her voice was low at first but steady, each word pronounced. "Senator, I did not *let* this happen. BostonFirst was the target of a coordinated assault—an attack on our liquidity, our stock, and our credibility. This was sabotage, not mismanagement."

Murmurs rippled through the gallery. Pens scratched furiously on reporters' notepads.

A heavyset man with a reputation for populist fervor signaled to Kellerman. "If I may, Mr. Chairman?"

Kellerman nodded, "I yield to the senior senator from Ohio."

Senator Jameson turned to Bobbi, his voice booming across the chamber. "Sabotage? You're claiming that a two-hundred-billion-dollar American bank, with one hundred fifty years of history, was brought down by... shadows? By rumors on the internet?"

Bobbi met his glare with steely resolve. "Not shadows, Senator. Algorithms. Bots. A coordinated campaign to first open thousands of bogus accounts, followed by a social media effort to trigger a run on the bank. False rumors were seeded and amplified to incite panic. This was not the market acting naturally. It was engineered."

Jameson slammed a palm against the desk. "Or maybe it was your mismanagement! Didn't you, Ms. Sullivan, enter into a platform agreement with Helvex Financial last year? Weren't those very contracts the weapon they used to gut your bank?"

The chamber murmured.

Bobbi's jaw was set, but her voice remained steady. "Yes, we partnered with Helvex. But partnership is not a crime. That contract was a bridge, not a dagger. The collapse of Boston-First was not inevitable; it was induced."

Jameson scowled, unimpressed. "I yield the floor."

Kellerman looked down the dais. "The junior senator from California."

Rachel Cho slid her glasses down her nose and flipped through a binder thick with papers. "Thank you, Mr. Chairman. Ms. Sullivan, the Helvex Bonds contained clauses that triggered control rights if your stock dropped by more than seventy-five percent. Did you, or did you not, understand those terms when you signed them?"

Bobbi hesitated long enough for the cameras to zoom in closer. Hendrix muttered under his breath, "Careful, Bobbi. They're baiting you."

She replied, "Senator, our counsel reviewed those documents. At the time, no one anticipated such a catastrophic collapse. The triggering event in those clauses was seen as highly remote. Hindsight makes it look obvious, but sabotage was not foreseen."

Cho's tone sharpened. "Highly remote, and yet here we are. So you admit your legal team failed? You admit you handed over the keys to one of America's oldest banks without fully appreciating the danger?"

Bobbi's eyes flashed. "I admit our legal counsel did not anticipate sabotage on this scale. No contract term alone justifies the destruction we saw. This was not just the fine print of a loan. This was an operation."

Cho shook her head. "I yield."

Kellerman nodded. "The senior senator from Texas."

John Burroughs leaned back in his chair, his drawl filling the room. "An operation, ma'am? Engineered by whom, exactly? Do you have names? Evidence? Or is this just a story to shift blame?"

Bobbi gripped her microphone tightly, her voice now fierce. "Senator, I don't have the smoking gun. But I know the signs: coordinated account manipulations followed by a social media campaign designed to bleed liquidity—malicious rumors igniting online like wildfire. Automated trading amplifying panic. Someone orchestrated this, and they profited."

The chamber hummed with noise, and the chairman pounded his gavel for order.

The barrage continued for over an hour. Senators took turns hammering Bobbi on a non-partisan basis—a rarity in the Senate, where most investigations unfold along party lines. There seemed universal outrage over the loss of a historic American bank to a foreign player. Some painted Bobbi as reckless, while a few implied outright incompetence. Through it all, she sat upright, her voice calm, refusing to buckle.

At one point, Jameson sneered, "So now you're the victim of a conspiracy, Ms. Sullivan? Isn't it more convenient to blame foreign ghosts than to admit you lost control of your bank?"

Bobbi locked eyes with him. "Senator, this is not about me. It's about the United States. If a coordinated attack can take down BostonFirst, it can take down any bank. That is what should concern you."

Her words reverberated through the marble chamber. Even the senators shifted uneasily. She sat back, her eyes unwavering.

Hendrix scribbled notes on his pad. She was cornered, alone, outgunned—but she was holding her ground.

The chairman banged the gavel. "Thank you, Ms. Sullivan. This hearing is adjourned."

Chairs scraped, aides swarmed, and cameras flashed. Bobbi gathered her papers quietly, rose, and walked out as she had entered— alone.

The screen faded to a panel of pundits arguing. Hendrix clicked it off. The room plunged into silence, save for the hum of the HVAC system. He sat back and let out a long breath. He had seen enough.

Bobbi had acquitted herself with more dignity, clarity, and fire than any lawyer her board had hired. But she was alone—no legal support in sight.

"This has to be ours now," Hendrix murmured.

He picked up his phone and dialed.

"Steven," he said when Shane answered. "Get ready. Unless you're living on another planet, you've got to agree we should be taking this on. The fight for BostonFirst may be over, but Bobbi has not finished fighting. And she's going to need us."

He set the phone down, leaned back in his chair, and stared at the dark screen. His only regret was arriving so late to the party—all the more reason to go full throttle now.

16

VINEYARD SOUND
MASSACHUSETTS

UNITED STATES OF AMERICA

The ferry rolled and pitched against the gray chop of Vineyard Sound. Jasmine Lin stood at the rail, watching the buildings of the Woods Hole Oceanographic Institution recede in the distance. One hand gripped the cold steel, the other pushed a few wind-whipped strands of hair from her eyes.

The sea spray stung her cheeks, sharp as pins, but she welcomed it. The salt air cleared her head, slicing through the haze of spreadsheets, encrypted messages, and the relentless hum of Washington.

Behind her, passengers had retreated inside to the warmth of the main cabin—tourists clutching paper coffee cups, weekenders hiding behind their phones.

The call from Jonathan Hendrix still replayed in her mind. It had come in the chaotic aftermath of BostonFirst's collapse. At the center of it all stood Bobbi Sullivan, trying to hold together the fragments of a shattered institution while the media gleefully tore her apart.

Hendrix had opened with courtesy—thanking Jasmine for her report, acknowledging her suspicions about Helvex Financial. But there'd been disappointment in his voice. "Suspicion isn't evidence," he'd said.

Jasmine had corrected him. After submitting the report, she hadn't stopped digging. Leveraging Treasury's supercomputer and a new suite of high-end analytical software, she'd breached BostonFirst's network.

Buried deep in the metadata was the digital fingerprint she'd been hunting—an encrypted signature linking the malware directly to Helvex. It was irrefutable proof. She hadn't penetrated Helvex's own mainframe. That would require an inside job—those Swiss vaults were digital fortresses. But she didn't need to. The data harvested from BostonFirst's servers was enough to map the attack back to Zurich.

When she told him, Hendrix's tone shifted from weary to excited. "That changes everything," he'd said. "Now we have a case." Then his voice softened. "I watched Bobbi at the Senate hearings. Brilliant performance—bravura, even—but she's swimming upstream. She needs help, Jasmine. The right kind of help."

That was when he'd told her about Law-Force—a legal strike force. It sounded almost cinematic, like something lifted from a Marvel screenplay, but Hendrix's gravity left no doubt it was real.

"You're close to Bobbi," he'd continued. "Convince her to meet with us. She needs allies who can match Helvex blow for blow."

Jasmine hadn't hesitated. "You're right," she said. "She's exhausted—and alone. I'll talk to her."

And now, as the ferry plowed through the churning sea toward Martha's Vineyard, Jasmine felt the weight of that promise pressing gently on her shoulders. She had tracked Bobbi down to her favorite hotel on Martha's Vineyard and invited herself over for a visit.

The wind shifted. The ferry's horn bellowed once. Ahead, Martha's Vineyard rose from the haze—low dunes, skeletal trees, gingerbread houses—like a chess piece set on the edge of the sea.

Jasmine smiled despite herself. Edgartown, she thought—trust Bobbi to pick the most discreet corner of New England to lick her wounds.

She remembered Bobbi's voice on the last call before everything unraveled—crisp, deliberate, but quivering at the edges.

"They're saying it was my fault, Jasmine—thousands of false accounts, insider trades. I don't even know where half the money went. We're being played."

Jasmine had wanted to believe it was just panic. Now she knew better. She stepped back from the rail, shaking droplets from her coat sleeve. The ferry listed slightly as it rounded the final buoy. Below, the churned water gleamed slate-green, flecked with foam. Above, gulls traced ragged arcs in the wind, riding thermals from the wake.

Inside, the loudspeaker crackled. "We'll be docking at Vineyard Haven in approximately fifteen minutes. Please return to your vehicles or prepare to disembark."

Jasmine took a last look as the island came into focus—the watercolor sweep of the harbor, yachts rocking on their moorings like nervous horses. She hurried to her car.

The ferry bumped the dock. Crewmen tossed lines to shore, the thick ropes coiling like snakes on the wet planks. Engines wound down. The air filled with the scent of diesel and brine. Jasmine drove off the ramp and headed for the narrow road to Edgartown, the asphalt twisting through marshland and pine. The afternoon sun flashed through the branches, strobing the windshield. Every so often, she caught glimpses of the ocean—a broad, cold shimmer.

When she reached the town, it was as if time had paused in a sepia frame: white clapboard houses, picket fences, a bakery exhaling cinnamon into the street. At the far end, the Harbor View Hotel rose like a grand old dame, its wraparound veranda cluttered with rocking chairs.

She parked near the front steps and killed the engine. For a moment, she sat in silence, watching the flag at the pier snap in the wind. So, this is exile, she thought—peace with a price tag.

Inside the lobby, a young clerk greeted her with island courtesy and directed her toward the Presidential Skyhouse Suite. "Ms. Sullivan's expecting you," he said.

Jasmine climbed the polished staircase, her fingers tracing the banister's curve. At the top, she straightened her coat, knocked twice, and waited.

17

MARTHA'S VINEYARD
MASSACHUSETTS

UNITED STATES OF AMERICA

The wind off Edgartown Harbor carried the tang of salt and the faint creak of moored boats as Bobbi Sullivan stood at her open window, gazing toward the low gray outline of Chappaquiddick Island. Everything looked so bare in the off-season, cold and soulless. The island felt strangely empty without all the tourists and beach worshipers. But for her, right now, it matched her mood perfectly. Her world was cold and empty these days. She sipped from a cup of lukewarm tea, eyes tracing the line where the channel met the sea.

Chappaquiddick. The name itself was a ghost, a whisper of scandal woven into American mythology. Ted Kennedy had his demons too, she mused, and he managed—mostly—to outlive them. Maybe not entirely. Some said that night had cost him the presidency, that no amount of charm or contrition could scrub away the stain. But still—he endured.

"Oh well," she muttered, setting the cup down on the sill. "Everyone has their Chappaquiddick." Hers had just come dressed in code and scandal—false accounts, digital fraud, and a media firestorm that refused to burn out.

The BostonFirst affair had left her reputation in tatters, her life under siege. The phone had stopped ringing weeks ago, except for reporters and lawyers. And then, out of nowhere, came the message from Jasmine.

Jasmine had been cryptic—no details, just that there were *significant developments* in her case and that she needed to speak with her in person. That alone was enough to stir both curiosity and dread. Jasmine wasn't one for drama; if she said something mattered, it mattered.

Bobbi stepped away from the window and glanced around the Harbor View Hotel's Presidential Skyhouse Suite—perched high with its panoramic view of the harbor and Chappaquidick Island. A vase of white hydrangeas sat on the dresser, wilting slightly in the warmth. On the writing desk, her laptop lay open, glowing faintly with unfinished drafts of letters she couldn't bring herself to send—to shareholders, to regulators, to her brother.

She caught her reflection in the window: the practiced poise of a banker who'd spent years being the calm center of the storm. But even she couldn't deny the fatigue in her eyes.

The soft creak of the floorboards, followed by two sharp raps, jolted her back to the present. She crossed the room and opened the door. There stood Jasmine, windblown from the ferry, her dark hair tangled, her expression serious but kind.

Bobbi managed a small smile. "Well," she said quietly, "you look like someone who's been through a storm."

Jasmine smiled back, just barely. "You have no idea."

The door closed softly behind her, sealing out the corridor's muffled chatter. For a long moment, neither of them spoke. Jasmine peeled off her coat and hung it over a chair, still glistening from sea spray. The faint hum of the harbor seeped through the windows—the sound of halyards clinking against masts.

Bobbi gestured toward the sitting area. "You made it through that ferry ride without getting sick? It looked like a rough one."

Jasmine smiled faintly. "I like a rough ride. Reminds me I'm still in control of something."

"That makes one of us," Bobbi replied, sinking into the sofa. "You said you had something important. Please don't tell me it's another subpoena."

Jasmine shook her head. "No subpoenas. This time, I'm here with hope. And help."

On the coffee table, Bobbi had arranged mugs, a French press filled with dark roast coffee, and a small plate of almond biscotti.

"Please, sit. Coffee?" Bobbi gestured toward the couch.

They sat together, with steaming mugs between them. For a moment, neither spoke. Jasmine set her mug down. "Bobbi, first let me say—I watched your testimony. You were remarkable. Holding your ground like that, alone in front of that panel..." She shook her head in admiration. "You showed more composure than most politicians I've seen."

Bobbi let out a short laugh. "Remarkable? They called me reckless and negligent. Half the country thinks I signed BostonFirst over to the Swiss in exchange for a yacht on Lake Como."

"That's just noise," Jasmine replied. "You carried yourself with strength. You spoke a truth that people needed to hear—that BostonFirst didn't collapse by accident. It was sabotage."

Bobbi seemed to relax slightly. "You believe me? But there's no proof."

"There is now," Jasmine said. She reached into her satchel, pulled out a thin folder, and slid it across the coffee table.

Bobbi hesitated before opening it. Inside were printouts—fragments of code, time-stamps, system logs, digital pathways that looked meaningless to anyone but Jasmine.

"What am I looking at?"

"The proof," Jasmine said softly. "Boston-First didn't collapse because of internal fraud. It was sabotaged. Helvex planted a malware chain in your client account system. That's what triggered the phantom accounts and fake transactions."

Bobbi's breath caught. "You're sure?"

Jasmine nodded. "We've traced the signature back to Zurich. It's theirs. No question."

For a moment, the room seemed to tilt. The weight of months—headlines, lawsuits, hearings—shifted into a single, clear focus. Bobbi leaned back, staring past Jasmine, seeing not the harbor but the faces of everyone who'd called her a liar.

"Jesus," she whispered. "Helvex... they really did it."

"They did," Jasmine said. "And now we can do something about it."

Bobbi looked up. "You said *we*."

Jasmine nodded. "You can't navigate this legal minefield alone."

Bobbi leaned back. "I've already had my fill of lawyers, Jasmine. If you saw how my counsel folded in our last meeting with Helvex, you'd understand why I'm hesitant to put my faith in another set of expensive suits."

She paused for a moment. "You see those ads all over Boston from that law firm making fun of our accent, boasting about its 'wicked smaht' lawyers? That's what I need, Jas."

Jasmine laughed. "Well, then these are the ones for you. Trust me, Bobbi, they *are* wicked smaht. And these aren't just lawyers. Let me explain. There's a task force—quiet, exclusive, under the radar—called LawForce. They were created to counterbalance inequities of counsel in cases of national importance."

Bobbi blinked. "LawForce? Sounds like a Saturday morning cartoon."

"I thought the same thing at first," Jasmine admitted. "But it's real. Jonathan Hendrix told me about them—handpicked lawyers, cyber analysts, former regulators. They're not a government agency, nor are they corporate. Think of it as a legal SWAT team."

Bobbi's brows furrowed. "A SWAT team of lawyers?"

"Yes," Jasmine answered, her voice steady. "They consist of some of the sharpest legal minds in the country and have access to all the resources of the U.S. government. I'm talking about the FBI, CIA, DEA, or any other alphabet soup agency you can think of, including Treasury. They don't just litigate; they strategize."

Bobbi studied her for a long moment. "And why me? Why now?"

"Because you're exactly what they were built for," Jasmine said. "A case too complex, too global, too radioactive for any single firm or agency. You've got the truth—but no army to defend it."

Bobbi sighed, staring down at her coffee mug. "You're assuming there's still a truth left to defend."

The Attorney General thinks LawForce will take your case," Jasmine continued. "They'll go after Helvex directly. Not just civilly—criminally, internationally, across jurisdictions. This isn't about a single bank anymore. It's about a financial war."

Bobbi turned toward the window again. The harbor was bathed in amber light now, the late afternoon sun slipping behind Chappaquiddick's low dunes. For a long time, she didn't speak.

"I'll admit," she said slowly, "I've been struggling with my counsel. They're terrified of Helvex, frightened of international litigation, and intimidated by regulators. Every time I ask them to push back, they look down at their shoes. The Senate hearing was the last straw. If this is the best legal help I can get, I might as well do it myself."

Jasmine's expression softened. "And you did. But imagine what you could achieve with the right team behind you."

Bobbi's eyes returned to Jasmine's. "So what's the catch? What does LawForce want from me?"

"Cooperation," Jasmine replied. "Transparency. And your willingness to stand with them as both client and partner. They don't take passengers; they take fighters."

The muffled sounds of traffic floated in from the harbor. Finally, Bobbi placed her mug down with a decisive clink.

"All right. I'll meet with them if they'll hear me out. At this stage, I need all the help I can get. If LawForce is as formidable as you say, then yes—I want their help."

Relief washed over Jasmine's face, though she maintained her composure. "Good. That's the right choice."

Bobbi arched an eyebrow. "But you'll be there, right? I don't intend to walk into another room full of skeptics alone."

"Of course," Jasmine assured her. "In fact, we need to pitch the case together. You—because it's your legacy and your story. Me—because I bring Treasury's data, analysis, and corroboration."

Bobbi nodded slowly. "Two fronts: personal and analytical. Emotion and evidence."

"Exactly."

They spent the next four hours at the coffee table, Jasmine's laptop open between them. Bobbi spoke with raw emotion about the night of the collapse—the call in the middle of the night, the flashing graphs, the sell-offs. Jasmine typed furiously, weaving Bobbi's account with data from the Treasury report: the massive account openings, the digital whisper campaign, and algorithmic triggers.

"This section," Jasmine said, turning the screen toward Bobbi, "we emphasize sabotage, not incompetence. You'll recount the lived reality, and I'll support it with charts and trade data."

Bobbi read the draft slide and shook her head. "Okay, but we don't want pity; we want conviction. I wasn't blindsided because I was careless—I was attacked because I was a threat. Phrase it that way."

Jasmine smiled approvingly. "That's the fire we need. LawForce respects strength."

By the time they finished, the French press was empty, and the biscotti reduced to a few crumbs. Bobbi leaned back on the couch, exhaustion etched on her face, but her eyes glowed with a newfound resolve. "I've been swinging blind," she admitted. "Now, for the first time, it feels like there's a way forward."

Jasmine met her gaze. "You're not alone anymore. Next, we convince LawForce."

Night had closed in, the lights of the harbor twinkling in the distance. Bobbi looked at her watch. "Wow, time flies. You missed the last ferry, Jas. You'll have to bunk with me tonight. Shouldn't be a problem, there's a nice guest bedroom."

"Sounds good," Jasmine answered. "I could even do a couch if I had to, but a bed sounds wonderful right about now."

Outside, the lighthouse beam swept slowly across the harbor, then back again—steady, unblinking, patient as the tide. Bobbi gazed at it and thought again of Ted Kennedy, of scandal and survival. He'd faced his Chappaquiddick. Now, perhaps, she would face hers—and this time, she wouldn't face it alone.

18

HOUSTON
TEXAS

UNITED STATES OF AMERICA

Shane surveyed the group gathered in the modest-sized room. This was definitely not a typical day at Shane & Lopez LLP. Seated next to Hendrix at the head of the oval conference table with turquoise inlays, Shane leaned in and whispered, "Jon, I'm mostly on board, but for the sake of due diligence, I'm going to have some tough questions for Ms. Sullivan. I might revert to cross-examination mode."

Hendrix nodded in agreement. "I expect nothing less from you."

Hendrix stood and addressed the assembled group: Shane, Val, Jasmine, and Bobbi. At this point, only the key players were required. If LawForce decided to take on the case, they would staff up accordingly.

"Thank you all for coming," Hendrix began. "We're here to determine whether the evidence warrants LawForce's involvement in a case against Helvex Financial. Steven, do you have any questions to start us off?"

Shane nodded. He was eager to see what Bobbi was made of. "Yes, thank you, Jonathan."

Turning to Bobbi, he said, "I've reviewed the basics of your case, Ms. Sullivan. You believe Helvex orchestrated the collapse of BostonFirst. That's a bold accusation."

Bobbi straightened her posture. "First of all, it's Bobbi for all of you. Ms. Sullivan is my mom. This isn't just an accusation; it's a fact. I have evidence."

Shane remained unimpressed. "So, you want us to take on Helvex, a bank that has spent decades hiding behind Swiss neutrality. Helvex is a fortress. Even if we could prove wrongdoing, jurisdictional issues would bury us in red tape."

"That's why I came to you. I understand that LawForce doesn't wait for permission; you find ways to win."

Shane smiled. "Flattery is nice, but it won't pay the court fees."

Bobbi's voice lowered. "I didn't just lose my bank; millions of shareholders lost their savings. And Helvex? They're laughing all the way to the bank—their new bank." She paused. "You've fought for the underdogs before. Fight for them now."

Shane's eyes sparkled at her passion. "Whoa, Bobbi, I haven't said no. I want you to understand the level of power you're up against."

Bobbi's eyes flashed. "I do. I also understand what happens if no one stops them. They've weaponized the system. If Helvex gets away with this, they'll do it again."

Shane folded his arms, fixing his gaze on Bobbi. "Pardon my directness, but how do we know you're not just in this for revenge, trying to take down those who took you down?"

"Yes, I can see how it may look that way. But even if there's a personal element in it for me, you can base your decision on the evidence. I mean, isn't that what lawyers are supposed to do?"

Shane laughed. "Touché, Bobbi. Okay, let's take a look at that evidence. The floor is yours."

She nodded and turned to face the group. "Thank you, Mr. Shane. And I want to express my gratitude to you and Mr. Hendrix for calling this meeting and hearing us out. I think once you have heard everything, you will understand the urgency of the matter.

"The takeover of BostonFirst by Helvex raised numerous red flags, but what I've discovered with Jasmine since then is far more disturbing. This is a pretty complex area, so I'm going to let her take it from here."

Jasmine stood with her laptop connected to the projection screen. "Thank you, Bobbi. This will be technical, so please interrupt with any questions as we go along. You all need to understand the implications of what may seem like a lot of computer jargon."

She tapped a key, and the first slide flickered onto the screen, rows of transaction logs scrolling in compressed type, timestamps precise down to the millisecond.

"BostonFirst didn't fall due to a single event," she began. "It was a two-phase attack. First, they fraudulently created thousands of customer accounts in their internal systems—an injection of digital rot to generate a scandal. Second, they leveraged that scandal with a coordinated whisper campaign that triggered a market run. Both phases tie back to Helvex's infrastructure."

Shane interrupted, "Whoa, hold on a second. I read your report; you suspected Helvex but didn't have its fingerprints yet. Has something changed?"

"Yes, Steve, sorry. This is a late-breaking development. I mentioned it to Jonathan the other day. I have now traced much of the activity back to Helvex. It took some time because they operate globally and route their data through hundreds of intermediary systems. However, some new software we developed at Treasury was able to follow the trail."

Shane stared at her. "Wow, that changes everything."

Hendrix interjected, "I had the same reaction, Steven, but let's allow Jasmine to finish her presentation."

Jasmine looked at Hendrix. "Everything we have is from the BostonFirst servers; we haven't been able to get into Helvex's system. If we could, I'm sure it would tell us a lot more. But I'm afraid that's beyond our capabilities. The good news is we have a fair bit just from the BostonFirst side."

She zoomed in on a section of code displayed on the screen. "These are database writes from BostonFirst's internal account management system. Notice the uniformity. Over a 48-hour window, 12,431 new accounts were opened. That volume, by itself, isn't impossible, but the entropy is wrong. The distribution of customer IDs is too uniform. In a typical environment, you'd see clusters around certain ranges, reflecting organic account creation. Here, the IDs are generated in a linear sequence—00039127, 00039128, 00039129. That's bot activity, not human."

Val looked up from her notes. "So, someone injected fake customers into the system?"

"Not injected," Jasmine corrected. "This was SQL injection at scale, utilizing elevated privileges stolen from inside BostonFirst's Active Directory. I traced the login tokens—spoofed Kerberos tickets forged using what's called a 'Golden Ticket' attack. Compromising the domain controller means you effectively own the entire system."

She flipped to the next slide. "The attackers' objective wasn't to steal but to plant fake accounts—thousands of them, many tagged with phony social security numbers or linked to dormant email addresses. There were enough anomalies to create a situation resembling a Wells Fargo-style fraud scandal. They anticipated exactly how regulators and the media would respond."

Hendrix grunted. "Which is precisely what happened."

Jasmine nodded and continued onto the next slide. "The second phase involved information warfare. Once the scandal broke—'BostonFirst Creates Fake Accounts'—the attackers launched a whisper campaign online. Social bots spread phrases like 'BostonFirst is insolvent' and 'Get your money out' across Reddit finance boards, WeChat groups, and Telegram channels.

"The campaign relied on coordinated amplification, with sockpuppet accounts retweeting, repeating, and cross-posting. Within twelve hours, the narrative shifted from BostonFirst having compliance issues to BostonFirst being broke."

Bobbi briefly closed her eyes, visibly pained. Shane noticed it but maintained a steady expression.

Jasmine continued, "I ran linguistic fingerprinting on the posts. They shared the same syntax quirks and punctuation anomalies—commas with spaces before them, double spaces after periods. These are classic markers of automated posting frameworks.

"More importantly, I traced the metadata on the images used in memes. The EXIF data indicated they were batch-created on servers geolocated to Zurich. Not just any servers—the IP blocks are owned by HelvData AG, a shell company that, surprise, resolves back to Helvex Financial. That's when we made the connection."

Shane looked around the table and then back at Jasmine. "Well, most of that's Greek to me, but the main thing is we've got the link we've been looking for. To be clear, you can show that the disinformation campaign originated from Helvex-controlled infrastructure?"

"Yes," Jasmine replied, her tone confident. "This isn't just smoke—it's fire."

She pulled up the final slide: a flowchart. At the top was Helvex Financial. Below it was

HelvData AG. Branches spread downward to servers, then to botnets, and finally to a flood of social media posts and market trades.

"The forensic trail clearly leads back to Helvex," Jasmine concluded.

Val broke the silence. "Will regulators accept this? You're talking about going up against a Swiss banking titan. They'll scream jurisdiction and sovereignty. They'll bury us in international law."

Jasmine glanced at her. "That's where you come in. I can prove the cyber attack. The law is your battlefield. But you asked for data, and now you have it."

Shane nodded. "You're right. This is actionable. Not conjecture, not paranoia—evidence. Enough to build a case. After what happened to Boston-First, the American public is primed to listen."

Shane hesitated to ask his next question, but it was necessary. "Bobbi, I understand that Helvex was able to buy the BostonFirst shares under the terms of a loan agreement with you. That part seems fairly above board. Can you help us with that?"

There was a long pause, and a tear trickled down Bobbi's cheek. "Yes, you're right. I bear responsibility for having made a deal with the devil. My lawyers didn't pay enough attention to the terms. It was stupid. It was incompetent. But it wasn't criminal."

Hendrix stood up. "Thank you for your candor, Bobbi. But I want to say you are not alone in carrying the blame for how things have played out. My office has been slow to respond. Inexcusably slow. We should have acted during phase one—the scandal campaign—instead of waiting for the market crash. If LawForce had gotten involved on time and given Dubois a fair fight, you'd probably still have your bank.

"So, enough said about the past. We need to focus on the road ahead. We had effectively decided to take on the case before this meeting, but wanted to confirm its legitimacy. What we've heard here today does that. LawForce is now officially on board. Agreed, Steven?"

"You bet. I also want to thank you for your honesty, Bobbi. Jonathan is right; we should have been on this sooner. But we'll do all we can to make up for lost time. From a legal standpoint, we'll need to figure a few things out. Who are we fighting now—the new BostonFirst or Helvex?"

Val raised an eyebrow. "I'd think both."

Shane nodded. "I agree. It raises some complex jurisdictional issues, but that's for the legal team to sort out."

Val nodded and took notes. She looked at Bobbi. "Speaking of that, what about the regulatory implications? Have you alerted any federal agencies about these findings?"

"Not yet," Bobbi replied. "We wanted to bring this to LawForce first to see if you'd be willing to take it on. I have to tell you, it's so good to hear you're joining the fight. The complexity of this case is evident. If Helvex has connections in Washington, as rumors suggest, this could complicate things significantly. I understand that Claudine Dubois, besides owning Switzerland, is about as well-connected in D.C. as anyone can be."

Hendrix leaned back in his chair, looking up at the Thunderbird on the ceiling, and commented, almost to himself, "You leave Ms. Dubois to us."

Shane stood. "We'll begin assembling our team and resources. Bobbi, Jasmine, you're obviously part of the team. I'd like you both to continue your investigations and gather as much data as possible."

Jasmine nodded, excited that the case was moving forward. "I'll dive deeper into the transaction patterns and work on tracing additional connections."

Bobbi added, "And I'll reach out to my contacts at BostonFirst to see if anyone is willing to share information. We may need to approach this delicately to avoid alarming those who might be involved."

As the meeting drew to a close, Hendrix cleared his throat. "And folks, stay on your toes. If Helvex has the connections we suspect, we need to tread carefully."

19

HOUSTON
TEXAS

UNITED STATES OF AMERICA

The offices of Shane & Lopez LLP buzzed with activity. Shane surveyed the team he had assembled around the long oak table. Val, Bobbi, and Jasmine.

At the far end of the table sat a newcomer, Marcus Patel. He looked as if he'd been carved from granite. At fifty-five, he sported a neatly trimmed salt-and-pepper beard, and his scalp gleamed under the overhead lights. He sat silently, eyes darting between the others, one hand rubbing the smooth dome of his head—a nervous tic that revealed the tension he tried to hide.

Shane stood and addressed the group. "I'm glad to have you all here together. You know each other, except for Marcus Patel," he gestured toward Marcus. "I'm sure you know Marcus by reputation. His enforcement battles at the SEC are legendary. He's just as nerdy as you are," Shane grinned at Jasmine, "but while you excel at coding, Marcus, while an exceptional coder himself, has a deep background on the regulatory side of cyber warfare. You two should balance each other out nicely."

Turning back to Marcus, Shane added, "We're glad you could join us, Marcus." He spoke in a warm, measured tone, hoping to make Marcus feel welcome without being overly indulgent.

Marcus responded with a low grunt. "Wouldn't miss it, Steve. Though I'd prefer quoting Keats to chasing down Swiss bankers." He rubbed his scalp again, a hint of wry humor playing on his lips. "Keats wrote 'Much have I traveled in the realms of gold,' but even he could never have imagined the gilded cages of Helvex Financial."

His dry wit broke the tension in the room. Val raised an eyebrow. "Surprisingly cheerful for someone about to tangle with one of the world's most powerful banks."

Marcus chuckled, a gravelly sound. "Cheerful? Let's say... motivated. Poetry helps keep the cynicism at bay. This road we're on is long and dark; a little light helps."

Val turned to Shane. "Are we able to speak freely?"

Shane nodded. "Of course. If there are any issues, let's hear them."

Val fixed Marcus with a steady gaze. "Mr. Patel, LawForce has access to anything in Justice's files. During my background check on you, I came across some sealed files from a few decades ago. Apparently, you were fired from the SEC under troubling circumstances. What were those circumstances?"

The room fell silent. Bobbi raised her eyebrows slightly, Jasmine tilted her head, and Shane waited, allowing Marcus to respond.

Marcus cleared his throat. "Yes, I was let go, and it was my fault. During an investigation, I inadvertently sent a confidential report to the wrong email address. This was back before we had the cyber safeguards we do today. That mistake caused a lot of damage—something I'll have to live with for the rest of my life. But it wasn't corruption. There was no bribery and no compromised integrity. It was simply a human mistake."

His voice took on an edge as he looked around the table. "And I will put my integrity up against anyone's. I always follow my own path, and it's a straight one. As the old bard said, 'This above all: to thine own self be true, and it must follow, as the night the day, thou canst not then be false to any man.'"

Shane intervened. "We ran a sweep, and Marcus is right—it was a costly mistake, but not a dishonest one. His integrity is intact, and his experience at the SEC is invaluable. He knows financial regulation inside and out, and more importantly, he knows the tricks."

Marcus nodded. "I do. If Helvex is engaging in the activities you suspect, I can help uncover them. I was one of the SEC's first cyber specialists."

Jasmine broke the tension. "Good enough for me. Let's get on with it. I've been analyzing their investment platforms. They have an unusually high level of exposure in the cryptocurrency sector. For a conservative Swiss bank, that's not typical. This suggests they might be using blockchain to disguise riskier bets."

Shane asked, "Can you trace it?"

Jasmine smirked, her fingers drumming on her tablet. "Give me a few weeks. Code doesn't lie; people do. That's why I trust algorithms more than lawyers."

Marcus snorted. "Algorithms alone won't be sufficient. Helvex's empire is built on loopholes. They don't play by the rules—they write them."

Jasmine bristled. "And you think the person who got fired from the SEC knows better?"

Marcus smiled faintly. "I know better than to think that code alone will win this fight."

Shane cut in sharply. "Enough. Jasmine, Marcus—you're working together. Leverage both tools: the code and the law. That's how we'll catch them, not through infighting."

Shane stood up and moved to a whiteboard at the far end of the room. With a marker, he drew three columns: *Cyber Evidence*, *Regulatory Pressure*, and *Legal Strategy*.

"Here's our plan," he said. "Jasmine, you're in charge of the cyber trail. We need the digital fingerprints tying Helvex to BostonFirst's sabotage."

Jasmine nodded, already jotting down notes.

"Marcus, you're in charge of financial regulations. Map every loophole they've exploited. We need to anticipate their defenses."

Marcus rubbed his scalp again, muttering, "There are plenty of those to find."

"Val," Shane continued, "you and I will structure the litigation. We'll handle contracts, jurisdiction, and causes of action. We'll build the skeleton."

Val smiled slightly. "I've always liked being the bones of the operation."

"And Bobbi," Shane said, turning to her, "you're our voice and heart. Your testimony, your documents, and your credibility as Boston-First's former CEO are the human stakes in this case. They can attack us lawyers, but you embody what they destroyed. You'll be our spear."

20

ZURICH

SWITZERLAND

Egli stood before the wide window of his corner office, staring at the panorama below. On a crisp winter morning, the pier at Bürkliplatz transformed into a scene of serene beauty with the hectic activity of summer departures for lake cruises scaled back for the season. The quay was now lined with silent, snow-covered benches. Long shadows from the lakefront trees stretched across the cobblestones, while a distant, snow-capped Uetliberg peeked above the horizon.

Looking back from the pier, Bahnhofstrasse intersected with the lakeside boulevard, and the elegant façades of city architecture rose beside the water, lights glowing in Helvex's executive offices.

In this city, time was of utmost importance; punctuality was a civic religion. But Egli knew Nadler would be late. He was unpredictable by nature, and Egli allowed him this breach of etiquette for one reason only: his usefulness.

When Nadler finally arrived, they skipped the pleasantries. After pouring them both a whiskey, Egli said, "BostonFirst is ours now." His voice carried the same neutrality with which he delivered quarterly earnings reports. "Stage four was an unmitigated success."

Nadler took a sip of his whiskey. "We dismantled an American pillar and made it look inevitable. The regulators shrugged. The markets swallowed the story. That's no small feat."

Egli steepled his fingers and allowed himself a faint smile. "Control," he replied, "is best exercised through inevitability. BostonFirst collapsed not because we forced it, but because everyone believed it would fail. Belief is stronger than proof."

The Ghost nodded. Egli understood that Nadler thrived on disruption and on watching systems unravel, but what he valued was different: orchestration. BostonFirst was not the prize; it was merely the doorway.

"Now," Egli continued, "we have their deposits, their infrastructure, their client base—it all becomes a gateway. Through them, we reach into the heart of the U.S. system. It is something we could never have achieved through Helvex, which the U.S. market still marginalizes as a foreign player."

"Yeah, yeah, I know all that," Nadler said impatiently. " I thought you asked me here to discuss what comes next."

Egli turned from the window and fixed his gaze on him. "Yes. Stage five." Egli savored this moment—the unfurling of the next act in his design, the pause before revelation.

He gave Nadler a lopsided grin. "Before I get into the details, I must admit my experience lies with tangible currencies—money you can see and feel—hold in your hands. I'm not well-versed in the new digital currencies. Perhaps you could give me a summary of crypto and blockchain as if you were explaining it to a five-year-old."

"Hans, you surprise me," Nadler said with a grin. "But it's wise to know your limitations. We techies sometimes forget that not everyone speaks our language.

"At its core, cryptocurrency is a form of digital money. The most well-known example is Bitcoin, created in 2009. Since then, many thousands of other cryptocurrencies—like Ethereum, Litecoin, and Solana, and now, Infinium—have emerged, each with its own features and uses. Unlike dollars or francs, cryptocurrencies aren't issued by a government or controlled by a central bank. Instead, they operate on computer networks that use blockchain technology to record ownership.

"So, what's a blockchain? Imagine a ledger—like a giant spreadsheet—that records every transaction ever made. Rather than being kept by a single person or bank, copies of this ledger exist on thousands of computers worldwide. Each time someone sends or receives cryptocurrency, the transaction is added to the ledger, and all copies of the ledger are updated. This makes the system transparent and very difficult to tamper with.

"Every new batch of transactions is grouped in a 'block.' These blocks are connected in chronological order—hence the name blockchain. Once information is added to the chain, it can't be changed without rewriting every subsequent block, which is nearly impossible. That's why blockchain is often described as 'trustless': you don't have to trust a bank or middleman because the system itself guarantees accuracy.

"Cryptocurrencies like Bitcoin and Ethereum use this system to allow people to send money directly to one another—quickly, globally, and without intermediaries. But crypto isn't just limited to money. Ethereum, for example, facilitates 'smart contracts,' bits of code that automatically execute agreements, similar to digital vending machines.

"Of course, cryptocurrency comes with risks: prices can be highly volatile, scams exist, and if you lose your private digital key, your coins are gone forever. Still, the idea of a secure, decentralized financial system is what makes crypto both powerful and controversial.

"In short: cryptocurrency is digital money; blockchain is the technology that makes it possible."

Nadler looked at Egli. "Does that help? Clear enough for a five-year-old?"

Egli chuckled. "Yes, Jerome, thank you. Now, onto the matter at hand. We have established a foothold within the American banking sector," he began. "But a foothold is not enough. We must scale our influence. What we build next will not simply occupy territory; it will redefine the landscape."

He let the silence linger. Nadler, ever impatient, broke it first. "You mean the fund?"

"Yes." Egli drew out the syllable with quiet satisfaction. "CryptoHelix." The name itself was modern, fluid, scientific.

"It will serve as the perfect fund for the world's newest and greatest cryptocurrency, Infinium." Another powerful name—timeless.

"This will be no ordinary investment product," Egli asserted. "It will attract investors like bees to honey. Institutions will flock to Infinium not because we demand it, but because they will feel compelled to do so."

Nadler tilted his head. "FOMO."

Egli nodded. "Precisely. The fear of missing out is the most reliable driver of greed. A handful of institutions will be enough—once they invest, the rest will follow. They will look at their rivals jumping on board and fear being left behind."

Nadler tapped the rim of his glass. "So, we seed it through BostonFirst?"

"Yes. We will position CryptoHelix as the natural development for the recovery of BostonFirst—an innovative fund emerging from a humbled bank seeking to reinvent itself. It's a story the media will love: traditional banking embracing new finance. Redemption sells."

Egli stepped closer, his silhouette sharp against the window. "We will dress Infinium in all the right attire: institutional-grade custody, white papers with dense footnotes, and compliance frameworks that seem robust. On the surface, it will be impeccable. Beneath—it will be entirely ours."

After a pause, he continued. "CryptoHelix and Infinium are a story they will write for us. We will provide the framework, the glossy promise. They will provide the greed. The more capital they invest, the less likely they are to perceive it as fragile. That blindness is the shield we require."

21

WASHINGTON
DISTRICT OF COLUMBIA

UNITED STATES OF AMERICA

Hendrix stared out the tall, arched window. It was one of those beautiful blue-sky days. From his vantage point, he could trace the grand axis of the capital: the curve of the National Archives across the street, the view down Pennsylvania Avenue past the Canadian Embassy to the Capitol Dome, and, looking the opposite way towards the White House, the Old Post Office Tower and Freedom Plaza.

He turned from the window and took a seat at the head of the conference table, tapping his cigar over the ashtray. Across from him, Shane waited in silence. The two men had spent countless hours together over the years—courtroom prep, late-night strategy sessions, urgent consultations—but the energy in the room felt different now.

The Helvex case had reached a turning point.

"The evidence is good," Hendrix began at last, his voice serious. "But it's scattered. Jasmine's work, brilliant as it is, has given us only half the puzzle. The digital trails point squarely to Switzerland—Zurich, specifically. That's the heart of it."

He set the cigar down and laced his fingers together, his gaze fixed on Shane.

"Helvex isn't just a bank. It's a fortress," Hendrix continued. "Its secrets aren't sitting on servers in Virginia or Delaware. They're buried deep in Zurich—hidden in vaults, in paper records, in the kind of testimony that can only be pried loose in person. We're not going to find the killer evidence sitting here in Washington or Houston."

Shane didn't flinch; he had expected this. The more they peeled back the layers of Helvex's schemes, the more obvious it became that Switzerland was the source of the problem.

"You're saying we need boots on the ground," Shane said quietly.

"I'm saying we need to plant a flag," Hendrix replied, reaching for his coffee. "LawForce needs a base of operations in Zurich—not Geneva, not Basel. Zurich. It's the home of Helvex Financial, the seat of their power, and the heart of Swiss banking. If we want to uncover the secrets, if we want to face down Claudine Dubois, we have to fight on her turf."

Hendrix rose from his chair and began to pace.

"Switzerland has protected its banks for centuries," Hendrix said, gesturing with his hand as he walked. "Banking secrecy there isn't just law—it's culture. It's tradition. Politicians defend it, regulators protect it, and courts enshrine it. Every trick we've seen from Helvex—every delay, every obfuscation—stems from that environment. You can't fight it from afar; you have to be there, in the corridors of Zurich, inside their fortress, to crack it."

He stopped pacing and turned, fixing Shane with an intense gaze. "This is their home ground. If we let them stay comfortable, they'll bury us in procedure and secrecy until this case dies of old age. But if we meet them in Zurich, if we show we're not afraid to operate in their backyard, then we change the game."

The silence stretched for a moment before Hendrix's tone shifted from explanatory to something sharper.

"You know why you're the one, don't you?" he asked.

Shane met his gaze evenly. "You bet. Because I have a Swiss background."

"Not just a background," Hendrix corrected. "You're a Swiss citizen. Fluent in Swiss German. You know the dialects, the courts, the culture. You've walked those streets. When you enter a courtroom in Zurich, you're not just another American lawyer parachuting in. You're one of them. That gives us credibility. That gives us cover."

Shane nodded. It was true; he had grown up straddling two worlds—his Swiss father and Navajo mother. Summers spent in the Bernese Oberland and winters in New Mexico. Swiss German and Navajo were spoken at the dinner table, and English was spoken in the classroom. He had always felt like he belonged to both places and to neither, but now that duality had become an advantage.

"Claudine Dubois will underestimate you," Hendrix said. "But what she doesn't know is that you speak her language."

"Claudine Dubois is from the French-speaking part of Switzerland," Shane nitpicked.

"But she speaks German fluently. Hell, she speaks English, too. Languages aren't an issue for the Swiss; you know that."

"True," Shawn acknowledged. "And the canton, or state, governs the language in court. So in Zurich, it would be German, or even English in special commercial cases."

Hendrix nodded. "Make no mistake: she'll hate you. You're the crack in her narrative—the American lawyer who can't be dismissed as an outsider because he knows Switzerland better than half the lawyers in Zurich."

Hendrix leaned across the desk, his voice dropping. "That makes you dangerous, Steven. And it makes you exactly who we need to take on Ms. Dubois. She's already handed Boston-First to Helvex on a silver platter. She's ruthless, and she's good."

Shane absorbed the words. Dubois was formidable, yes, but she was also fallible. He had studied her cases, knew her style, and understood the cultural levers she leaned on. If anyone could disrupt her rhythm, it was someone who could speak her language—in and out of court.

Hendrix straightened. "I want you to establish a LawForce office in Zurich. Not a token presence—a real working office. Recruit local counsel as needed. Build relationships with regulators. Find witnesses—whatever it takes. This isn't going to be a quick skirmish; it's going to be a campaign."

He paused, then added, "I know you have that chalet in Wengen."

Shane blinked. The chalet was his sanctuary, a retreat in the Bernese Oberland. He had never considered it an operational asset.

"It might be useful as a secondary base," Hendrix said. "Zurich for operations, Wengen for strategy and unwinding. When the city closes in on you, when the pressure mounts, you'll need a retreat. Just stay off those bloody mountains. That escapade on the Eiger should have taught you a lesson."

Shane grunted. "Low blow." But he had to admit, Hendrix made sense. Wengen was remote, yes, but that remoteness could become a shield. The mountains had always sharpened his mind. "It's possible," he conceded. "Zurich will be the base; Wengen the escape."

Hendrix nodded. "And since Valentina will be with you, maybe bring Cody along. It's going to be a long engagement."

Shane perked up at that. "Yeah, that would be cool. Cody's only been over a few times, when he was too young to really understand anything. It's time he got to know his roots. That's a great idea, Jon."

"Good," Hendrix's voice softened slightly. "Then it's settled. LawForce moves to Switzerland. Zurich is Ground Zero."

22

ZURICH

SWITZERLAND

Shane looked out at the lights shimmering along the tarmac as the plane touched down at Zurich-Kloten Airport. He felt a jolt of recognition. He was home—not America-home, not his Navajo mother's desert mesas, but the other half of himself—his father's world. This was the part of him that had grown up hearing the clipped syllables of Swiss German, eating rösti and fondue in small Bernese kitchens, and playing along the narrow streets of alpine villages.

"Welcome to Switzerland." Shane guided the team through customs—Val beside him, sharp-eyed and steady as ever; Jasmine, lugging a backpack full of portable servers and encrypted drives; Bobbi, drawn but resolute, wearing a tailored coat that gave her the air of a general returning from exile; and Marcus, grumbling about the cold, nervously rubbing his smooth scalp.

* * *

A few hours later, they stood outside Talstrasse 65, a mid-rise building next to the Old Botanical Garden. A month ago, they had leased the top two floors beneath an exclusive rooftop club restaurant. The space was promptly gutted and rebuilt. The upper floor contained a suite of offices, while the lower floor was the heart of the operation, variously called the war room, command center, ops center, or nerve center.

Rows of heavy desks ran the length of the main room, each equipped with high-powered machines, triple monitors, and ergonomic chairs. Server racks hummed, connected to a satellite uplink that Jasmine insisted was non-negotiable.

On one wall hung a sprawling projection screen, currently displaying the blockchain transaction maps Jasmine had assembled—glowing rivers of color snaking across a black background, pulsing with the rhythm of money in motion.

Another wall bore Val's handiwork: photographs of Helvex executives, with Hans Egli at the center like a spider, red yarn linking him to subsidiaries, shell companies, regulators, and politicians. The air smelled of fresh paint and ozone from the servers, and a faint hum vibrated through the floor.

"This is it," Shane said, his voice carrying through the room. "Our new home. Buckle down, folks; we'll be here for months, if not a year or more."

Shane had personally chosen the location. He wanted to be close to Paradeplatz but far enough away not to attract attention. The office tower on Talstrasse fit the bill nicely.

Ah, yes, Paradeplatz. At the heart of Zurich, the square seemed unremarkable to the casual tourist—trams screeching, banks rising in stone and glass. Yet Paradeplatz, just off the famed Bahnhofstrasse, was one of the most symbolic intersections of money in the world.

For centuries, this district had been both a literal and an emblematic ground zero for Swiss finance. The area was compact, elegant, and understated—the antithesis of Wall Street's loud aggression. Here, power moved in whispers, behind heavy oak doors, in boardrooms lined with art and guarded by centuries-old secrecy.

Zurich's role as a financial center began long before the elegant sandstone buildings of the late 19th and early 20th centuries lined Bahn-hofstrasse. In the Middle Ages, the city was home to guilds that controlled trade and crafts. Power was concentrated not only in the church and local nobles but also in guild halls, where merchants and artisans combined political authority with financial muscle.

By the sixteenth century, Zurich had become a Protestant stronghold under Huldrych Zwingli, and with the religious reformation came a certain austerity. Banking here lacked the flamboyance seen in Florence or Venice. Instead, Zurich cultivated a reputation for diligence, order, and probity—the qualities that would, centuries later, become the backbone of Swiss finance.

During the nineteenth century, Zurich began its transformation into a financial power-house. Switzerland's neutrality and stability attracted capital during the Napoleonic Wars. As industrialization swept through Europe, Zurich emerged not only as a hub for textiles and machinery but also as a banker for those industries. By the time the Gotthard railway was completed, connecting northern and southern Europe in the 1880s, Zurich was already flush with capital, ready to lend to projects that would reshape the continent.

The true symbol of Zurich's wealth was Bahnhofstrasse, a mile-long boulevard stretching from the central train station to Lake Zurich. Once a moat surrounding the city walls, it was filled in during the nineteenth century and became the grand avenue of finance.

Over time, Bahnhofstrasse became lined with luxury boutiques—Tiffany, Cartier, Hermès—but its real treasures lay behind discreet façades. The banks exuded understated elegance. Their approach was not one of ostentation but of discretion: no flashing ticker boards or chaotic trading floors like on Wall Street. Here, fortunes moved invisibly, recorded as entries in ledgers, then replaced by encrypted digital connections.

The notion of Swiss banking secrecy was well known, but in Zurich it became more than just a legal principle; it became part of the city's identity. Since the Banking Act of 1934 codified secrecy into law, Swiss bankers have regarded client confidentiality not merely as a privilege but as a sacred duty. Until recently, breaking this confidentiality was punishable by imprisonment.

This secrecy proved especially valuable throughout the tumultuous twentieth century. During both World Wars, capital flowed into Swiss banks, safeguarded by the nation's neutrality. In the Cold War, Zurich's vaults became a refuge for money that could not find safety in Moscow, New York, or London.

By the late twentieth century, Zurich was managing not just Swiss wealth but also the wealth of the world. For every official account, there were shadow structures: trusts, shell corporations, and foundations—arrangements designed to obscure ownership and the origins of capital.

For a team like LawForce, this environment meant navigating a labyrinth built to repel intrusion. Each trail could vanish into a shell company in Liechtenstein, a trust in Panama, or a proxy account in Singapore. The genius of Zurich's financial district lay not in the money itself but in its invisibility.

At the symbolic center of this world sat Paradeplatz, where the two great titans—Credit Suisse and UBS—once faced each other across the tram lines. Since then, UBS absorbed Credit Suisse, leaving Switzerland with only one major bank. Now, after several taxpayer bailouts, this bank was threatening to move its headquarters to New York City.

The real heartbeat of Zurich's finance, however, was the smaller, more discreet private banks that served dynasties and sovereigns, clustered on quiet streets. Institutions such as Julius Bär, Pictet, Vontobel, and, of course, the enigmatic Helvex Financial, prided themselves on discretion, offering not just financial services but also protection, camouflage, and sometimes even impunity.

Helvex's main headquarters was on a side street off Paradeplatz, but that wasn't good enough for Herr Egli. Shane knew that he maintained special executive offices further down Bahnhofstrasse, near Lake Zurich. Apparently, he was too special to share office space with the workerbees.

Helvex's rise seamlessly fit into this ecosystem. It operated with the same restraint and invisibility until its ambitions expanded from quiet wealth management into the realm of geopolitical influence.

Physically, Zurich's financial district mirrored its philosophy. The buildings were not brash towers but restrained palaces. The old Credit Suisse headquarters on Paradeplatz boasted Renaissance Revival façades that resembled a city hall more than a bank. The lobbies were understated: featuring marble floors, muted lighting, and discreet artwork.

For Shane, Zurich was not just another city; it was personal. He could navigate the terrain like no other American lawyer could. He understood how the regulators thought, how the courts operated, and how the cultural gears turned. He knew when "yes" meant "perhaps" and when "perhaps" meant "never."

Setting up in Zurich gave LawForce proximity not only to Helvex but also to the networks that supported it: the lawyers who drafted impenetrable contracts, the regulators who turned a blind eye, and the auditors who left just enough ambiguity to avoid liability.

The real battle would be fought not in the hearing rooms of Washington, but in the narrow streets and glass-fronted offices of Zurich. Unlike in centuries past, when Swiss banking revolved around paper ledgers and gold bars, the battlefield had been digitized. Zurich was wired with encrypted channels, server farms hid in unremarkable office parks, and blockchain ventures flourished in the "Crypto Valley" stretching toward Zug.

This is why the LawForce office in Zurich resembled more of a data center than a traditional law firm—rows of monitors, firewalled servers, and forensic tools. It mirrored the environment they needed to infiltrate.

Bobbi stood in silence for a moment, watching them. Then she walked to the wall of photographs and pinned a picture of her old office at BostonFirst above Hans Egli's portrait. The meaning was clear: this was personal.

23

BOSTON MASSACHUSETTS

UNITED STATES OF AMERICA

He looked around his new office with admiration. It was a significant upgrade from the loft in Greenwich. A polished maple desk sat before him, adorned with framed photos showcasing BostonFirst milestones.

The spectacular view over Boston's harbor—once Bobbi Sullivan's morning consolation—captured the slow blue of the river and the distant glint of a storied skyline. Nadler had reorganized the photographs, adding a few of his own. He liked how BostonFirst's past blended with the Ghost's future.

He sat in the chair that used to belong to her and relished the small, private pleasure of occupying someone else's command post. To his right, a glass-fronted bookcase held the books that executives display for show—strategic theory, leadership, financial histories—titles that illustrated how power looked when presented politely. His own books—cryptography tomes, intrusion manuals, vintage hacker zines—were tucked away in a locker beneath the desk.

Across from him, a bank of wall-mounted monitors displayed lines of market data streaming in ribbons. Social media chatter flowed across feeds like a thread, and sentiment analysis graphs rose and fell in predictable human rhythms. However, Nadler's gaze rarely focused on the global noise. Instead, he concentrated on the private parts of the displays, monitoring backchannels.

He had been in the office for a few weeks, discreetly transforming BostonFirst's executive wing into the nerve center for the new architecture of the CryptoHelix Fund—the state-of-the-art digital fund featuring the latest cryptocurrency, Infinium.

While investment could be made directly into Infinium, purchasing through the CryptoHelix Fund was marketed as providing extra protection for parties still unsure of the stability or legitimacy of cryptocurrencies.

BostonFirst would guarantee fifteen percent of the purchase price for any investment in CryptoHelix. BostonFirst pocketed a handsome premium on the sale through CryptoHelix, with no intention of ever standing behind the guarantee. Through this minimalist "safety blanket", the CryptoHelix Fund would dramatically accelerate investment into Infinium.

The plan, though complex in its execution, was devilishly simple in principle. Lure at least ten percent of the Western banking sector's cash reserves into an investment (CryptoHelix, Infinium). Then devalue that investment, thereby triggering the failure of enough financial institutions to bring down the whole interconnected sector through further cascading failures.

The half-truth behind the plan was that Infinium was a secure investment, implemented through blockchain technology. The whole truth—something no outsider needed to know—was that the blockchain technology had been compromised. Nadler's program could artificially increase supply. There was no limit, like Bitcoin's 21-million-coin limit, to preserve its value. Economics 101 taught you that if you control supply, you control price. At the right time, the market would be flooded with new Infinium coins, cratering its price.

Helvex had underwritten the fund and handed Nadler the keys to BostonFirst's name and resources. It had paid for the rebranding, the presentations, and private dinners in elegantly lit rooms. It also arranged proper introductions to middle management in banks that still liked to pretend they shaped the future rather than merely followed it. The deal was simple: lend a fallen American bank some credibility; use that credibility to seed an investment vehicle; and invite the rest of the world to join in.

Nadler scrolled through the list of subscribing institutions, letting the names settle in his mind like a map. A regional bank in the Midwest—modest assets but an ambitious board; two European private houses looking for "innovation"; a sovereign wealth desk in a small, compliant state; and three American banks eager to get in early with a "strategic partnership" press release.

He had crafted the launch exhibit with the taste of someone who understood theater. A white paper, delivered at the right cadence—technical enough for quants, yet warm enough for wealth managers—was included in the investor packets. Institutional custody partnerships were detailed in glossy sub-clauses. A thin list of advisory board members lent the impression of respectable oversight: one retired regulator, a neutral-voiced professor in tokenomics, and the obligatory brand-name CEO who owed Egli a favor from a past funding round.

At the top of the packet, in a font suggesting science and stability, read the promise: Infinium—an institutional-grade store of value, compliant by design. That word—"compliant"—served as a crucial selling point. It allowed Nadler to invite cautious, conservative boards into the future while preserving their reputations intact.

He had encountered hesitation. Men with moderate appetites for risk had asked questions about volatility, counterparty risk, and perceived connections to Helvex. Nadler responded with measured patience. "We are providing a pathway," he told them in his private meeting room, with the Boston harbor in the background. "This is not speculation. This is infrastructure. It's the kind of investment you make to ensure you're not left behind."

He infused the conversation with notions of scarcity and exclusivity—the Bernie Madoff approach: early access, invitation-only opportunities, a minimum investment threshold, a governance token available only to accredited buyers. The sense of scarcity generated excitement, while the exclusivity fostered a fear of missing out. FOMO was a market force Nadler had come to revere.

Although he might be considered a nerd, he was a nerd steeped in history. When it came to finance, history demonstrated that financial scandals often stemmed less from exotic instruments than from human behavior. Again and again, the same pattern unfolded: a new opportunity promised riches, early adopters gained spectacular returns, and everyone else rushed in, anxiously trying to avoid being left behind. FOMO transformed ordinary markets into speculative frenzies.

In eighteenth-century England, the South Sea Company persuaded investors that immense wealth awaited from trade with South America. Share prices soared, not due to actual trade but because everyone else was buying. When reality struck, the so-called "South Sea Bubble" burst, and fortunes evaporated overnight.

The Roaring Twenties saw a similar mania. Ordinary Americans purchased stocks on margin, convinced that prices could only rise. When the market crashed in 1929, the world plummeted into depression.

The cycle repeated during the 1980s Savings & Loan crisis, when deregulated institutions promised high returns, and during the 1990s dot-com bubble, when startups with little more than a ".com" in their names attracted billions of dollars.

Most recently, the U.S. housing boom led investors, banks, and homeowners to believe that real estate was foolproof. Securitized subprime mortgages spread this illusion globally. When defaults increased in 2008, the entire system fractured, triggering a global financial crisis.

What connected these episodes wasn't the specific asset—be it trade monopolies, stocks, internet startups, or mortgages—but the psychology that drove them. Investors observed neighbors or competitors getting rich, and caution gave way to panic buying. FOMO acted as the accelerant, pushing markets beyond their fundamentals until collapse became inevitable.

The lesson was timeless. CryptoHelix would be the latest vehicle to exploit two enduring aspects of human nature: greed and FOMO.

There were technical hurdles to overcome—custody bridges, KYC arrangements, and a registered vehicle that would take the fund's name into markets where vain regulators wanted to be seen as progressive. Nadler delegated the details with an executive's confidence—he left the technicalities to the experts. He operated in the realm of perception and appetite.

However, he was more than just a salesperson. When the timing was right and liquidity had been gathered, the hammer would drop.

"Too big to fail," Nadler mused, was an assumption rather than an absolute truth. It was a doctrine binding governments, reputations, and markets together; it implied that institutions would be supported because the cost of their collapse was greater than the political ramifications of inaction.

Yet, this doctrine had an edge: if one *could* engineer the failure of such an institution or set of institutions—topple a small but significant series of dominoes in a controlled manner— the rest would follow, not through force, but because they were tied to the fallen institutions through a myriad of financial instruments. That was the philosophy behind "too big to fail," the fear that allowing one domino to tumble would result in a cascading crash of the other, highly interconnected, dominoes. With Infinium's value plunging, the CryptoHelix Fund would be gutted—its investors losing everything.

If you topple the right first dominoes—targeting ten percent of the system—the entire structure would be unable to absorb the stress. Nadler argued this point to Egli like an engineer calculating collapse points. It was mathematical: once enough actors' balance sheets relied on the same fragile trust, the deflation of that trust would propagate with geometric severity.

Of course, there were contingencies. People were messy and unpredictable. There would be regulators making noise, law professors writing op-eds about market manipulation, and senators calling for hearings—distractions that Nadler welcomed. All of that attention would only fuel the panic.

Nadler supervised the media rollout of CryptoHelix's launch with the same meticulous attention he applied to coding. The PR firm's statements were approved in advance, and the guest list for the launch dinner was a carefully balanced mix of bankers, fund managers, and neutral-sounding academics. Claudine Dubois herself delivered a short public broadcast from Geneva, praising the "prudence" of the fund and promising stringent governance standards. To the public, she sounded like a guardian of European markets.

* * *

Over the following days, Nadler tracked the buy-ins. Initially, the numbers trickled in— small allocations from cautious treasurers. But the flow increased steadily: a significant tranche from a regional player; a private desk that quietly upped its allocation after its peer boards did the same. He watched, glassy-eyed, as the fund's pool expanded.

From time to time, he thought of Jasmine. She had been the one to walk away and was subsequently ruined by the first iteration of his appetite for profit. He had envisioned different futures then—some kind—but none had come to pass. He could feel the old ache of rejection, but now, as he observed the world bending to his creation, it felt like a distant bruise.

Nadler rearranged the photos on Bobbi's shelf to his liking, adjusted a paperweight shaped like a lighthouse, and leaned back—the city below pulsed, placid and unsuspecting. That evening, the fund's custodians called to report that another institution had signed up—a name Nadler had been waiting for: JP Morgan Chase Bank, N.A.

If CryptoHelix was good enough for Jamie Dimon, it was good enough for anyone. The floodgates had opened.

24

ZURICH

SWITZERLAND

The command center felt smaller at night. Gathered around a table filled with screens and notes, the LawForce team sifted through data on the CryptoHelix Fund. It was growing remarkably fast. Banks that usually took months to adopt a new product were throwing money at the fund. The collapse of BostonFirst—once the talk of scandal—was being rewritten as a story of rebirth.

Bobbi sat apart from the group, her back to the glass, listening as Jasmine and Marcus debated in hushed tones. Since her Senate testimony, she had been inundated with calls from sympathetic strangers, journalists eager for scandal, and interview requests she declined. That evening, however, her inbox held something stranger: a message so cautious she took several minutes to grasp its meaning.

It was a few lines, written in careful, formal English:

> **I work for Helvex Financial. I have followed your words in Washington. You are not wrong. We must speak, but with discretion.**

No name, no address—just a warning:

> **Do not reply to this channel. If you are willing, place a small Swiss flag outside the mailbox at your building. I will contact you.**

Bobbi stared at the screen long enough for Shane to notice. "What is it?" he asked.

"Something... unusual," Bobbi replied, closing her laptop. "I'm not sure yet."

* * *

Regula Rivella sent the message. A lawyer she knew had recently interviewed with a foreign firm setting up shop in Talstrasse, looking for local counsel. He mentioned they were working with the former BostonFirst CEO. Regula found her email address online.

At thirty-four, Regula was not someone who stood out in the polished halls of Helvex Financial. She wore simple gray suits, kept her black hair cropped short, and rarely spoke in meetings. Her one nod to fashion was a pair of Cartier rose-gold hoop earrings—understated, elegant, circular. When deep in thought, her hand would rise unconsciously to one earring, tracing its smooth edge between her fingers.

As a compliance officer—a mid-level executive charged with ensuring institutional integrity—Regula had not set out to become a whistleblower. Born in Zug, in a modest family apartment overlooking the lake, Regula grew up in one of Switzerland's most discreet neighborhoods. Zug was known for its tax shelters and, more recently, its self-branded Crypto Valley. The world came to Zug to hide money; to Regula, this seemed perfectly normal.

Even as a child, she was serious; her classmates teased her for being *die Professorin*—the professor—because of her meticulous note-taking. By her teenage years, she was already teaching herself to code. The Eidgenössische Technische Hochschule (ETH)—Swiss Federal Institute of Technology—was a natural fit for her. There, she pursued cybersecurity and graduated with distinction, one of only a handful of women in her class.

She was delighted when Helvex Financial offered her a compliance position after graduation. She would be joining one of the most prestigious banks in the country. Her parents were proud, and her professors congratulated her.

Initially, the work was satisfying, and everything seemed normal: designing audits, monitoring transactions, and double-checking that departments followed cybersecurity protocols. She liked rules and systems.

However, over the past few years, she began to notice cracks. Reports were rewritten to downplay risk, and clients with political influence were protected. Cyber flags—suspicious patterns, repeated anomalies—were quietly marked as "not material."

She told herself that all banks bent the rules. But when she saw the internal communications regarding BostonFirst, she could no longer ignore the situation.

It started with a single memo. While reviewing an internal audit trail, she came across language that sent chills down her spine: "controlled devaluation vector." Another document referred to "leveraging contagion risk."

To anyone else, these phrases might have seemed abstract, but to Regula, they were smoking guns. They didn't describe risk management; they described a plan that was to unfold in defined stages—a strategy aimed at destabilizing world markets.

Determined to act, she began discreetly copying documents, building her own archive: emails between Hans Egli and Jerome Nadler, sanitized draft reports, and spreadsheets mapping "liquidity events" against targeted institutions.

Fear gripped her with every click. Helvex did not tolerate betrayal, and she had seen colleagues quietly removed, their reputations shredded overnight.

For months, she hesitated, doing nothing, aware that she was sitting on dynamite. Then she saw the American banker Bobbi Sullivan on television testifying before the U.S. Senate—ruined and humiliated—but refusing to be silenced. The banker's voice had trembled only slightly, her jaw clenched as she spoke of sabotage. Regula whispered to herself, "She knows. She dares to say it out loud." In that moment, something inside her broke.

When Regula first drafted the message, her hands shook so violently she had to step away from her desk. She deleted it. Wrote another. Deleted that one too.

She understood the risks: losing her job, her career, her safety. Helvex had friends in politics, law enforcement, and the press. One wrong move could mean professional exile, or worse.

But she also knew that silence would make her complicit. Her father, a highly religious man, had often reminded his children that all it takes for evil to prevail is for good men or women to do nothing. She had to act, or she could never live with herself.

Finally, she settled on a few cautious lines. No name. No details. Just enough to test whether Bobbi Sullivan would listen.

She pressed send and then sat in the dark of her apartment, listening for footsteps in the hallway that never came.

* * *

Bobbi read the message three times before showing it to Shane. "She says she works for Helvex," Bobbi murmured. "She doesn't give a name. She wants to meet."

Shane furrowed his brow. "It could be bait, or it could be the first honest hand we've seen extended."

Val leaned back in her chair. "If she's real, she must be terrified. Switzerland doesn't do a great job of protecting whistleblowers. She's risking everything just by sending this."

The team was divided. Marcus wanted to treat the message as a potential lead, but not as a lifeline. "We don't know who she is, what she has, or if she'll follow through."

Jasmine outright rejected it. "A few lines from an anonymous account? Helvex could be playing with Bobbi. It could be Nadler himself. I mean, a compliance officer? That's too rich. It feels like they're trying to set Bobbi up."

Bobbi shook her head. "I don't think so. The tone—it's not bait. It's fear."

Val was curious. "But if it's real... A compliance officer inside Helvex would see everything. They might know where the bodies are buried."

Shane ended the argument. "Then we treat it as legitimate, for now. Put up a flag at the office tomorrow morning. If she really wants to meet, she'll find a way to follow up. If she's genuine, we'll proceed carefully. If she's not, we'll know soon enough."

* * *

The next day, from her desk inside Helvex's sleek Zurich headquarters, Regula watched the internal chatter about CryptoHelix with growing dread. Her colleagues spoke of it with pride— an innovation, a breakthrough, a way to cement Switzerland's dominance in digital finance.

But she knew better.

Every time she glanced at Bobbi's testimony replayed online, she felt a mixture of admiration and guilt. *She dares, and you hide.*

During her morning coffee break, she slipped outside for a quick walk. She strolled along Talstrasse and poked her head into the lobby where the mailboxes were located. A small Swiss flag hung from the boxes for the penthouse suites. She felt weak-kneed. Okay, contact made. She hurried back to the office and decided to set up the meeting details from home. She would not do anything from inside Helvex's offices.

While she felt butterflies in her stomach, she also experienced a curious sense of relief, as if she was finally turning a page—in a good way.

25

KLOTEN

SWITZERLAND

The Radisson Blu Hotel at Zurich-Kloten Airport was a monument to anonymity. It was designed to serve travelers moving between flights, featuring sleek, modern, and deliberately impersonal architecture: white walls, brushed steel, and glass.

The vast lobby housed a massive wine tower that, in the hotel's earlier days, was serviced by acrobatic cocktail waitresses strapped into harnesses, flying up and down to retrieve that special bottle of wine—all reminiscent of Cirque du Soleil.

Those wine angels were gone now. The lobby hummed with the sounds of rolling suitcases and tired footsteps, but in the upper levels, in the private meeting rooms that could be rented by the hour, silence reigned. It was the perfect place for a conversation no one could overhear.

Shane stood by the window of one such room, gazing at the tarmac where planes taxied to their gates. The glass was thick, muting the roar of jet engines. He checked his watch. They had agreed on absolute discretion: no names, no unnecessary signals, and a meeting that would feel more like an accident than an arrangement.

Behind him, Bobbi sat stiffly at the conference table. She looked composed in a tailored beige blazer, but Shane could see the tension in her clenched jaw. This was her first real glimpse into Helvex from the inside, and she knew that whatever they learned tonight might confirm her worst fears.

The door opened with a soft click. A woman entered quickly, closing it behind her. She was of medium height, with short black hair and a deliberately plain suit. Her dark eyes scanned the room before settling on Shane and Bobbi, appearing as though she had rehearsed this moment a dozen times but still wasn't sure it was wise.

"Grüezi," Shane said softly, slipping into Swiss German. "Danke, dass Sie cho sind." (Thank you for coming.)

Her shoulders relaxed just slightly at the familiar cadence of her mother tongue, which put her at ease in a way that English could not.

"Sie sind Schwyzer?" she asked, surprise flickering across her face. (You're Swiss?)

Shane nodded. "Dual citizenship. I was born in the States, but my father was from Cham. I grew up speaking Swinglish." He allowed himself a thin smile. "I know how to order a good Züri Gschnätzlets, if that helps my credibility."

Regula let out the faintest chuckle, and the ice began to break.

She sat down opposite them, folding her hands together on the table. "My name is Regula Rivella. I work in Helvex's compliance division."

She glanced at the door, lowering her voice. "What I'm about to tell you could end my career—maybe more. Swiss secrecy laws continue to be draconian in some respects. Banking secrets are aggressively protected, without clear public interest exemptions. Ironically, reporting on crooks can land you in jail. Just recently, a journalist was charged under Article Forty-Seven of the Swiss Banking Act. Whistleblowers are not a protected species in Switzerland. Do you understand?"

Bobbi leaned forward. "We understand. And we'll protect you. But we need to know what we're facing."

Regula hesitated, then drew a slow breath. "CryptoHelix. You've heard of it in the press?"

Shane nodded. "A dazzling new investment fund built around a cryptocurrency called Infinium, supposedly the future of digital finance, rumored to be bigger than Bitcoin. Every major bank seems desperate to buy in. We've seen the hype. What's beneath it?"

Regula's lips pressed into a thin line. "Beneath it is a weapon. One designed to bring down the Western financial system."

She opened a slim folder she had brought with her, though she kept it close, unwilling to hand it over just yet. She tapped one page with her finger.

"Infinium is not just a currency. Helvex controls it. The blockchain has hidden vectors, centralized nodes disguised as distributed ones. It is not truly decentralized, despite the marketing."

Bobbi frowned. "So they can manipulate it at will?"

"Exactly. They've built the fund to attract massive buy-in from Western institutions— your Bank of Americas, your Barclays, your Deutsche Banks—driven by the fear of missing out. Once a few invest, the rest will follow. The herd is powerful."

Shane leaned forward, narrowing his eyes. "And when the herd is large enough?"

Regula's voice dropped. "They plan to devalue Infinium deliberately. They'll cause its collapse. Every bank that invested will lose it all."

A silence stretched across the table. The rumble of a plane taxiing outside suddenly seemed louder, a mechanical growl pressing against the glass.

Shane finally spoke. "How many banks are we talking about?"

"Enough to represent at least ten percent of the Western system's cash reserves," Regula stated flatly. "That's the threshold. Once those banks fail, the domino effect will take over. Do you know what a G-SIB bank is?"

Shane looked at Val, who shrugged. "Please, enlighten us. We only just read *Finance for Dummies.*"

Regula chuckled. "Global Systemically Important Banks—the so-called 'too big to fail' institutions. The Financial Stability Board determines them based on four main criteria: size, cross-jurisdiction activity, complexity, and substitutability. Currently, there are about thirty banks on that list."

Regula paused to take a drink. "Think about it. With its balance sheet total twice Switzerland's GDP, some people argue that UBS, with that concentration of wealth and power, represents the greatest threat to the Swiss Confederation's existence since the Second World War. If Helvex can get a few of those big guys to go down, confidence will vanish. Liquidity will dry up. Panic will ensue."

Bobbi spoke up. "You said this will bring down the Western system. What about Eastern banks?"

"Largely unaffected," Regula replied. "They are insulated. Any Eastern bank buying in will be allocated a matching amount of another crypto-currency—one that will not share the same fate as Infinium. While some Eastern banks will suffer the domino effect, toppling due to financial interconnections, the large, state-run enterprises will survive. This isn't just about profit; it's about power. When the West collapses, the East will seize the opportunity."

For a long moment, no one spoke. Then Regula's voice softened, her professional facade slipping just enough to reveal her humanity. "I'm here not only as a matter of professional duty. My sister—she lives in Savannah, Georgia. She lost everything in the BostonFirst collapse: her savings, her retirement... all gone. And it was my fault."

Bobbi blinked. "Your fault?"

"I recommended BostonFirst to her," Regula whispered. "I told her it was strong, safe. I honestly believed it at the time. When it fell, she called me, devastated. Do you know what it feels like to have your sister fall apart because of you?"

Her eyes glistened, though no tears fell. She blinked hard, steadying herself.

Bobbi reached across the table, resting her hand lightly on Regula's. "I understand. My brother lost everything, too. He's a firefighter. He invested his pension in BostonFirst. He trusted me. Now he's ruined."

Their eyes met—two women from different worlds, united by the same wound.

"It can't happen again," Bobbi insisted. "We won't let it."

Regula nodded, her jaw set. "Then you'll need my help. I can testify. I can show you the documentation. But you must move carefully. Helvex is watching everything. If they suspect me, I'll disappear."

Shane leaned back in his chair, arms folded, studying her. He had spent a lifetime assessing witnesses, allies, and enemies. Regula Rivella did not exude opportunism or deceit; instead, she radiated exhaustion, disillusionment, and just enough courage to push past her fear.

Switching to Swiss German, he said softly, "Sie sind sehr mutig, aber Vorsicht isch alles." (You are very brave, but caution is everything.)

Regula exhaled, relief flickering across her face.

"Tell me," Shane continued. "Why now? Why come forward at this moment?"

She hesitated before answering, "Because I saw Ms. Sullivan's Senate testimony. And because I cannot stand by and do nothing in the face of this corruption. Our country's secrecy laws should not be used to shield acts like this. I believe it was one of your chief justices who said that 'Sunshine is the best disinfectant.' This case needs sunshine. And finally, I come to you now because CryptoHelix is almost ready. Once the first wave of investments closes, it will be too late. The trap will be sprung. That's not years away; it's months."

The meeting concluded with logistics—plans for Regula's testimony and the documentation she might be able to provide.

As she rose to leave, she paused at the door and turned back to Bobbi. "You said your brother lost everything too," she said quietly. "Then you understand. This is not just about law or politics. It's about family. It's about lives."

Bobbi nodded, her voice steady. "And that is why we will stop them."

* * *

Shane stood in silence, his hands resting on the back of his chair, staring at the seat Regula had just vacated. "Well," he finally said, "we wanted answers. Now we have them."

Bobbi met his gaze. "And a witness."

"More than that," Shane added grimly. "We have a clock. And it's ticking."

26

BERNESE OBERLAND

ZURICH

SWITZERLAND

Shane stepped onto the balcony of his apartment at Chalet Bergkristall, coffee mug in hand, and breathed in the scent of pine and distant snow. Val followed, zipped into her bright red jacket, with Cody bundled beside her, tugging at his mittens. Down in the Lauterbrunnen Valley, the white ribbon of the Lütschine River shimmered in the sunlight.

"Perfect day for the mountains," Val said, squinting toward the peaks that formed a jagged crown above the valley.

"The kind of day that makes you forget there's a case anywhere in the world," Shane replied.

He wanted that to be true today—for Cody, for Val, for himself. The Helvex case had consumed every waking moment of the last month. Even here, among the placid chalets and bell-wearing cows of the Bernese Oberland, his mind refused to release its grip on Helvex and the tangled web behind it. But today, he reminded himself, belonged to family.

The bus ride from Lauterbrunnen to Stechelberg followed the valley's contour, flanked by waterfalls that descended like strands of silk. When they reached the base station of the Schilthorn cableway, the sleek glass façade looked almost out of place against the rustic barns and snow-laced meadows.

Cody pressed his nose against the window. "Is that the one that goes to the top of the world, Daddy?"

Shane smiled. "That's the one, cowboy—the Schilthornbahn. And today, we're going all the way to Piz Gloria. Exiting the bus, they tried not to get trampled by the horde of skiers and boarders, anxious to hit the slopes.

Inside the station, the cable car hung motionless, a gleaming red-and-silver capsule tethered to impossibly thin steel ropes stretching upward into the mist. He remembered when these cars had been smaller—rattling aluminum boxes with rubber floors and a human operator inside who told stories to passengers as they climbed. He had once been one of those operators.

After high school, before law school and a career in the courtroom, he had spent a year as a Kabinenführer—the man who operated the cable car, checked the doors, and narrated the ride. His father's old friend, Paul Eggenberg, had been the first director of the Schilthornbahn. Eggenberg loved telling stories—how they had run low on money building the top station in the late 1960s, and how a British film crew had arrived just in time with an offer that helped them finish the project.

"They were filming On Her Majesty's Secret Service," Eggenberg had said, pride gleaming in his eyes. "James Bond paid for our viewing platform, amongst other things. Without him, Piz Gloria as you see it today might never have existed."

To a young Shane, Eggenberg had seemed larger than life. He was not only accomplished in business, but also an author of children's books in the Bernese dialect. Shane had been overjoyed to get the invitation to visit the Schilthorn, not realizing that the "visit" would stretch into a year. The Bernese Oberland had that effect on people; once you experienced it, you didn't want to leave.

Now, decades later, Shane watched the tourists and skiers file into a car so advanced it seemed to have been pulled from a Bond film. No levers, no operator's booth—just digital screens, sensors, and voiceovers in three languages.

They stepped aboard; the cabin's glass walls curved like the surface of a lens. Shane glanced around for the operator, but the woman in uniform stood outside, holding a small handheld keypad. She waved, pressed a sequence of buttons, and the doors glided shut.

Val blinked. "Wait—she's not coming?"

"Nope," Shane replied, shaking his head with a mixture of awe and sadness. "These new cars don't need anyone on board anymore. They're all automated. I'm a little surprised the code allows it. Operators weren't just there for technical reasons. If there was ever any problem, the presence of a uniformed employee provided some comfort to passengers, if only psychological."

Cody tugged at his sleeve. "Who drives it then?"

"The computer, buddy. A brilliant one."

As the car rose, it seemed to scratch the adjacent cliff, and Shane stared down at the valley floor shrinking beneath them. Another job replaced by technology. Another sign that the world was moving faster.

He thought of Helvex's algorithms, Nadler's malware, and the cyber underworld that could topple empires with a few lines of code. Progress was a double-edged sword—cutting through inefficiency on one side, slicing away humanity on the other.

The cableway's new section from Stechelberg to Mürren was an engineering marvel; it was the steepest cableway in the world, climbing at a gradient that made even Shane draw a sharp breath. The cabin rose above cliffs that plunged 2,500 feet.

"Cody squealed with delight, 'We're flying!'"

Val gripped the railing tightly. "Feels more like falling," she replied.

Shane chuckled. "That's the thrill of the Schilthorn. Just think—when they built this thing, they had to haul supplies up by helicopter. Every single beam, every pane of glass."

From Birg, the final leg to Piz Gloria swept across barren alpine rock and ice. Above them, the jagged triangle of the Schilthorn rose into the blue sky, its summit crowned with the futuristic dome of the revolving restaurant.

When the cabin eased into the top station, Shane stepped out into dazzling sunlight. A gust of cold wind caught his jacket and whipped Cody's scarf sideways.

"Welcome to Piz Gloria!" Val said dramatically, pointing to the sign carved in brushed steel.

Inside, the Bond World exhibit shimmered with light and sound, instantly captivating Cody. He darted from the snowmobile simulator to the virtual helicopter chase, shouting, "Look, Daddy, I'm 007!"

Shane followed him with an indulgent grin, reminiscing about his own boyhood awe at this place. In those days, the "Bond" theme had been understated—a few still photos and a couple of posters. Now, it was a multimedia spectacle. Yet the charm of the mountain remained unchanged.

A recorded voice narrated snippets from *On Her Majesty's Secret Service*, while scenes of George Lazenby racing down the mountain flickered on the screens. Shane smiled at the memory of Eggenberg telling him it was a low-snow year, and when the production crew ran out mid-shoot, they had to import fresh flakes from eighty miles away.

While Cody steered a virtual bobsled, Shane drifted toward the glass doors leading to the outdoor viewing platform—the original helipad built for the movie's climactic escape scene. The wind bit hard. The Alps stretched out in every direction, with the Eiger dominating the skyline, its snowy peak sharp against the cobalt sky.

He leaned against the railing, the sunlight reflecting off his sunglasses, and tried to clear his mind. Yet thoughts intruded anyway. Helvex. The trial. They had come a long way, but something still nagged at him—an unfinished piece of the puzzle. This went deeper than Helvex; it had to. But they were stuck.

He thought about Jasmine's frustration—how she had said that breaking into Helvex's new system was impossible without inside access. "They've sealed themselves tighter than Fort Knox," she had told him. "Short of someone on the inside, there's no way in."

His gaze traced the slowly revolving restaurant behind him—a symbol of a world that never stopped spinning. A sudden gust swept past, carrying the echo of Val's words from breakfast: "Cracking Helvex would take an insider."

Shane straightened, his heartbeat quickening. They now had an insider. Regula Rivella.

"Son of a gun," he muttered.

He hurried back into the restaurant, where Val and Cody were seated by the window, Val's playing cards spread out before her and Cody sipping hot chocolate from a white mug that dwarfed his small hands.

Val looked up. "Hey, where did you go? You missed the best part—Cody's bobsled run. He set a record!"

Shane kissed her forehead. "You two stay and enjoy dessert. I need to head back to Zurich."

"Zurich? Now?"

"Something's clicked, Val. I think we can finally get inside Helvex's fortress."

She studied him for a moment and saw the old fire in his eyes—the look that had both thrilled and terrified her since the day they met.

"Go," she said softly. "But promise me one thing."

"What's that?"

"Don't lose sight of what matters." She glanced at Cody, who was now humming the Bond theme. "This—" she nodded toward their son—"is the future you're fighting for."

Shane smiled, kissed her cheek, and turned toward the exit.

* * *

The ride down felt faster than the ascent, perhaps because Shane's mind was racing. With each tower they passed, he felt himself drawing closer to Zurich and the team.

The cable car glided through thin wisps of cloud. Below, the Lauterbrunnen Valley opened like a white ribbon, stitched with waterfalls shimmering in the afternoon sun. He recalled his first solo run as a Kabinenführer, back in the days before automation, when he felt the thrill of command each time he closed the doors and called out, "Abfahrt!" (Departure).

Now, there was no voice, no human touch—just sensors and silence—a fitting metaphor, he thought, for Helvex's digital empire: efficient, soulless, and inhuman.

By the time Shane reached Stechelberg, the plan had crystallized in his mind. As a compliance officer, Regula would have access to Helvex's innermost sanctum. Jasmine would know how she could compromise them. She could engineer a covert link—something subtle, undetectable, yet powerful enough to lift the veil.

* * *

The drive back to Zurich took two hours, winding through the emerald pastures of the Oberland, past chalets adorned with flower boxes, and into the sleek metallic skyline of the city. When he arrived at the LawForce office on Talstrasse, dusk had fallen. He walked straight into the operations center, where Jasmine sat hunched over her monitors.

She looked up, startled. "You're back early. Everything okay?"

"Better than okay," Shane said, dropping his jacket onto a chair. "Do you remember what you told me about needing an insider to crack Helvex's system?"

Her brow furrowed. "Of course. Helvex's encryption tree regenerates every twenty-four hours. Without internal authorization keys, we're locked out permanently."

Shane smiled—a rare grin that came when puzzle pieces finally fell into place. "Then let's talk to Regula Rivella. Because as of a few days ago, we've got ourselves an insider."

Jasmine's eyes widened as realization dawned.

"That might just work," she whispered. "She has access. We could mirror Helvex's key pattern. You're serious?"

"Dead serious," Shane replied. "The view from the Schilthorn gave me some perspective. Sometimes, to see the whole picture, you have to climb higher."

Jasmine chuckled. "Trust you to have an epiphany at ten thousand feet."

"Hey," he said, grinning, "Bond had his revelations up there. Why can't I?"

* * *

Later that night, after briefing the team, Shane strolled down the Limmatquai, admiring Zurich's night lights. The river glowed like liquid silver, the cathedral towers piercing the night sky. Somewhere out there, in encrypted vaults and hidden servers, lay the truth that would bring Helvex to its knees.

27

ZURICH

SWITZERLAND

They called it the quiet room—a small conference space off the main operations floor where Jasmine liked to spread out network maps, legal briefs, and printed chain-of-custody logs. Around the table sat Shane, Val, and Regula Rivella. Hendrix was on the large screen video feed from Washington.

"You understand the stakes," Shane said quietly. "Helvex's systems are closed to outsiders and rigorously audited. If we could see into those systems, even passively, we could prove the orchestration we've alleged. But you will be exposed if something goes wrong."

Regula let out a breath that might have been a laugh if not for its rawness. "I have children," she said. "An older sister. My parents live in Zug. This is not how I pictured myself serving my country. But I cannot stand by and do nothing."

Val reached for a paper and slid it across to Regula: a letter from Swiss counsel promising to protect her and advocate for whistleblower protection if required. "This won't make you bulletproof," Val said, "but it will provide the best legal shield we can offer. We'll file immediately if anything goes sideways. Jonathan's on board. The Attorney General's office will act if necessary."

Hendrix's voice came through the speaker. "Regula, I can promise you U.S. federal support, rapid relocation if necessary, and the full weight of the Department. We will not abandon you. But I'll be frank: if we're going to take Helvex down, this is the next step. Your testimony will be instrumental, but that could devolve into a she-said-he-said fight. We need concrete evidence."

Jasmine set a tablet in front of Regula; its screen displayed a slim schematic silhouette of a server rack and a high-level depiction of the probe they intended to plant.

"We're not asking you to 'break in,'" she said. "We're asking you to place a monitoring probe in a location that only someone with privileged audit access could reach. Think of it as leaving a recorder in a meeting room.

It will listen to and copy metadata and transaction signatures that are already flowing past that node. There will be no destructive payload and no exfiltration that leaves a trace. It simply watches and timestamps the activity."

Regula nodded slowly. "I can get to a diagnostic aggregator in the back office," she said. "There is a rack they use for troubleshooting, configured for temporary connections. I can plant something small there."

Shane watched her intently. "We'll be listening on our end," he said. "You need to get in, make the placement, and get out before anyone sees you."

"How exactly do I get in?" Regula asked.

"Your usual compliance credentials," Jasmine replied. "They trust you enough to let you into diagnostic areas on a semi-regular basis. You'll be doing this as part of a scheduled verification. You'll carry the device as a 'portable logging module' for the audit. We'll provide the casing to make it look legitimate. You'll sign the standard receipt."

Regula's eyes narrowed. "What if they ask where I'm taking it? What if someone asks for serial numbers? How do I plant it? I'm not an engineer."

"Easy, Regula," Val replied. "Take a breath. You have the authorized inventory list. You'll present a barcoded tag that matches our internal records. And the installation is straightforward. The module clicks into one of the server's slots. Jasmine will show you where to put it."

Shane leaned forward, resting his forearms on the table. "Regula, you know their routines—the afternoon hand-offs, the complacent vetting, the people who never look beyond their checklists. Use that knowledge. Move with the crowd. Don't try to be heroic. We need you to be invisible."

She smiled faintly, almost sadly. "Invisible," she repeated. "I know how to be invisible."

"Okay, that's enough work for now. Ms. Rivella, with a last name like that, would I be correct in guessing that your ancestors came from Italy?"

"Well, yes and no. I don't have roots in Italy per se, but my mother is from Bellinzona, in the Italian-speaking part of Switzerland. I grew up speaking and eating Italian."

"Perfect," Shane replied. "Then I hope you'll join us for lunch. We have a nice Italian restaurant downstairs—Luigia. Their spaghetti bolo is delizioso."

"Sì, grazie mille," she said with a smile. "I'd love to get to know you all better."

* * *

Two evenings later, under a sky dim and heavy with the threat of rain, Regula walked into Helvex's headquarters. Security screens glowed behind a reception desk staffed by bored professionals.

She inserted her pass, and the turnstile card reader blinked green. Shane had insisted she carry a simple personal item—a photo of her sister, who had lost everything in the Boston-First collapse—a constant reminder of why she was taking this risk. She touched the photo once and then slid it back into her coat.

Her route took her to the "diagnostic bay," a narrow room a floor below the main trading hall. It housed rows of racks, filled with the engineering smells of new plastics and ozone, and hummed with the steady sound of computing equipment. The room was guarded by a wall of windows overlooking a seldom-used corridor, a door equipped with numerous card readers, and a single bored engineer's station beside it.

Regula continued to breathe slowly. She greeted the technician on duty—a man she had nodded to during compliance drills a dozen times. He barely looked up.

"Evening, Peter," she said, handing him her inventory log. "I'm here to swap in the portable logger as scheduled."

Peter scanned the log, printed a sticker, and tossed it to her. "Follow the port map. You know the drill."

She smiled; the sticker in her hand felt warm. It bore a barcode that matched the entry Val had prepared. She walked among the racks as if she belonged there. Her palms were damp, gripping her handbag tightly.

When she reached the designated rack—an unremarkable array labeled AUD:03—she slid the faux module from her bag. Jasmine had designed the outer shell to mimic the vendor's maintenance hardware—a pocket-sized aluminum pod with a clip and no visible ports when closed.

She worked methodically. Attach the bracket. Confirm the mechanical latch. Her hands trembled slightly as she looked behind her. All clear. The module locked into place with a final click that sounded unbearably loud to her.

Only one more step. She tapped the unit's face once, sending the handshake code with her palm token—a procedure that appeared, to everyone else, to be a routine diagnostic boot. In the room beyond the glass, a security guard paced past the windows, phone to his ear.

Regula's world narrowed to the click of the latch, the thudding of her heart, and the slight vibration as the probe warmed up and transmitted. She whispered a soft prayer in Italian.

At that moment, a pair of footsteps approached down the far corridor. Initially, she didn't hear them; the room's acoustics played tricks on her—but then a hushed voice rose, followed by a laugh. The door to the diagnostic bay swung open, framing the silhouettes of two men in the light.

Her breath caught in her throat. She froze, telling herself to remain still. From spy movies, she had learned that movement draws attention; staying motionless helps you blend into the surroundings.

The men didn't glance in her direction at first. They walked past the rack where she stood, speaking in low tones. One of them spoke in clipped German. Regula understood enough to know they were discussing an unexpected audit—a surprise security sweep of the maintenance areas triggered by a flagged login down the hall. A flicker of panic shot through her.

The footsteps halted. The man near the door glanced at the rack line and then towards Regula. Her lungs burned. The probe's edge protruded from the rack; she needed to hide it. She couldn't pull it out; that would be noisy, and the slot latch would leave a mark. Instead, she slid forward, her hand brushing the face of the probe, pressing it back. The man's eyes flicked inches away from her fingers before he turned to join his colleague. They chuckled as their voices faded down the corridor.

It was only when the door closed and their footsteps receded that Regula allowed herself to breathe again.

* * *

In the LawForce nerve center, Jasmine monitored screens full of watchfaces and meters, her fingers poised above her keyboard. On her screen, a single green heartbeat blinked: AUD:03—module active—handshake complete—00:00:13. The timestamp landed in their logs like a detonating bomb. The room erupted in loud cheers. Val tried not to leap out of her chair.

* * *

Regula made it onto the street minutes later. The threatening skies had fulfilled their promise. She opened her umbrella against the downpour, waving at a colleague she barely knew and smiling at nothing. Her legs felt like lead.

28

**BOSTON
MASSACHUSETTS
UNITED STATES OF AMERICA**

- - -

**ZURICH
SWITZERLAND**

With another working day coming to a close, Nadler stretched and gazed out over Post Office Square. Despite the priceless view, he usually kept the blinds closed. Sunlight and monitors did not mix well. After a moment, he flicked them closed again. He was focused on CryptoHelix, tracking the fund's sales.

Then it happened.

A soft ping. It wasn't the jarring alert of an external assault—no alarms or loud warnings. Instead, it was the subtle heartbeat of a foreign presence on his network, a listening post try-ing to tap into Helvex's internal systems. Nadler bit his nail and smirked, more curious than sur-prised.

His defense program—a hybrid AI mesh he'd designed himself, codenamed *BlackBriar*—chirped softly from the corner of the screen. It had been crafted in layers to accomplish two simultaneous tasks: protect Helvex's assets and learn the language of probes. It had been watch-ing with the cold patience of a predator. The probe's signature was unfamiliar in its specifics but recognizable in its intent: someone wanted to listen.

He tapped a few keys to isolate the anom-alous session. The data flow wasn't originating from an external node, which piqued his inter-est. It was coming from within their own net-work.

A cold grin spread across his face. "An in-side job."

BlackBriar was already tracing the signal. Within moments, a digital map appeared—a schematic of Helvex's Zurich mainframe, illu-minated with green threads representing regular traffic and one pulsing red dot.

There it was—Rack AUD:03, a maintenance unit in the diagnostic bay. Whoever had plant-ed the device knew what they were doing. That bay wasn't high-security, but it was connected to systems that monitored internal transactions—perfect for someone trying to listen quietly.

"Clever," he whispered, almost admiringly.

He pulled up the device's signature. The coding wasn't Helvex's. After running a few cross-checks, he recognized the authentication pattern: a micro-timing sequence identical to one he had encountered months ago during a hack of BostonFirst's systems. He muttered under his breath, "So, Jasmine, my dear, back with your merry band of vigilantes for round two. How very predictable."

At first, his plan was straightforward: isolate and destroy. He typed a quick sequence to activate *BlackBriar's* purge protocol. Within ten seconds, the foreign hardware would be fried, and every trace would be erased. But as his finger hovered over the enter key, Nadler hesitated. Something about the breach intrigued him.

He could see the line of code running through his network like a silver thread. It wasn't malicious; it was listening, monitoring. Whoever had planted it wasn't there to cause damage—they wanted to observe. That made them vulnerable.

If he killed the device, the opportunity would be lost. But if he kept it alive, he could exploit it to gain access to their system. The intruders would be blocked, while simultaneously allowing Helvex to penetrate them—whoever they were. *BlackBriar's* boomerang module had been designed for precisely this purpose.

He wrote a short line of code—six words, elegant and deadly:

```
init_reverse_bridge(tether:
INTRUDER_ZH)
```

BlackBriar processed the command instantly, tunneling back through the data handshake initiated by the device. In seconds, Nadler had established a silent backdoor connection into LawForce's Zurich command hub.

"Hello, Jasmine," he whispered. "Let's see what secrets *you've* been hiding."

* * *

In the LawForce command center, Jasmine sat at her console, watching as the heartbeat from AUD:03 stabilized.

"Signal looks good," she murmured. "Regula did it."

Shane leaned over her shoulder. "What are we seeing?"

"Transaction pings from the internal compliance servers. Mostly checksum chatter for now. We'll need a few hours before the probe fully syncs." As she spoke, a flicker crossed the screen—a ghost pulse.

She frowned. "That's odd."

"What?" Shane asked.

"There's a mirrored feed... a latency spike on the inbound route. Something's—"

Before she could finish, the signal froze. The probe's indicator light went dark.

"Damn it," Jasmine hissed. "We've been cut off. Blocked."

Shane's expression hardened. "They found it?"

She didn't answer. Her fingers flew across the keyboard, running diagnostic traces. The probe still existed on the network, but it was now unresponsive. A firewall had slammed down between them and the Zurich mainframe.

"Yes, Steve. They found it. This operation is over."

He exhaled sharply. "Goddamn it. Nadler?"

Jasmine nodded grimly. "Only the Ghost could turn an intrusion back on us this fast."

* * *

Once *Blackbriar* had established an open gateway into the intruder's system, it was time to identify the intruder. Nadler knew Jasmine was behind it, but who else?

He isolated one of the digital signatures on a system folder labeled "Task Force Helvex." With a few keystrokes, he tore through obfuscation layers until he hit pay dirt: a real-world metadata trail—an IP block registered to Zurich.

Then came the identity: Marcus Patel.

The name appeared on his monitor like a trophy. Nadler leaned back, savoring the moment. He traced the metadata deeper: Zurich network, Swiss business license filings, and connection points tied to an office leased under an American LLC—LawForce International.

He froze. "LawForce," he said aloud. "Well, well."

His fingers blurred again, pulling up databases, scraping dark-web registries, and running pattern analyses. Within moments, he was staring at a dossier of a top-level legal task force.

LawForce—an independent, elite consortium of lawyers, investigators, and cyber experts operating with the blessing of the U.S. Government, including the Departments of Justice and Treasury. They were known internally as a "legal SWAT team" specializing in cases of national and global significance, tackling issues where the rule of law was under attack and where the good guys' lawyers weren't up to snuff.

He scrolled through the public façade of the organization: its founders, its signature initial high-profile case, *Green Action Coalition v. Wildcat Oil & Gas*, and its ethics charters. It was impressive—idealistic, even. But Nadler wasn't fooled.

"They think they're the white knights," he said with a smirk. "Everyone's a knight until they're on the wrong side of the castle walls."

Then he dove deeper, beyond public data. His private algorithms mined internal communications, cached pages, and leaked server fragments from government sources. Within an hour, he had the skeleton of their structure and all key personnel, including Marcus Patel, a former SEC cyber auditor. Nadler's smile widened. "There you are, dude."

He opened Marcus's personnel records and cross-referenced them with his U.S. database. An SEC file popped up. The file was sealed. Nadler smirked. Sealed to most people, but not to the Ghost. After thirty minutes, he'd bypassed the layers of protection and began reading. It described a leak of classified financial records that had cratered an investigation and derailed Marcus's career.

Nadler chuckled, low and sharp. "Oh, Marcus, you poor bastard."

He turned back to the LawForce file, scrolling through images of the team: Steven Shane, Valentina Lopez, and Jonathan Hendrix—the so-called legal eagles. They were assisted by his old nemesis, Jasmine Lin, and the sharp ex-SEC operator, Marcus Patel. All were now aligned with Bobbi Sullivan.

He studied Bobbi's face longer than the rest. "You just couldn't stay down, could you?" His smile faded.

He saved the data, encrypting it under a classified directory marked "LawForce_Dossier." Information like this—identities, personal histories—wasn't just power; it was leverage.

He picked up his encrypted satellite phone and dialed a secure line. It rang once before connecting.

"Hans," Nadler said smoothly. "You're not going to believe what I've found."

On the other end, Egli was calm but irritated. "Jerome, you were supposed to be handling containment. Are you telling me there's a problem?"

"Oh, there's a problem," Nadler replied, almost cheerfully. "Not with us, but with a group chasing us that, until now, we knew nothing about. They just infiltrated us—temporarily. But I traced it back and shut them down. The silver lining is that I was able to use their connection in reverse to gain access to their system. You'll want to hear this."

Egli's tone was impatient. "Who are you talking about?"

"An entity that calls itself LawForce," Nadler said, savoring the name. "A U.S. government-sanctioned task force—legal, financial, cyber. They're working with Bobbi Sullivan."

Silence crackled for several seconds. Then Egli said, "And you're certain?"

"Absolutely. I have names, locations, and profiles. Their entire team is in Zurich at the moment, except the U.S. Attorney General."

Egli's voice was low and strained. "It goes that high? That complicates matters."

"Not necessarily," Nadler said. "It also gives us an opportunity. I'll forward the files I compiled. I suggest we let Claudine handle the legal angle while I take care of the rest."

Egli's tone shifted. "You've done well, Jerome. Send me what you have. And make sure this LawForce learns what happens when they meddle in affairs beyond their pay grade."

Nadler grinned. "Oh, I already have."

He opened the folder labeled LawForce_ Dossier, encrypted it twice, and uploaded it to Egli's private terminal on the secure Helvex line.

He closed the file and flicked open the blinds. Outside, dawn was breaking over Boston Harbor. Nadler stood, stretched, and poured himself a cup of black coffee.

He smiled faintly. The Ghost had met his adversaries—capable ones at that.

29

ZURICH

SWITZERLAND

Egli enjoyed the morning hour. He surveyed Bürkliplatz as it came to life—trams moving smoothly, bankers hurrying through the morning mist. His musings were interrupted by a ping from his encrypted terminal.

Incoming secure transmission: Nadler – Priority One.

Egli entered his credentials, and a data packet opened on the screen, full of metadata, IP logs, digital schematics, personnel files—LawForce. He scrolled through the information quickly, his brows furrowing in concentration.

Jonathan Hendrix—Attorney General, founder.

Steven Shane—Lead Counsel, dual U.S.-Swiss citizen fluent in Swiss German.

Valentina Lopez—Litigator, logistics command, Shane's wife.

Jasmine Lin—Cyber and crypto specialist at the U.S. Treasury Department.

Marcus Patel—Former SEC cyber auditor.

Each name was accompanied by comprehensive dossiers—backgrounds, security clearances, and internal communication snippets—a complete and unfiltered profile of the group that had been probing Helvex's networks.

For a moment, Egli stared blankly into space. He had sensed something brewing—the breaches, the rumors, the digital disturbances across their firewalls. But this—LawForce—was more formidable than he had anticipated. He leaned back, letting out a slow breath through his nose.

"Nadler really did it. He caught them at their own game," he murmured.

Egli opened the memo attached by Nadler. The Ghost had written it with his usual precision:

Subject: Infiltration Neutralized. Target Identified.

- Opponent is a U.S. task force codenamed LawForce International.

- Operates under the direct mandate of the U.S. Attorney General.

- Base of operations: Zurich.

- Core personnel attached. (See file LAWFORCE-001).

- Suggest immediate counter-narrative—public exposure.

- If they hunt in the dark, drag them into the light.

Jerome N.

A chill ran through Egli, followed by a surge of grim satisfaction. Nadler was correct—Law-

Force was targeting Helvex. But the gift Nadler had provided was invaluable: intelligence and opportunity; chapeau, Jerome, chapeau.

He poured himself a measured finger of Kirsch, the burn sharp at the back of his throat.

"Know your enemy," he said aloud, quoting one of his favorite sayings by Sun Tzu. "And you need not fear the result of a hundred battles."

He skimmed the dossiers again, pausing at Shane's file—dual Swiss-American citizen, educated at Yale and the University of Zurich. Interesting. Fluent in Swiss German. Connections within the Swiss Federal Tribunal. So, the Americans had sent one of their own to wage war against his motherland's financial core.

Egli smiled thinly. "A Judas with a passport," he muttered under his breath.

For a moment, he contemplated the implications—then the strategist within him took over. This wasn't a crisis; it was leverage.

He pressed the intercom. "Claudine Dubois. Get her on the line. Priority call."

Dubois answered on the second ring. "Good morning, Hans. I assume this isn't a social call?"

"No," Egli replied. "Nadler just sent me something extraordinary: the complete profile of our adversaries—an American group called LawForce. Every member, every tie, every thread. They're operating out of Zu-

THE CYBER SANCTION 229

rich, and they already attempted to breach our systems. Nadler turned the tables on them. They're exposed, and now we're in their systems."

A pause. "You're sure about this LawForce entity?"

"I'm looking at their files, including internal emails. They've been building a case against us for months."

Dubois inhaled sharply and then laughed. "Then let's not wait for them to go public. We'll go first."

Egli frowned. "Meaning?"

"Meaning," she said, "we drag this LawForce creature out of the shadows and into the light. If they take pride in secrecy, we will make it their liability."

Egli turned his chair toward the window, watching as the morning sun bathed Lake Zurich in golden light. "Yes, Nadler suggested the same thing: a counter-attack."

"A legal and public one," she replied. "While it may connect us to them, they are clearly going to act against us soon, so there's little downside. We need an immediate press conference to get the jump on them. Paint them as an American deep-state task force meddling in sovereign nations. That narrative will resonate here, as well as in Brussels, Singapore, and Dubai. The world despises U.S. overreach."

He paused for a moment. "Perhaps Paradeplatz? It's symbolic."

"No," she said immediately. "Too small. Too Swiss. This can't appear to be a local dispute."

After a brief silence, she continued, "I've got it—the ETH terrace. It's above the city, commanding, and has a global view. You can see all of Zurich and the Alps beyond. We'll rise above national borders. Paradeplatz is associated with bankers, while ETH represents innovation, science, and progress. Plus, it's larger; we could get quite a turnout."

Egli reflected, tapping a pen against his chin. "ETH. Yes, that's a clever choice."

"Of course it is," she replied, a hint of amusement in her voice. "We'll frame LawForce as an ideological virus—America's attempt to dictate global financial morality. We'll ask the obvious questions: Why are they here? Why the secrecy? Who authorizes their actions on Swiss soil? If they're legitimate, why do they operate behind encrypted servers and offshore shells?"

Egli started to smile again. Dubois always had a rare combination of legal brilliance and political instinct.

"Claudine," he said softly, "you sound positively delighted."

"I am," she confessed. "This is the kind of fight I was born for. And if we handle it correctly, we won't just discredit LawForce—we'll rally international sympathy for Helvex. We'll be seen as the victims of cyber imperialism. Isn't the irony delicious?"

* * *

Within the hour, Dubois had mobilized Helvex's communications team. Press liaisons drafted invitations to global media outlets, including Reuters, Bloomberg, Nikkei, *Inside Paradeplatz*, *Le Monde*, the *Financial Times*, and *The New York Times*. The subject line was crafted to intrigue and alarm:

Global Banking Sovereignty Under Threat by Shadow U.S. Agency – Helvex Financial Responds

Inside Helvex's executive offices, Egli paced while Dubois orchestrated efforts from Geneva via video link.

"We go public at noon tomorrow," she stated. "The ETH terrace will be perfect at that hour. The sun will hit the dome behind us, and the photographers will capture a great spectacle. You'll start by expressing gratitude to the Swiss people, reaffirming Helvex's commitment to transparency, stability, and global trust. Then, you'll pivot: introduce LawForce as an unknown, unsanctioned, extrajudicial task force targeting sovereign banks."

Egli nodded, absorbing her plan like doctrine. "And the evidence?"

"We'll reveal just enough—organizational charts, mission statements, snippets of their internal communications. No classified documents, but enough to substantiate our claims."

"And the tone?" he asked.

"Serious," Dubois replied. "Not defensive—righteous. Helvex isn't just protecting itself; it's safeguarding the integrity of international banking. And if anyone claims this is deflection, remind them of the BostonFirst hysteria—that it was American panic that destabilized markets, not Swiss prudence."

Egli smiled. "You've already written my speech, haven't you?"

"I'm halfway through," she admitted. "You'll be the calm statesman, and I'll be the outraged defender of sovereignty. Together, we'll control the narrative."

30

ZURICH

SWITZERLAND

The Polybahn funicular clattered loudly as it began its steady ascent from Zurich's bustling Centralplatz, its scarlet cars gleaming against the gray morning mist. The short climb was one of the city's oldest rituals—a daily link between the modern heart of Zurich and its intellectual crown. Inside, Egli braced his feet to counteract the gentle swaying of the carriage.

He had taken this funicular every morning as a student, clutching his notes and ambitions, his head full of equations, rising toward the heights of the ETH. Now, decades later, the same view passed before him, but the climb felt heavier.

The Polybahn still creaked with the same mechanical honesty, yet its ascent now carried the weight of reputations and markets rather than dreams. He looked through the fogged glass, past Dubois's reflection, toward the ETH dome looming at the top.

"Still a beautiful city," Dubois remarked.

"Yes," Egli replied softly, "but it was simpler in my student days. Equations didn't lie."

The funicular jolted slightly as it reached the top station. The doors slid open, revealing the sun-dappled terrace of ETH Zurich. Egli straightened his tie. The student had returned—not for lectures this time, but for battle.

At midday, the terrace was a hive of activity. Technicians erected podiums and cameras under white canopies; sound crews tested microphones against the wind sweeping up from the Limmat. The view stretched spectacularly—Zurich's Old Town below, the spires of Grossmünster and Fraumünster gleaming, the Alps distant but unmistakable.

Dubois climbed the dais first, flanked by an aide and a photographer. Reporters recognized her instantly; she had been head of the Swiss Federal Department of Finance before joining the private sector. Cameras swiveled.

"Madame Dubois, is this about the Boston-First investigation?"

"Why ETH? Why now?"

She smiled, offering no answers. "All will be clear soon," she said, moving gracefully toward the podium.

When Egli joined her, the crowd thickened. Helicopters circled at a distance, and news drones hovered above the balustrade. His silver hair gleamed; his composure radiated quiet confidence. Dubois handed him a folder, whispering, "Stay on script. And remember—LawForce isn't an American hero; it's an American mistake."

He nodded.

The cameras clicked to life as Egli stepped up. His image filled screens around the world within minutes—Zurich's skyline behind him like a stage.

"Good afternoon," he began in calm, deliberate tones. "Helvex Financial has stood for over a century as a symbol of financial integrity and global cooperation. We have weathered wars, recessions, and revolutions. But never have we faced what we face today."

He paused, allowing the murmurs to settle.

"A clandestine organization, operating out of Zurich, has infiltrated the global banking network. It calls itself LawForce—a secretive task force operating under the United States Department of Justice. Its mission: to police and, when convenient, destabilize foreign institutions under the guise of justice."

Reporters stirred. Cameras zoomed closer.

Egli continued, his voice gaining strength. "LawForce claims to defend fairness in global markets. In reality, it operates without accountability, jurisdiction, or transparency. Its agents have engaged in cyber intrusions on Swiss soil—acts that, by any definition, constitute espionage."

He gestured subtly to Dubois, who approached with a thick dossier. "This," she said, addressing the microphones, "is evidence of LawForce's operations. It includes names, locations, and communications. Their Zurich base is located within a few kilometers of where we stand."

Gasps rippled through the crowd.

Egli resumed, "Switzerland is a sovereign nation. We respect the law, but we will not tolerate foreign interference. To our partners around the world, understand this: if it can happen to us, it can happen to you."

The questions came rapidly.

"Mr. Egli, are you accusing the United States government of espionage?"

Egli replied, "I am accusing them of arrogance."

"Is this LawForce team investigating Helvex as a result of the BostonFirst takeover?"

Egli responded, "Not to my knowledge. I don't know what they are doing here. But I do know that justice cannot be served through secrecy and subterfuge."

Dubois stepped in, her voice carrying effortlessly. "Ask yourselves why LawForce hides. Why do its members conceal their identities even from allied governments? Transparency is the currency of democracy—why are they bankrupt?"

The crowd erupted in overlapping shouts. Cameras flashed.

Dubois leaned toward the microphones. "Helvex will not remain silent while shadow forces rewrite the rules of global finance. This is about the sovereignty of every financial system on earth." She let her words linger before delivering the final blow. "I am calling for an inquiry into LawForce's activities by the Swiss Federal Council. My contacts there share my concern that the U.S. Department of Justice has created an unaccountable monster—a legal Frankenstein."

The line landed like thunder. Reporters shouted; some cheered. Egli and Claudine exchanged a subtle glance. It was working. Within minutes, the first headlines were being pushed out:

Helvex Financial Accuses U.S. of Global Espionage

Secret DOJ Unit Operating in Zurich, Claims Helvex CEO

U.S. Legal Frankenstein Loose on the Streets of Zurich

As the press dispersed, Dubois and Egli stepped to the edge of the terrace. Distant church bells chimed one o'clock. "That," Dubois said, exhaling, "was flawless."

Egli nodded. "We've forced them into the open. From this moment, LawForce isn't a righteous crusader; it's a scandal."

He smiled. "Your ETH idea was inspired."

"I thought so. Paradeplatz would've made us look like cornered bankers. ETH made us look like visionaries." She paused, a gleam of excitement lighting up her dark eyes. "I'm already getting calls from Bern. I know members of the Federal Assembly from the past. If we feed them the right details, we can spark a hearing in the Assembly—imagine the optics."

Egli laughed softly. "You're enjoying this far too much."

"I told you," she replied, "I was born for this."

They stood silently for a moment, the wind tugging at their coats. Egli's phone buzzed with a new message from Nadler.

Helvex systems are secure. Have breached the LawForce network. Awaiting next orders.

– Ghost

Egli's satisfaction deepened. "Our phantom performs well," he said quietly.

Dubois tilted her head. "Jerome Nadler. I've never met him. Is he as brilliant as they say?"

"Brilliant," Egli said. "And dangerous. A man who believes in chaos as justice."

She smiled faintly. "Then he fits right in."

* * *

That night, news feeds across Europe and North America pulsed with Helvex's revelation. Financial anchors dissected Egli's speech, and pundits debated sovereignty and surveillance. Hashtags trended: #LawForce, #BankingEspionage, #USBigBrother.

At LawForce's Zurich command center, Shane and his team watched in stunned silence. The screens that once displayed market data now streamed news footage of Egli's press conference.

Bobbi slammed her fist on the table. "They flipped the script. They made us the villains."

Jasmine's face was pale. "His breach of our system was more serious than I thought. It wasn't just Marcus who was burned; we all were, as was LawForce. They know everything."

Marcus, still nursing the sting from Nadler's counterattack, muttered, "The Ghost. He's feeding them our playbook."

Shane stared at the footage—Egli's composed face and Dubois's fiery rhetoric. "Then we adapt," he said quietly. "They want war in the light of day? We'll meet them there. Remember, folks, we are the good guys here. Jonathan and I discussed this at the inception of LawForce. We decided then to operate under the radar for strategic reasons. That ends now."

He turned off the screen.

* * *

Later that evening, Egli sat alone in his office. On one monitor, stock tickers danced—Helvex's shares were up four percent. The press loved a good underdog.

He replayed the press conference footage, lingering on the moment Dubois declared LawForce a global menace—Frankenstein! He smiled; she was magnificent.

He opened his encrypted inbox and found a message from the Chinese liaison—short, coded, and promising continued progress.

**Excellent progress. Maintain narrative.
Stage six authorization forthcoming.**

Egli deleted it immediately, then poured himself another glass of kirsch. Everything was aligning: Helvex was untouchable again, Law-Force was exposed, and Nadler was hunting in the shadows.

He raised the glass toward the skyline. "To the ghosts," he said softly. "May they never rest."

31

ZURICH

SWITZERLAND

Inside the nerve center, Shane stood at the window. The press conference on the ETH terrace a few days earlier was a masterpiece of manipulation. Claudine Dubois had turned the tables with surgical precision. The headlines followed her narrative like sheep:

U.S. Legal Inquisition Targets Swiss Sovereignty

LawForce or LawFarce?

Shane had witnessed smear campaigns before, but never one this quick and efficient.

Dubois controlled the optics perfectly—every camera angle, every quote. Even Zurich's famously reserved populace was stirred into nationalistic indignation. But Shane knew that propaganda could only delay the inevitable. Facts were stubborn, and Regula Rivella's testimony was more than damning—it was dynamite.

He turned away from the window. "All right," he said, "enough damage control. It's time we went on the offensive."

Val looked up from her tablet. "You're serious about filing today?"

"You bet. I was serious yesterday," Shane replied. "We're filing in the Handelsgericht—Commercial Court. Based on Regula's testimony and what Jasmine was able to pull off the BostonFirst servers, we have grounds for fraud, market manipulation, and conspiracy to defraud foreign investors. It's showtime."

Bobbi leaned forward, her hands clasped on the conference table. "Do you really think we'll get a fair hearing here? This is Claudine Dubois's playground. Every clerk in that courthouse probably owes her a favor."

Shane smiled slightly. "All the more reason to walk straight into her backyard and light the fire."

* * *

The main courthouse of the Commercial Court of the Canton of Zurich stood on Hirschengraben, a gray neo-Renaissance structure whose carved stone façade and wrought-iron balconies exuded permanence and restraint. It was a building that had seen centuries of financial disputes, inheritance wars, and international litigation pass through its arched doors.

At nine a.m., the LawForce team arrived— Shane, Val, and a small group of Swiss counsel they had hired as local advisors. The street smelled of roasted chestnuts from a nearby stand and wet cobblestones from the morning drizzle.

Inside, murals depicting allegories of justice adorned the high ceilings: Veritas, blindfolded, held her scales above a gleaming brass plaque that read Einigkeit vor dem Gesetz (Equality before the law).

At the counter, their documents were inspected with characteristic Swiss thoroughness. The clerk, a young man in horn-rimmed glasses, looked up after stamping the documents. "You're here for case 2025-CF-148, yes? BostonFirst shareholders et al. versus Helvex Financial Aktiengesellschaft?" His eyes flicked back up again.

Shane's expression remained steady. "Yes, that's correct."

The clerk nodded, but his slight smirk betrayed recognition. Claudine Dubois's influence extended even here.

In Switzerland, filing a civil action wasn't the theatrical event it was in American courts. There were no camera crews, no court officers announcing the arrival of a case. It involved paperwork and procedure.

Still, as Shane handed the bound complaint, with flash drives containing a complete digital copy, across the counter to the court registrar, he felt the gravity of the moment. The document was two hundred pages of meticulous detail, outlining Regula's testimony regarding CryptoHelix, Infinium, and the planned sabotage of Western markets.

The registrar stamped the final page with the court's red seal. "Case accepted," he announced.

* * *

By midday, the court server had delivered a copy of the lawsuit to Axos GmbH at their marble-and-glass offices overlooking the Limmat. From her office window, Dubois could see the top of the courthouse. She smiled faintly as she sipped her espresso.

"They filed so soon after that beating they took at the press conference?" She turned to her junior partner, Luca, shaking her head. "This Mr. Shane is bold, I'll give him that."

After scanning the first pages of the filing, her expression turned ashen. "My God," she stammered. "It can't be." But there it was, in black and white: "The scheme aims to destabilize the West through strategic marketing and subsequent devaluation of the CryptoHelix Fund and the cryptocurrency, Infinium."

"Where, in God's name, did this Regula Rivella get her information?" she said to no one. "Those morons at Helvex really blew it this time." She sat at her desk, tugging an earlobe, trying to process the ramifications of what she had just read.

An associate poked her head in the door. "Frau Dubois?"

"Yes, what is it?"

"I just thought you should know that the lawsuit we were just served with is all over town. Apparently, the plaintiffs released it to the media."

"*Damn*," Claudine banged a fist on the desk. "I was hoping we'd have time for some damage control. This Mr. Shane is a sharp operator. Get back to the filing. I want a full brief on my desk before you leave today."

"Yes, ma'am."

She waved at Luca. "We're done here. Go help the rest of them comb through that filing."

After he shut the door, Dubois sat for a few moments collecting her thoughts. Then she grabbed the phone.

Within seconds, Egli came on the line. "Yes, Claudine, still basking in the glow of our press conference?"

"Hans," she hissed, "you've been caught with your pants down. I just received a filing from LawForce initiating litigation at the Commercial Court. They know everything. And they've gone public with it. They're aware of stage six, the devaluation of Infinium. I'm sure it's affecting the markets now. You may want to check your fund balances. I can guarantee that by tonight, there won't be a single investor left."

"But they haven't proven a thing," Egli rasped.

"Hans, you know as well as I that markets don't move on proof; they move on fear. There's enough in that filing to scare anyone holding Infinium."

She could hear frantic typing through the phone, followed by a shout. The venerable Mr. Egli had lost it. "Claudine," he yelled. "People are dumping Infinium. CryptoHelix is bleeding out. What the hell is going on? How did LawForce find out?"

Dubois held the phone away from her ear while his tirade continued. After a minute, she spoke again. "Hans, do you know a Regula Rivella?"

"No, I don't think so. Who the hell is she?"

"She's an executive in your compliance department. She's the one who spilled the beans. I don't know how she got her information, but you ran a leaky ship."

There was a long pause before Egli returned to the line. "Verdammt, Claudine, this is an unmitigated disaster. I have to make some calls. I assume we can still mount a defense?"

"Yes, of course. We're going to look into this Rivella character, and we'll dig up some dirt—believe me. No one survives my investigators. We'll fight the litigation and go for damages. But Infinium, I'm afraid, will never live up to its name. It's finished."

She heard the line go dead as Egli scrambled to address the fallout. Turning to the table where her partners were reviewing the lawsuit, one of them looked up and asked, "Should we move for dismissal?"

"In due course," Claudine replied. "But first, we need to challenge jurisdiction, the evidence chain, Rivella's credibility—every procedural angle. This isn't about winning just yet. It's about exhausting them."

Her assistant entered quietly with a file. "The court clerk called, Madame Dubois. The presiding judge will be Rolf Bärtschi."

Claudine managed a slight smile. "Ah, dear Rolf. I coached his daughter through her clerkship exams. This should be... civil."

* * *

While Swiss courts generally respect privacy in commercial actions, Shane and the team needed transparency. In particular, to alert the markets about Infinium. At the time of filing, they'd also issued a media package with a sanitized summary, omitting any sensitive or confidential information. By evening, Zurich was buzzing with speculation. *Inside Paradeplatz* released a special online bulletin, while the *Neue Zürcher Zeitung* featured the headlines:

American LawForce Files Suit Against Helvex Financial—Swiss Sovereignty at Stake?

Investors Abandon Infinium—Is Law-Force a Villain or a Hero?

Commentators on Swiss television debated whether this situation represented a new form of economic imperialism. Near the Hauptbahnhof, a bank of screens displayed the coverage. Some people labeled LawForce a vigilante legal cartel, while others admired its boldness. Amid it all, the markets reacted negatively, punishing Helvex. The contrast was perplexing.

Back at the LawForce offices, the mood was mixed. There was relief at the market's reaction; they had just averted a collapse of the Western financial sector. However, there was also concern about some adverse reactions to LawForce.

"A lot of them are framing us as the enemy," Val said, her frustration evident.

"Let them," Shane replied. "Public opinion shifts. The truth doesn't."

Bobbi joined them and set a stack of documents on the table. "Regula is ready to take the stand. We've prepared her thoroughly. She's a natural. I think Dubois will have her work cut out for her."

Shane nodded. "Good. We'll need her to turn the tide."

He moved to the whiteboard at the far end of the room and sketched out a plan. *Phase One: Establish credibility. Phase Two: Show motive. Phase Three: Explain the fraud.*

Val leaned against the wall, looking concerned. "And if she gets the case dismissed on jurisdictional grounds?"

"Then we'll take it to the Swiss Federal Supreme Court, if necessary. Reason will prevail sooner or later, Dubois or no Dubois. She doesn't own the whole country."

32

ZURICH

SWITZERLAND

Dubois reacted with remarkable speed. Just two weeks after the LawForce filing, she had persuaded the court to hold a preliminary hearing on jurisdictional matters. Shane realized she intended to dismiss the case before it gained any traction, and with her influence, she might succeed.

The courthouse was set back from Hirschengraben, behind a small plaza lined with chestnut trees. Shane paused for a moment before the wide oak doors. "Remember," he said to Val and Bobbi, "today is important. We lose jurisdiction, and this effort is over before it starts. We need to stay calm and focused. No theatrics."

Inside, the courthouse smelled faintly of waxed floors and old wood. The marble steps curved upward. Courtroom One was a study in Swiss minimalism—pale wood panels, muted lighting, and a crucifix mounted high above the judges' bench. Behind the judges, a wood-paneled wall displayed the Coat of Arms of Zurich, featuring white and blue diagonal stripes. Three judges were present, as was typical in the Swiss system, which favored panels over a single judge and reflected a belief in collective deliberation. Shane hoped this would work in their favor.

The presiding judge, Rolf Bärtschi, was in his late fifties and had the calm demeanor of someone who had seen every trick counsel could play. His gray hair was cut short, and his wire-rimmed glasses rested halfway down his nose as he reviewed the docket. He wore no robe, just a charcoal suit and a blue tie, embracing the Swiss tradition that judges do not distinguish themselves from the citizens they judge through attire. In this courtroom, authority stemmed not from grandeur but from quiet discipline.

To his right sat Verena Graf, a petite woman with sharp eyes. A former finance professor turned judge, she was rumored to be knowledgeable about every derivative instrument ever devised. To his left sat Lukas Schmid, a younger lay judge and accountant from Zollikon, appointed for his financial expertise. Although he appeared slightly uncomfortable in the formal setting, Shane knew that Swiss lay judges held significant influence.

* * *

At precisely ten a.m., the clerk announced, "Case 2025-CF-148: BostonFirst shareholders et al. versus Helvex Financial Aktiengesellschaft."

Shane rose, buttoning his dark gray suit. Across the aisle, Dubois stood, immaculate in a tailored charcoal jacket and her trademark red silk scarf. The room buzzed with quiet anticipation as legal observers from across Europe crowded the small gallery. The case was already being dubbed "The Trial of the Century" in financial circles.

Judge Bärtschi opened the proceedings. "We are here to determine whether this court has jurisdiction over claims brought by foreign and national plaintiffs against a Swiss financial institution regarding actions allegedly undertaken through subsidiaries in the United States. Mr. Shane, although this is a defense motion, the court will hear from you first. You may proceed."

* * *

Dubois sat at the defense table with her Axos GmbH team. She looked at home—this was her court, her turf.

She watched as Shane approached the lectern. It was her first look at her adversary. She noted he cut a dashing figure, with a dark complexion inherited from his mother's side and a trim, powerful physique. The ponytail was a surprise, but it suited him well. She had read he was half Navajo, which seemed quite exotic to the Swiss, who had a peculiar fascination with Native Americans, fueled by all those Karl May westerns.

His German was precise and fluent—a product of his dual heritage. While Swiss German was commonly spoken on the streets, there was no uniform written form; what the Swiss called "High German" was used in all formal proceedings. His command of that language impressed the court, and Claudine noticed it too, a faint flicker of respect crossing her face.

* * *

Shane noticed Dubois studying him carefully. He realized she'd been surprised by his grasp of German. *Stay tuned, Ms. Dubois, there might be a few more surprises before we're finished.* He turned to face the bench squarely.

"Good morning, Herr Präsident, Judges Graf and Schmid," he began, "this case concerns a Swiss corporation. Its world headquarters are just a few blocks from here. While BostonFirst is a bank based in Boston, it is wholly owned by Helvex and operates under its direction. Furthermore, while a portion of the plaintiff pool includes Americans, it also includes Swiss citizens. Several investors in the Infinium cryptocurrency are Swiss. The connection to Switzerland is strong and obvious. While this case has international aspects, it is fundamentally Swiss in nature—dressed in Swiss clothing. Zurich, and your court, are the natural venue."

When he finished, Dubois rose gracefully. "Good morning, Herr Präsident, Judges," she began, her voice smooth yet sharp, "with respect, the Court should reject this case outright. The alleged harm occurred in the United States, not here. If Mr. Shane wishes to add drama to his case, he should file in Hollywood."

A ripple of laughter spread through the gallery. Even Judge Schmid allowed himself a faint smile.

She continued, "Mr. Shane speaks of Swiss shareholders. Let's examine the facts, as they are crucial here. Only five percent of the plaintiffs are Swiss residents—just five percent. As for the Infinium investors, again, only a small number are Swiss, accounting for just eight percent of total investment. Therefore, it should be clear that if this case is dressed in Swiss clothing, it is naked."

A few muffled laughs escaped from the gallery. Shane made a mental note. Despite the quiet reputation of Swiss courts, Madame Dubois had a flair for the dramatic.

After she finished, Judge Bärtschi closed the hearing. "The court will render its decision on jurisdiction within ten days. Until then, proceedings are suspended."

Shane masked his frustration. The delay was expected—but annoying. Every day gave Dubois more time to consolidate her advantage. As they left the courtroom, she brushed past him, leaning close enough for only him to hear. "Welcome to Zurich, Mr. Shane. You're playing on my chessboard now."

Shane smiled faintly. "Then I hope you don't mind losing a queen."

* * *

That evening, Dubois retreated to her office to review the transcript. She had expected Shane to be competent, not charismatic. His command of German had caught her off guard. He wasn't the brash American caricature she had painted at the press conference; he was disciplined, intelligent—and dangerous. She knew the jurisdictional action was a long shot, given all the ties to Switzerland—Helvex's home base, and Swiss shareholders and investors—but she had to try. She was used to winning long shots, usually against average lawyers. She now realized there was nothing average about Steve Shane.

She would enjoy this battle. A worthy opponent always raised the stakes.

She poured herself a glass of Chasselas and dialed Egli.

"He's better than I expected," she admitted.

Egli's voice was calm, almost amused. "Then destroying him should be that much more satisfying. Have at it."

She smiled. "With pleasure."

* * *

At the same hour, LawForce's Zurich team reconvened in their glass-walled office. Shane stood by the window, his jacket off and sleeves rolled up.

"We made it through the first round," Val said, dropping a folder on the table. "But Dubois is already working the judges. Our local counsel saw her bumping into Bärtschi outside the courthouse."

Shane raised an eyebrow. "Any social contact with counsel would be improper for the judge. At this point, I'll have to assume it was just an accident. We keep everything clean on our end. No drama, no leaks. We win this on evidence."

Bobbi looked up. "And if we lose jurisdiction?"

Shane turned from the window. "Then we make it political. We'll take it to the European Parliament if we have to. Helvex wants this buried in procedural mud; we'll drag it into the open."

* * *

Ten days later, Judge Bärtschi delivered the court's decision with typical Swiss precision— measured and deliberate. The courtroom was silent as he adjusted his glasses and read from the written ruling.

"The court has reviewed the submissions and finds sufficient connection to the jurisdiction of Switzerland," he said. "Helvex Financial is domiciled in Zurich, and the alleged acts of misrepresentation and manipulation originated, in material part, from its Swiss operations. Furthermore, several of the plaintiffs in this matter are themselves Swiss nationals, establishing both territorial and substantive links to this jurisdiction. Accordingly, this court affirms its competence to hear this case."

Shane exhaled quietly, exchanging a glance with Val. Across the aisle, Dubois remained composed, her expression unreadable, though there was a faint tightening around her mouth.

Judge Bärtschi concluded, "The court will proceed to scheduling evidentiary hearings in due course. Counsel will be advised. I should give you all a heads-up that we have set the trial date for July fourteenth."

Shane glanced at Val. "That's pretty fast by Swiss standards," he whispered. "Not bad."

But Dubois was already on her feet. "Herr Präsident, given the international complexity, we propose a longer preparatory period—say, October for trial."

Bärtschi frowned slightly. "Frau Dubois, the court will not permit undue delay. This matter has already drawn significant attention. The schedule stands."

It was a small victory, but a visible one. Shane caught the flicker of annoyance in Dubois's eyes. The Queen of Zurich rarely heard "no" from the bench.

The judge turned to the clerk. "Please mark the calendar: the evidentiary hearing in Boston-First et al. versus Helvex Financial Aktiengesellschaft will begin on July fourteenth at nine a.m."

The clerk nodded crisply.

Bärtschi faced the room. "Thank you all, we are adjourned."

Shane leaned back, letting out a breath he hadn't realized he was holding. They had survived the first test. Better than that, they now had a trial date. In Swiss litigation, securing a trial date was half the battle. More importantly, Shane had developed some respect for Bärtschi. It appeared they would have a fair hearing from him, which is all any lawyer could ask for.

Outside the courtroom, Dubois approached, flanked by two associates in sleek black suits. "Efficient morning," she said lightly, switching to English. "You have to admire how our courts keep things tight."

Shane smiled politely. "I was thinking the same. It's a nice change from the chaos of American procedures."

Her eyes glinted. "You may find Swiss precision less forgiving than American improvisation."

"Or perhaps," Shane replied, "it's exactly what this case needs."

For a moment, they stood eye to eye—two tacticians who understood that law was just another form of warfare, fought in syllables instead of bullets.

Then Dubois inclined her head. "See you in July, Mr. Shane."

"And before that, I suspect," he replied.

She smiled faintly, then swept down the corridor, her heels striking the stone in perfect rhythm.

The group started back to the office, crossing the Münsterbrücke to Paradeplatz and the adjacent Confiserie Sprüngli. Bobbi followed a step behind, her expression thoughtful.

"I can't believe how calm it all was," she said. "No objections, no shouting—just... precision."

"That's Switzerland," Shane replied. "They believe courtrooms should be civilized arenas. But make no mistake—Dubois will fight hard; it's just that you'll barely see the blood."

Val smiled faintly. "You almost sound like you admire her."

He didn't answer right away. The truth was, in a way, he did. She was brilliant, disciplined, and ruthless. In another life, they might have been allies.

They reached the café and sat down at the outside terrace, overlooking the tram tracks on Bahnhofstrasse. Steam rose from their coffees, curling into the cold air. "Well," Shane said quietly, "we're on the calendar. That's all that matters for now."

Val lifted her cup. "To July fourteenth."

33

ZURICH

SWITZERLAND

Hendrix hated transatlantic flights, but this one felt longer than usual. As Air Force One's smaller counterpart— the DOJ's Gulfstream G550—descended over the snow-tipped Alps, the Attorney General pressed his palm against the window, watching the clouds break over the blue-grey waters of Lake Zurich. Below, the old city unfurled in ordered beauty—church spires, cobbled lanes, and the Limmat River cutting clean through its heart.

But he wasn't here for the scenery. He was here to steady the ship. The aftermath of the Helvex press conference had been chaotic. Cable pundits, op-ed writers, and digital warriors were tearing into LawForce, branding it everything from "a globalist legal militia" to "America's shadow hand in Europe." The president wanted control of the narrative, and Hendrix had been tasked with delivering it.

He knew this moment would come. The secrecy that gave LawForce its edge also made it a target. Dubois, with her silken Geneva charm and photogenic disdain, had exploited that perfectly. Her press tour after the ETH conference had turned LawForce into a symbol of American arrogance.

* * *

Shane was already waiting when Hendrix entered the LawForce command center. He rose from the conference table.

"Jon," he said, offering a hand. "Long flight?"

Hendrix grinned, setting down his briefcase. "About as long as our public relations nightmare."

They shook hands firmly, old comrades in a new war. Shane looked every inch the Swiss-trained lawyer—crisp dark suit, restrained tie, and no hint of the exhaustion that had dogged the team for weeks. Still, Hendrix could see it in his eyes. The Zurich litigation, the press conference ambush, and the endless battle with Dubois were grinding them all down.

"Let's walk," Hendrix said. "I need some fresh air."

* * *

They stepped out into the late afternoon chill. Hendrix tugged his coat tight and breathed in the clean air. "The president's not happy," he said as they walked a loop across the Rathausbrücke, through a segment of the Old Town, and back across the Münsterbrücke that connected the Fraumünster and Grossmünster churches. "He says every time he turns on the television, LawForce is being painted as an unaccountable cabal of vigilante lawyers. He wants clarity—public, moral, and legal."

Shane nodded. "We knew this was coming. The minute we stepped onto Swiss soil, we stopped being invisible."

"Dubois forced our hand," Hendrix said. "That press conference—she framed us as the villains before we even got started."

"Which is exactly why we need to stop playing defense," Shane replied. "LawForce was never about hiding. It was about rebalancing the scales when power tilted too far."

In the Old Town, they ducked into a café in Niederdorf, the old student quarter. Warmth and espresso steam filled the air. Hendrix ordered coffee, while Shane opted for mineral water.

"This city hasn't changed much," Shane said, gazing out the window. "When I studied here, it always felt like the center of gravity—where finance, law, and intellect all collided. Now it's our battlefield."

Hendrix stirred his coffee slowly. "And it's the right battlefield. The world's watching Zurich. The markets, the banks, the regulators—it all flows from here. If you win this case, Steven, you don't just take down Helvex; you redefine what accountability means in global finance."

Shane smiled faintly. "No pressure, then."

"Pressure's the point," Hendrix replied. "If this were easy, anyone could do it."

They sat in silence for a moment, the espresso machine's rhythmic hiss filling the gap. Outside, students hurried across the cobblestones, their laughter mingling with the clang of a distant tram.

"You know," Hendrix said finally, "the president told me something before I left. He said, 'LawForce is like the Manhattan Project for justice: brilliant minds, dangerous mission, all in the dark. The question is, can they survive the light?'

"And we can," Hendrix continued. "You just need to show people what you're fighting for. You've got victims, shareholders, small investors—human faces behind this mess. Make them the story."

Shane nodded slowly. "I never did like the secrecy. In a way, it's a relief to move beyond that. We'll need media coordination."

On the way back, they paused at the edge of Münsterhof Square. The cobblestones were slick with a fine drizzle. Before them, the Fraumünster church rose in pale stone. Its stunning stained-glass windows by artists Marc Chagall and Augusto Giacometti glowed faintly in the dimming light.

Hendrix motioned toward a plaque set in the cobblestones at their feet as a ray of sunshine broke through. "Do you know what this is?"

Shane looked down, surprised at what he was standing on. The inscription read:

Hendrix smiled faintly. "Churchill's 'Arise Europe' speech. He stood right here, saying the world had to learn from its collapse, that unity and courage would rebuild civilization after the ruin of war."

"I've read it," Shane said quietly.

"Then you know what he meant when he said, 'Let Europe arise.' He wasn't talking about governments or armies. He was talking about will, resolve, and the guts to start again."

Hendrix turned to him, his eyes steady. "If the old bulldog could rally Europe, you sure as hell can rally your team. Dubois may have taken the first swing, but we're the ones with the moral high ground. Don't forget that."

Shane exhaled, feeling the weight of Hendrix's words. "Do you think the public can see that?"

"They will," Hendrix replied. "If we show them. Right now, all they see is secrecy. You have to make them understand what LawForce stands for."

* * *

Back at the office, the two men gathered the senior team—Val, Jasmine, Marcus, and Bobbi. "Here's the situation," Hendrix began, pacing in front of the main display. "We're being hammered in the press. The public thinks we're some secret cabal meddling in global markets. That ends today."

Marcus nodded his head vigorously. "Dylan Thomas said it best. 'Do not go gentle into that good night...; Rage, rage against the dying of the light.'"

"Thank you, Marcus, you clearly get the point," Hendrix said wryly, then pointed to Shane. "Steven's leading the litigation, and I need everyone behind him. Beyond that, we need to win hearts and minds. History offers many examples of good causes that failed because they didn't explain themselves properly."

Jasmine frowned. "Are you suggesting we go public about our operations?"

"Not in detail," Hendrix replied. "But we need transparency where it matters. We must show our purpose, explain why we exist, and reveal who we protect."

Bobbi crossed her arms. "And what about Helvex's smear campaign? Dubois has every journalist in Europe eating out of her hand."

"Then we change their diet," Shane replied. "We'll release the first wave of human stories—real people who lost everything because of Helvex's schemes. Regula Rivella's sister. My own cousin's pension fund. Bobbi's brother."

Jasmine nodded. "That could work. Make it about the victims, not the lawyers."

"Exactly," Hendrix said. "LawForce isn't a power grab; it's a shield. We need to remind the world why we picked up that shield in the first place."

Val, who had been quietly taking notes, looked up. "What about the lawsuit?"

"Proceed as planned," Shane replied. "But in addition, we'll hold our own press conference—fight fire with fire. It will be in Washington. Let Dubois play defense for a change."

A murmur of agreement rippled through the room. Hendrix watched them and said softly, "This is your Churchill moment. When he stood in this city and told Europe to rise again, nobody believed it could happen. But belief is what starts everything. LawForce doesn't need to apologize for existing; it needs to remind the world why it is essential."

* * *

After the meeting, Hendrix and Shane took one last walk through the quiet city. "I have to get back to Washington tomorrow," Hendrix said. "The president wants weekly updates. He'll support us—but only if we hold the moral high ground."

Shane nodded. "We will."

They stopped at Bellevueplatz, where the city opened up toward the lake. Across the water, the Alps loomed faintly in the moonlight.

"You know," Hendrix said, "when Churchill gave that speech here, he was just a washed-up politician out of office—no power, no army. But he had words, and words can move worlds."

He turned to Shane. "You have your words, Steven. Use them."

Shane looked out toward the distant mountains. "We'll win this," he said. "Not just in court, but in the court of public opinion. LawForce isn't the enemy; it's the conscience."

Hendrix smiled. "That's the headline I want to read. Now, do you know a good place to eat?"

Shane pointed to the square. "You bet. The Kronenhalle is just a few steps away. It's a Zurich institution."

* * *

The next morning, Hendrix's motorcade made its way to the airport. As the car climbed the gentle rise past ETH Zurich, he glanced out the window at the terrace where, just days before, Dubois had declared LawForce a threat to global sovereignty—time for a reckoning.

The old bulldog had once told Europe to rise. Now it was America's turn to stand tall.

34

WASHINGTON
DISTRICT OF COLUMBIA

UNITED STATES OF AMERICA

The late-winter air swept over the House Triangle, the open-air podium on the East Front of the U.S. Capitol. A forest of microphones surrounded the sleek wooden lectern, while reporters from every major outlet crowded into the cordoned-off area, their breath fogging in the cold. The marble steps of the Capitol gleamed behind them, and the dome loomed overhead.

At the center of it all stood Shane, with Val behind him and flanked by members of the LawForce team—Jasmine, Bobbi, and Marcus—alongside a handful of congressional allies who had weathered the media storm of the past few weeks. To their left, a row of TV cameras blinked red lights in anticipation. The world was watching.

For days, the airwaves had been dominated by the fallout from Dubois's Zurich press conference. The theatrical performance had gone viral. Her blend of moral indignation and continental charm resonated with an international audience hungry for scandal.

In Washington, this translated into outrage. Headlines blared:

LawForce: Rogue Justice or Legal SWAT Team?

Secretive U.S. Legal Unit Operating Abroad—Who's Funding This?

LF: America Demands Answers

Shane knew there was only one way to combat a propaganda war: head-on. The public was largely undecided on LawForce; it was time to win their hearts and minds. He stepped up to the microphone as a reporter shouted, "Mr. Shane! Is LawForce a covert operation under the Department of Justice?"

Shane smiled thinly. "I'll be answering that—and more—in a moment," he said, "But first, thank you all for coming."

He gripped the podium and took a brief pause. "Let me start by saying this," he began. "There is nothing sinister about LawForce. There never was."

A low hum rippled through the crowd as cameras clicked.

"LawForce was created to level the playing field in cases of national importance that risk being decided by the size of one party's wallet rather than the strength of their case. It exists for one simple reason: to ensure fairness. That's it—nothing more, nothing less."

He paused to let that sink in. "You've all seen the headlines—the claims that we're some legal hit squad, that we operate in the shadows, that we're accountable to no one. That's nonsense. LawForce is fully sanctioned, transparent to Congress, and funded through a joint mechanism involving the Department of Justice and the Treasury. We file our disclosures, we follow the law, and we serve the public."

He raised a folder in his hand—a visual prop for the cameras. "These are the public filings for LawForce's creation. They've been on the record for over six years. No one paid attention then because it wasn't controversial."

He scanned the lawn filled with journalists. "You've seen this before: a billion-dollar corporation hires a dozen top-tier law firms to bury its opponents in motions, delay tactics, and billable hours. Heck, they will sometimes hire firms just to deny their opponents access to them—essentially try to lock up all the Tier One legal talent.

"Meanwhile, victims—small businesses, whistleblowers, even governments—run out of money and give up. Justice becomes a commodity sold to the highest bidder. That's not the rule of law; that's the rule of leverage."

A murmur of agreement rippled through the crowd.

"LawForce exists to correct that imbalance. We bring parity to the cases that matter most. It's not a secret army; it's a safeguard."

He leaned slightly forward, his passion rising. "Let me remind you of our first case six years ago—the Explorer Seven offshore oil disaster. A billion-dollar energy company deliberately blew up a well in the Gulf of Mexico to undermine a competitor.

"Multiple lives were lost, and thousands of barrels of oil were spilled into the Gulf. An army of top lawyers protected that company. Their competitor—the innocent party under attack—couldn't match those resources. So we stepped in to even the scales."

He paused. "Had LawForce not intervened, that company would have walked away owning its competitor and profiting from a scheme involving murder and the destruction of a fragile ecosystem. Instead, we forced accountability. We won full compensation for every family that lost a loved one. We compelled the creation of a restoration fund that is now rebuilding the Gulf ecosystem. And we did it all within the rule of law."

Applause broke out from a small group of onlookers behind the press corps, cutting through the tension.

"That's not sinister; that's not secretive. That's justice done right."

A *Financial Times* journalist raised his hand. "Mr. Shane, Claudine Dubois has accused Law-Force of acting as an instrument of American overreach—of imposing U.S. legal values abroad under the guise of fairness. How do you respond to that?"

Shane's eyes narrowed slightly. "Ms. Dubois is an excellent lawyer. However, she is also the lead counsel for Helvex Financial, the Swiss bank at the center of one of the largest financial scandals in decades. I respect her skill, but I question her motives."

The crowd stirred.

"Let's not pretend this is about principles. Ms. Dubois represents an institution currently being investigated for orchestrating a cyberattack and a market manipulation campaign that brought down one of America's oldest banks. She's not defending justice; she's protecting her client. That's her job. This," he gestured toward the Supreme Court, "is ours."

He took a breath and continued, "Every nation has special units to safeguard its interests. The police have SWAT, the military has Rangers, the Navy has SEALs, and even the IRS has special enforcement teams. Why should the law—the very institution meant to uphold fairness—be left without one? LawForce is that team."

A ripple of camera flashes illuminated the podium.

He smiled faintly, his tone softening. "You've all seen the image of Lady Justice—blindfolded, holding her scales. That blindfold represents impartiality. But sometimes, those scales are tipped by money, power, and politics. When that happens, Lady Justice needs a steady hand to balance them again. That's what LawForce does."

Another voice shouted from the back, "But why all the secrecy? If you're so aboveboard, why weren't you public before?"

Shane nodded. "Fair question. LawForce was initially designed to handle sensitive, high-stakes litigation—situations where premature publicity could jeopardize a case. The secrecy wasn't about avoiding scrutiny; it was about maintaining a strategic advantage."

He paused for a sip of water. "But now that LawForce has been thrust into the spotlight, we welcome the scrutiny. We welcome transparency."

He closed his speech with conviction. "Law-Force isn't an empire. It's a promise. A promise that no one is above the law—not a corporation, not a government, not a millionaire CEO directing operations against a U.S. bank from the shores of Lake Zurich. We exist to ensure that justice isn't a luxury good."

He paused again to survey the crowd.

"To those who've asked whether LawForce has a right to exist, I'll say this: LawForce has a *duty* to exist. Because when justice is outmatched, the law must have its champions. So don't be fooled by the melodrama you hear from Ms. Dubois and her masters. Look at the facts and make up your own minds. And yes, we will pursue those who have defrauded U.S. citizens or companies, no matter where they are in the world."

As he stepped away from the microphone, the crowd erupted with questions. Val placed a reassuring hand on his arm. Marcus strode up to him and declared, "I am the master of my fate, I am the captain of my soul."

Shane poked him in the ribs. "Where does that come from?"

"Invictus—Unconquered—from William Ernest Henley. Thought it was appropriate," Marcus replied.

Shane laughed. "It may be, my friend, it may be."

* * *

Across the street, in a black sedan idling near the Capitol Reflecting Pool, Hendrix watched the scene unfold live on his phone. He allowed himself a rare smile. Shane had done it. Against every smear and insinuation, he had reset the narrative.

"Good work, Steven," Hendrix muttered to himself.

* * *

By mid-afternoon, the networks were buzzing with highlights from the speech:

LawForce Chief Defends Operation: Justice Needs a Fighting Chance

From Shadow Team to Public Defender: LawForce's Case for Legitimacy

Dubois's Swiss Offensive Backfires as Shane Charms Washington

Cable hosts debated the finer points. Pundits who had once called for investigations now acknowledged that the team's mission was noble—if unnecessary. Even skeptics conceded that, for the first time in weeks,

LawForce looked less like a rogue outfit and more like what it was: a modern check on runaway power.

35

FELSENEGG

ZURICH

SWITZERLAND

She spotted Regula on the terrace of Restaurant Felsenegg, enjoying the fabulous views over Lake Zurich and the city. Jasmine strolled up to the table, shedding her jacket. Spring had arrived early, and it was unseasonably warm, even at 2,500 feet above sea level. She was grateful for the cable car that had whisked her up the hill from Adliswil.

Catching her breath as she took her seat, Jasmine smiled at Regula. "It's a little out of the way. A bit of a cloak-and-dagger routine?"

Regula grimaced. "I didn't want to meet on Bahnhofstrasse. I'm feeling a little exposed these days."

Jasmine noticed Regula's tight grip on her cup of tea. She kept her answers measured, her eyes occasionally flicking to the forest behind them, as if she expected someone to emerge from the trees.

"No worries, I understand. And what a beautiful day to get out of the city," Jasmine replied.

Regula nodded. "You understand what you're asking of me," she said, her voice low and careful. "As you predicted, once your initial court filings revealed me as the whistleblower, they fired me. They claimed it was for cause, citing incompetence and incriminating allegations from some of my former colleagues, whom I had considered friends. Thankfully, they never tied me to that probe planting fiasco, but pardon me if I feel a bit paranoid before taking the stand."

"I understand," Jasmine said softly. "And rest assured that we will do what is necessary to restore your reputation post-trial, ensuring the industry doesn't blacklist you. We have considerable resources, as you know. You may even want to consider a career move to the United States."

Regula smiled slightly. "Thank you."

Jasmine ordered an espresso and a slice of Zuger Kirschtorte. "Back to the matter at hand. I wanted to meet with you because you see Helvex from the inside. You told me once that they don't act on rumors—they act on data. That's where you can help."

Regula's fingers tightened on the porcelain cup. "They're obsessed with measurable signals. If they see a risk score spike tied to a particular kind of regulatory action, they move—fast. They don't respond to editorials or leaks; they respond to numbers."

"Exactly." Jasmine leaned forward. "When you planted that probe in their system, it backfired. We didn't manage to get in, but they accessed our system instead. Jasmine can sometimes see Nadler's digital footprints. That's how they learned about LawForce. Once we realized that, we didn't react because the damage was already done. We want to use that to our advantage now by planting misinformation on our servers to smoke them out. It needs to be something irresistible. You know how they think. Can you help us?"

Regula took a sip of her tea. "Perhaps an external regulatory notice? A court filing?"

"No," Jasmine shook her head. "That's too mundane. They won't react to that. They already track public filings."

Regula toyed with her earring. "If they believe the president of the United States is about to sign an order that could freeze assets or impose sanctions, they will act immediately. They'll try to preempt any such measures."

"Wow, that could work. Something originating from the heart of American power: the White House. Something they would see as an existential threat." Jasmine paused to collect her thoughts.

"What if we create a memo that looks like it's from the president's chief of staff?" she suggested. "Not an executive order—something lower profile and more plausible: a working paper circulated internally that announces a principals' meeting to sign off on an emergency order to freeze Helvex's assets in the U.S., including those held by BostonFirst."

Regula's eyes narrowed. "They'd want to be proactive," she said. "They'll attempt to trace the memo back to its source."

"Where should we plant it?" Jasmine asked.

Regula took a bite of her Nussgipfel. "Tuck the false lead in a place where a meticulous, data-obsessed intruder like Nadler would instinctively search—not in the obvious firewall logs, but deep within the bureaucratic belly of your system. It shouldn't look like it originated with you, but rather as if it came directly into your servers from the White House. Helvex cannot suspect that you planted it."

Jasmine took Regula's hand. "Thank you, Regula. We know how hard this is for you. But this is useful. It's going to help us achieve justice for many, including your sister."

Regula nodded. "I know. I'm okay with it all now. In fact, I should have done it sooner. I watched the corruption unfold and told myself that small compromises were the price of a stable career. But the faces of those who've lost everything—retirees, families—have begun to haunt me. Just make sure you catch these guys."

* * *

Three monitors glowed blue in the dim light of the war room: a SIEM dashboard, a terminal window devoid of identifying output, and a document editor featuring a single line of text blinking in the center.

Jasmine stood at the front of the room to brief the team on her meeting with Regula. She outlined the plan to lure Helvex to pull the memo from their system. "If and when that moment comes, we'll have the chain of custody: ledger entries and server access logs from their intrusion," she explained.

Val's lips tightened. "So you expect Claudine Dubois to drag the president's chief of staff into court?"

"That's precisely the point," Jasmine replied. "We need him to be the final, incontrovertible authority that refutes the memo's authenticity. When Dubois raises the memo, we'll achieve a twofold objective: first, evidence that Helvex's operatives illegally hacked our systems to obtain it; and second, a public denial, under oath, from the White House."

"Jasmine, how do we prove it wasn't leaked?" Shane asked from the doorway, his legal mind already working through the implications. "If Helvex claims someone else told them, we'll need a chain of custody."

"I mentioned that we'll have proof they hacked our system. We'll maintain a data trail of their intrusion. We'll timestamp the memo, snapshot the file system, retain the exact copy in our write-once archive, and capture the access control list and event stream when it's moved. If anyone opens or exfiltrates the file, the SIEM will record the IP address, user agent, and behavior."

Val nodded. "What about the White House? How will you ensure the chief of staff's cooperation to appear at a trial in Switzerland?"

Jasmine glanced at Shane. "We've already spoken to Hendrix. He's floated it with his contacts, and they're on board. We won't bother the White House unless and until Helvex takes action."

Shane stood up. "Alright, team, let's make this happen."

Marcus popped out of his chair. "In the words of William Wordsworth, 'To begin, begin.'"

He sat down next to Jasmine, shoulder to shoulder, as they attacked the keyboards. They had been an awkward pairing—the meticulous young Treasury cyber specialist and the grizzled ex-SEC operative whose career had been scarred by one forgettable mistake. But tension, when honed correctly, made them complementary. And a strong mutual respect was moving a business relationship into the realm of friendship.

They planted the document in the directory of an employee with the highest security clearance. Instead of placing it in the standard, encrypted vault, they put it in the analyst's temporary inbox, which was accessible from the outer subnet but was supposedly protected. Parking the memo there would look like the kind of mistake a distracted employee might make.

By 2:00 a.m., they had finalized the trap: a tidy suite of documents, including the memo, watermarked with subtle artifacts identifying them as LawForce property, then sealed into a mimic folder.

The hook was set. Now the waiting began.

36

ZURICH

SWITZERLAND

S hane stood at the window of the nerve center, hands in his pockets. His team was ready, but they were out of their element. They were Americans preparing to fight in a Swiss court, and Shane knew that their lack of understanding could jeopardize the case before it began.

He turned to face the team. "Okay, everyone, the evidentiary phase of our case starts in a few hours. Let's be clear: we're not in D.C. anymore, and this isn't the U.S. District Court. Swiss civil litigation operates differently. If we walk in thinking it's the same, Claudine Dubois will eat us alive."

Bobbi spoke up. "So what's the biggest difference?"

"Control," Shane replied. "In the States, the lawyers control the pace—discovery, witness preparation, cross-examination. In Switzerland, the judges have much more control over the proceedings. There's no jury. The presiding judge—sometimes a panel, as in our case—manages the questioning, directs the evidence, and can stop a witness mid-sentence. It's a system built on efficiency, not theatrics."

Val smirked. "So, no grandstanding?"

Shane smiled faintly. "Not unless you enjoy being reprimanded on the record. The Swiss judges want facts—no rhetorical flourishes, no emotional appeals. Think of it as more like a surgeon's approach than a showman's."

Jasmine twirled her pen. "What about procedure? Who goes first—us or them?"

"As the plaintiffs, we open," Shane explained. "However, there won't be a grand opening statement. We already submitted our Schriftliche Klage, the written claim. It's detailed and includes the facts, evidence, and legal reasoning—all upfront. The defense replied in writing, known as the Klageantwort. We've gone through a few Instruktionsverhandlungen—pre-trial hearings—to clarify several issues before trial. But that might not interest you non-lawyers. The bottom line is that civil litigation in Switzerland is less like a duel, as it can be in the States, and more like a chess match."

Marcus asked, "So, no Matlock 'gotcha' moments?"

"Exactly," Shane said. "Discovery, as we know it, doesn't exist. Each side submits what's relevant from the start. If you hide something, the judge will likely find out, and that could be disastrous. Transparency is the currency of Swiss courts."

Bobbi frowned. "And what about witnesses?"

Shane walked to the whiteboard and wrote, *Witnesses = Judge's Domain*. He continued, "The judge questions first. We can propose questions, but we can't badger or lead. Witness testimony is formal, often pre-recorded, and sometimes even submitted in writing. The Swiss value civility—interrupting is taboo. So Val and I will hold our comments until we're invited to speak."

Jasmine raised a hand. "And cross-examination?"

Shane nodded. "It's limited. The court may allow follow-up questions if they are relevant, but it's nothing like what we're used to. Think of it as a matter of clarification rather than confrontation."

Val tapped her pen. "So our approach is to be slow, steady, and methodical."

"Exactly," Shane agreed. "Dubois thrives on control. She's a master of Swiss procedure. Our advantage has to come from preparation—and understanding her overconfidence. She'll assume we're uncultured litigators stumbling through her system. Bulls in a china shop. We'll let her think that."

A faint smile crossed his lips. "Then we'll out-Swiss the Swiss."

The team chuckled softly, the tension breaking for a moment.

"When I say there won't be any big dramatics, I'm not talking about the consequences of what Ms. Dubois herself might set in motion. Remember, if she calls the president's chief of staff as a witness, I suspect this Swiss court is in for some fireworks, despite its best efforts to keep things low-key.

Alright, that's all. Into the forum."

* * *

Shane adjusted his tie—calm on the surface but inwardly tense. He was ready for the start of the evidentiary phase of *BostonFirst et al. v. Helvex Financial AG*.

Judge Bärtschi entered briskly, followed by Judges Graf and Schmid. Once they were seated, Bärtschi addressed the courtroom. "This court is now in session," he said in German before repeating in careful English, "We will proceed with the first day of evidentiary hearings in the matter of BostonFirst et al. versus Helvex Financial Aktiengesellschaft."

Bärtschi nodded toward Shane. "Mr. Shane, your opening statement, please."

Shane rose, buttoning his jacket. Val sat next to him, while the rest of the team—Bobbi, Jasmine, and Marcus—sat behind them. Shane took a breath. "Thank you, Herr Präsident."

He strolled toward the bench, not pacing but anchoring his presence. "This case is about trust," he began. "Trust that was betrayed at the highest levels. The plaintiffs—ordinary shareholders and employees—placed their faith in a venerable institution, BostonFirst Bank. They believed in its integrity, its systems, and its leadership."

He paused, glancing toward Bobbi.

"What they did not know," he continued, "was that BostonFirst's partner, Helvex Financial Aktiengesellschaft—a Swiss institution of immense global reach—was engineering that trust into a weapon. A weapon used to seize control of BostonFirst from within, manipulating digital systems, falsifying account data, and launching a coordinated campaign designed to destabilize the banking sector itself."

He allowed that information to sink in. The courtroom was still; even Dubois's expression tightened slightly. He laid out the structure of the CryptoHelix Fund, the marketing of the Infinium cryptocurrency, and the plan to devalue it and crash Western financial markets.

"We will show, through documentary evidence and testimony—including from one of Helvex's own employees—that this was not an accident. Every step was carefully planned and executed."

Dubois shifted slightly, pen poised, her lips pressed into a smirk.

"Herr Präsident," Shane continued, "our key witness, Ms. Regula Rivella, will testify to internal memoranda, encrypted communications, and executive-level directives that outlined the precise mechanisms of the fraud. She was there. She saw the code. She risked her life and career to bring the truth here."

He stepped closer to the bench.

"Mr. Shane," Bärtschi interrupted. "In Swiss courts, it is not necessary for counsel to pace the floor. We can hear you just as well from behind the counsel table."

Shane nodded, accepting the slight reprimand. "My apologies to the court. I mean no disrespect. It is difficult to change mannerisms developed over many years of practice across the pond."

As he returned to the counsel table, he glanced at Dubois, who winked at him. *You will not get me off my game, Ms. Dubois.* He faced the bench and continued.

"This court will see that Helvex's hands are not clean. What they did speaks for itself. They may call it innovation, competition, or digital restructuring. But we will prove it was something else entirely."

He placed both hands on the lectern.

"It was betrayal—algorithmic, deliberate, and devastating. And at the end of this trial, the evidence will show that the trust they built their name upon is the very thing they destroyed."

He nodded to Judge Bärtschi and the panel. "Thank you, Herr Präsident, Judges."

There was no applause, no murmurs—only the quiet scratching of pens and the hum of the recorder.

Judge Bärtschi looked toward Dubois. "Ms. Dubois, please."

"Thank you, Herr Präsident."

She turned slightly to address the courtroom. "My learned colleague paints a compelling story," she began. "It is filled with intrigue, betrayal, and grand conspiracies. But, as with most stories of this kind, it is built on imagination, not evidence. Helvex Financial is not the villain in this drama; it is one of Europe's oldest and most respected financial institutions. What my colleague calls 'fraud' is, in fact, a series of standard commercial transactions—executed transparently, documented, and reviewed by international regulators."

She paused, meeting Judge Bärtschi's gaze directly. "The plaintiffs would have this court believe that a global bank conspired to destroy its own clients, its own capital markets, and its own reputation. That, Herr Präsident, is absurd."

Shane watched her, his expression unreadable. He had expected this—every denial, every deflection.

Dubois continued, her voice taking on a cool edge. "And the so-called 'evidence'—the foundation of this elaborate theory—rests entirely on the testimony of a man skilled in breaking the law and a disgruntled employee."

She emphasized the word "disgruntled," letting it hang in the air. "Ms. Regula Rivella," she continued, "a mid-level compliance officer, was dismissed for cause. A woman who, having lost her position, seeks vengeance under the guise of whistleblowing. Her allegations are unsubstantiated. Her documents are unverifiable. And her motives are highly suspect."

A faint murmur rippled through the gallery. Bobbi tensed. Shane shot her a small, warning look: don't show emotion.

Dubois pressed on. "Herr Präsident, the plaintiffs will attempt to weave a tale of digital espionage, of malware, and of secret banking conspiracies orchestrated from Zurich. But where is the hard evidence? Unfortunately for my esteemed colleague, this court does not deal in fairy tales."

She glanced briefly at Shane, a razor-thin smile on her face. "We will demonstrate that there was no plot, no sabotage, and no intention to destabilize anything. BostonFirst's collapse was self-inflicted—an internal mismanagement crisis, not a Swiss conspiracy."

She paused deliberately, allowing silence to emphasize her point.

"Helvex Financial acted in good faith. As this court will see, the plaintiffs' allegations are a desperate attempt to shift blame, to recast incompetence as victimhood, and to vilify a respected institution that had the misfortune of being associated with an American failure."

Her tone softened, but the knife edge remained. "We look forward to dismantling these allegations over the next many days."

She inclined her head to Judge Bärtschi. "Thank you, Herr Präsident, Judges."

The courtroom fell silent again. Shane could feel the air change—a slight shift, the weight of her words settling. Bärtschi leaned forward, his face unreadable.

"Thank you, Ms. Dubois. Thank you, Mr. Shane."

He turned to Shane. "Mr. Shane, you have indicated that your first witness will be Ms. Regula Rivella?"

"Yes, Herr Präsident," Shane replied. "She is prepared to testify."

Bärtschi nodded. "Very well. The court will adjourn for today and reconvene at nine o'clock tomorrow morning. The testimony of Ms. Rivella will commence at that time."

As the judges and clerks filed out, low conversations filled the hall. Shane gathered his papers slowly, feeling the adrenaline ebb. Val leaned over. "She went right for Regula. We knew she would."

"She's trying to poison the well before we start," Shane said quietly. "She wants to make the court question our foundation."

Bobbi looked up, her voice soft but edged with conviction. "She called Regula 'disgruntled.' That's not fair. That woman lost everything because she tried to do the right thing."

Shane nodded. "Which is why she's the key. Dubois knows that if Regula stands firm, Helvex's facade will crumble."

Marcus, seated in the back row, spoke quietly, "I didn't like what she said about me being skilled in breaking the law."

"She's trying to rattle both of you—knock you off your game. It's an old litigator's trick. Don't let it work. You'll be fine."

37

ZURICH

SWITZERLAND

The atmosphere felt electric, like the moment before a storm. This was the day everyone had been waiting for: the testimony of Regula Rivella, the soft-spoken compliance officer who had turned against her powerful employer.

Shane sat at the plaintiffs' table, his expression composed, but his pulse racing. This was it: the heart of the case. All the data, filings, and digital forensics had led to a single witness with the power to expose an empire. Across the aisle, Dubois, immaculate in black and silver, her signature crimson scarf folded with military precision, appeared as calm as a surgeon preparing for an incision. Her pen was poised, and her eyes were fixed on the witness chair.

At the center of it all sat the panel, Judge Bärtschi, flanked by Judges Graf and Schmid. When Bärtschi called the session to order, the room fell silent.

Regula approached the stand. At thirty-four, she looked younger than her resume suggested. A murmur rippled through the room; everyone knew who she was—the insider who had dared to speak out.

Shane stood. "Ms. Rivella, please introduce yourself to the court."

"My name is Regula Rivella. I was employed by Helvex Financial Aktiengesellschaft in Zurich as a compliance officer in the cybersecurity and internal audit division. I hold a master's degree in Cybersecurity from ETH Zurich."

Her voice was steady, and Shane felt a flicker of relief. No amount of preparation could predict how a witness would handle the pressure of the courtroom.

"Ms. Rivella," Shane continued, "how long did Helvex Financial employ you?"

"Nearly ten years," she replied. "I was hired in 2014, after completing my degree."

"And what were your responsibilities?"

"I was part of the compliance division responsible for digital integrity reviews—essentially, ensuring that our systems and our clients' data conformed to Swiss financial regulations and international security standards."

"Did your duties involve the fund known as CryptoHelix?"

She hesitated briefly. "Yes. CryptoHelix was developed for Helvex's BostonFirst Bank subsidiary in Boston. But all the critical work on the fund took place in Zurich. I was assigned to review aspects of the fund's structure and compliance certifications."

Shane's voice softened. "Can you explain to the court what you discovered during that review?"

Regula nodded. "At first, I thought it was a routine fund—an investment vehicle designed to capitalize on digital asset growth. But as I examined the internal documentation, I found inconsistencies. The fund's liquidity model relied almost entirely on one cryptocurrency: Infinium. Helvex had created and controlled it. While that in itself is not illegal, it raised questions."

"What kind of questions?"

"Questions about control," she replied. "When you control both the underlying asset and the investment mechanism, you control the market. In the internal communications I reviewed, it became clear that the intent was not merely to profit, but to manipulate."

She paused, as if weighing each word carefully. "Helvex intended to use CryptoHelix to attract massive investments to Infinium from external institutions—banks, pension funds, even national reserves. Once a threshold of dependency was reached, the plan was to devalue Infinium. The loss of at least ten percent of the Western banking sector's cash reserves would trigger a domino effect."

Murmurs swept through the courtroom.

Judge Graf leaned forward. "Ms. Rivella, are you suggesting that Helvex intended to engineer a financial collapse?"

"Yes, Frau Richterin. That was the clear implication of the internal communications."

"And who authorized such a plan?" Graf pressed.

"The directives originated from the office of CEO Hans Egli, with cyber operations managed by Jerome Nadler—known on the internet as the Ghost."

Shane noticed Dubois's jaw twitch.

Judge Schmid interjected, his tone calm yet pointed. "Ms. Rivella, these are serious allegations. Did you confront your superiors?"

"Yes, Herr Richter. I raised my concerns with my department head," she replied. "The next day, I was reassigned."

"And you retained copies of these communications?"

"I preserved encrypted backups, yes. They were provided to this court through counsel."

Judge Bärtschi made a note, then looked up. "You mentioned that Helvex sought external investors. Which institutions were targeted?"

"Western banks—BostonFirst itself invested. They wanted to provide credibility to the fund, to show outside investors that Boston-First believed in its own product and had some 'skin in the game,' as they say. Several European banks invested, and JP Morgan Chase was also courted, though I cannot confirm whether they invested."

"Thank you," Bärtschi said, leaning back. "Please proceed, Mr. Shane."

Shane nodded. "Ms. Rivella, let's focus on a question that the court will naturally be curious about." He turned slightly toward the bench. "Why would BostonFirst participate in a scheme that, on its face, appears self-destructive?"

She hesitated, choosing her words carefully. "That remains unclear to me. Possibly, they thought they would benefit by eliminating competitors—smaller banks unable to withstand volatility."

Judge Graf raised a brow. "So you are speculating."

Regula's voice lowered slightly. "Yes, Frau Richterin. On that specific point, I cannot say more."

Shane felt his gut tighten. He knew this would be a problem, but there was no way to feign certainty here. Better to let honesty prevail.

Dubois's pen tapped softly against her legal pad, and he sensed her anticipation.

When Shane concluded his questioning, Judge Bärtschi nodded toward Dubois. "Ms. Dubois, do you have any questions for this witness?"

She rose smoothly. "Indeed, I do. Thank you, Herr Präsident."

She drummed her fingers on the lectern, her voice dripping with cordiality. "Ms. Rivella, you've painted quite a picture—corporate conspiracies, planned collapses, global ruin. It's fascinating, truly."

Regula met her gaze calmly.

Dubois continued. "You claim that Helvex sought to bring down the Western banking sector—do you understand how absurd that sounds? Why would BostonFirst engineer its own destruction?"

"I said I do not know the reason," Regula replied.

"Exactly," Dubois said, turning toward the judges. "You don't know. So this entire theory rests on your assumption that a multinational bank intended to engage in financial suicide because—why? They wanted to hurt their enemies, too?"

She turned back to face Regula. "Do you realize how ridiculous that sounds, Ms. Rivella?"

Shane began to rise, but Bärtschi raised a hand. "Please, Mr. Shane. The witness will answer."

Regula's voice, though quiet, remained firm. "I am not a mind-reader. I cannot imagine what they were thinking. However, I would note that by this time, BostonFirst was owned by Helvex. Perhaps Helvex was willing to sacrifice Boston-First for a greater purpose."

Dubois slammed her fist on the podium. "And here we go again. Innuendo, speculation, but no facts. You do understand, Ms. Rivella, that this court deals in facts."

Regula stared at Dubois but remained silent.

Dubois shook her head. "All right, let's talk about you for a moment, shall we? You worked for Helvex for seven years, correct?"

"Yes," Regula replied.

"And you were, by your own admission, reassigned?"

"Yes."

"And ultimately terminated?"

"Yes."

Dubois's tone sharpened. "So, you were a disgruntled employee."

"I was a concerned employee," Regula corrected softly.

Dubois smiled thinly. "Of course. Concerned. Tell me—how does a compliance officer with limited access to executive correspondence obtain internal memos and encrypted communications from the CEO's office?"

"I was tasked with auditing the digital integrity systems," Regula replied evenly. "That included access logs and archival servers."

"So you stole information."

"No," she said firmly. "I preserved evidence of criminal activity."

Dubois feigned surprise. "Criminal activity? Proven by your own interpretation of data, perhaps? Because no Swiss regulator—FINMA, for instance—has found wrongdoing."

Regula's face remained unreadable. "Not yet."

The courtroom murmured again. Dubois tugged an earlobe before recovering her smirk.

"Ms. Rivella, as a banking professional, you would be aware of Switzerland's secrecy laws, in particular, Article Forty-Seven of the Swiss Banking Act, correct?"

"Yes," Regular replied simply.

"Then you would also be aware you breached those laws in talking to LawForce."

"You may not understand this, Ms. Dubois, but I did it for our country." Regula turned to look at the judges directly. "I did what was right. If there is a price for doing so, I will pay it."

Dubois rolled her eyes. Her final jab came with surgical cruelty. "You were fired, Ms. Rivella. You're angry, aren't you? This is all about revenge."

"No," Regula said. "It's about responsibility."

Dubois turned crisply to the bench. "No further questions."

Judge Bärtschi adjusted his glasses. "Mr. Shane, redirect?"

Shane stood slowly. "Yes, Herr Präsident. Just a few questions."

He turned toward Regula. "Ms. Rivella—when were you terminated from Helvex?"

"On March thirty-first of this year."

"And when did you first contact my office?"

"On February eighteenth."

"And when did we file your testimony with this court?"

"On March twenty-sixth."

For a split second, there was silence. Then the entire courtroom erupted. Reporters whispered furiously. Someone dropped a laptop. The sound of it hitting the resin floor reverberated through the room. One of the clerks gasped aloud. Dubois froze, her pen suspended mid-air.

Judge Bärtschi pounded his gavel. "Order! *Order in this court!*" When the noise subsided, he leaned forward, his voice lower but edged with disbelief. "So, Ms. Rivella—you came forward and your testimony was filed *before* Helvex terminated you?"

"Yes, Herr Präsident."

He nodded slowly, his expression shifting from neutrality to incredulity, then respect.

"Then your coming forward was not an act of vengeance for your dismissal."

"Precisely," she said. "It had nothing to do with my termination. It was an act of conscience."

Bärtschi sat back. "Thank you, Ms. Rivella."

The judges conferred briefly, whispering among themselves. Shane caught a flicker of something like admiration in Lukas Schmid's eyes. Even Verena Graf's professorial calm seemed to falter for a moment.

Dubois, however, sat utterly still. Her knuckles whitened around her pen. For once, she had nothing to say.

Shane glanced across the aisle. The great Claudine Dubois—Zurich's courtroom queen—looked like a statue carved from disbelief. No rebuttal. No pivot. Just silence.

He leaned slightly toward Val and whispered, "That's checkmate for today."

Val grinned faintly. "Who'd have thought a mid-level pencil pusher could take down Switzerland's finest?"

Shane's eyes remained on Dubois. "Never underestimate the quiet ones," he said. "They're the ones who keep the receipts."

Outside, the bells of the nearby Grossmünster began to chime noon. Inside, Helvex's empire had started to crack.

38

ZURICH

SWITZERLAND

The spires of Fraumünster and Grossmünster pierced the early light, their bells chiming across the old city as Shane and the LawForce team stepped out of the car and approached the courthouse. It was late July, but the morning air in the courtroom felt unseasonably cold.

Shane stood at the plaintiff's table, his eyes fixed on the witness stand. He had seen many courtroom battles, but few filled him with such unease. Ever since Marcus appeared on the Helvex witness list, a sense of foreboding had settled over him. They briefed Marcus thoroughly, and he was undoubtedly a formidable intellect, but he also had a troublesome past. While records of his time at the SEC were sealed, Shane feared they might not be beyond the Ghost's reach.

Across the aisle, Dubois adjusted her cufflinks and smiled faintly, exuding an air of control.

Shane glanced at Marcus, who sat stiffly in the front row. His bald head caught the light streaming through the tall courtroom windows. He appeared calm—perhaps too calm—in that fatalistic way a soldier does before battle.

The judges entered and were seated. Judge Bärtschi's gavel came down softly. "Ms. Dubois, you may call your next witness."

Dubois rose, her voice smooth and unhurried. "The defense calls Mr. Marcus Patel."

A ripple passed through the courtroom. Marcus rose and walked slowly to the witness box, glancing at Shane as he passed. After taking the oath, he settled in the chair. Shane met his gaze and gave a slight nod—steady now.

Dubois began her questioning with a warm tone. "Mr. Patel," she said, tapping the file before her, "you are currently employed by Law-Force, correct?"

"I'm employed by the Department of Treasury, on secondment to LawForce," he replied.

"And before that, you worked at the United States Securities and Exchange Commission?" Dubois continued.

"Well, before that, I was in private practice. I did a stint at the SEC, but that was many years ago."

Dubois smiled faintly. "So one might say you have... expertise in identifying and tracing digital irregularities in the financial sector?"

"Yes."

"Excellent," she said brightly, turning to the judges. "You see, Judges, Mr. Patel is not just a witness—he is an expert. A man of credentials, integrity, and great insight. Wouldn't you agree, Mr. Patel?"

Marcus hesitated before answering, "I do my job as best I can."

"Of course you do," Dubois replied. "Now, let's discuss how you came to be part of this case."

Marcus explained how he joined LawForce as a consultant to assist in the forensic analysis of BostonFirst's systems. He described working alongside Jasmine to dissect the blockchain networks behind Infinium. He detailed their discoveries: falsified transaction nodes, artificial liquidity trails, and hidden caches of data—each thread drawing closer to proof of Helvex's global conspiracy.

Judge Schmid leaned forward, intrigued. "Mr. Patel, can you explain how these falsifications were masked in the blockchain, from a scientific standpoint?"

Marcus nodded, relieved to receive a technical question. He launched into a detailed yet understandable explanation of distributed ledger forensics, encryption masking, and metadata cloaking—a digital cat-and-mouse game.

The judges nodded appreciatively. For a moment, the courtroom belonged to Marcus.

Dubois remained patient, poised like a serpent. After a few minutes, when the time felt right, she smiled and flipped a page in her notes.

"Mr. Patel," she said softly, "let's step back for a moment to your time at the SEC."

Shane's stomach tightened; he could sense the trapdoor opening.

Dubois continued smoothly, "You were with the SEC's Enforcement Division for how many years?"

"Almost twelve," Marcus replied.

"What was the nature of your work at the SEC?" she asked.

"I was on various minor committees and task forces focused on cybersecurity issues."

"You are too modest, sir. You were, in fact, one of the first specialists brought in to help the SEC modernize its cyber enforcement protocols," Dubois remarked.

Marcus nodded. "I guess you could say that."

"Impressive. And during that time, you were involved in several high-profile cases, correct?"

"Yes."

"Some of these involved the misuse of digital assets and the theft of market-sensitive data?"

He hesitated. "Yes, some did."

Dubois nodded, her tone still friendly. "In fact, one such case—the Halcyon Capital investigation—ended rather abruptly, didn't it?"

Marcus froze. "How do you know about that case? Those records are sealed."

Shane began to rise, but Bärtschi waved him off. "The court is interested in this testimony, Mr. Shane. Please continue, Ms. Dubois."

"You don't need to trouble yourself with my sources. Just answer the question, Mr. Patel," Dubois urged, enjoying the buildup.

"What was the question again?" Marcus asked.

"I asked you to confirm that the Halcyon Capital investigation ended abruptly."

Marcus frowned and whispered, "That was... a difficult case."

"I imagine so," Dubois replied. "Because that was the case in which you—how shall we put it?—compromised the entire investigation?"

"Objection," Shane said immediately, rising. "Argumentative."

Judge Bärtschi nodded. "Sustained, Ms. Dubois. Please rephrase."

"Of course, Herr Präsident," she said, unruffled. "Mr. Patel, is it true that during your time at the SEC, an email containing confidential investigative data was sent from your account to an unauthorized external recipient having no security clearance?"

Marcus inhaled sharply. "Yes. By mistake."

"A mistake," Dubois echoed, tilting her head. "And this email—what did it contain?"

"Internal reports," Marcus replied, his voice low. "It was a draft case summary."

"With classified attachments?"

"Yes."

"And that email, once sent, was irretrievable?"

"Yes."

Dubois smiled almost sweetly. "So, to summarize, you—one of the top cyber experts in a federal agency—sent confidential SEC documents outside the agency's network."

"It was an accident."

"Of course," she said, her voice smooth as glass. "A simple... slip of the keyboard."

Marcus tried to steady himself. "You have to understand—this was a long time ago, before the security safeguards we have today. I owned that mistake. It caused damage, yes, but it was never malicious."

Dubois turned to the judges. "Damage. That's one way to put it." She flipped another page. "The SEC estimated that this *mistake* compromised an entire network of cooperating institutions and forced the shutdown of a three-year investigation, didn't it?"

Marcus clenched his hands. "Yes, that's true."

"And following that, you were—what is the term—'terminated for cause'?"

Marcus's throat was dry. "Yes."

A stillness fell over the courtroom, broken only by the faint shuffle of papers.

Judge Graf leaned forward. "Mr. Patel, if I may—did the SEC conduct a review before dismissing you?"

"Yes, Judge Graf."

"And after reviewing the incident, they still concluded that dismissal was warranted?"

"Yes."

Her tone was clinical. "So the agency determined your actions, whether intentional or not, had irreparably damaged a federal investigation?"

"Yes."

Judge Bärtschi scribbled something in his notes, his lips pressed tightly together. To anyone watching, the message was clear: they were troubled.

Dubois, sensing victory, circled like a shark.

"So, Mr. Patel," she said softly, "you expect this court to accept your conclusions about our systems—about our integrity—when you were dismissed from your own regulatory agency for breaching theirs?"

Marcus's face hardened. "It was a mistake, not corruption."

"But it was a breach, wasn't it?"

"Yes."

"And you were unceremoniously fired after a thorough review by the SEC?"

"Yes."

Dubois smiled faintly. "Then we are in violent agreement."

Shane wanted to object, to shout, to defend his colleague, but in Swiss civil court, objections were rare, and arguments had to be raised afterward, not during testimony. He sat stone-faced as Dubois turned to the judges with a practiced sigh.

"No further questions, Herr Präsident, Judges."

The silence that followed was heavy. Even the spectators seemed to hold their breath.

Judge Bärtschi cleared his throat. "Mr. Shane, any redirect?"

Steve hesitated. "Yes, Herr Präsident, one question."

He faced Marcus. "Mr. Patel, in its closing report on the incident, did the SEC reach any conclusions regarding intent with respect to the misdirected email?"

Marcus nodded. "Yes, they found there was no intent to leak it. They concluded it was a mistake, but one with such consequences that they felt they had no choice but to terminate me."

Shane sat down. It was the best he could do.

Bärtschi nodded at Marcus. "Thank you, Mr. Patel. You may step down."

Marcus rose, his expression hollow, and walked past Shane without a word. Dubois leaned back in her chair, crossing one leg elegantly over the other. And then—because she could and was careful to ensure the judges didn't see—she winked at Shane.

* * *

After the court adjourned for the day, Shane and the team gathered in the quiet of the Zurich office. Bobbi sat with her hands clasped, staring out at the gray sky. Jasmine stood by the window, arms folded.

Marcus sat apart, rubbing his forehead, the lines on his face deeper than usual. He groaned quietly. "Things fall apart; the center cannot hold."

"Yeats?" Shane asked.

Marcus nodded.

Shane walked over to him, sat down, and put an arm around his shoulder. "You did fine," he said softly. "They know it was a mistake."

Marcus gave a bitter laugh. "Yeah, but they think I'm a washed-up fool. Maybe not a criminal, but certainly incompetent."

Val leaned against the wall. "She was brutal, Marcus. But you handled yourself as best as anyone could."

"It wasn't enough," he muttered. "I can feel it—they don't trust me anymore. The judges. They looked at me like I was contaminated."

Jasmine crossed the room, her tone gentler than usual. "You made a mistake, Marcus. You owned it. That counts for something."

He looked up. "Not in this world, Jasmine. Not in Dubois's world. To her, I'm leverage. She just used me to discredit all of us."

Shane exhaled. "She did. But this isn't over. The judges might doubt you, but we still have Regula's testimony and the data we recovered from the BostonFirst servers. We hold the truth, and that's still our best weapon."

Marcus shook his head slowly. "The truth only wins if someone believes it."

Shane looked at him for a long moment, then placed a firm hand on his shoulder. "Then we'll make them believe it."

Despite his forced optimism, Shane knew they'd lost a lot of ground. And he knew Dubois knew. That wink was a kick in the gut.

39

YANQI LAKE

CHINA

Inside the Yanqi Lake International Conference Center, Chairman Liang Ze sat at the head of a long oak table, his fingers resting lightly on a small porcelain teacup. The faint aroma of jasmine wafted upward. Across from him sat Gao Feng.

Liang's expression was contemplative as he watched the sunlight filter through the room's latticework screens. "Feng," he finally said, his voice calm but edged with steel. "The Swiss trial has taken a troubling turn."

Feng nodded respectfully, eyes blinking. "Chairman Liang, you refer to the LawForce revelation, I presume?"

Liang gave a slight nod. "Among other concerns, yes. This organization—LawForce—is not merely a private legal team. Their methods, coordination, and resources..." He trailed off, his eyes narrowing. "Mr. Egli's press conference has fully exposed them. They have the backing of the Department of Justice and, in fact, the entire United States government. One could even consider them an extension of that government."

Feng chose not to interrupt; he knew better than to fill Liang's silences. The Chairman's pauses were deliberate, meant to make others think and squirm.

"This situation," Liang continued, "means we are now facing something far more formidable than a Swiss courtroom or an American corporate investigation. It signifies that the United States has chosen to make us—and Helvex—a proving ground. A weaponized legal offensive masquerading as justice."

He looked directly at Feng. "And that, Feng, cannot be ignored."

Feng nodded slowly. "Yes, Chairman. We have already begun reinforcing our operational firewalls. Our partners in Zurich remain committed. Despite setbacks, morale remains strong."

Liang exhaled through his nose, unimpressed. "Setbacks," he repeated, "are a convenient euphemism." He sipped his tea and set the cup down. "I have read every report from the Swiss courts. This so-called whistleblower—Regula Rivella—has disclosed the essence of DragonBreath without knowing its origin. I fear our plans have been thwarted. Her testimony paints Helvex and BostonFirst as saboteurs of Western finance. In light of that testimony, investors are fleeing Infinium as if it were the plague. And LawForce has leveraged its position skillfully. The CryptoHelix Fund has collapsed."

He paused again to take a sip of tea. "But all is not lost. DragonBreath may be stalled for now, but we shall keep the infrastructure in place. BostonFirst still exists and has the potential to rise like a phoenix once these ill winds blow over."

Feng nodded. "Brilliant, Chairman. BostonFirst will rise from the ashes when the time is right."

Liang acknowledged him with a nod. "That time will come. Western memories are short. The Dragon is patient. And they have yet to prove their claims."

He leaned back slightly. "But tell me, Feng, do you still believe that our esteemed advocate in Zurich—Madame Dubois—is the right choice for this fight?"

Feng hesitated for a fraction of a second. "Chairman, Claudine Dubois remains the most effective counsel in Europe. Her record speaks for itself. She single-handedly destroyed BostonFirst's defenses. Without her, Helvex would not hold that American crown jewel."

Liang gave a faint, sardonic smile. "Yes, she dismantled BostonFirst adeptly enough. But this is no longer a simple corporate raid. This is war in another form. Ms. Dubois is a creature of the courtroom—a predator in silk—but she is not a strategist. She fails to understand the battlefield that lies beneath the law."

Turning his gaze toward the window, he watched a pair of cormorants skim low over the lake. "And worse," he said, "she has allowed herself to appear desperate. The treatment of Ms. Rivella—portraying her as a disgruntled employee—was a mistake of arrogance.

"My seven-year-old son would understand that I cannot be 'disgruntled' based on something that hasn't happened yet. To attack credibility, one must do so with precision, not carelessness."

Feng bowed his head slightly. "Your wisdom is clear, Chairman. In hindsight, that strategy was flawed."

Liang's voice softened but still carried a weight of command. "Hindsight is for historians, Feng. We deal in foresight. The next misstep will not be tolerated. If Dubois falters again, she must go. Do you understand?"

"Yes, Chairman."

The two men sat in silence. Outside, a pair of PLA naval drones glided across the surface of the lake, their small rotors whirring softly.

Feng cleared his throat delicately. "If I may, Chairman, there is still reason for confidence. Despite LawForce's theatrics in court, Dubois has effectively struck back. Just before the Swiss recess, she undermined the credibility of Law-Force's cyber expert, Marcus Patel. He was revealed to be a disgraced former SEC officer, dismissed for incompetence. That revelation damaged LawForce's reputation, especially with the panel of judges."

Liang's eyes flicked toward him. "Patel," he said slowly. "Yes, I read the transcript. An unfortunate weakness in their chain." He allowed himself a thin smile. "After the rain, the sky clears."

Feng's tone grew more confident. "Indeed, Chairman. The Western media have already begun questioning LawForce's legitimacy. Dubois has framed them as an overreaching American entity meddling in European sovereignty. That narrative plays well among the neutral states. We expect it to gain traction."

Liang clasped his hands behind his back. "I disagree. The LawForce press conference in Washington effectively countered that avenue of attack." Feng remained silent, watching the

Chairman. After a while, Liang turned from the window and walked back to Feng, placing a hand on his shoulder.

"Do you know why I prefer to meet here, Feng?"

Feng blinked, uncertain if it was a rhetorical question. "Because of the security, Chairman?"

Liang let out a faint chuckle. "That too. But mostly because of the symbolism. The Yanqi Lake complex was built for the APEC summit in 2014—the first great international gathering hosted by the People's Republic in this century. Here, beneath these mountains, we showed the world that China was not merely a participant in global affairs—but the axis around which they would one day turn."

Liang sat down and poured himself another cup of tea. "Project DragonBreath exists for the same reason: to remind the world that economic power can achieve what armies once did. Helvex, and now BostonFirst, are our instruments—our reach, our Western front."

Feng bowed his head. "Your vision is unmatched, Chairman."

Liang waved a dismissive hand. "Flattery is unnecessary. Results are all that matter." He smoothed the cuff of his tailored jacket. "I want a full review of Helvex's legal strategy. I want contingency plans for Madame Dubois's replacement. And I want a comprehensive risk analysis on LawForce."

"Yes, Chairman. I will see to it immediately."

"Good," Liang said, his tone cooling. "And tell our Zurich operatives to monitor this Law-Force attorney—Steven Shane. He is not to be underestimated. I have seen his type before: men who fight not for money, but for ideals. They are the most dangerous."

Feng carefully noted the order. "It will be done."

* * *

The meeting concluded an hour later, and the two men stepped onto the terrace. The warmth of a beautiful summer day washed over them. Feng breathed deeply, inhaling the clean air, which carried a faint scent of pine mingled with the earthy tang of the forest bed.

A convoy of black Hongqi sedans waited discreetly at the base of the hill. Before leaving, Liang paused by the railing, gazing across the placid expanse of water. "Do you hear it, Feng?"

Feng frowned. "Hear what, Chairman?"

"The silence," Liang said softly. "It is the sound of control. True power does not roar—it whispers. It moves unseen, like a current beneath the surface."

Feng bowed deeply. "Yes, Chairman."

Feng allowed himself a private smile. The Chairman's confidence had returned. Dubois's sharp cross-examination of Marcus had bought them some breathing room. Yes, things were looking up. The east wind rises again.

40

BERNESE OBERLAND

SWITZERLAND

Shane woke before dawn in the serene quiet of Chalet Bergkristall, the pale gold of early light filtering through the shutters and illuminating the exposed beams. For two days, the chalet had served as a refuge—filled with the scent of wood smoke and coffee. An unfinished novel lay open, face down on the table. Shane intended to let the mountains continue to work their magic, simplifying the noise inside his head.

Marcus padded into the living room in socks, rubbing the sleep from his eyes. Shane had brought him here after his court appearance went awry under the cruelty of a master cross-examiner. Marcus needed the fresh air, the mountains, and the steady, simple routines of life in the alpine.

"Coffee?" Marcus offered, already moving toward the kitchen.

"Please," Shane replied. Outside, the valley began to awaken: the distant sound of cowbells, the gentle rumble of the morning train, and the silver ribbon of a waterfall cascading down the cliffs. With each breath, he felt the tension in his shoulders ease.

Ten minutes later, Val emerged from the bedroom. "Ready to go, boss? The cable car is running. It's too perfect a day to waste indoors."

"You bet. Take care, Marcus. Don't spend all your time on that laptop."

Marcus waved them off. "Just a little work today, but tomorrow I'm going to try that Via Ferrata across the valley."

* * *

They strolled up the path to the village center, which was a bit of a climb. In alpine villages, it was always uphill or downhill. They passed the "Three Amigos"—three young cows in the pasture next to the chalet. At night, they would graze directly below their bedroom balcony, the sound of their bells serenading them to sleep.

As Val stroked one of the Amigos, who had come up to the electrified fence to say hello, she turned to Shane. "Cody would have loved to come; he can't get enough of these guys."

Shane nodded. "You bet, babe. He's a real cowboy, literally. But I need to devote some time to Marcus this visit, and frankly, I could use a bit of peace myself in the middle of this trial. Cody's a typhoon. We'll bring him up here when it's all over."

He paused for a minute. "I really miss my loom. There's no better way to unwind than weaving a few more lines on the latest rug. But no room for that in Bergkristall, it's a mouse-hole."

Val laughed. "It's tiny, for sure. But that means cozy. Switzerland may not have as much room as the Bar C, but it's got its own charms."

As they turned the corner under the railroad tracks and past the Coop, Shane pointed to the Downhill Hill Only (DHO) clubhouse at the base of the Eiger apartments, next to the train station. "The Brits have been in Wengen for over a century."

Val whistled. "Wow. Nearly as old as Wengen itself."

Shane shook his head. "Not quite. Wengen town's been around since the mid-thirteenth century."

Val laughed. "Okay, okay. I keep forgetting how old things are over here."

They caught the Männlichen cable car at the ground station off the main street, though calling it a street seemed a stretch. With a capacity for seventy-five passengers, the cabin rose like a metallic pod over the alpine meadows. Wengen fell away beneath them, the village shrinking to a charming, miniature version of itself. The community swimming pool appeared at the edge of town like a small, blue postage stamp.

At Männlichen, they stopped briefly for coffee at the Berghaus before tightening their boots and heading out on the Panoramaweg. The trail was aptly named; every few steps invited a pause to take in the breathtaking views. To the south, the famous mountain trio—Eiger, Mönch, and Jungfrau—towered like sentinels, their snowfields sparkling under a sun so bright it was blinding. The gently sloping trail meandered in switchbacks toward Kleine Scheidegg.

The path hugged ridgelines and meadows, crossing over gentle streams and patches of alpine flowers. Snow still lingered in sheltered hollows, bright and stubborn against the sun; marmots whistled, and far below, the valley transformed into a fresh carpet of green.

Cows grazed on the slopes, their bells clanging melodically. Tourists meandered past with walking poles and GoPros, while a paraglider silently spiraled down into the valley. Val walked with an easy rhythm, her boots crunching on the gravel. "You needed this," she remarked.

"I did," Shane admitted. "The air in Zurich was starting to taste like printer toner."

They chatted about lighter topics. Val began telling her favorite tale about the famous trio of mountains. He'd heard it countless times.

"You know the story?" she asked casually.

Shane feigned ignorance and shook his head.

Val grinned. "It's almost too perfect. The Eiger—ogre—has the wild, rugged face; he's the one who devours climbers in old stories. The Mönch is the monk, the calming figure in the middle. And the Jungfrau—virgin—she's the protected one at the end. The monk's job is to keep the virgin safe from the ogre, which is why he stands in the middle; he's the buffer. It's charming and entirely unscientific, but it makes the mountains feel like they have a certain order."

Shane smiled, rubbing his shoulder. "After that last climb, I've learned to leave the ogre alone."

"Good," Val replied. "The Eiger doesn't like being challenged. He's eaten better climbers than you."

As they crested a rise, Kleine Scheidegg spread out before them—a small cluster of chalets, the train station, and the promise of a cold beer and hot food.

Restaurant Eigernordwand sat just above the pass, a modern chalet made of glass and steel—alpine chic, combining clean Scandinavian lines with Swiss coziness. Its large picture windows framed the Eiger's north face. They chose a table on the deck, their jackets off in the midday sun, taking in the panoramic view.

Lunch was one of those uncomplicated mountain meals that Shane preferred over a dining experience at a three-star Michelin restaurant. He ordered Älpler Hörnli—a favorite of his: macaroni caramelized in cheese, cubes of bacon, soft potatoes, and a side of tart apple sauce. It was the kind of hearty, honest fare that the mountains called for.

Val, fork poised, tilted her head and said, "So, you're smiling again." Just then, a buzz interrupted her. "That's either the cheese working its magic or the phone in your pocket about to ruin your day."

He grinned, wiped his mouth, and checked his phone. It vibrated again—a new message from Zurich—a FedEx notification, forwarded by their clerk. The subject line stopped him cold.

> **From:**   **Claudine Dubois**
> **Re:**   **Supplemental Witness List**
> **– BostonFirst Shareholders v. Helvex Financial AG**

He tapped it open.

The note was brief:

Pursuant to Chapter 3, Article 175 of the Swiss Civil Procedure Code, the Defense hereby gives notice of its intent to add the chief of staff of the president of the United States, Mr. Edward Langford, to its witness list.

Shane blinked once, then again. Then a slow smile spread across his face.

Val leaned forward. "Good news?"

"The best news we've had in months."

Val stared. "You'll have to explain that."

Shane set down his fork, wiped his hands, and took a long sip of his beer before answering. "Dubois just added the chief of staff to their witness list."

Val shrieked, almost knocking her rösti off the table. She leaped up and gave Shane a huge hug.

"Easy, babe," Shane saw the looks of surprise from the neighboring tables."

"They fell for it, Steve. They really did." Val couldn't contain her excitement.

"You bet." Shane grinned.

Val let out a low whistle. "Hook, line, and sinker."

They ordered two celebratory shots of Poire Williams. Shane's grin was wolfish. "I can't wait for Dubois to call him to the stand."

* * *

The deck filled with hikers. The waiters moved among the tables with practiced grace. The Eiger's shadow crept slowly across the perforated steel grating of the deck floor.

Shane sat quiet for a moment, watching a thin plume of cloud slide across the mountain's shoulder. The last time he was up here, he was almost killed by another kind of battle—a climb from hell. Now, he felt that same tremor of adrenaline, but in a good way.

He turned to Val. "You know what the best part is? Dubois thinks this will be her knockout punch."

Shane tapped the phone screen to forward the message to Jasmine and Hendrix, tagging it with a short note:

Subject: Game On.

Dubois just listed Langford. She's taken the bait. Confirm access logs, prepare authentication trail, and brief White House.

He hit send and pocketed the phone. They finished lunch and ordered espresso, reluctant to leave the sunlight. The waitress brought a tiny plate of chocolate truffles with the check, the kind of Swiss grace note that made you believe the world wasn't such a hard place after all.

41

BERNESE OBERLAND

SWITZERLAND

From the balcony of Chalet Bergkristall, Marcus could see across the great U-shaped Lauterbrunnen Valley. At night, he had gazed in awe at the massive lights trained on Staubbachfall—Dust Stream Fall—across from the chalet. In the daytime, the fall lived up to its name, plunging nearly 1,000 feet from a sheer limestone cliff in an ethereal mist, making it one of Europe's highest free-falling waterfalls. The poetic beauty of the fall inspired Johann Wolfgang von Goethe, who immortalized it in verse, earning it the affectionate nickname "Goethe's waterfall." The valley was also credited with inspiring J.R.R. Tolkien's Rivendell.

On a ridgeline on the opposite side of the valley sat the Palace Hotel, in the cliffside village of Mürren, gleaming like a toy set across from the snow-capped Jungfrau.

Marcus had been restless all week. He couldn't get the Zurich courtroom out of his mind—Dubois's elegant dissection of his past at the SEC, the polite disdain on the judges' faces, and Shane's grim silence afterward. Law-Force had survived the day, but not Marcus's credibility. And worse, he knew Nadler—the Ghost—was still out there. The man had humiliated them in cyberspace, costing them countless hours of work. Marcus couldn't shake the thought that he was still watching.

So when an email pinged in his inbox a few days ago, he was grateful for the distraction.

Subject: Exclusive Offer — Via Ferrata Mürren: Half-Day Adventure, 50% Discount for Late Cancellation Group Slot.

The message came from an outfitter Marcus didn't recognize, but the email looked legitimate—complete with logos, insurance details, and a scanned permit from the Interlaken Adventure Office. The sender's name, Kletterteam Jungfrau AG, matched a listed company. The trip included five spots and a guide, with all gear provided. Departure was from the Intersport Mürren shop by the tennis courts at 10:30 a.m.

Shane had invited him up to his chalet in the Bernese Oberland for a few days. Marcus grimaced. Maybe after the courtroom fiasco, Shane wanted to keep him on suicide watch. He laughed off the crazy thought. But he knew he deserved a break, so he booked the Via Ferrata. It was just what he needed—something outside his comfort zone.

He boarded the train from Wengen to Lauterbrunnen, then took the cable car up to Grütschalp on the opposite cliff face, followed by a cogwheel railway to Mürren itself. Each leg of the journey from Lauterbrunnen lifted him higher, into cleaner air and a sense of lightness he hadn't felt in months. The valley floor dropped away 5,000 feet below, and the sound of waterfalls filled his ears.

At the Intersport shop, a group of four awaited him with their helmets clipped to their packs. Their guide—a wiry Swiss in his thirties—was checking carabiners and harnesses.

"Marcus Patel?" the guide called out. "You're our last guest?"

"Yes," Marcus replied, nodding.

"Come with me to the back room, and we'll get you geared up."

The others looked like tourists—two men and two women, dressed in bright synthetic clothing and slathered in sunscreen. One of the men stood slightly apart, tall and quiet, with a friendly presence. He wore mirrored sunglasses and sported a faint smile. He turned toward Marcus, and the smile deepened. "Welcome, Marcus. You're in for a treat today. The Mürren Ferrata is one of the most spectacular in the Alps."

Marcus grinned back. "I've heard that."

"I'm Johan," he said. "Johan Keller."

The group moved out, clanking their gear as laughter echoed against the cliff walls. The trail led them to the start of the Via Ferrata, a steel-laddered path anchored into a vertical world. From the first step, the ground seemed to vanish beneath them—a sheer drop to the green meadows of Lauterbrunnen Valley, the sound of cowbells faint and surreal far below.

The guide briefed them: keep two carabiners attached to the safety cable, never unclip both at once, and maintain at least one meter between each person. Simple, absolute rules. Then they began.

Marcus felt his fear melt away into exhilaration. The exposure was terrifying—steel pegs drilled into raw rock and narrow ladders dangling over nothing—but it felt pure. Each movement was measured—his body, his breath, his will.

The guide led the way, followed by the two women, then one of the men, and finally Johan. Marcus brought up the rear, silent and steady. Occasionally, he glanced at Johan, who would return a brief thumbs-up.

By midday, the sun had warmed the rock to the touch. Below them, paragliders drifted like colorful seeds in the valley air. Marcus couldn't remember the last time he'd felt this alive.

Halfway through the route, they reached the airy traverse—a notorious section where the cliff face cut inward, leaving climbers hanging over the open void, with steel pegs spaced widely apart and the valley yawning below. The guide was twenty meters ahead, helping one of the women navigate the area while the others lagged behind him. Marcus noticed that Johan had stopped to fiddle with his harness.

"Is anything wrong?" Marcus called.

"No, no. My rig was just twisted up and digging into my chest. I've got it straightened out now," Johan replied.

Marcus saw that the group had disappeared around the corner, leaving only him and Johan momentarily alone, suspended between heaven and death.

"Beautiful day for it," Johan called out.

Marcus turned his head slightly, panting. "Yeah, it's unbelievable. But we should probably catch up to the group."

"Do you like heights?" Johan asked.

"They scare me," Marcus admitted with a smile. "But that's the point, right?"

Johan's smile widened. "I guess."

Marcus moved closer to Johan, who had slowed down again. The metal cable rattled between them as the wind rose from the valley, creating a cool breath that made their harnesses hum.

Marcus didn't notice the first carabiner being unclipped; he thought the tug was merely the wind. But he heard the unmistakable click as the second carabiner released. Turning towards Johan, confusion morphed into horror.

"What the—?" Marcus began.

Johan's face was calm, almost kind. "Greetings from the Ghost," he said softly.

And then he pushed.

It wasn't violent; it didn't need to be. A slight, deliberate nudge—the kind one might give a door. Marcus's eyes widened, his mouth open but soundless. For half a second, his hand brushed against the cable. Then he felt himself falling in a wide arc through the air—his scream echoing off the cliffs, fading into the thunder of the waterfalls below.

* * *

Nadler started breathing hard, in and out, in and out. He hugged the cliff tightly, grasping the iron bars, not moving, the picture of a man in severe shock. The guide's frantic shout came seconds later, accompanied by the metallic clatter of someone hurrying along the ladder. Nadler turned and shouted hysterically.

"He slipped!" he exclaimed. "He lost his footing!"

By the time the guide reached him, Nadler was breathing like a man in a panic, one hand on the rock, trembling. "He... he wanted to go faster; he said I was too slow. So he unhooked both biners to move around me. I told him not to—then he was gone."

The guide stared at the empty stretch of cable, white-faced. Far below, there was only the shimmer of distance. "I should have stayed closer to you," he said.

Nadler shook his head. "It's not your fault. You warned us never to unclip both. He was just... just in such a hurry."

* * *

Rather than return via the cogwheel to Grütschalp and the connecting cableway, Nadler took the Schilthorn cableway at the other end of town. He was on the new, steep section that went straight from Mürren to the valley floor. Had he taken the old line, still in use for servicing the hamlet of Gimmelwald, he would have seen the "Nepal Bridge," an eighty-meter-long suspension bridge that served as the grand finale of the Via Ferrata. It was an hour ago that he and his fellow adventurers had crossed that bridge. The others had been in total shock, with one of the women clinging to Nadler, who was happy to play the hero.

* * *

As he reached the valley floor, the cabin dropped dramatically through the ceiling of the base station due to the steep angle. He saw the Air-Glaciers helicopters scouring the valley. Their operations base was located between Lauterbrunnen and Stechelberg, not far from where Marcus had fallen. The response time was excellent, but unfortunately, it did Marcus no good. This was a recovery, not a rescue mission.

* * *

They found Marcus an hour later, at the base of the cliff near Gimmelwald—his body crumpled among alpine flowers, the helmet shattered. The official report would call it "a tragic recreational accident." The safety line had not been compromised, and the climber had "apparently acted negligently while adjusting his gear." No one suspected otherwise.

* * *

Evening had settled over Interlaken by the time Nadler boarded the train to Zurich. The carriage's rhythmic motion was calming. In the reflection of the window, his face appeared ordinary, anonymous—a businessman heading home after a long day.

In his lap, his phone vibrated once, then twice. Encrypted messages, auto-deleted after reading. Updates from Dubois's office were being prepared for the next day's brief, while Egli was waiting for a call. Everything was moving according to plan.

He couldn't resist the impulse. He opened his secure email channel, his fingers dancing with muscle memory, and composed a short note to LawForce's anonymous contact address. It felt childish, he knew, but the Ghost was sentimental about his triumphs.

To: shane@lawforce.sec
From: theghost@nullnode.ch
Subject: Marcus Patel — Dive into Retirement

Regrettably, Mr. Patel will be unable to continue his duties at LawForce—a tragic fall from grace.

— The Ghost

He encrypted it, hit send, and closed the device. Outside, the lights of Lake Thun slid by in mirrored ribbons. Nadler leaned back and exhaled. For the first time in months, his mind was quiet.

Jasmine, Marcus, Shane, Bobbi—they had all underestimated him. These righteous warriors thought they could win a war fought in the shadows with ethics. Fools. The Ghost had written the rulebook on shadows.

And Marcus—poor Marcus—had been his favorite piece to move. The seasoned genius with his guilt, his eagerness, and his clean moral compass had intrigued Nadler. He had seen it in Marcus from the beginning: that need for redemption. He had taken everything from him—his credibility, his dignity, and finally, his heartbeat.

He smiled faintly as the train wound its way toward Zurich. Soon, the LawForce team would read that message. Jasmine would see it; her breath would catch, and her eyes would widen. Perhaps she'd cry. He hoped she would. She had scorned him, only to accept a loser like Marcus into her life. Well, she would soon know how that worked out for her.

He remembered Jasmine's face from their last meeting—in Shanghai, years before LawForce—when she had walked away from him after their brief, volatile collaboration. She had

called him "reckless," "untrustworthy," "corrupt." He had laughed then, but her rejection
had festered like acid in the dark corners of his
pride.

Now, she had lost someone she cared for
because of him. Balance restored.

42

BERNESE OBERLAND

SWITZERLAND

Early evening clouds hung low over the Jungfrau massif, shrouding the peaks in a fine blanket. From the balcony of Chalet Bergkristall, Shane watched a lone paraglider trace lazy arcs above the valley before vanishing into the mist. It should have been peaceful. It wasn't.

His phone buzzed on the wooden table beside him—one new message, encrypted, from an anonymous sender. The subject line was short, almost mocking:

Marcus Patel — Dive into Retirement

Shane's thumb hovered over the screen as he opened it. The message was a few lines long:

Regrettably, Mr. Patel will be unable to continue his duties at LawForce—a tragic fall from grace.

— The Ghost

No attachments. No GPS metadata. No traceable link—just a calling card. The Ghost's signature. Shane read it twice, then looked out over the valley again, a knot tightening in his stomach. What the hell did it mean? He knew Marcus was in Mürren today to tackle the Via Ferrata.

He called Marcus's cell. No answer. From the balcony, he could see helicopters buzzing around the valley below, which was typical since Air-Glacers did a good business with tourist flights during the summer season.

His phone buzzed again, this time with an incoming call.

"Shane."

"Mr. Steven Shane?" A voice with a heavy Swiss accent crackled through.

"Yes."

"This is Klaus Meier, Leiter der Polizei Lauterbrunnen—er... chief of police in Lauterbrunnen. Do you know a Marcus Patel?"

"Yes. He's a colleague." Shane's heart raced.

"I have some terrible news. Mr. Patel was killed in a climbing accident this afternoon."

Shane let out a sharp breath and held the phone away for a moment, tears welling in his eyes. "What happened, exactly?"

"From what we can ascertain at this stage, he fell from the Via Ferrata that runs from Mürren to Gimmelwald. The guide reported a tragic accident—Mr. Patel's safety clips detached mid-traverse. Recovery teams located the body this afternoon and transferred it to the morgue in Interlaken. Will you be able to come down to the police station in Lauterbrunnen to discuss logistics? We found this number on a card in his wallet, and we have no other contacts for Mr. Patel."

Shane was trying to process everything. He needed time to gather more information and ensure the right people were contacted.

"Yes, of course. I can be down there in two hours, if that works for you."

"That will be fine. Thank you very much, Mr. Shane. My sincere condolences for your loss."

* * *

Minutes later, Shane was on a Zoom call with Hendrix, who appeared on screen in his Washington office, his tie loose and his eyes red-rimmed.

"Jesus Christ, Steven," Hendrix said as the connection stabilized. "Tell me it's not true. I just got a message from the U.S. consul about a fatal accident in the Oberland involving Marcus Patel. What the hell is going on?"

Shane exhaled slowly. "Not sure of all the details yet, but Marcus is dead. You won't believe it, but I received an email from the Ghost about Marcus taking a high dive. That son of a bitch actually sent an email gloating about it. The police in Lauterbrunnen just confirmed his death."

There was a long pause before Hendrix asked softly, "Details?"

"Marcus went climbing yesterday—a Via Ferrata in Mürren. He received an email offering a discount for a group booking, and he took it." Shane's voice hardened. "It was Nadler. The bastard was on that climb with him. He pushed him off a cliff."

Hendrix swore under his breath. "No witnesses?"

"None, other than Nadler. He convinced the guide that Marcus unclipped himself. They're calling it an 'accident.' And there's nothing to prove otherwise."

For a moment, neither of them spoke. Finally, Hendrix looked straight into the camera, his voice low and deliberate. "All right. We keep this between us for now. We can't conceal his death, but don't tell the team about Nadler.

Jasmine's already under enough pressure; she needs to stay focused."

Shane nodded. "Understood."

Hendrix's expression darkened. "And Steven, let me be clear: this isn't just about another cybercriminal anymore. Nadler crossed a line. Manipulating data is one thing. But this?" He shook his head. "This is cold-blooded murder. It will not stand."

After the call, Shane sat at his desk, staring at the wood grain until the lines twisted into nonsense. Outside, fog rolled through the valley, erasing the mountains. He thought of Marcus's laugh—the way his latest line of poetry would crack the tension in the Zurich war room at 2:00 a.m.—and the quiet pride on his face when he finally earned Jasmine's respect. Marcus had been awkward, brilliant, and too earnest for the game they were playing. But he had saved them more than once. And now he was gone.

* * *

Shane headed out to catch the train to Lauterbrunnen. On the way, he ducked into his favorite watering hole—the Crystal Bar in the center of Wengen. A few locals sat on the stools along the U-shaped wooden bar, its polished surface worn smooth by years of elbows and stories. He ordered a "Stange"—a standard 3-decilitre glass of draft beer, named after the tall, slender cylindrical glass it's served in. The bar's hum—a mix of Swiss-German and English, along with the clink of glasses and an old Procol Harum song playing softly from a corner speaker—faded as Shane stared into his glass. After a minute, he raised the glass and whispered a name only he could hear: "Marcus."

* * *

That night, Hendrix called again—no video this time, just a low, grim voice. "I've spoken with the president," he said. "We're classifying Nadler as a Tier-One international threat: cyberterrorism with extrajudicial homicide."

"You're going after him?" Shane asked.

"You better believe it. I'm done letting this ghost play puppet master. We've traced one of his proxy chains through a shell company in Lisbon. That's our window."

Shane felt the old prosecutor's instinct flare—the part of him that wanted justice carved clean, no matter the cost. "And you think you can bring him in?"

"No." Hendrix's tone was cold and final. "I think we can finish him."

Shane said nothing.

"I've got a small JSOC detachment already read in," Hendrix continued. "SEALs. Tier-One operators. Off the books. No paper trail. If Nadler's hiding in Zurich, we'll flush him out. If he runs—well, we're good at chasing ghosts."

There was no bravado in his voice, only resolve.

Shane leaned back, rubbing the bridge of his nose. "Jon, if this goes sideways—"

"It won't," Hendrix interrupted. "This is for Marcus and for everyone else Nadler has hurt. You focus on the trial. Bring down Helvex. We'll handle the Ghost."

The line went quiet for a moment.

"Steven," Hendrix said finally, softer now. "You okay?"

Shane hesitated. "No. But I will be."

"Good." Hendrix exhaled. "Because when this is over, I want to see you standing on those courthouse steps with a verdict in your hand. Don't let Marcus's death be in vain."

* * *

The next day, Shane forced himself into a routine: coffee, emails, notes for the Zurich hearing. The court date loomed, and the trial would resume soon. There was no time for grief in the war they were fighting. He drafted a short message to the team in Zurich:

Subject: Marcus Patel

Marcus was killed in a climbing accident in Mürren. Please keep your focus on the trial prep. He'd want that.

He read it twice before sending it. He hated keeping the whole truth from them, but Hendrix was right. Mentioning the Ghost's involvement now would only destroy their concentration, which had to remain on the trial.

* * *

Later, he called Jasmine privately. She answered from the Zurich war room, her voice ragged.

"Hey," he said gently. "How's the prep going?"

"Long nights," she replied. "Oh, Steve," he heard her crying softly. "I just can't believe it. Poor Marcus. He was so down after the court appearance, and it was so unfair. Then this. Do you think he jumped or what? It just doesn't make any sense."

Shane sucked in some air. "No, Jas, he didn't jump. He was in relatively good spirits. The mountain escape was doing him good. It was just one of those things."

Shane hated to get back to business, but time was short. "Are you going to be okay without him?"

"Yes, I think so," she said, blowing her nose as she regained her composure. "We're preparing for the Helvex witnesses next week. Marcus was supposed to handle the data exhibits, but Val and I are rebuilding them."

"Okay, keep it up, Jas. And remember, they really put Marcus through the ringer. If there's anything we can do for him, it's to give them a taste of their own medicine."

* * *

That evening, as the sun dipped down behind the peaks, another encrypted message arrived. This one bore the Department of Justice seal.

From: **Jonathan Hendrix**

Subject: Update — Operation Specter's End

Target's proxy chains confirm activity in the Bern area. Intelligence assets tracking movement. Engagement window: imminent.

You focus on the trial. Leave the rest to us.

Shane read it, then closed the laptop slowly. The name—*Specter's End*—was typical of Hendrix's wry humor. The Ghost lived on borrowed time.

* * *

The formalities took longer than Shane had expected. The Swiss authorities were efficient and compassionate, but the bureaucracy still had to run its course. Since Marcus had no family in the United States—no next of kin to claim his remains and no one to call—it fell to Shane. He signed the papers in a small municipal office in Lauterbrunnen, where the clerk's voice was gentle as she explained the process.

* * *

A day later, the ashes were ready, sealed in a modest urn made of polished pine. Shane held it for a long time, feeling the weight—or rather, the lightness—of what was left of Marcus. It didn't feel real. Not yet.

That afternoon, Shane and Val made their way to the banks of the White Lütschine. The river thundered through the Lauterbrunnen Valley, a ribbon of milky turquoise fed by glaciers high above.

Some of that water formed the famed Trümmelbach Falls, which spectacularly carved their way through the cliff walls to the valley floor. Tourists experienced the raw power of the water from tunnels and viewing platforms carved into the rock.

Marcus loved that river. On their earlier trips, he often wandered the path beside it, sitting for hours on the riverbank boulders, watching the water braid and unbraid itself. He said it reminded him of code—simple patterns hiding infinite complexity.

They found a quiet bend where the water slowed for a moment before rushing onward to Zweilütschinen, where it joined its twin, the Black Lütschine, flowing down from Grindelwald. Together, they became the Lütschine proper, winding its way to Lake Brienz near Interlaken.

Shane uncapped a small vial. He looked at Val and managed a faint smile. "Marcus would've liked this spot," he said.

Val nodded silently.

"Do you remember his favorite joke?" Shane asked. "The one about the villagers on the two rivers?"

She smiled through her tears.

"The people on the White Lütschine used to say the others were so dirty that when they washed, it turned their river black," Shane said, chuckling softly. "And the villagers on the Black Lütschine claimed that the others never washed—so their river stayed perfectly white."

He shook his head, eyes glistening. "Vaya con Dios, my friend."

He tilted the vial, watching the white flakes scatter into the turquoise current, swirl once in the shimmer of sunlight, and disappear into the glacier-fed water—bound for the lake below and the sea beyond.

43

ZURICH

SWITZERLAND

The courtroom felt unusually tense. Even Judge Bärtschi, typically as impassive as the mountains beyond the Limmat, seemed more deliberate in his movements as he adjusted his glasses and glanced toward the doors.

"Please bring in the witness," he said, his voice echoing softly against the wood-paneled walls.

When Edward Langford entered, the low murmur among the spectators fell silent. The president's chief of staff cut an impressive figure—tall, silver-haired, impeccably dressed in a dark gray suit that suggested diplomacy rather than politics. Despite the long flight from Washington and the swirl of media speculation surrounding his appearance, he exuded calm authority.

Judge Bärtschi nodded respectfully. "Mr. Langford, the court thanks you for making the journey to Zurich and accommodating your schedule for this matter. You may be seated."

Langford inclined his head slightly. "I consider it my duty, Herr Präsident."

Bärtschi shuffled through a few pages. "Ms. Dubois, the court has permitted your request to question the witness. Please proceed, but confine yourself to relevant matters."

Dubois rose gracefully. "Of course, Herr Präsident." She approached the witness stand with a faint smile. "Mr. Langford, good morning."

"Good morning," Langford replied evenly.

"You are the chief of staff to the president of the United States of America, correct?"

"Yes."

"And as such, you would be briefed on international financial developments, particularly those involving U.S. institutions and foreign banks. Is that fair?"

"To the extent relevant to my duties, yes."

Dubois drummed her fingers on the lectern. "Then you are aware of the situation involving BostonFirst Bank and Helvex Financial?"

"I've read about it," Langford replied. "I'm familiar with the situation in general terms."

"In general terms," Dubois repeated as if weighing the phrase. "But surely, Mr. Langford, your awareness extends beyond what an ordinary citizen might glean from newspapers?"

Langford smiled faintly. "I wouldn't say so. I read the Financial Times and The Wall Street Journal, just like everyone else."

A few chuckles rippled through the room, but Dubois ignored them.

"Let's not be modest," she pressed. "You're one of the most powerful men in Washington. Are you seriously asking this court to believe that you have no deeper knowledge of the U.S. government's interest in this matter?"

Langford's tone hardened slightly. "I said I'm aware of the situation, Ms. Dubois. I didn't say I'm involved."

Dubois's voice sharpened. "So you deny that the U.S. government has targeted Helvex Financial and its affiliates for investigation, sanctions, and asset freezes?"

The courtroom buzzed.

"Absolutely," Langford said firmly. "No such actions have been ordered by the president or any of his departments, to my knowledge."

That was Shane's cue. "Objection, Herr Präsident," he said, standing. "Counsel is testifying through her question. There's no evidence before the court of any such targeting."

Judge Bärtschi nodded. "Ms. Dubois, do you intend to support this line of questioning with evidence?"

Dubois's lips curled slightly. "As a matter of fact, I do."

She turned, picked up a leather folder from her table, and produced a paper bearing the seal of the executive office of the president. "May I approach, Herr Präsident? This evidence is not on the record; we only received it a few days ago."

"Yes, please," Bärtschi replied.

Dubois strode to the bench, delivering three copies of the memo to Bärtschi and one to the court reporter. She then provided copies to Langford and Shane before returning to her counsel table.

"Mr. Langford, I'm going to give you a minute to read this." The silence was electric as the judges and Langford reviewed the memo. Shane had to admit, Dubois was a master of suspense.

After a few minutes, she continued, facing the bench. "Herr Präsident, my client obtained this memo through an independent source. It details a coordinated plan to sanction and freeze the assets of Helvex Financial and its affiliates, including BostonFirst. Mr. Langford is its author."

The courtroom erupted in whispers. Word spread to reporters in the hallway.

Judge Bärtschi's gavel struck the bench. "*Order!* Order in the court.*" He turned to Dubois. "You may proceed, but remember that the authenticity of this document must be proven."

"Of course," she said smoothly. Then she turned to Langford, holding the memo up like a sword. "Have you had a chance to read this memo, sir?"

"Yes," he replied.

"So, your memory is refreshed?" she pressed.

"No," Langford answered.

Dubois raised an eyebrow. "And why not?"

Langford remained as cool as ice. "You can't refresh something that didn't exist to begin with."

A blush appeared on Dubois's face. "You deny the authenticity of this document?"

Langford's gaze was steady. "Yes. Categorically."

"So, you claim you never authored or signed this?"

"I've never seen it before this moment."

Dubois tugged an earlobe; her voice grew sharp. "Mr. Langford, you are under oath. Are you accusing my client, Helvex Financial, of fabricating evidence?"

"I'm saying this document is not genuine," Langford replied calmly. "Where you obtained it, how it was produced, and by whom, I cannot say."

Dubois stepped closer, her eyes flashing. "You're being disingenuous, Mr. Langford."

Before Langford could respond, Shane stood up. "Objection, Herr Präsident! Counsel is out of line. This is highly inappropriate."

Judge Bärtschi frowned. "Ms. Dubois, refrain from personal attacks. This is your warning."

Dubois turned toward the bench, feigning contrition. "My apologies, Herr Präsident. But I believe the witness is withholding information vital to this case."

"The witness has answered," Bärtschi said curtly. "Move on or present proof."

Dubois hesitated. She had played her card, but it hadn't landed as she'd hoped.

Shane watched her for a moment before standing again, his voice calm but edged with authority. "Herr Präsident, may I request permission to ask Ms. Dubois a few clarifying questions?"

Dubois's head snapped toward him. "You can't cross-examine opposing counsel!"

Judge Bärtschi regarded him thoughtfully. "It is a highly unusual request, Mr. Shane."

"Unusual, yes," Shane replied, "but necessary. I believe I can clarify the origins of this so-called memo—and, in doing so, demonstrate its significance to this case."

After a lengthy consultation with the rest of the panel, Bärtschi nodded. "Given the serious nature of Ms. Dubois's allegations, I will allow you some latitude, Mr. Shane. Proceed, but keep it relevant. Ms. Dubois, you need not take the witness stand for this; remain seated at your counsel table."

Shane turned to Dubois and saw the confusion in her eyes. "Ms. Dubois, could you please tell the court where Helvex obtained this document?"

Her chin lifted. "As I said, from an anonymous source."

"An anonymous source," Shane repeated. "Someone who just happened to deliver a classified memo from the U.S. president's chief of staff to your client's doorstep?"

"I can't reveal sources," Dubois said crisply. "Professional confidentiality."

Shane's tone sharpened. "Would it surprise you, Ms. Dubois, to learn that this memo—this very one—originated not from Washington but from inside LawForce's own secured servers?"

Dubois blinked, surprised. "That's absurd."

"Absurd?" Shane said, lifting a small folder from his table. "Then allow me to refresh *your* memory. A week ago, your client, Helvex Financial, hacked into LawForce's systems. We detected the breach, logged the access, and recorded the download of this very document."

Dubois tensed. "You're accusing Helvex of espionage?"

"I'm not accusing," Shane said evenly. "I'm presenting evidence."

He gestured toward the monitor beside the bench. Jasmine's prepared report appeared on-screen: timestamps, server logs, and a forensic chain of data connecting the intrusion to Helvex's IP addresses.

The judges leaned forward.

Verena Graf adjusted her glasses. "Mr. Shane, are you saying this file was *planted?*"

"Yes, Frau Richterin," Shane replied. "It was a honey trap—a decoy document placed within LawForce's private archives after we discovered Helvex had infiltrated our network. We wanted to see if they would take the bait. They did."

Judge Lukas Schmid frowned. "And you can prove this?"

"Every keystroke," Shane stated. "Every packet of data. Our logs are time-stamped, cryptographically signed, and verified by neutral third-party systems."

The courtroom was silent, except for the faint hum of the monitors.

Dubois broke the silence. "This is entrapment, Herr Präsident. It cannot stand."

Shane quickly followed up. "So, now you do not deny that Helvex hacked our systems?"

Dubois realized her mistake too late. "Well, I don't know what the technical folks at Helvex did. I only know they told me they obtained the memo from an outside source."

Shane smirked. "And now we're throwing our client under the bus, are we, Ms. Dubois?"

Judge Bärtschi's angry voice rang out. "Enough. Our cyber experts will review the forensic data immediately. If Mr. Shane's assertions are confirmed, this court will consider sanctions against Helvex and may refer the matter for criminal investigation."

The color drained from Dubois's face.

Langford, still seated in the witness box, turned to face Bärtschi. "For what it's worth, Herr Präsident," he said quietly, "the United States appreciates the court's diligence. I trust the facts will speak for themselves."

Judge Bärtschi nodded gravely. "You are excused, Mr. Langford. The court thanks you for your cooperation."

Bärtschi addressed the room. "These developments were not anticipated. As noted, the court will review everything that happened here today. We will issue further directions at a future date. We stand adjourned."

Langford rose, offered a courteous nod to the bench, and left the room.

Dubois gathered her files with stiff, mechanical movements. The murmurs in the courtroom grew louder as journalists rushed out to relay the breaking news.

Shane allowed himself the faintest of smiles.

44

ZURICH

SWITZERLAND

A month later, the trial resumed. Judge Bärtschi and his colleagues entered the courtroom with measured calm, the anticipation in the air fading to silence as they took their seats.

The court clerk rose.

"Handelsgericht des Kantons Zürich, the Commercial Court of the Canton of Zurich, is now in session."

Judge Bärtschi spoke in his even, deliberate cadence—his voice filling the room.

"The Court has completed its deliberations," he began, glancing briefly at the two counsel tables—Shane's team seated in composed anticipation; Dubois alone, her expression unreadable.

"We are ready to render our final decision in this matter."

A stunned silence swept the room.

Dubois rose, her voice trembling. "But, Herr Präsident, you have not heard final argument."

Bärtschi scowled. "Argument is at the discretion of the court. We have heard enough in this proceeding, especially from you, Ms. Dubois."

Shane noticed the crimson flush rise on her face—an ignoble end to what had been, for her, the trial from hell.

Bärtschi gazed across the room. "At the outset, the Court acknowledges that the evidence presented by LawForce demonstrating a cyber intrusion by Helvex Financial into its systems has been verified. Independent experts, both from Switzerland and internationally, have examined the forensic trail and confirmed its authenticity beyond a reasonable doubt. Helvex Financial's unauthorized access and use of confidential LawForce data is hereby established as fact. The intrusion was real, deliberate, and targeted."

A low murmur rippled through the gallery. Bärtschi raised a hand for silence.

"However," he said deliberately, "this Court also notes that the plaintiff's counsel—LawForce—and its investigative team did not conduct themselves entirely with clean hands."

Shane tensed. He knew what was coming.

"The evidence obtained from the servers of BostonFirst Bank was acquired through unauthorized access. Under Swiss law, such an act constitutes a violation of data protection statutes and cybersecurity ordinances. It was, in plain terms, an illegal hack."

He looked directly at Shane when he said it. Shane's expression did not change, but his hand tightened on the edge of the table.

"In the United States," the judge went on, "there exists what is known as the 'fruit of the poisonous tree doctrine,' whereby evidence obtained through illegal means is automatically excluded. It is considered tainted. In Switzerland, however, our legal philosophy differs. We assess the probity—the reliability and value—of the evidence. Illegally obtained material may, under specific circumstances, still be admissible, provided it serves to establish the truth in a matter of public and systemic importance."

He let that sink in.

"That does not mean, however, that the misconduct of the party obtaining such evidence goes unpunished. This court shall sanction LawForce appropriately for its actions in that regard. Justice must never be achieved through lawlessness, even in pursuit of righteousness."

At the defense table, Dubois allowed herself the faintest flicker of a smile.

Bärtschi returned his gaze to Shane. "In this instance, while the Court condemns the unauthorized access by the plaintiffs' agents, it finds that excluding the data in question would not serve justice. Nevertheless, the Court emphasizes that its ultimate conclusions do not depend upon this evidence."

Dubois' smile faded.

Bärtschi continued, "With respect to the testimony of Ms. Regula Rivella, the Court finds that Ms. Rivella breached Switzerland's secrecy laws in her testimony, specifically Section forty-seven, subsection one, paragraph (a) of the Swiss Banking Act. However, the Court finds that Ms. Rivella's testimony has proven decisive. As a mid-level compliance officer of Helvex Financial, Ms. Rivella provided a detailed, coherent, credible, and internally consistent account of events, supported by internal correspondence, and corroborated by financial transaction data reviewed independently by court-appointed auditors."

At the plaintiff's table, Shane and Val exchanged a quick look. Behind them, Jasmine sat motionless, eyes fixed on the bench. Across the aisle, Egli's face was expressionless, though his fingers tapped an unsteady rhythm on the table. Dubois, her lips thin, stared straight ahead, defiant to the last.

Bärtschi continued, "Even without the evidence retrieved from the BostonFirst servers, the testimony of Ms. Regula Rivella and the documents she produced provided the court with more than sufficient grounds to reach its conclusion. "

He turned a page in his notes.

"Her evidence establishes a pattern of conduct by Helvex Financial intended to manipulate markets and mislead regulators through the creation and collapse of financial instruments—most notably the CryptoHelix Fund and its underlying cryptocurrency, Infinium—with the ultimate objective of destabilizing Western banking institutions."

Judge Graf nodded faintly, signaling concurrence.

Bärtschi continued, "Such actions violate Swiss banking regulations, international financial laws, and constitute a grave breach of fiduciary duty to shareholders."

He lifted his gaze, looking directly at Egli now.

"Mr. Egli, as Chief Executive Officer of Helvex Financial, this Court finds that you knowingly authorized and oversaw actions that undermined both Swiss and international financial integrity. Your conduct has not only damaged the reputation of one of Switzerland's most venerable banking institutions but also threatened the stability of the global financial system."

Egli shifted in his chair. His face was pale, his composure cracking.

Bärtschi drew a deep breath. "Accordingly, the Court finds in favor of the plaintiffs."

Dubois's pen slipped from her fingers and clattered softly onto the table. The sound echoed in the still courtroom.

Bärtschi reached for the written judgment before him.

"In consideration of all admissible evidence, both documentary and testimonial, the Handels-gericht Zürich renders its judgment as follows. LawForce is fined fifty thousand francs for its illegal hack of the BostonFirst computer systems. Ms. Regula Rivella is fined one franc for her breach of Swiss secrecy laws."

He paused to survey the courtroom. "Helvex Financial Aktiengesellschaft is ordered to pay damages of twenty-five billion francs to the plaintiffs, representing losses directly attributable to its fraudulent and manipulative activities."

Bärtschi turned a page.

"Furthermore, the Court orders that Helvex Financial shall immediately divest itself of its ownership in BostonFirst Bank. All shares are to be returned to the shareholders of record as of the date of Helvex's acquisition, at the same valuation Helvex paid at that time. This order effectively nullifies Helvex's acquisition of BostonFirst."

The reporters' pens scratched furiously. Shane exhaled—slowly, controlled—but a tremor of relief passed through his shoulders.

Bärtschi raised his hand once more.

"Finally," he said, "Helvex Financial and its principals, most notably Mr. Hans Egli, are hereby banned for life from participating in any aspect of the Swiss financial markets—directly or indirectly, through proxies, subsidiaries, or affiliates. Any violation of this order shall constitute a criminal offense under Swiss law."

The courtroom buzzed.

Bärtschi rapped his gavel once for order.

"This Court recognizes the gravity of its decision. Financial institutions are the backbone of our global economy. Their integrity must be beyond reproach. In Switzerland—whose name has long been synonymous with financial probity—we can afford nothing less."

He looked squarely at both tables.

"Let it be understood," he said gravely, "that this Court takes no satisfaction in dismantling a Swiss institution of Helvex's historical stature. But the integrity of our financial system demands transparency, accountability, and adherence to law. When those principles are violated, no legacy, however grand, will shield the guilty from justice."

He removed his glasses and looked over the courtroom, his eyes momentarily softer.

"The Court also emphasizes that while the plaintiffs' conduct in securing certain evidence was irregular, their overall pursuit served a legitimate public interest. They have been sanctioned proportionally.

"As for Ms. Rivella's breach of Swiss secrecy laws, the Court has exercised its discretion in a manner appropriate to the circumstances. We call on the Swiss authorities to consider amending these laws in light of cases like this, where existing provisions can operate to frustrate justice.

"Justice must weigh not only the means, but the ends."

He raised the gavel again.

"This session of the Handelsgericht Zürich is concluded."

The gavel struck.

The courtroom erupted—journalists sprinting for the doors, flashbulbs strobing. Dubois sat frozen, staring straight ahead. For a moment, the unflappable queen of Swiss litigation looked small, almost fragile.

Egli himself sat motionless, pale, as if the floor beneath him had dropped away. The ban alone was a death sentence in the world of Swiss banking; the damages merely salted the wound.

Across the aisle, Shane stood, expression sober but eyes alive. Val squeezed his arm. Jasmine smiled faintly through tears.

For all the months of warfare, the sleepless nights, the compromises, the losses—it had come down to this moment.

45

WENGEN

SWITZERLAND

The chalets and narrow streets glowed in the low autumn sun, their wooden facades taking on a warm, honey-like color. Shane observed it all from the terrace of Hotel Schönegg.

The hotel's façade exuded an old-world charm, featuring a stone base, chestnut timbers, and large windows with painted shutters. Inside, however, it embraced a quiet modernity: a polished lobby, plush wool rugs, and a library filled with law journals and travelogues, faintly scented of beeswax.

Shane had booked a block of rooms for the team since his apartment at Bergkristall was too small to accommodate everyone. The Schönegg offered something different: ample space to breathe and a neutral public place for their planning—far from the chaos of a war room or the hum of servers—just the mountains and the distant sound of cowbells.

Val arrived first, her cheeks flushed from the hike up from Bergkristall. Bobbi followed, still showing faint fatigue in her eyes but steadier than Shane had seen her in months—battle-scarred and pragmatic. She had been thrilled when the Swiss Court ordered the unwinding of the BostonFirst transaction, allowing her to reclaim control of the family legacy.

Jasmine lingered for a moment at the terrace door, a wistful look crossing her face as she surveyed the group. Marcus was still heavy on her mind. Shane felt it too. It was strange to see Jasmine without him; the pair had been inseparable in the trenches of the cyber wars in Zurich.

They took their seats at a round table beneath a striped awning that provided cool shade. The main street of Wengen unrolled below them, winding between hotels and shops, full of tourists and locals. Tourists enjoyed happy hour while the locals scurried to complete their end-of-day tasks, sometimes joining the tourists for a drink in a favorite locale.

Shane took off his jacket and folded it across his knees. He had asked them to come for one reason: the fight in Zurich had been a victory, but their work was not finished.

"First things first. Shall I order a round of Champagne? I think that judgment calls for it."

Bobbi threw up her hand. "I'll have an Aperol Spritz... no, wait, make that a Bellini, please."

Shane looked at her with a raised eyebrow. "That's a bit whimsical."

Bobbi giggled, "I'm feeling whimsical. I just got my bank back!"

Everyone laughed. When the drinks arrived, they all stood and raised their glasses in Bobbi's direction. Shane led the toast. "To just returns."

After they'd all taken their seats, Shane remained standing. "We did what we had to do. The Swiss court ruled in our favor. It was an impressive judgment. I have a newfound respect for Swiss jurisprudence. The court was scrupulously fair and dissected a complex case with incredible competence. While we got a slap on the wrist, deservedly so, Helvex took a hit." He paused for emphasis.

"But Helvex still exists. Egli still controls capital, channels, and the kind of legal muscle that this judgment won't deter." He looked at each of them. "The Swiss ruling was essential. It represents a legal and moral watershed. But it doesn't address the broader global issue. Our response must be commensurate with that."

He sat down, surveying the table. Bobbi took a sip of her Bellini. "At least they've been stripped of BostonFirst. The divestment order and the damages were significant. But you're right—Helvex's balance sheet is robust. They can rebuild, restructure, and litigate the ruling into oblivion. We need to ensure they don't just buy themselves another chance."

Shane grabbed a few slices of Bünderfleisch. "Frankly, I never expected the court to go so far as to unwind the BostonFirst takeover, but I'm very happy for you that they did. However, Bobbi, while I know you want to focus on rebuilding your bank, we need you to stay with us until we finish the job."

Bobbi nodded. "I get it. I've thought about that. I'll definitely devote some time to BostonFirst, but you're still my priority. I have a strong team that can manage BostonFirst in my absence. I want to see Egli and his associates stopped for good."

Shane put his glass down. "Thanks, Bobbi. So, team, what's our next step?"

Val tapped her finger on the tabletop, her eyes sharpening. "We need to consider international forums. What about the International Court of Justice? A complaint to the United Nations? Global pressure like that could impose a reputational cost on them."

Shane shook his head gently. "The ICJ handles disputes between states—one sovereign against another."

"What about the International Criminal Court?" Val asked, not giving up. "They prosecute individuals for international crimes—like crimes against humanity or crimes of aggression. Do we have anything that could fit?"

"No," Shane replied calmly. "The ICC's jurisdiction is narrow. It's an important court, but it deals primarily with systemic violence related to military actions or war crimes. A case of financial sabotage would be rejected on jurisdictional grounds."

Val's mouth thinned with frustration. "So, are we limited to national courts?"

"Not necessarily a bad thing," Shane said. "Look: the world's financial centers—New York, London, Frankfurt—are where capital flows, and reputation matters most. If we target a financial institution in a way that hits them where it hurts—through asset seizures, regulatory sanctions, or criminal indictments for individuals—we can change the calculus."

"You mean the U.S.?" Bobbi interjected.

Shane nodded. "One word: RICO." He noticed Val's brow raise; she understood exactly what he meant. Shane continued for the others' benefit. "RICO stands for the Racketeer Influenced and Corrupt Organizations Act. It's a powerful tool, a legal bazooka. And we need a legal bazooka."

"That's a U.S. statute," Jasmine pointed out. "Can it target a Swiss bank?"

"It can if there are sufficient domestic contacts," Shane explained.

Val gestured to Shane for a refill from the bottle in the wine chiller beside him. "So, we bring them to the U.S. We force them into federal court, using the full weight of American discovery and grand jury powers."

"You would be operating on familiar ground, without the constraints of a more cautious court," Bobbi added, her eyes narrowing. "And with the potential for criminal exposure for the individuals involved, Egli and Dubois would surely start to get nervous."

Shane finished pouring Val's drink, gesturing around the table to see if anyone else needed a top-up. "RICO requires patterns. Once we establish the existence of an enterprise, we gain access to powerful tools: asset restraints, forfeiture, civil treble damages, grand jury subpoenas, and extradition pressure."

"Treble damages," Val murmured. "That could reach the financial scale of Helvex."

"Exactly." Shane grabbed another slice of Bünderfleisch—he couldn't get enough of that air-dried beef. "Civil RICO could be initiated by private plaintiffs—shareholders, creditors—

while the U.S. Attorney's Office could pursue criminal RICO. If we combine both, we can make the cost of doing business for Helvex unbearable."

Jasmine joined in. "We also need cooperation from Swiss authorities. The Zurich court's ruling will help us politically; it gives foreign authorities cover to act. This isn't just about legal muscle—it's diplomatic chess."

Val nodded. "We'll need plaintiffs ready in the U.S.—BostonFirst shareholders, pension funds, and unions. They can file civil RICO suits. We'll coordinate with Hendrix on the criminal referrals." She turned to Shane. "Have you discussed this with him?"

"I have," Shane replied. "He's on board— he called it 'a test of American jurisdiction over global financial malfeasance.' He's practical, too; he knows the political pressure involved. But the Attorney General's office is willing to open channels if we present irrefutable evidence." Shane tapped the folder. "We have that: the Swiss judgment and Regula's evidence. We can build the RICO enterprise element from that."

After a long silence, Val spoke up. "I like it. Yankee justice."

Bobbi's mouth twitched. "It also comes with a slew of reporters and more political pressure than a barbecue in July. Are we prepared for that?"

"We are," Shane said. "We've already been through the PR grinder in Zurich. This time should be easier. It's our language and our rules. We'll put together the prima facie RICO outline this week. Val and I will investigate the RICO elements. Bobbi, you'll organize the shareholder plaintiffs and notify the trustees and pension funds. Jasmine, your team needs to ensure that the logs and timestamped evidence are admissible under U.S. rules."

Bobbi wrapped a strand of hair around her finger. "And what about the human angle? The pensions that were wiped out—my brother's 401(k), Regula's sister's nest egg—people need to see the faces behind this story. RICO will involve numbers and statutes, but we should prepare a narrative that places the victims at the center."

"Absolutely," Shane said. "Law and morality need to work together. We'll incorporate the human cost into every filing and press briefing.

"Okay, team, that's a wrap. I'm buying the next round at the Crystal."

46

BERN

SWITZERLAND

The moon hung over Bern, casting its soft light across medieval rooftops. From the high ridge above the Aare River, the city appeared timeless, with arcades, clock towers, and sandstone facades that whispered of old power and older secrets. Founded in the twelfth century by Duke Berchtold V of Zähringen, the Swiss capital had survived fires, wars, and political upheaval. Its core, the Old Town, remained a living museum of history, inside a great loop of the river coiling around it like a serpent guarding its hoard.

Tonight, though, that hoard was not gold. It was the Ghost—Jerome Nadler, once a phantom behind digital curtains, now flesh and blood hiding inside a Helvex safe house.

SEAL Team Six moved like shadows. They wore black tactical suits equipped with night optics, their movements so rehearsed that they acted as one. The Swiss authorities had not been informed; this was a deniable operation, green-lit from the top. Hendrix himself made the call from Washington after Marcus's death. The message was clear: Find the Ghost. Terminate him.

Team leader Commander Jack "Falcon" Harlan crouched at the edge of a narrow street that smelled of old stone and wood smoke. He raised his hand, and the team froze. Across the cobblestoned lane stood a grotesque statue illuminated by a solitary streetlamp—its form half-human, half-monster.

"The hell is that thing?" whispered Lieutenant Cole.

Harlan smirked. "That," he murmured, "is the Kindlifresserbrunnen—the Child Eater Fountain."

They all looked up. The ancient fountain, dating back to the sixteenth century, depicted a hulking ogre sitting cross-legged, shoving a small child into its mouth while a sack of other children slumped beside it. A ring of armored bears circled the base, as if guarding the atrocity.

"Local legend," Harlan continued softly. "No one knows if it's supposed to scare kids into behaving or warn nobles to watch their greed. Either way, that ugly bastard makes us look like Boy Scouts."

The Helvex safe house occupied the upper floors of a narrow sandstone building just off Kramgasse, the main artery of Bern's Old Town. From the outside, it looked like a respectable investment firm—complete with a neat signboard, flower boxes, and old shutters. Inside, however, it was a fortified shell of reinforced glass and encrypted fiber channels.

Thermal scans showed two heat signatures. One was seated at a workstation—the Ghost, almost certainly. The other patrolled the hallway with the slow rhythm of a professional guard.

Harlan quietly spoke into his throat mic. "Alpha and Bravo flank north and east. Charlie covers the alley. No collateral damage. Our target's a ghost—let's make him one."

The SEALs fanned out.

Through the second-floor window, Harlan could see Jerome Nadler—thin and intense, fingers darting across multiple screens. He worked with eerie calm. Through his high-resolution scope, Harlan could read a message on one of the monitors being sent to Zurich—presumably to Hans Egli himself. The subject line read, "Post-trial measures to deal with LawForce."

Harlan tightened his jaw. "Target confirmed," he whispered. "Execute."

A soft thup marked the silenced round that shattered the guard's visor. He collapsed wordlessly. Before his body reached the carpet, the SEALs charged through the door.

The room was bathed in pale blue monitor light, with cables snaking across the floor. Nadler looked up, startled but not panicked.

"So," he said softly, his voice dry, "they finally sent soldiers."

He reached for a key on his keyboard—an emergency purge command—but Harlan was faster. A burst from his suppressed MP7 tore the keyboard apart, shredding Nadler's hands.

"Don't bother," Harlan said. "We're here for you, not your toys."

Nadler screamed in pain, looking at his mangled hands. His eyes flicked between the intruders. "LawForce," he hissed. "Of course. Shane's pet thugs. He can't win in court, so he sends killers."

"No," Harlan replied evenly, stepping closer. "We're here for justice. Marcus Patel's justice."

At the mention of Marcus's name, something flashed in Nadler's eyes—a glint of recognition, almost pride. "Ah," he murmured. "The old coder. He was... talented."

"And now he's dead," Harlan said, raising his weapon. "Thanks to you."

Nadler snorted. "He chose to play my game. He lost. Isn't that what your kind calls natural selection?"

Harlan rolled his eyes. "You talk too much."

Nadler lifted his arms in surrender, blood dripping from his wounds. "You can't shoot me, you're officers of the law."

Harlan's voice hardened. "We have our own law. This is for Marcus. He lived with honor. You'll die without it."

Nadler's smirk faltered as Harlan's finger tightened on the trigger—one suppressed shot. The Ghost jerked backward, his head snapping to the side. A crimson bloom spread across the desk. For the first time in years, the Ghost was silent.

"Clear!" called Lieutenant Cole.

"Device?" Harlan asked.

Petty Officer Lang moved to the desk, careful not to disturb the bloodied keyboard. "Found the primary unit. Military-grade encryption. Looks like he was in the middle of something big."

"Bag it," Harlan ordered. "And clean things up."

* * *

Within minutes, the laptop was sealed in an EMP-proof container, along with two external drives and a burner phone. The data would be sent straight to Shane's Zurich office under diplomatic pouch.

They carried Nadler's body in a duffel bag under the cover of darkness, moving down narrow alleys and across the Nydegg Bridge, where the city opened into the BärenPark—the famous Bear Pit.

Bern's name itself came from Bär, the German word for bear. Since the sixteenth century, the city had kept live bears as mascots and symbols of strength. The pit had once been a cruel attraction—a stone enclosure where bears were chained for tourists' amusement. But in modern times, it was transformed into a lush, sloped habitat overlooking the river, a monument to nature reborn.

Harlan stood at the railing, looking down at the darkened enclosure. Two great brown shapes moved below, their heavy bodies swaying in the moonlight.

"Poetic," Lang murmured. "Feeding a monster to the bears."

"Fitting," Harlan replied.

They heaved Nadler's body over the edge. The splat was muted, followed by the faint sound of curious snuffling. One of the bears ambled closer. Harlan didn't watch the rest.

"Mission accomplished," he said quietly. "Let's go home."

* * *

The next morning dawned over Bern—a clear autumn day. Commuters filled the trams, and tourists strolled beneath the Old Town's arcades, stopping to photograph the fountains and the medieval clock tower. Life went on, unaware of what had transpired during the night.

At the Bear Pit, caretaker Urs Meier began his morning routine early. Carrying buckets of fruit and vegetables, he called softly to his furry charges. They lumbered toward him, noses twitching.

Then one stopped and growled.

"Was isch los, Balu?" (What's up, Balu?) Urs called, setting down the bucket. He followed the bear's gaze—and froze.

There, half-buried among the rocks and leaves, was a mangled human form. The face was unrecognizable, the body torn. Only the shredded U2 T-shirt and faint glint of a watch hinted at who it might have been.

Meier backed away, trembling, and fumbled for his phone.

* * *

By the time the Bern city police arrived, a crowd of onlookers had gathered at the railings. The officers cordoned off the area, muttering in hushed tones.

The forensic team worked quietly, removing what remained of the body. One of them noted that the man's hands were severely damaged—perhaps from trying to defend himself. Another pointed out the faint smell of gun oil.

They had no idea this was Jerome Nadler—the Ghost—the man behind the collapse of BostonFirst, the architect of financial chaos.

But far away, in Zurich, Shane would soon receive a secure package—a laptop sealed in a black case, bearing a note inside:

"For Marcus. The Ghost has been eliminated."

* * *

By evening, the Bern police issued a short statement:

A deceased male was discovered early this morning in the BärenPark. Identification pending. No threat to public safety.

In the soft light of dusk, as the bears returned to their den and the tourists drifted away, the Kindlifresser loomed silently above the cobblestones.

Bern kept its secrets well.

47

ZURICH

SWITZERLAND

Shane stood at the head of the table, jacket off, sleeves rolled up to his forearms. The rest of the LawForce team—Bobbi, Jasmine, Val, and Hendrix, who was on a remote feed from Washington—waited silently. Shane's expression was unreadable.

He set a black briefcase on the table, unlatched it, and laid out three sealed evidence bags: a laptop, two external drives, and a burner phone.

"It's over," he said quietly. "Nadler's gone."

A ripple passed through the room. Jasmine's fingers froze above her tablet. Bobbi blinked twice, uncertain she had heard him correctly.

"Gone?" Val asked. "As in—arrested?"

Shane shook his head. "As in killed."

The words hung in the air.

"SEAL Team Six tracked him to a Helvex safe house in Bern," Shane continued. "They recovered these from the scene: two drives, one laptop, and one phone—all encrypted and in use at the time of his death."

He paused. "The Ghost is dead."

Jasmine let out a long, slow breath. "You're sure?"

"Positive," Shane replied. "DNA confirmed by the Swiss authorities." He didn't mention that the Swiss had no idea who the dead man was—officially, Jerome Nadler didn't exist.

Hendrix's voice crackled through the video feed from Washington. "This is a good thing, team. The president's been briefed. It doesn't bring Marcus back..." His voice caught briefly. "But it means the world is rid of its most dangerous cybercriminal."

Bobbi's sharp Boston accent cut through the stillness. "Wait—Bern? Did you say Bern?"

Shane nodded.

"I just read something about that," Bobbi said, scrolling through her phone. "A local Swiss outlet reported they found a body in the Bear Pit. Mauled. Authorities haven't identified it yet." She looked up, her eyes narrowing. "That wouldn't have anything to do with Nadler, would it?"

Shane hesitated. "No comment."

The way he said it—flat and final—told them everything they needed to know.

"No way," Val gasped. "Was he alive when they dropped him into the pit?"

Shane shook his head. "I doubt it. Our Navy boys don't operate like that. They're tough, but not sadistic. I think the pit was just a disposal site, and maybe they wanted to make a point."

Jasmine gave a small sigh. "Too bad; it would have been the perfect ending for that bastard."

Bobbi nodded. "Justice takes different forms."

Val pointed at the sealed laptop. "What about that?" she asked. "Do you think there's something useful on it?"

Shane nodded slowly. "There might be. But before we dig into it, I want to raise a bigger question."

He walked to the window, looking down at the glass-and-steel skyline of Zurich's financial district. "Think about it," he said. "What was in this for Helvex? What was the point of all this chaos?"

No one spoke.

Shane turned to face them. "Let's recap. Helvex—supposedly a neutral Swiss bank—creates a fund and cryptocurrency with the intention of destabilizing Western financial markets. But in every version of the plan, one detail never changes."

He paused. "Eastern banks are spared."

Val frowned. "You mean the Chinese, Russian, and state-owned Asian consortia?"

"Exactly," Shane replied. "This wasn't about random disruption. It was selective. Controlled demolition."

Hendrix leaned closer to the video screen. "You're thinking geopolitical, not financial."

"I'm thinking strategic," Shane said. "Every document Regula gave us, every move Nadler made, was designed to topple institutions in New York, London, Frankfurt... but not Beijing, Shanghai, or Singapore."

Jasmine was quiet for a long time. "Do you think Helvex is working on something bigger?"

"I think Helvex isn't at the top of the pyramid," Shane said. "I think they're just the façade. While we managed to crack the Boston-First servers, we never could get into Helvex's system."

He nodded toward the evidence bags. "That's why this matters. Somewhere inside that laptop, those drives, or that phone is the answer. Who was pulling the strings? Who was Nadler really working for? And why were Eastern banks untouchable?"

Jasmine reached for the laptop, turning it over in her hands like a jeweler inspecting a rare gem. "If he kept his playbooks digital, they're in here somewhere. Nadler always documented his brilliance—guys like him can't resist doing that."

"Be careful," Shane warned. "You saw what he did when we tried to infiltrate their system. He may be dead, but his programs are still running. Treat that laptop like it's radioactive."

"I will," Jasmine said, biting her lip. "I'll start with a forensic mirror—no live environment, air-gapped system only. I'll extract metadata before touching the content. If there's anything booby-trapped, we'll catch it before it bites us."

"Good," Shane said. "I want you and Val to lead the analysis. I've already arranged a secure lab at ETH. Their cyber division will provide you with isolated compute clusters. No network, no cloud."

Bobbi smirked. "Going academic, huh?"

"ETH's labs are safer than Langley's," Shane replied. "Right now, we can't risk another hack."

Jasmine placed the evidence bag back on the table and looked up. "So that's it? Nadler's gone, but Helvex is still out there."

Bobbi crossed her arms. "They just lost their wizard. No more Ghost. That's got to slow them down."

"Maybe," Shane said. "But Nadler was only one piece. If you take down a wolf, the pack scatters—but if there's an alpha behind them, they'll regroup quickly."

Val tilted her head. "So, what do we do while Jasmine digs?"

Shane gave a thin smile. "We keep the legal fires burning. We move forward on that RICO case in the U.S. and start winding down this office. We'll handle any appeals of the Swiss case from the U.S. We need to get back home for the next chapter."

For a moment, silence reclaimed the room. Shane looked down at the evidence bags again—the physical remains of a ghost. It was strange how something as intangible as digital terror could come down to a few pounds of plastic and circuitry.

He remembered Marcus's voice—steady, sardonic, always a step ahead of everyone else in the room. The way he had defended Jasmine during the counter-hack, taking the digital hit to save her system.

"Rest easy, Marcus," he murmured. "We're not done yet, but the tide is turning."

48

ZURICH

SWITZERLAND

Typing away at mach speed in front of the main terminal of ETH Zurich's secure cyber lab, Jasmine was surrounded by the Ghost's digital legacy—the laptop, two external drives, and a burner phone recovered in Bern.

Around her, the LawForce team waited in quiet anticipation: Val was playing solitaire, Bobbi stood watching with her arms crossed, and Shane paced at the back of the room like a lawyer awaiting a jury's verdict.

This was the moment Jasmine had been waiting for—the chance to unmask the final layer of deception that had haunted their investigation from the start. "His encryption is good," she muttered, typing furiously. "Really good. He used custom AES layering with staggered salting. He probably built the cipher himself."

"Of course he did," Val replied under her breath. "Nadler never trusted anyone else's genius."

They had spent fourteen hours peeling back layers of his digital armor. The Ghost had been a perfectionist—using redundant encryption, false file paths, and even self-deleting data clusters designed to vaporize upon incorrect password attempts. But Jasmine had learned to think like him.

"He always viewed security as an art," she said. "He'll have left a flaw—something elegant, something he considered too beautiful to destroy."

Her fingers danced across the keyboard, navigating directories within directories, until she found it: a folder hidden deep within a system file marked innocuously as *drivers/logs/sys32-temp*. The folder name appeared as:—
Project DragonBreath.

Jasmine froze. "Got it."

Val leaned closer. "DragonBreath?"

Jasmine's voice was low. "That's our missing link."

They began opening the decrypted files one by one. Emails. Financial ledgers. Communication logs. And then—a corporate registration document.

Helvex Financial AG – 100% Owned, Through Intermediary Companies, by Zhonghua Capital Holdings Co., Ltd.

Followed by a memo with a broad diagonal watermark: **TOP SECRET**.

PROJECT DRAGONBREATH — SIX STAGES

1. **Partner & Finance** — *Helvex loan to BostonFirst for investment in EigerNet (Helvex fintech platform).*
   Code name: 龙合 (Lóng Hé) — *Dragon Union.*

2. **Seed Scandal** — *Cyber operation manufactures a fraud/false-account scandal implicating BostonFirst.*
   Code name: 龙孽 (Lóng Niè) — *Dragon's Seed / Dragon Scourge.*

3. **Bank Run** — *Amplify panic via whisper/cyber campaign to trigger a run on BostonFirst.*
   Code name: 龙吼 (Lóng Hǒu) — *Dragon's Roar.*

4. **Takeover** — *Exercise loan rights to buy devalued stock and seize BostonFirst.*
   Code name: 龙爪 (Lóng Zhǎo) — *Dragon's Claw.*

5. **Capital Lure** — *Attract ≥10% of Western bank capital into CryptoHelix and Infinium (BostonFirst's crypto investment fund and controlled cryptocurrency).*
   Code name: 龙饵 (Lóng ěr) — *Dragon Bait.*

6. **Collapse** — *Devalue Infinium (under Helvex control) and crater CryptoHelix to topple targeted banks → systemic cascade.*
   Code name: 龙坠 (Lóng Zhuì) — *Dragon Fall / Dragon Plunge.*

Bobbi inhaled sharply. "It's all here, just as Regula laid it out, except we didn't have that last piece—the identity of the true puppet master: Zhonghua Capital. That's a Chinese state financial corporation."

Shane stopped pacing. "You're saying Helvex isn't a Swiss bank at all—it's a shell company?"

"Not a shell," Jasmine replied, her eyes scanning lines of Mandarin text. "It's a vessel. Zhonghua Capital is registered directly under the State Council of the People's Republic of China. Its board includes members from the Ministry of Finance and the People's Liberation Army's Technology Division."

Val swore under her breath. "So that's why the plan targeted Western banks. This was never about profit; it was economic warfare."

Jasmine nodded grimly. "When the Western sector collapsed, Chinese state banks would move in with liquidity support—'rescue funds'—effectively taking control of the post-crisis economy."

Bobbi shook her head in disbelief. "So Helvex was the Chinese Trojan horse all along."

Shane laughed. "Actually, there's a Russian element to all this."

They looked at him quizzically.

"It's like those Russian Matryoshka dolls—nesting dolls. Multiple Trojan horses—BostonFirst, inside Helvex, inside Zhonghua Capital."

Val rolled her eyes. "We're getting a little off track. What else did you find, Jas?"

Jasmine opened another folder. "Travel logs, itineraries, hotel receipts, visa scans. All belonged to Gao Feng, the so-called 'international investment director' of Helvex Financial."

"There's your courier," Val said. "He was the go-between."

The screen filled with movement records spanning five years—Zurich, Geneva, Hong Kong, and Beijing's Yanqi Lake, appearing repeatedly.

Jasmine set her coffee down. "Yanqi Lake... that's not just a resort."

"No," Shane replied. "It's one of China's most fortified government compounds. The State Council meets there. It's where the first Belt and Road Forum was held. If Feng was going there, it was on direct government orders."

Val brought up satellite imagery. The massive Yanqi Lake complex sprawled like a modern fortress—glistening water, private villas, and the enormous Yanqi Lake Hotel, its golden-domed tower reflecting the surrounding mountains. Razor-wire fencing and patrol roads circled the perimeter.

"They call it the 'Dragon's Retreat,'" Jasmine said quietly. "Only the most senior officials are permitted entry. It's where China's top leadership holds its confidential summits. That means—"

"—Project DragonBreath was born at the Dragon's Retreat and sanctioned at the highest level," Shane finished. "By Chairman Liang Ze himself."

The room fell silent as they absorbed the implications.

Jasmine exhaled and opened the final set of communications. "Here's the chain," she said. "Nadler's correspondence with Hans Egli. And Egli's with Gao Feng."

The emails scrolled across the monitor:

From: **Jerome Nadler (ghost@ helvexfinancial.ch)**

To: **Hans Egli (hegli@ helvexfinancial.ch)**

Subject: **Phase Transition**

The system is stable. Infinium architecture is absorbing liquidity faster than modeled. Will confirm once Western participation exceeds 10% of capital pool.
-J

Egli's response was curt and clinical:

Maintain schedule. DragonBreath will not tolerate delay.
-HE

Then came a second message, routed through a secure server in Beijing:

From: **Gao Feng (g.feng@ zhonguacapital.cn)**

To: **Hans Egli (hegli@ helvexfinancial.ch)**

Subject: Directive 7

Confirm readiness for Stage 6-Lóng Zhuì. Chairman Liang expects full Western collapse within the quarter. Yanqi Lake meets next week. Results will be reported.

Val leaned back, cracking her knuckles. "They weren't even subtle."

"They didn't need to be," Shane said. "They thought they were untouchable."

"Until Nadler got sloppy," Jasmine said. "His arrogance saved us. He couldn't resist documenting everything. The ego of a man who thought his brilliance would rewrite the world."

She scrolled through more of his files—detailed breakdowns of Western banks, asset vulnerability models, and cross-border capital flight simulations. In one folder, labeled "End Scenario Projections," Nadler had calculated the percentage of global GDP that would shift eastward after the collapse: twenty-one percent within six months.

He had titled the file "The Second Century of the Dragon."

As they reached the end of the directory tree, Jasmine noticed one last folder—marked only with her initials: JL.

Her stomach dropped.

"Open it," Shane said gently.

She hesitated, then clicked. The folder contained personal photos, transcripts, and an old press clipping—her face from a Treasury symposium years ago, when she'd spoken about blockchain regulation. There were also fragments of code from their failed startup.

A short note accompanied the files:

> **To J.L.**
> **You could have been part of this. The Ghost never forgets his best student.**
> **–J.N.**

Jasmine bit her lip. She closed the folder, her hand trembling slightly.

"That sick son of a bitch," she whispered. "He's been watching me for years. And still taunting me from the grave."

Shane stepped closer. "He's gone, Jasmine. He can't hurt you anymore."

They spent the next six hours cataloguing, hashing, and timestamping every file into an evidentiary ledger. By dawn, they had constructed a digital chain linking Helvex Financial → Zhonghua Capital → the Chinese State Council → Chairman Liang Ze himself.

Jasmine compiled the data into an encrypted dossier for Shane to deliver personally to Hendrix in Washington. The first section contained corporate filings and ownership structures tying Helvex to Zhonghua Capital. The second section summarized the communications between Egli, Nadler, and Feng, establishing a timeline of coordination. The third section—her own addition—was titled simply: "Yanqi Lake – The Dragon's Nest."

In it, she detailed the evidence linking Gao Feng's movements to government-level planning. She included translated excerpts from Mandarin emails, financial transfers routed through Beijing's state investment authority, and satellite photos of Yanqi Lake labeled **CONFIDENTIAL – PLA PROTECTED ZONE**.

Finally, she added a one-page executive summary:

Subject: Chinese State Involvement in Western Financial Destabilization

Summary: Evidence recovered from Jerome Nadler's encrypted devices confirms that Helvex Financial AG functioned as a front for Zhonghua Capital Holdings Co., Ltd., a Chinese state-owned corporation. The operation—codenamed *Project Dragon-Breath*—was conceived to collapse Western financial markets through controlled liquidity manipulation, thereby strengthening Eastern economic influence.

Recommendation: Immediate escalation to the U.S. National Security Council. Request coordinated sanctions under the International Emergency Economic Powers Act (IEEPA).

She encrypted the dossier under triple-key signature and slid it across the table to Shane. "All verified. All admissible," she said quietly. "The world needs to see this."

She stared at the Ghost's laptop one last time before powering it down. He had thought himself invincible, untouchable—a god in the machine. But in the end, his own vanity betrayed him.

Bobbi, ever the realist, broke the silence. "So what's next? We drop this on the Senate? The U.N.? The Financial Stability Board?"

Shane shook his head. "Not yet. We go to Washington first. Hendrix will brief the president. After that, we move forward on that RICO case. But we have to be very careful how we out the Chinese. We move too soon, and they'll be able to take counter measures."

Val smiled faintly. "Guess LawForce isn't done bending the arc."

"No," Shane said, watching the city wake below. "We're just getting started."

* * *

That night, after the others had left, Jasmine sat alone in the lab. The drives were sealed and the phone disassembled and stored. But one small file on the laptop lingered on her secondary monitor—a recording buried deep within Nadler's personal cache.

She hesitated, then played it.

A voice, faint and distorted, spoke through static.

"Hello, Jasmine. If you're listening to this, then I'm gone. But remember, systems never die. They replicate. Somewhere out there, someone else is watching, learning, building. Ghosts don't vanish—they multiply."

The recording cut to silence.

Jasmine closed the window and shut down the machine. "Not this time," she whispered. "Not your system."

49

WASHINGTON
DISTRICT OF COLUMBIA

UNITED STATES OF AMERICA

Hendrix sat at the head of his small conference table, watching the flames flicker in the fireplace. It was a beautiful January day in Washington, perfect for a fire to create a more comfortable environment for the team. They needed a break from those cyber-prisons they usually worked in. The ones that crush the spirit and smother the soul.

Across from him, Shane sat at the table, the afternoon light cutting sharp angles across his face. Next to him, Val sorted through a pile of papers, while Ollie—the youngest of the group and the team's resident researcher—fidgeted with a pen that clicked too often for Hendrix's liking.

"Thank you all for coming to D.C. on such short notice. I thought it was important to bring the legal team together in person to review our next steps. We have some crucial decisions to make. With the Swiss ruling, we've taken the first bite. Now it's time for the main course. The question is: where should we bring the RICO action?"

Val spoke first. "The obvious answer is Boston. BostonFirst's headquarters are there, it's where this all started, and the local courts are familiar with the institution."

Shane's expression remained noncommittal. "I'm not so sure. While Boston makes sense on paper, optics matter. BostonFirst is back in friendly hands, under Bobbi's control. So, BostonFirst isn't the enemy anymore. And this isn't just about Boston; it's about the entire Western financial system."

Ollie chimed in. "Then where? D.C.? Treasury has been looped in, and Jasmine is already coordinating from there."

Hendrix shook his head. "D.C. makes it political. We don't want this framed as a government vendetta, even if the government is behind us. We need the appearance of impartiality and the muscle of experience." He paused, glancing at Shane. "That's why I believe we both know where this belongs."

Shane's lips twitched into a faint smile. "New York. The Southern District."

"Exactly." Hendrix smiled back. "Ground zero for the financial world. The Southern District of New York has been the venue for some of the biggest financial and organized crime cases in history—Mafia, Enron, Credit Suisse, UBS—you name it. Every one of them went through the SDNY."

Val looked thoughtful. "It's also a good fit legally. Helvex has a major presence in New York. They have a branch on Park Avenue, a satellite office in the Hudson Yards complex, and they transact daily through the New York Fed's system."

Ollie frowned. "But what about jurisdiction? Helvex is Swiss. Doesn't that complicate it?"

Shane tapped his pen against the table. "Not with them having a primary place of business in New York City. On top of that, New York's long-arm jurisdiction under CPLR 302 covers foreign entities doing business in the state. Beyond their physical presence, Helvex has correspondent accounts in Manhattan, regularly transacts in U.S. dollars, and uses clearinghouses in New York. That's more than enough of a nexus. They've put themselves squarely under U.S. jurisdiction."

Val raised an eyebrow. "And what about the judges?"

Hendrix smiled. "Some of the best in the country. The SDNY bench is battle-tested. They've handled cybercrime, securities fraud, money laundering—you name it. They won't blink at a case with international implications. Plus, the prosecutors there—those men and women live and breathe financial crime."

He glanced around the room. "There's another reason. RICO."

Val folded her arms and said, "RICO is usually associated with mobsters and drug cartels. How do we adapt it to fit Helvex?"

Hendrix's eyes gleamed with excitement. "That's the beauty of it. RICO was designed to dismantle criminal enterprises, not just target individuals. While it was originally aimed at organized crime, courts have since applied it to corporations, financial networks, and even foreign entities. Remember, the statute defines a 'person' as any entity capable of holding property, including corporate entities."

Ollie nodded in understanding. "So, if Helvex and its Chinese owners are acting as a criminal enterprise..."

"We connect them," Shane interjected, completing Ollie's thought. "Every fraudulent act they committed—every transaction, every shell company, every wire transfer—becomes part of a coordinated pattern of racketeering activity."

Hendrix smiled approvingly. "One enterprise, multiple actors, shared intent. This allows us to charge them as a unified operation. Think of it as the legal equivalent of connecting all the dots in a global spiderweb of conspirators."

Val's pen hovered above her notebook. "What's the Chinese connection here? That part really worries me."

Hendrix folded his hands and replied, "Zhonghua Capital Holdings Company Limited." He let the name hang in the air for a moment. "The parent company, through a tangled web of intermediaries, behind Helvex Financial. Based in Beijing, owned by the Chinese government."

"State-owned?" Val asked.

"Fully," Hendrix confirmed. "This isn't a rogue private actor; this is the Chinese state operating through a financial front. And make no mistake—our discovery from the Ghost's laptop confirms it."

Ollie, who had been trying to balance a pencil on the edge of his coffee mug, let it clatter loudly onto the table. "That's significant. But can we really go after a Chinese state-owned entity under RICO?"

"That's the question," Shane replied.

Hendrix stood up and began pacing toward the window overlooking the Capitol Building. "Our reach has extended in the last few years," he said quietly. "We've prosecuted Chinese corporations before—like Huawei Technologies. The Department of Justice charged them under RICO with bank fraud, wire fraud, and trade secret theft. That sets a precedent. That's our pathway."

He turned to face them. "We can make Zhonghua Capital a co-defendant alongside Helvex, just as the DOJ tied Huawei and its subsidiaries together under one RICO enterprise. The statute allows it. Corporate entities can conspire, and if they do, every act committed by one becomes attributed to the enterprise as a whole."

Val nodded slowly, her eyes narrowing in thought. "So if Helvex committed banking fraud, Zhonghua Capital would be implicated too."

"Right," Hendrix affirmed. "RICO enables us to break down the barriers between subsidiaries. We don't have to pursue each offense separately; we present the entire network as one corrupt organization. That's what makes it such a powerful tool. We can bring the whole Chinese financial apparatus into a single courtroom."

Ollie let out a low whistle. "That's ambitious."

"Ambitious is what this case demands," Shane said. "The Swiss ruling was important, but it was limited to property and restitution.

It didn't address the core of the conspiracy. If we want to take down Helvex, we need to demonstrate that it's part of a broader criminal enterprise—an extension of state-sponsored economic warfare."

Val looked up. "We'll need airtight evidence."

"We'll have that," Hendrix assured her. "Our digital forensics team is already preparing affidavits to verify the integrity of the Ghost's data. The Swiss police cooperation agreement gives us admissibility under mutual legal assistance treaties. Once we file the RICO case, we can subpoena any U.S.-based intermediaries—banks, clearinghouses, and investment firms—that facilitated Helvex's transactions."

There was a pause, and Hendrix's expression hardened. "But remember, this isn't just another lawsuit. Once we file RICO, we're declaring open season on Helvex and its backers. The Chinese government will see it as a direct challenge."

"So be it," Shane said. "They've been pissing in our sandbox for too long. It's time we built a wall around it."

Val still looked skeptical. "Do you think the administration will let us go that far? Suing a Chinese state-owned company could ignite a diplomatic firestorm."

Hendrix nodded. "The White House is on board. After Huawei, the Justice Department made it clear—the China Initiative wasn't just symbolic. We're not acting alone here."

Ollie nodded slowly. "So, we have political cover."

"And more than that," Hendrix continued. "We have momentum. The world's financial press is still covering the Swiss verdict. Public sympathy is on our side. Western investors and small shareholders all want accountability."

Ollie leaned forward, knocking a stack of files halfway off the table. Papers were scattered across the carpet. He bent down to pick them up, banged his head on the underside of the table, and then reemerged, rubbing his temple. "I'm good," he said, squinting at Hendrix. "I was just wondering about their assets here? Helvex has billions parked in U.S. accounts. If we sue, won't they move it all offshore before judgment?"

Hendrix nodded grimly. "That's the next step—an emergency injunction. We can't let them shift assets once they see us coming. The Swiss ruling, combined with the ongoing investigation into their hacking of LawForce, should meet the threshold for asset preservation."

Val twirled her pen. "So, we file in SDNY and simultaneously petition for a pre-trial asset freeze?"

"No. That won't work. We can't afford to give Helvex a single second of warning," he said, scanning the faces around the conference table. "Once the RICO indictment is filed, they'll know we're onto them. In the digital world, billions can be moved out of reach in seconds. If those transfers hit a labyrinth of offshore accounts, shell entities, and crypto conduits, we'll never see that money again."

He tapped the folder in front of him marked "Mareva Application—Draft." "That's why we need a Mareva Injunction, and we need to bring it ex parte—without notice to Helvex. They can't see it coming."

Bobbi frowned. "Do you think the court will grant it without notice?"

Hendrix nodded slowly. "The bar is high, no doubt. We'll need to show solid evidence that Helvex has assets within our jurisdiction and that there's a real risk of dissipation. But between Jasmine's cyber forensics, the Swiss judgment, and Nadler's laptop evidence, we have a strong foundation. The Mareva is designed exactly for cases like this—where delay equals defeat."

Val leaned back. "So we go in under seal?"

"Yes," Hendrix said. "Quietly. We file the injunction first, freeze everything, and only then does the grand jury file its indictment with the court. Helvex will wake up one morning to find its empire, at least that part within U.S. jurisdiction—which is the vast majority—locked tight by court order. That's how we hit them where it hurts—before they even realize the fight has begun."

For a long moment, the only sound was the faint hum drifting up from Pennsylvania Avenue. Then Shane spoke. "New York, it is."

Hendrix nodded. "Good. I'll coordinate with DOJ and SDNY." He handed Val his Mareva folder. "You prepare affidavits and asset schedules for the injunction; that's the first order of business. And keep things tight. A leak before we can get that injunction will make the rest of the process meaningless. Steven, you'll finalize the brief for the grand jury. Ollie, start compiling financial data on Helvex's U.S. operations, especially its real estate holdings. Jasmine will handle digital evidence authentication. I think we're finished here."

The war against Helvex—and now Zhonghua Capital—was moving to New York City.

50

BEIJING

SHANGHAI

CHINA

The haze over Beijing hung heavy as dusk fell on Zhongnanhai, the compound housing the offices of the Chinese Communist Party and the residence of its leader. From his office window, Chairman Liang Ze could make out the walls of the Forbidden City—a reminder of empires that endured and of rulers who punish failure without hesitation.

On his desk lay the report from State Security. Its words stung:

Helvex Financial / Zhonghua Capital
— assets frozen.

Zhonghua Capital — named in U.S.
RICO indictment.

He drummed his fingers on the rosewood surface and then picked up the phone. He was breaking his own rule against using alternative forms of contact, but given recent developments, it was clear their cover was blown. "Get me Gao Feng on the secure line."

When the line connected, Feng answered immediately. "Yes, Chairman Liang."

"Feng," Liang said coolly, "all of Helvex's assets within reach of the Americans are frozen. How could this happen under your supervision?"

"Chairman, the Americans obtained an ex parte Mareva injunction. We had no idea our security had been compromised or that a lawsuit was coming. We could not have anticipated these events. I assure you..."

"Anticipated?" Liang interrupted him. "You swore our financial architecture was impenetrable. And now Hans Egli informs me that Zhonghua Capital is part of the RICO case. That means they know about us. Do you remember what I told you about leaks at our first meeting?"

"Chairman, there was no leak," Feng said quickly. "Their Navy SEALs killed Jerome Nadler, our cyber operative in Switzerland. They must have extracted data from his devices. That's how they found us."

Liang's silence was long and suffocating. "You think that comforts me? You think Beijing can excuse humiliation because of a dead mercenary?"

Feng's voice cracked. "Chairman, if you allow me some time, our core assets in Hong Kong remain intact. We can reposition. I'll rebuild the network."

Liang's reply was calm but lethal. "Tell me, Feng, what is your title?"

"Director of Project DragonBreath," he answered, barely a whisper.

"Exactly. *Director*. As one of those American presidents liked to say—'The buck stops with you.' When things went well, you accepted praise and whispered promises of the Order of the Republic. Now, when things collapse, do you expect someone else to carry your blame?"

"Chairman—please—"

"You have failed the Motherland," Liang said softly. "Goodbye, Feng."

The line went dead.

* * *

Feng stood in his office, overlooking the Huangpu River, the phone still in his hand. Outside, Shanghai's skyline glittered—a crown of light mocking the darkness within him.

He poured a measure of Maotai, savoring its bitter warmth. The room was too still, too quiet. He replayed the Chairman's voice in his mind: "You have failed the Motherland."

He thought back to their first meeting at Yanqi Lake—the elegant calligraphy hall, the still water, the quiet confidence of Liang Ze as he laid out the plan. Feng had believed in that vision. He built Project DragonBreath. Now, his creation was unraveling, all because of that egomaniac Nadler. It all felt so unfair.

He turned from the window and sat at his desk. Slowly and deliberately, he took out a piece of parchment and began to write. His penmanship was immaculate, the strokes elegant and unwavering:

I have failed in my duty to Chairman Liang, the Party, and the Motherland. My actions have disgraced my comrades and dishonored my ancestors. In betraying trust, I have disturbed the balance of righteousness and virtue that binds us all.

I can only seek to restore harmony through my own end. May my death cleanse the stain I have left behind.

—When the Way is restored, the realm is at peace."

He set down the pen, eyes blinking furiously. The characters gleamed in the lamplight. He read them once more, then folded the paper neatly and placed it on the table beside an untouched cup of tea.

He changed into a simple white shirt and black trousers. No tie. No watch. He opened the balcony doors, and the faint roar of the city below drifted in.

He looked out toward the Oriental Pearl Tower, glowing crimson against the smog. He remembered his father's words: "In China, honor is heavier than life."

Taking the cord from the armoire, he tested the knot. His hands didn't tremble as he whispered a final word—"Motherland"—before stepping forward.

* * *

The maid arrived the next morning at 7:45. She found him hanging in the living room. The letter lay on the desk, perfectly aligned beside the teacup.

Within an hour, unmarked sedans lined the curb. Officials arrived, sealed off the apartment, and carried the note away in an evidence envelope. The press release came by noon:

Senior executive Gao Feng passed away suddenly this morning from a cardiac event.

No mention of ropes or shame. But within Party circles, everyone understood: failure is unforgivable.

* * *

Two days later, Chairman Liang stood on the balcony of his private villa overlooking Yanqi Lake. He reread Feng's letter—the calligraphy flawless. He traced the final line with his forefinger: "When the Way is restored, the realm is at peace."

He folded the note and slipped it into his pocket. "Loyal to the end," he murmured.

51

NEW YORK CITY
NEW YORK

UNITED STATES OF AMERICA

A steady flow of yellow cabs and pedestrians seemed indifferent to the global turmoil LawForce had unleashed. It was midday: attorneys in dark suits hurried between the Thurgood Marshall Courthouse and the Jacob K. Javits Federal Building, journalists clustered around camera tripods, and food trucks sent up curls of steam that mingled with the scent of roasted nuts and pretzels.

High above, the late afternoon light streamed through the tall windows of LawForce's temporary headquarters in Manhattan—a war room on the thirty-second floor of the Ted Weiss Federal Building, overlooking Foley Square.

Just beyond the square, the Manhattan Detention Complex loomed—a reminder that justice here was both an aspiration and a business. The plaza itself was anchored by a fountain at its center, flanked by Art Deco spires and modern glass towers. In the distance, the faint echo of traffic over the Brooklyn Bridge could be heard.

Hendrix turned away from the window and approached the conference table, setting down his coffee next to a stack of documents. Shane, Val, and Bobbi were bent over a printed draft of the latest motion in *United States v. Zhonghua Capital and Helvex Financial*. Jasmine's dual monitors glowed with code traces from Zurich—fragments of digital evidence salvaged from the Ghost's encrypted drives.

The phone on the table buzzed—a call from overseas. Hendrix answered on speaker. "Jonathan Hendrix."

"Mr. Attorney General, this is Swiss Finance Minister Renata Blaser. Thank you for taking my call." Her voice was low and deliberate, carrying the soft inflection of Zurich German tempered by years of diplomatic experience.

"Madame Minister," Hendrix replied. "I appreciate you reaching out. I have you on speakerphone with some of my team, if that's alright."

"Yes, that's fine. In fact, I welcome the opportunity to speak with them as well. Hello to all."

Hendrix provided a quick introduction. "Thank you, Minister. For your benefit, 'all' consists of Steven Shane, Valentina Lopez, and Bobbie Sullivan. So, what's on your mind?"

"I have reviewed the RICO indictment handed down by the grand jury. I have spoken with your Secretary of the Treasury. Still, given LawForce's direct involvement in the Swiss proceedings, as well as this new RICO development, I felt it necessary to discuss this with you as well."

The team exchanged glances. Shane mouthed "Blaser—Federal Finance Minister. That's top-level."

"Please continue, Minister," Hendrix said, encouraging the others to listen.

Blaser exhaled softly, "Switzerland is deeply shocked by these revelations. Mr. Egli is an embarrassment to all of us, certainly to the Swiss. From the indictment, we see that there is nothing Swiss about this man. He is little more than a Chinese puppet. As you would have seen in the Swiss Commercial Court's ruling, Helvex Financial and its principals have been banned from conducting business in our country. That judgment is unprecedented in our financial history. I felt it necessary to clarify that the Confederation does not tolerate this sort of behavior."

"Understood," Hendrix said. "But may I ask why the court didn't go further? Was there no mechanism for liquidating the company?"

A brief pause followed before a crisp reply emerged from the career bureaucrat, who weighed every word carefully: "The judiciary in our system operates independently, Mr. Attorney General. I have no control over the judges, as I'm sure you can understand. The court may have taken into account the proportion of Helvex's domestic assets to its global holdings when calculating damages. Furthermore, the court has no means of enforcing its order beyond our borders."

Hendrix nodded grimly. "Yet Hans Egli remains relatively untouched. He is sitting on a fortune, most of which is parked in jurisdictions far beyond our reach."

Blaser's voice remained calm. "Mr. Egli has been banned from participating in any Swiss financial markets. As this was a civil matter, the court lacked the authority to imprison him. However, Mr. Attorney General, I must emphasize—he is a pariah in Swiss finance. You understand, our penalties often stem not from the law but from social ostracism. He will not find another board seat in this country."

Bobbi spoke softly, more to herself than to anyone else: "That's small comfort."

Blaser continued, "As I've mentioned, and as you can appreciate, our courts' jurisdiction does not extend beyond our borders. I notice that Helvex continues to operate rather freely in your country."

Silence lingered for a moment before Hendrix chuckled. "An excellent point, Madame Minister. As outlined in the RICO indictment, we intend to address that—let me assure you."

"Yes, I see that," Blaser replied. "I wish you fortitude, Mr. Attorney General. The eyes of the international banking community are upon you."

She hesitated briefly, as if deciding whether to end the call formally or personally. "Godspeed, Mr. Attorney General," she finally said. "We will... how do you say... squeeze our thumbs for you."

Hendrix blinked, caught off guard. "Pardon me, Madame Minister?"

A genuine, warm laugh bubbled through the speaker. "It's a Swiss thing," she said. "Look it up. It's the equivalent of keeping our fingers crossed."

And with that, the line went dead.

For a moment, the only sound in the room was the hum of the city below. Hendrix stared at the receiver as if the faint echo of the Minister's voice might still hold meaning.

"Squeezing thumbs," Val repeated with a slight grin. "I like that. It sounds determined."

Shane leaned back in his chair. "Better than crossing fingers. It's more deliberate—less about luck, more about willpower."

Jasmine looked up from her screen. "Do you think she was sincere?"

"Oh, she was sincere," Hendrix replied. "Look, the Swiss have a great democracy, and I'd put their integrity up there with the best. They needed this like a hole in the head. She's worried about the fallout. Switzerland's reputation for neutrality and discretion is crucial. The idea that one of their flagship banks was essentially a Chinese Trojan Horse? That's an existential threat to their image."

Bobbi nodded. "She's probably fielding calls from every private banker in Zurich and Geneva right now, reassuring her that it could never happen to them."

Hendrix walked to the window, hands in his pockets. "You know, for decades, the Swiss built their global brand on secrecy. It made them rich and indispensable. Now, that same secrecy has made them vulnerable." He turned to Shane. "You did good work over there, Steven. I know the court didn't give us everything, but it gave us enough."

"Enough to take it across the Atlantic," Shane said quietly. "But the real question is whether we can keep it here."

Val frowned. "Meaning?"

"Meaning," Shane explained, "that freezing assets is one thing. Keeping them frozen against a wall of international lawyers is another."

* * *

They worked late into the evening, reviewing discovery timelines and deposition requests. Outside, dusk deepened over the Hudson. When the room finally began to empty, Hendrix lingered with Shane by the window. "Renata Blaser," Hendrix mused. "Did you ever meet her in Zurich or Bern?"

Shane shook his head. "No. But I know the type. Precise, cautious—probably plays chess three moves ahead of everyone else. If she's squeezing her thumb for us, she's also hedging her bets."

Hendrix smiled faintly. "That's what makes her good. She's doing her job—protecting Switzerland's position. And we're protecting ours."

He paused, glancing out at the shimmering lights of lower Manhattan.

"Have you ever stopped to think how close they came? If LawForce hadn't cracked the Infinium scheme thanks to Ms. Rivella, if the Swiss court hadn't acted as it did... The Swiss are done with Helvex, but the machine behind it—Zhonghua Capital—is still spinning. We've cut off one arm, but the other is still reaching."

Shane studied him, recognizing the prosecutor and the patriot beneath. "Do you think we can actually dismantle them?"

"I think," Hendrix said quietly, "we have to try."

He turned from the window, stopping at the door to look back at Shane. "Squeeze your thumb, Steven. We're going to need it."

52

**NEW YORK CITY
NEW YORK**

UNITED STATES OF AMERICA

The marble columns of the Daniel Patrick Moynihan U.S. Courthouse stood like solemn sentinels above Foley Square. Flags flapped lazily in the spring breeze. The courthouse, home to the Southern District of New York, had hosted its share of titans—mob bosses, Wall Street moguls, and political kingpins—but few trials promised stakes like this one.

Shane looked at the row of twelve binders neatly lined up on the counsel table. A lot of work condensed to this moment. Next to him sat a copy of the fifty-page indictment.

UNITED STATES DISTRICT COURT
SOUTHERN DISTRICT OF NEW YORK

UNITED STATES OF AMERICA
v.
ZHONGHUA CAPITAL HOLDINGS CO., LTD.
and
HELVEX FINANCIAL AG,
Defendants.

INDICTMENT

(18 U.S.C. §§ 1961–1968; Racketeer Influenced and Corrupt Organizations Act)

COUNT ONE

(Racketeering Conspiracy)

The Grand Jury charges:

1. Beginning in or about 2022, and continuing through the date of this Indictment, within the Southern District of New York and elsewhere, the defendants **ZHONGHUA CAPITAL HOLDINGS CO., LTD.**, a Chinese state-owned financial conglomerate, and **HELVEX FINANCIAL AG**, a Swiss private banking institution, together with others known and unknown to the Grand Jury, did knowingly and intentionally conduct and participate, directly and indirectly, in the conduct of the affairs of an enterprise, the activities of which affected interstate and foreign commerce, through a pattern of racketeering activity, in violation of **Title 18, United States Code, Sections 1962(c) and (d).**

2. The enterprise (the "Zhonghua-Helvex Enterprise") constituted an association-in-fact of corporations and individuals engaged in financial, cyber, and economic acts designed to undermine the stability of Western monetary markets and to secure unlawful control over U.S. banking assets.

3. The enterprise's objectives included:

   • the acquisition and control of **BostonFirst Bank**,

   • the creation, manipulation, and planned devaluation of a digital currency, **Infinium**, and associated financial fund, the **CryptoHelix Fund**,

   • and the destabilization of Western financial systems through coordinated cyberattacks and misinformation campaigns.

4. The defendants, through agents including **Jerome Nadler, a/k/a "The Ghost,"** used electronic communications and international banking networks to execute wire transfers, launder proceeds, and conceal their control through shell entities and proxy accounts.

Inside the courtroom, the press gallery buzzed with activity. Reporters jostled for seats, their murmurs echoing off the high, coffered ceilings. "United States of America v. Zhonghua Capital Holdings Co., Ltd. and Helvex Financial AG" splashed across the morning's headlines, accompanied by grainy photos of Shane and Hendrix on one side, and Dubois and Egli on the other. The world was watching, eager to see whether American justice could reach across oceans and pierce the armor of secrecy woven by Swiss bankers and their Chinese counterparts.

At the government's table, Shane sat calmly, flipping through his notes. They had decided to lead with the criminal case; the civil case could come later. If he did his job right here, they wouldn't need a civil case. They were going for broke—total annihilation. The thick RICO complaint lay open beside him, its pages marked with color-coded tabs. To his left, Val and Bobbi whispered about last-minute strategy points. Hendrix, seated just behind, wore his usual half-smile—the expression of a man who had seen too many Washington battles to be easily rattled.

Dubois entered the courtroom in a tailored black suit, trailing her signature crimson scarf. Behind her, a small group of Axos GmbH attorneys carried sleek leather binders embossed with Helvex's crimson emblem. Accompanying Dubois was an Asian gentleman with two assistants; Shane guessed he was the attorney for Zhonghua Capital, which had its own representation at this point.

Dubois crossed directly to the government's table.

"Mr. Shane," she said softly in her French-Swiss accent. "Your Mareva application was inspired. And so fast. You must have worked through a few nights."

Steve looked up, his expression unreadable. "We've had practice with urgent matters."

Dubois leaned closer, her perfume sharp, her voice low. "But winning a battle isn't the same as winning the war. You'll soon find that freezing assets is easier than keeping them frozen. After we're through, we'll have our funds back—with interest. And, naturally, we'll be seeking damages for malicious prosecution."

Shane's reply was flat, almost bored. "Good luck with that."

She smiled. "Oh, Monsieur Shane, I do not rely on luck." With that, she turned and glided back to her table.

* * *

At precisely nine a.m., the bailiff, a broad-shouldered man in a navy jacket, stepped forward and struck his gavel once.

"All rise," he intoned, his voice echoing through the chamber. The chatter evaporated.

"Court is now in session. The United States District Court for the Southern District of New York is convened, the Honorable Judge Eleanor Markham presiding."

He paused, scanning the courtroom before reading from the docket in crisp, deliberate tones.

"The matter before the court: United States of America versus Zhonghua Capital Holdings Company, Limited, and Helvex Financial Aktiengesellschaft."

Judge Markham entered the courtroom and took her seat behind the towering mahogany bench. In her early sixties, she had silver hair neatly coiled and round, silver-rimmed glasses. She was known as one of the toughest judges in financial crime.

"Be seated," she said. She glanced over her notes. "Counselors, this court recognizes the gravity of this case. We will proceed with professionalism and courtesy. Are you ready to begin?"

Shane stood up. "Ready for the United States, Your Honor."

Dubois followed suit, "My colleague, Zhao Wenhai, and I are ready for the defense, Your Honor."

Markham nodded. "Very well. I will hear the opening statements now. Mr. Shane?"

Shane rose slowly. "Thank you, Your Honor."

He buttoned his jacket, took a deep breath, and walked over to the jury box, scanning the jurors—a mix of professionals, retirees, and small-business owners—ordinary citizens being asked to weigh a case of global consequence.

"Good morning," he began. "This case is about power—and what happens when power forgets its limits."

He leaned on the railing of the jury box. "Helvex Financial and its master, Zhonghua Capital, operated under a shield of secrecy, exploiting a system to protect power, not justice. They didn't just break laws; they broke lives. Families lost their savings. Workers lost their pensions. Investors lost faith in the very markets that sustain our economy. And all of it—every single bit—was orchestrated through an enterprise of deception that spanned continents."

He paused, allowing his words to resonate in the courtroom.

"Our burden under the Racketeer Influenced and Corrupt Organizations Act—RICO—is to establish the existence of an enterprise that engaged in a pattern of racketeering activity. Essentially, we must show that the operations of Zhonghua Capital and its subsidiaries, including Helvex, were regularly supported by criminal acts such as fraud, wire manipulation, and cyber intrusion."

Turning slightly, he gestured toward the defense table. "Characterizing the Zhonghua Capital group's business in this way is no small step. It means their misconduct was not incidental; it was institutional. It permeated the organization like a cancer."

Dubois raised an eyebrow but remained silent.

Shane continued. "RICO was designed for cases just like this—for organizations so powerful and interconnected that traditional law enforcement could not hold them accountable. It has been used against the mafia, against cartels, and against corrupt corporations. Now, it must be used against the most sophisticated financial conspiracy of our time."

He picked up a single sheet of paper from the podium—the Swiss judgment. "This court will hear evidence that Helvex engaged in a deliberate campaign to destabilize the U.S. financial sector through cyber manipulation, using BostonFirst Bank as both a pawn and a weapon. You will hear from whistleblowers, forensic analysts, and government officials who will trace the flow of money and data—from Beijing to Zurich to Wall Street."

His gaze swept the room. "And at the center of it all, you will see the unmistakable fingerprints of Zhonghua Capital—a Chinese state-owned enterprise masquerading as a neutral Swiss investment firm. This was not commerce; it was economic warfare."

A murmur rippled through the gallery.

"Ladies and gentlemen, Helvex Financial and its masters at Zhonghua Capital believed they could hide behind money, distance, and silence—that justice itself could be bought, manipulated, and buried. But justice is here, in this room, in your hands. In this trial, you will prove that the law still belongs to the people, not to those who think they stand above it. Thank you."

Markham adjusted her microphone. "Thank you, Mr. Shane." She turned to Dubois. "Will the defendants be making a joint opening statement, or will I hear from you individually?"

Dubois stood. "Your Honor, I will be presenting the opening statement jointly on behalf of both Helvex Financial and Zhonghua Capital. I have a bit more experience with this case than Mr. Zhao, who is relatively new to the proceedings."

Markham nodded. "Very well, Ms. Dubois. Please proceed."

Dubois faced the jurors. "Ladies and gentlemen," she said, "what you just heard from Mr. Shane is not an opening statement; it is a manifesto."

A few nervous laughs rippled through the gallery.

"This case," she continued, "is a witch hunt—a political crusade disguised as a pursuit of justice. My clients, Helvex Financial and Zhonghua Capital, are being persecuted not for their actions but for who they are: successful, foreign entities that operate independently of American control."

Her tone sharpened. "The United States Department of Justice is attempting to criminalize standard banking operations and international investments. These institutions have injected billions into the U.S. economy, created jobs, funded startups, and supported communities. Yet today, they are portrayed as villains."

She paced slowly. Shane sensed her discomfort with the freedom of a U.S. courtroom. Used to staying anchored behind the counsel table, she recognized her disadvantage if she didn't get closer to the jury. "The latest charges reveal nothing new. Instead, they recycle a civil dispute. The same evidence, the same witnesses, the same allegations—only the forum and the politics have changed. As we lawyers say, it is res judicata—already judged—by the Swiss courts."

Her eyes flicked toward Shane. "The government is now attempting to use RICO as a weapon because it lost its case in the court of public opinion."

She returned to the counsel table, tapping the podium with a manicured finger. "The case should be dismissed."

Judge Markham regarded her coolly. "You will have the opportunity to preserve your motion for later argument, Ms. Dubois. For now, please continue."

Dubois nodded. "Thank you, Your Honor."

She softened her tone, addressing the jurors. "You will see no conspiracy here. No criminal enterprise—just a series of complex financial transactions that the government does not understand, along with a story too sensational to resist. When this trial is over, you will see that Helvex and Zhonghua Capital are guilty only of success."

She bowed slightly toward the bench. "Thank you, Your Honor."

Judge Markham glanced at the clock. "We'll recess until tomorrow at 9:00 a.m. Counsel will be prepared to proceed with witness testimony." She struck her gavel lightly. "We are adjourned."

The gallery erupted in whispers as the judge left the bench. Reporters bolted for the doors, phones already out, crafting headlines before they hit the street.

Dubois returned to her table, collected her papers, and flashed Shane a tight smile. "À demain, Monsieur Shane. Tomorrow, we begin the dismantling of your fantasy."

Shane didn't look up from his notes. "We'll see who gets dismantled when the evidence comes in."

As she walked away, Val leaned closer. "She's good."

"Yeah," Shane admitted. "But she's overconfident. That res judicata argument is just a smokescreen. Swiss civil findings don't bar U.S. criminal prosecution. She knows that—she's just playing for headlines."

Bobbi added quietly, "And she's going to get them. Every outlet in the world will spin her 'witch hunt' quote."

Hendrix, who had remained silent through most of the morning, spoke for the first time. "Let them spin. The truth will come out faster once we start presenting our exhibits."

Shane nodded. "We just need to survive the noise."

* * *

Outside, on the courthouse steps, the crowd had swelled. Cameramen clustered like vultures as Dubois gave a brief, carefully calibrated statement in English, denouncing "lawfare masquerading as justice." The microphones flashed and clicked.

A few minutes later, Shane exited with Hendrix and Val. Reporters surged forward, but he raised a hand. "We'll do our talking in the courtroom, thank you," he said.

They pushed through the chaos down the granite steps to the waiting car. As the doors closed, Shane looked back toward the courthouse, where the flags were fluttering vigorously against a rising wind. He opened his notebook, the words of his opening still fresh in his mind: *They didn't just break laws; they broke lives.*

Outside, thunder rolled faintly over the Hudson.

53

NEW YORK CITY
NEW YORK

UNITED STATES OF AMERICA

The courtroom was packed—reporters jammed shoulder to shoulder, lenses fixed on the witness stand where Hans Egli adjusted his cufflinks with deliberate movements. He looked every inch the European banker: tailored black suit, silk tie, and hair slicked with precision—the man who had once ruled Zurich's financial scene with the cold composure of a chess master.

But Shane saw something different: a man standing on a trapdoor, with his arrogance being the only thing keeping him upright.

Judge Markham's gavel rested loosely in one hand, her gaze fixed on Shane. "Mr. Shane," she said, "you may proceed with your cross-examination."

Shane rose slowly. His tone was measured—almost friendly. "Good afternoon, Mr. Egli."

Egli smiled faintly. "Good afternoon, Counselor."

"You are the Chief Executive Officer of Helvex Financial, correct?"

"Yes."

"And Helvex is a major Swiss banking institution?"

"Indeed. Among the largest private wealth managers in Europe."

Shane nodded, pacing before the jury box. "Tell me, Mr. Egli, who owns Helvex Financial?"

Egli hesitated for a second. "Our ownership structure is complex. Primarily private investors."

"Private investors," Shane repeated, glancing toward the jurors. "Would that include Zhonghua Capital Holdings Company Limited?"

The courtroom went still.

Egli's expression didn't change, but a muscle twitched near his temple. "I don't believe Zhonghua Capital has any direct interest in Helvex."

"No *direct* interest," Shane said in a loud voice. "How about indirect?"

Egli shifted in the chair. "Again, the ownership is complex. I cannot recall the pedigree of all our investors."

"Well, maybe the evidence can help us out. According to documents recovered from Jerome Nadler's laptop—your own head of cybersecurity—Helvex isn't just partially owned by Zhonghua Capital. It's wholly owned, through a complex web of intermediary companies. Does that refresh your memory?"

Dubois sprang to her feet. "Objection! The provenance of that laptop is contested—"

Judge Markham cut her off. "Overruled. The court has already admitted the forensic evidence. Proceed, Mr. Shane."

Shane nodded politely and turned back to Egli. "Let's be clear, sir. Zhonghua Capital is ultimately your parent company. Correct?"

Egli's tone became clipped. "On paper, that appears to be what the evidence shows, yes."

"Okay, and who owns Zhonghua Capital?"

Egli exhaled slowly. "It's a consortium of shareholders."

Shane stepped forward, his voice tightening. "A consortium controlled by the State Council of the People's Republic of China. Isn't that true?"

The gallery murmured, and reporters leaned forward.

Egli's steely calm was cracking. "I believe so. I am not familiar with the internal structure of

Zhonghua Capital," he said stiffly. "And, frankly, I don't understand the relevance. I am the CEO. I take orders from no one."

Shane held up a printed email chain—one of the many that Nadler had hoarded. "Let's talk about who gave what orders. Please pull up Exhibit Two Fourteen—an internal memorandum dated June 4, 2023. It bears your signature. The subject line reads, and I quote, 'Directive from Chairman Liang Ze—approval for BostonFirst acquisition strategy.'"

He handed the document to the clerk. "Your Honor, request to publish."

"Granted."

The email appeared on the large courtroom screen, the text in harsh black-and-white.

Shane let the silence stretch.

"Mr. Egli," he said finally, "Chairman Liang Ze isn't a private banker. He's the head of the Chinese Communist Party. Do you still wish to claim you didn't know where your orders came from?"

Egli's fingers twitched against the wood of the witness box. "This is being taken out of context."

Shane stepped closer. "Please—provide the context. Because, from where I stand, it looks like you took your marching orders from the People's Republic of China. Correct?"

Egli looked toward Dubois, who sat rigid at the defense table, tugging an earlobe. She gave the faintest shake of her head.

Shane waited.

Egli swallowed. "I followed business opportunities. Nothing more."

Shane's voice rose, sharp as glass. "Business opportunities directed by Beijing and funded by Zhonghua Capital. That's not entrepreneurship, Mr. Egli—that's state-sponsored racketeering."

Dubois stood up again. "Objection! Counsel is testifying."

Judge Markham didn't even look at her. "Overruled. Mr. Egli, please answer the question."

Egli hesitated, his composure slipping fast. "We took strategic direction from our investors, yes."

"Your investors," Shane repeated. "By investors, do you mean the Chinese state?"

Egli tensed. "I don't accept that characterization."

Shane leaned on the witness rail, his voice low but fierce. "You don't get to characterize facts, Mr. Egli. They are what they are. And they show you're not a CEO—you're a marionette. Your strings are pulled in China."

Dubois rose again. "Objection! Argumentative—"

Shane turned, eyes flashing. "He's the one who admitted he takes direction from Beijing."

Judge Markham rapped her gavel once. "Overruled. The witness will answer."

Egli's face was pale now. "Helvex has Chinese ownership. That's all I can confirm."

"Ownership, direction, control—it's all the same when you're just a puppet," Shane said softly.

The jurors were riveted. Egli, once the picture of poise, was unraveling thread by thread.

Shane circled once more. "Let's talk about Project DragonBreath."

Egli blinked rapidly. "I'm not that familiar with it."

"Oh, I think you are," Shane replied, sliding another document onto the screen—a file recovered from Nadler's external drive. "Your own name appears on its coordination roster alongside Zhonghua Capital executives and one Director, Gao Feng."

At the mention of that name, Egli froze.

Shane pressed on. "Project DragonBreath was a plan to create liquidity crises in Western banks while shielding Eastern counterparts. Correct?"

Egli's lips parted, but no sound came out.

"Mr. Egli?"

"I—"

Shane stepped closer. "Did you approve it?"

"I—did not authorize any such program."

"But you executed transfers supporting it. One billion through shell accounts in Hong

Kong, routed via Helvex's Zurich node. We have the records, and you signed them."

Egli's voice broke. "I was following protocol—"

Shane cut him off. "Protocol written in Beijing by people whose language you don't speak but whose orders you never questioned. Isn't that right?"

The courtroom was silent except for Egli's uneven breathing.

Finally, he whispered, "I did my duty, yes."

Shane let the word hang in the air like a thunderclap. Then he turned to the jury. "Ladies and gentlemen, that's what racketeering looks like in the twenty-first century. It wears cufflinks instead of brass knuckles, but the crime is the same. I'm finished with this witness."

Judge Markham looked at Dubois. "Any redirect?"

Dubois shook her head. "No, Your Honor."

Markham glanced at the clock. "We'll adjourn for the day. Mr. Egli, you are excused pending recall. Court will reconvene at nine a.m. tomorrow."

* * *

Shane was collecting his notes when he heard the familiar click of heels behind him.

"Mr. Shane," came the smooth, calm voice.

He turned to see Dubois, looking immaculate, but there was a tremor beneath her composed exterior—a controlled implosion.

"Counselor," he replied.

She folded her arms. "You were ruthless in there."

"You make it sound like an insult."

Her eyes narrowed. "It's a compliment, begrudgingly. But I came to tell you something."

Shane raised an eyebrow. "I'm listening."

"I had no advance knowledge of the Chinese involvement," she said quietly. "None. Egli kept me in the dark. I found out when you did."

Shane studied her for a long moment. Her voice was steady, but her pride was evident in every syllable.

He finally said, "You expect me to believe that?"

"It's the truth."

He gave a small, humorless laugh. "That's what happens when you sleep with snakes."

For a moment, she stood still. The words landed like a physical blow. Her composure cracked briefly—a flicker of hurt in her eyes before she straightened her shoulders.

"Goodbye, Mr. Shane," she said softly, turning to walk away.

Shane watched her go. For the first time in a long while, he almost felt sorry for her. Almost.

* * *

In a conference room two floors above, Egli sat with his head in his hands. The television on the wall replayed the cross-examination in clipped sound bites. Each answer sounded worse than the last.

He could see the headlines forming:

The Marionette Banker

China's Man in Zurich

The walls seemed to close in around him. He had spent a lifetime mastering control—of numbers, of people, of perception. Yet in one afternoon, an obnoxious lawyer had stripped it all away.

Far across the world, he imagined the cold silence of Yanqi Lake—and the men who sat there, watching. They would not forgive him.

* * *

Shane stood on the courthouse steps, the warm breeze tugging at his coat. Below, the lights of lower Manhattan shimmered against the Hudson River.

Val came up beside him. "You got him good today."

"Yeah," Shane said quietly. "But we're not done. There's still the verdict, and then—whatever comes after."

She nodded. "Dubois won't go down easy."

"No," Shane agreed. "I had the strangest encounter with her. She came over and told me she hadn't known anything about the Chinese connection. It's incredible, but I believed her."

Val was unsympathetic. "She made her bed. She has to lie in it."

"That's what I told her, but still, I felt a bit sorry for her."

Val snorted. "You're losing it. Keep your sympathy for those people out there rebuilding their lives because of her and her clients."

"Touché." Shane wrapped his arm around her waist. "We have to celebrate. What do you say we grab a spinalis dorsi at Gallagher's?" He loved that cap of the ribeye. It wasn't cheap, but he figured the U.S. government owed him one.

Val snuggled up to him. "And I'll have the other soup."

"What the hell is that?"

Val smiled mischievously. "So, you don't know everything. Here's a neat fact about your favorite restaurant: It opened as a speakeasy during Prohibition, founded by Helen Gallagher, a former Ziegfeld girl, and gambler Jack Solomon. During those secret-drinking days, patrons would order 'the other soup' as a code phrase—and receive a soup cup filled with liquor.

"After Prohibition ended, Gallagher's transitioned into one of Broadway's first steakhouses.

From illicit beginnings to an enduring culinary icon, its roots remain part of its legend."

Shane laughed. "The crazy stuff you come up with, Valentina Lopez. I think that's why I married you."

For the first time, Shane felt truly relaxed. The weight of the world was no longer resting solely on his shoulders.

54

ZURICH

SWITZERLAND

The rain over Zurich fell as a thin, persistent drizzle, blurring reflections in the Limmat River and dulling the city's sharp lines. From Helvex's executive headquarters, Claudine Dubois stood by the window, arms crossed, watching the umbrellas drift by below.

She had arrived without an appointment, walking straight past reception and ignoring the startled assistant's protests as she pushed through the glass doors of the corner office. Hans Egli was on the phone, his back to her. He didn't turn immediately; instead, he lifted a finger as a casual acknowledgment, the arrogance of a man accustomed to controlling time itself. When he finally ended the call, he pivoted slowly.

"Claudine," he said, his voice smooth as lacquer. "To what do I owe the pleasure?"

Her eyes flashed angrily. "Pleasure, Hans? You must be joking. You knew."

He blinked. "Knew what?"

"Don't play games with me," she snapped. "You knew all along that the Chinese were behind Helvex. That the so-called 'Swiss' bank was merely a puppet for Zhonghua Capital. And you didn't tell me."

Egli's lips curved into the faintest of smiles. "You didn't need to know. Nobody was ever meant to know. But that egomaniac Nadler couldn't help leaving a paper trail—more accurately, a digital trail—of his accomplishments. Some ghost! But it doesn't affect you."

Her voice rose with indignation. "I didn't need to know? I am your counsel, Hans! You don't get to decide what I need to know. I've built my reputation on winning impossible cases and controlling every variable. You've made me a pawn in your little geopolitical charade. Now I have to defend the Chinese in a U.S. RICO case," she spat the last word as if it were poison, "a case that names Zhonghua Capital as a co-defendant. Do you understand what that means? I choose my clients, Hans. I didn't choose treason."

"Treason?" He laughed softly. "No, my dear. Treason requires loyalty to something greater than yourself."

Claudine no longer tried to control her fury. "Do you know what I gave up for Helvex? I turned down seats in Parliament and the Federal Council. I could have been Switzerland's president. But I moved to the private sector because I believed in what we were building—an institution that stood above politics. And now you tell me it was all an illusion."

Dubois exhaled sharply and turned away, pacing back toward the window. Her reflection stared back at her, trembling.

"I've had enough," she finally said. "I'm finished. I'm firing you as a client."

Egli chuckled, a low, humorless sound. "You can't fire me, Claudine."

Her eyes narrowed. "Watch me."

"No," he said, rising slowly. "You don't understand. You can't fire me—because you've already been terminated."

He walked around his desk. "You know those Chinese masters you seem to have no time for? They ordered me to let you go. They don't trust you anymore. Frankly, I can't blame them."

"You're bluffing," she said.

Egli smiled thinly. "Am I? After your pathetic performance in Zurich, why would anyone in this town—or anywhere else, for that matter—

still want to be associated with the *great* Claudine Dubois?"

He moved closer, savoring the moment. "No one forgets the woman who lost to a whistleblower and a ragtag team of American lawyers. You've gone from being the queen of Swiss litigation to the face of defeat."

He paused. "I may be done, Claudine, but so are you."

For a long time, neither spoke. The rain tapped faintly against the glass. Dubois's expression was unreadable. Slowly, she reached for her bag and drew out a thick leather folder—her copy of the Helvex file. She placed it on the desk between them.

"So, this is how it ends," she said quietly. "You'll let the Chinese run your bank. You'll sell out your country's legacy for a seat at their table. Tell me, Hans—when they're done with you, do you think they'll still call you CEO, or just another Western dupe?"

His jaw tightened. "Careful."

"No," she replied, her voice suddenly calm. "You be careful. Because when this all comes crashing down, and it will, I'll be the one testifying."

Egli's smile returned, but his eyes were cold. "You overestimate your importance. They don't need to ruin you, Claudine. You've already done that yourself."

He walked up behind her and whispered in her ear, "You were brilliant once, but brilliance fades when pride blinds you. You thought you could dance with wolves and remain untouched."

* * *

Down on Bahnhofstrasse, Dubois stepped into the fading light. The rain had left the cobblestones slick. She pulled her coat tight and walked toward Paradeplatz, where the cafés were filling with the after-work crowd. The world continued as usual—orderly, precise, indifferent.

She felt strangely weightless, as though something enormous had finally broken free inside her.

55

NEW YORK CITY
NEW YORK

UNITED STATES OF AMERICA

Months of testimony, weeks of cross-examination, and countless late nights had led to this moment. Following four days of deliberation, the jury sent notice it had reached a verdict. Shane reflected on how fitting it was to be ending here, in the Moynihan building. The famous senator's signature line, "Everyone is entitled to his own opinion, but not his own facts," still resonated in a building where fact-finding was paramount.

Every seat was occupied—by reporters, regulators, Wall Street analysts, and a gallery of curious foreign diplomats. At the government's table sat Shane, flanked by Val, Ollie, and Hendrix.

Across the aisle, the once-invincible fortress of Helvex had crumbled. Dr. Fabian Mettler, the Swiss attorney flown in at the last minute to replace Claudine Dubois, joined Zhao Wenhai at the defense table. Both had a sense of what was coming. Dubois had walked out weeks earlier, unable—or unwilling—to face the mounting disgrace. Her exit sent shockwaves through Zurich's legal community.

At the far end of the defense table sat Egli, his once-proud face ashen, his eyes hollow from months of humiliation. His empire was gone, his wealth frozen, and his Chinese masters unreachable.

Judge Eleanor Markham entered from her chambers, her black robe flowing behind her as the bailiff called out:

"All rise. The United States District Court for the Southern District of New York is now in session, the Honorable Judge Eleanor Markham presiding."

The room rose to its feet. The judge took her seat, nodding to the bailiff.

"Please be seated."

Judge Markham's gaze fell to the twelve men and women in the jury box. "Members of the jury," she began evenly, "have you reached a verdict?"

The jury foreman, a middle-aged man in a gray suit, stood. His hands trembled slightly as he held a folded note.

"We have, Your Honor."

A clerk approached, took the note, and delivered it to the bench. Markham unfolded the paper, reading its contents in silence. Then she nodded and looked up.

"Mr. Foreman," she said, her voice steady, "will you please rise?"

He did.

"We have two defendants, so on each charge, I would like you to respond first with respect to Zhonghua Capital Holdings Company, Limited, and then with respect to Helvex Financial Aktiengesellschaft. Understood?"

The foreman nodded.

"Very well, how do you find the defendants on Count One, racketeering in violation of Title 18 of the United States Code, Sections 1962(c) and (d)?"

The foreman's voice was clear, though his Adam's apple bobbed once before he spoke.

"Guilty and guilty, Your Honor."

A rustle moved through the gallery.

Judge Markham continued.

"On Count Two, willful market manipulation resulting in financial destabilization?"

"Guilty and guilty."

A flicker of expression crossed Shane's face. Val's hands clenched around her pen. Across the aisle, Hans Egli shifted in his chair, jaw tight, eyes forward.

"On Count Three, cyber intrusion and unauthorized access to U.S. financial infrastructure?"

"Guilty and guilty."

"On Count Four, acting as an agent of a foreign power in a conspiracy to defraud the United States?"

"Guilty and guilty."

Markham continued methodically down the list to the eighth and final count. Each count carried its own echo. All guilty. Eight for eight.

For a moment, silence reigned. Then came a collective intake of breath, followed by muffled murmurs from the gallery.

Judge Markham raised her hand. "*Order.* Order in the court."

The whispers died.

She turned once more to the jurors. "Members of the jury, the Court thanks you for your service in this matter. Your duty has been long and your responsibility great. You have fulfilled it with diligence and honor. You are now formally discharged."

A few jurors exchanged weary, relieved smiles. One woman dabbed her eyes.

"You are free to speak about your experience," Markham continued, "though the Court reminds you that discretion remains the better part of valor when justice itself has been tested."

She paused, letting that settle. "The Court will now proceed to sentencing. Before I do that, I see we have a new face this morning. I did receive the notice of change of counsel; thank you. I suspect, Dr. Mettler, that you have even less history with this case than your colleague, Mr. Zhao. I mention this only because prior counsel, Ms. Dubois, emphasized this during the opening statements. Since we are at the sentencing stage, I trust that this last-minute change will not give rise to any claims of unfairness. I want your assurance on that."

Mettler stood. "Yes, your Honor. You have my word, on behalf of my client, that the change of counsel prior to the decision being made will not be grounds for any appeal from Helvex."

"Thank you, Dr. Mettler. Mr. Zhao, can I have a similar assurance from Zhonghua Capital?"

Zhao rose slowly. "While this change of counsel has nothing to do with my client, I can also assure the Court that it will not form any grounds for an appeal from Zhonghua Capital."

"Thank you, Mr. Zhao. The court appreciates your cooperation."

Shane leaned over and whispered to Val, "She's dotting her i's and crossing her t's. She wants this decision to be bulletproof.

Markham adjusted her glasses and scanned the room. "This case has revealed one of the most elaborate financial conspiracies in modern history."

She paused, glancing toward Egli, who did not look up. "The defendants weaponized finance—an act akin to economic warfare. In light of the global nature of the offenses, the extensive damages caused, and the willful attempt to destabilize the U.S. financial system, this court orders the following."

The room fell still.

"One—all Zhonghua Capital and Helvex assets within the reach of the United States government—including, but not limited to, funds, securities, and property—are hereby seized and declared property of the United States.

"Two—all cash assets are to be immediately transferred to the U.S. Department of the Treasury.

"Three—all non-liquid assets are to be sold through court-appointed receivers, with the proceeds likewise remitted to the Treasury."

A collective murmur rose before she raised her hand for silence.

"Four—Zhonghua Capital Holdings, its subsidiaries, and its principals are permanently barred from conducting business in the United States, directly or indirectly, including participation in any U.S. or U.S.-regulated financial markets.

"Five—Helvex Financial, its subsidiaries, and its principals are similarly barred."

Shane exchanged a glance with Hendrix. The magnitude of the ruling was sinking in.

"Six—in addition to the asset seizure, the court imposes a monetary penalty of $150 billion against the defendants, jointly and severally."

Judge Markham turned, fixing her gaze on Egli. "As for you, Mr. Hans Egli—your role in directing and implementing these operations is well documented. The evidence demonstrates not only complicity but leadership in a conspiracy to manipulate international markets, fix prices, and enable hostile foreign interests. You are sentenced to fifty years in federal custody, without the possibility of parole."

The color drained from Egli's face. He was sixty-three years old.

Mettler leaned in to whisper, but Egli didn't move.

"That concludes the Court's judgment," Markham said, closing the leather-bound docket before her.

Mettler's eyes flashed. He rose to address the bench. "Your Honor," he said firmly, "we reserve the right to appeal—"

"You may file your appeal, Dr. Mettler," Markam replied curtly. "However, it will not stay the execution of this judgment."

Markham struck the gavel.

For a moment, no one moved. Then the gallery erupted—reporters whispering fiercely, phones lighting up, headlines being drafted.

At the plaintiff's table, Hendrix exhaled deeply, his fingers steepled in silent thanks.

Across the aisle, Egli was being led away by U.S. Marshals, wrists bound. For a moment, his gaze locked with Shane's—hatred and humiliation blazing behind his eyes. Shane met it calmly.

"Game over," he whispered.

As Egli disappeared through the side door, Mettler gathered his papers with mechanical precision, muttering to himself. Shane could almost hear the words: *Unglaublich* (Unbelievable).

* * *

Outside, Shane and the LawForce team paused on the courthouse steps, greeted by a storm of microphones and flashing lights. Hendrix raised a hand.

"No statements today," he said firmly. "Justice has spoken."

Fabian Mettler emerged from the courthouse, flanked by two assistants. Reporters turned to him.

"Dr. Mettler, any comment?"

He paused, his English crisp and emotionless. "Helvex will appeal. We believe a gross miscarriage of justice occurred here today. Thank you."

Spotting Zhao exiting the building, a reporter rushed over. "Mr. Zhao, any comment?"

Zhao blinked at the lights. "This case was politically motivated. Despite the soaring rhetoric from opposing counsel about justice and fairness, this is a blatant attack on China. The United States clearly fears the rising financial power of the People's Republic and seeks to weaken it through its judicial system."

One reporter yelled out, "Will China retaliate? If so, how?"

Zhao gave a wry smile. "It is not only Chinese companies that operate in the United States; the reverse is also true. We have always treated your companies with fairness and respect. I fear that may be about to change."

He turned sharply and walked away.

* * *

Hours later, the LawForce team regrouped in their Manhattan office. Hendrix poured a round of coffee from a dented steel pot. "To the end of Helvex," he said.

Shane raised his cup. "And the beginning of something better."

Val, ever the realist, countered softly, "Better for a while, maybe. But there will always be another Helvex."

"Then we'll always be employed," Shane replied.

Ollie grinned. "And that's a good thing."

They all laughed.

* * *

Later, as night descended over the city, Shane lingered at the window alone. The courthouse below was now dark, save for the floodlit flag that still fluttered faintly in the wind.

He thought of Marcus Patel, of the price paid in blood to reach this day. He thought of Regula Rivella, whose courage had sparked a chain of events. And he unexpectedly thought of Claudine Dubois, brilliant yet damned, who had vanished into exile somewhere in Geneva.

Val approached quietly. "We should get back to the hotel. You need some sleep," she said.

Shane shook his head. "Not yet. I keep thinking—fifty years for Egli. But the ones in Beijing... they'll sleep in silk tonight."

Val touched his shoulder. "Maybe. But tonight the world knows. That has to count for something."

* * *

By dawn, the verdict had spread around the globe.

In Washington, the Treasury Department issued a statement confirming that the seized Helvex assets were already being processed into federal accounts.

In Zurich, the Swiss press lamented the fall of "a once-great institution undone by greed."

And in Beijing, behind closed doors at Zhonghua Capital's headquarters, there was silence—cold, calculating silence.

The *South China Morning Post* headline read:

Zhonghua Capital Found Guilty in U.S. Court—Historic Judgment Against Chinese State Enterprise

Markets trembled. The yuan slipped. But inside the U.S. Department of Justice, champagne corks popped.

56

YANQI LAKE

CHINA

Within the conference pavilion—where Project DragonBreath had been conceived—Chairman Liang Ze sat at the head of a long, lacquered table, flanked by his remaining inner circle.

A single red folder lay before him, its cover embossed with the gold characters — **Project DragonBreath Final Report**.

No one spoke. Only when Liang opened the folder and read the first line did he exhale slowly and deliberately. "Project DragonBreath did not go well."

Around the table, aides avoided his gaze. Minister Hu Ren, his national security adviser, shifted uncomfortably. General Chang Jun, commander of the PLA's Strategic Cyber Division, cleared his throat but remained silent. Finally, the chairman closed the folder, folded his hands, and looked toward the window.

"The Western court has spoken," Liang said. "The assets of Zhonghua Capital and Helvex Financial have been seized—Zhonghua Capital has been named and shamed. And our agent—" he paused, "—the Ghost—is dead." His tone carried neither anger nor surprise, only fatigue. "Thus ends our dragon's breath."

No one dared to respond.

Liang's gaze shifted to the empty chair at the far end—the seat once occupied by Gao Feng. "He chose the honorable exit," Liang murmured. "At least he understood shame."

General Chang nodded. "A necessary cleansing, Chairman. He failed the Motherland."

Liang waved the comment aside. "Failure is not what concerns me, Comrade Jun. Failure is temporary. What troubles me is exposure. The Americans now know about DragonBreath. Their so-called 'LawForce' has unmasked us."

Minister Hu finally spoke. "With all due respect, Chairman, the Western press will eventually lose interest. Their attention span is short. They will turn to new scandals, new elections, new wars."

Liang's mouth tightened—almost into a smile. "That, Comrade Ren, is precisely why we will prevail in the long run."

He rose and strolled toward the wide window overlooking the lake. Beyond it, the autumn trees burned red and gold against the gray mountains of Huairou. "The Americans think in seasons; we think in dynasties. They rotate leaders every few years—presidents every four, senators every six, members of Congress every two. And with the president subject to a two-term limit, they make him a lame duck from the start. Everyone knows his shelf life."

Liang shook his head in disgust. "Their government is a house of cards propped up by opinion polls. Ours," he tapped a finger on his chest, "is built on centuries of continuity."

He turned back to them, his eyes bright. "They celebrate change. We cultivate endurance. And endurance wins every contest."

The words hung in the air.

Hu ventured cautiously, "Then you do not view this as a defeat?"

Liang's laugh was low. "Defeat? No. Just a pause. Even dragons sleep between storms." He resumed his seat and poured himself a small glass of Maotai, its sharp, medicinal fumes filling the air. "We lost a battle. But history is not written in battles; it is written in patience."

He raised the glass slightly toward the others. "To patience." They murmured their assent and drank, though none dared to match the Chairman's measured calm.

After a moment, Liang gestured toward the folder. "The Americans think they have triumphed. They celebrate their RICO prosecutions as if they have slain a beast. But tell me—what has truly changed? Western markets still crave liquidity. Their banks still depend on Chinese capital. Their supply chains still run through our factories, and their debts still run through our bonds. They have cut one head from the dragon, but they forget that dragons are creatures of renewal."

General Chang leaned forward. "So, we rebuild?"

Liang nodded. "In time. Quietly. Not with Swiss fronts or Western proxies. The next architecture will be born here, under our full control. The West will invite it again—greed always opens the gate."

A faint chuckle rippled through the room. Even in loss, the vision of eventual dominance held its own intoxicating pull.

Hu opened a tablet and scrolled through the summary report. "Chairman, what about Helvex's former directors? Shall we silence them?"

"No," Liang replied. "Let them talk. The more they protest their innocence, the guiltier they will appear to the West. The Americans love scandal—let them feed on it."

He looked back at the lake, where the mirrored hotel reflected the faint outline of the Chinese flag above its roofline. "They think exposure weakens us. It does not. It purifies us. It reminds us that our destiny cannot depend on foreigners, not even Swiss intermediaries."

There was a pause as aides took notes.

"Chairman," General Chang asked carefully, "shall we reconstitute the cyber division's foreign operations?"

"In time," Liang replied. "For now, we observe. Let the West fight its own shadow. Inflation, debt, elections, social unrest—these are more powerful weapons than any virus or hack. We will not need to destroy them. They will destroy themselves."

He drained the glass of Maotai and placed it upside down on the table, a deliberate gesture of closure. "Project DragonBreath is concluded."

The room remained silent. Finally, Hu asked, "Chairman, what about our message to the Central Committee?"

Liang took a pen and wrote in the margin of the report:—**ended between honor and shame**. Suitably contradictory. He handed the page to Hu. "Tell them the dragon rests. And when it wakes, it will breathe fire again."

He looked toward the door. "Now leave me."

The officers filed out. The door closed with a soft click, leaving Liang alone with the panoramic view of Yanqi Lake.

He stood for a long time, hands clasped behind his back. He allowed himself a single sigh as he turned toward the portrait of Mao on the far wall, framed in gold. "Do not despair, Great Helmsman; the empire is not dead; it merely sleeps."

57

WASHINGTON
DISTRICT OF COLUMBIA

UNITED STATES OF AMERICA

The flag stood centered behind the Resolute Desk, its folds pressed and illuminated from above. He sat behind the desk, hands clasped in front of him, staring straight into the camera.

"My fellow Americans and citizens of the world. Tonight, I address you not merely as your president, but as a steward of the international order that has maintained peace and prosperity for more than eighty years. That system has come under attack—not with tanks or missiles, but with keyboards and code. It is a conflict not over territory, but over trust."

He paused, allowing the words to linger.

"For generations, America's strength has rested not only on our power, but on the confidence the world places in a simple truth—that our markets are open, our institutions honest, and our laws sacred. That trust has been tested before. But never has it been tested as profoundly as it has been in recent months."

He straightened, narrowing his eyes slightly.

"A plot was uncovered. A coordinated attempt to bring down the Western financial system. This operation—conceived by foreign actors, executed through Swiss banking proxies, and directed by elements within the Chinese state—sought to destroy confidence in our banking institutions, ignite panic, and seize control of the global economic order.

"Through malware, misinformation, and market manipulation, they came perilously close to success. The goal was not profit, but dominance—to replace the free world's trust in open markets with fear, dependency, and control."

A brief pause followed, just long enough for the audience to imagine the consequences of what might have been.

"But they were stopped by a group of lawyers, technologists, and investigators working under the banner of LawForce."

He looked down for a moment, before returning his gaze to the teleprompter.

"Yes, LawForce—the same organization that came under heavy scrutiny from our own Senate and the press mere months ago. We bear some responsibility for that. But the truth has a way of emerging."

The camera slowly zoomed in as his tone shifted from admonition to determination.

"Tonight, the United States stands resolute. The Department of Justice, acting under the RICO statute, has held the Chinese actors accountable for their crimes. Their assets have been seized, their influence dismantled, and their leader convicted.

"This is not an attack on the Chinese people. It is a stand against those who weaponize economic systems for control, against those who exploit openness to undermine the very freedoms that sustain global prosperity."

Behind him, the faint ticking of the Oval Office clock punctuated his words.

"But let me be clear—this is not just an American victory. This is a defense of every honest trader in London, every banker in Frankfurt, every investor in Tokyo. This is a defense of integrity itself.

"The threat we face is not confined by borders or language. The Internet knows no boundaries; cyberwarfare respects no sovereignty. A keystroke in one hemisphere can erase fortunes in another. And so, no nation—no matter how powerful—can stand alone in this fight."

He lifted a folder from the desk—a symbolic prop embossed with the Great Seal of the United States.

"That is why, tonight, I am calling on all nations—our allies and our rivals—to join us in forging a new Alliance for Financial Integrity. Its mission: to defend the arteries of the global economy from the toxins of corruption, theft, and digital sabotage.

"Together, we will build new safeguards.

"We will share intelligence across borders.

"We will hold every nation to the same standard of transparency, accountability, and truth.

"Those who question our resolve do so at their peril."

The president's voice softened.

"When I was a young man, I read the preamble to our Constitution and was struck by its first three words—'We the People.' It didn't say 'We the Government' or 'We the Powerful.' It said 'We the People.' Because in a democracy, power is not inherited; it is entrusted. And trust is what was almost destroyed here.

"We do not seek confrontation. We seek cooperation rooted in respect and reciprocity. However, if you exploit our openness, you will face consequences. If you weaponize our trust, you will lose it. And if you undermine our systems, you will have to answer for it."

He reached forward, resting both hands on the desk.

"To our friends in Europe, in Asia, in Africa, and beyond—I say this: the pursuit of prosperity must never come at the expense of trust. The free exchange of goods and ideas depends on the integrity of those who move them.

"To the government of China, I say: your nation has the talent, the intellect, and the history to lead through innovation, not subversion. The world welcomes your participation in fair competition—but it will not tolerate digital warfare masquerading as commerce.

"And to the American people: our vigilance must not wane. The enemies of freedom are patient. They study us. They probe our weaknesses. But our greatest strength has always been our unity.

"From the courtroom in New York where justice was served, to the Treasury monitors tracking illicit funds, to the engineers hardening our systems tonight—the message is the same: democracy is not fragile. It is fortified by those who defend it."

His tone hardened slightly.

"We will invest in cybersecurity the way previous generations invested in steel and ships. We will train a new generation of defenders—not with rifles, but with firewalls and code.

"We will ensure that every transaction, every transfer, every digital bridge that connects our global economy is guarded by law, by ethics, and by truth.

"The story of LawForce is not one of vengeance—it is one of vigilance. It reminds us that courage can still bend the arc of history toward justice, even when the battlefront is invisible."

He looked directly into the camera.

"And so, let this be remembered not as the day we won a single case, but as the day we reaffirmed our collective promise—to one another and to the generations that follow—that honor, not deceit, will govern the marketplace of nations.

"Thank you and good night. May God bless you, and may God bless the United States of America."

As the camera light faded to amber, the president exhaled. His chief of staff stepped into the room.

"Sir," he said softly, "that was... exceptional."

The president looked out through the Oval Office windows toward the South Lawn, where the Washington Monument glimmered in the distance.

"Let's hope they were listening."

58

WENGEN

SWITZERLAND

The mountains surrounding Wengen were dusted with early snow, the high ridges of the Jungfrau and Silberhorn catching the last amber light—Abendrot—of late afternoon. In the valley below, cowbells chimed faintly. The sound drifted upward through the open window of Chalet Bergkristall, where the autumn air carried the scent of pine and distant wood smoke.

At the Eckbank, Shane sat with Val, two cups of coffee between them, steam rising in thin, silver threads. Papers from Zurich, Washington, and New York lay stacked nearby, but neither had touched them all day. The case—the

RICO verdict, the sanctions, the unraveling of Project DragonBreath—was finished. For the first time in months, there were no calls to take, no filings to review, and no crises demanding attention.

Just silence. And the mountains.

"Strange, isn't it?" Val said softly, staring out toward the Jungfrau. "How something so big, so world-shaking, just stops. One moment it's consuming everything, and the next..." She gestured toward the peaks. "It's gone. Into the mist."

Shane smiled faintly. "That's justice for you. The fight feels endless, and the peace is fleeting."

She turned to him, catching the shadow of weariness behind his eyes. "You did it, Steve. You took on the dragon and walked away with the world still standing. You should feel proud."

He sipped his coffee, thoughtful. "Pride's a dangerous thing, Val. I'm just grateful it's over. For now."

Outside, the distant sound of a cowbell grew louder. Then came a child's voice—high, excited, and full of wonder.

"Daddy! They're coming down tomorrow! The cows are coming!"

Shane looked up to see Cody bounding in the doorway, his cheeks flushed from the cold, and his small hands clutching a carved wooden cow they had bought from the village shop.

"They're coming down from the high pastures!" Cody declared, his words tumbling out. "Ruedi said they'll have flowers, bells, and ribbons! Real bells, Daddy! Not like this one." He shook his toy for emphasis, the little bell tinkling.

Val smiled, brushing his hair back. "Yes, sweetheart. Tomorrow's the Alpabfahrt, the big parade. You'll see all the cows come down for winter."

Cody's eyes widened. "Do they walk all the way down from the clouds?"

Shane laughed. "Just about. They're Swiss cows—they can do anything."

Cody nodded solemnly. "They're not like the Texas cows, huh?"

"No," Shane said, pretending to ponder it. "Swiss cows don't have those long horns. But they're friendlier, and smarter too. They know when it's time to head home."

Satisfied with that wisdom, Cody clambered into his father's lap, his little legs swinging. He leaned against Shane's chest, while Val watched them with quiet amusement.

"See, Steve?" she said softly. "He's got it figured out. Life's simple when you don't complicate it."

Shane rested his chin lightly on his son's head. "Yeah," he murmured. "I think Cody's got the right idea."

For a while, they sat in easy silence. The bells from below grew louder as herders guided small groups of cows through the meadows toward the village.

Shane's thoughts drifted to Zurich, where the judges had rendered their verdict. To New York, where the final order had come down. To Bern, where the Ghost had met his end. And to Wengen, here, where all roads—legal, moral, and personal—seemed to converge. And to a grizzled old coder who loved to quote verse.

Val watched him. "You're thinking about Marcus again, aren't you?"

He nodded slowly. "I can't help it. It seems like just yesterday he came padding out of that bedroom looking for coffee." Shane gestured at the guest bedroom. "Every victory feels smaller without him. He should've been part of this."

"He is," Val said gently. "Every line of code he wrote. Every firewall that held. Every document you used in court. He's here, Steve, just not in the way we hoped."

Cody had dozed off against Shane's shoulder, the small wooden cow still clutched in his hand. Shane shifted carefully to avoid waking him.

The faint murmur of voices carried up from the pathway below. Tourists and villagers gathered in the evening, and the smell of raclette and fondue wafted up into the cool air.

Val rose to fetch a blanket and draped it over Cody. "You know," she said, "the Swiss have it right. They celebrate endings as much as beginnings. Bringing the cows down from the Alps is a way of saying, 'We made it through another season.'"

Shane smiled faintly. "A good reminder for us, too."

"Exactly."

He looked toward the distant ridgeline, where the sharp peaks of the Lobhörner glowed rose-gold against the deepening blue sky. Somewhere, a church bell began to toll.

"Do you think it's really over?" Val asked quietly.

Shane considered the question. "For now," he replied. "But peace isn't permanent. It's borrowed time. The Chinese will regroup. There'll be another plan, another scheme. There always is."

They watched the sky fade to twilight. Below, the last of the herders guided their cattle into barns, the bells now muffled. The stars began to appear—first one, then a dozen, and soon a thousand more.

Shane looked at the lights in the Lauterbrunnen Valley flickering far below. "There's something about these mountains," he said quietly. "They don't care who wins or loses. They... endure."

"Kind of like justice," Val said.

He smiled. "Kind of like Cody's cows."

Val laughed softly.

For a long moment, neither spoke. Then Val turned toward him, her voice a whisper. "You know, I think we've earned tomorrow."

Shane looked down at his sleeping son, his small chest rising and falling in perfect rhythm. "Yeah," he said softly. "Tomorrow's for him."

* * *

The next morning, the streets of Wengen filled with laughter, music, and the resonant clang of cowbells. Children ran ahead of the herd, waving wildflowers. The cows, draped in garlands of alpine blooms and crowned with brass bells, clopped proudly through the cobblestoned streets.

Shane stood with Val and Cody on the curb, sunlight warm on their faces. Cody waved at every passing cow, his grin wide and innocent.

"Look, Daddy! That one's smiling!" Cody exclaimed.

Shane laughed. "So she is."

Val squeezed his hand. "See? All is well in his world."

Shane nodded, his eyes following the cows as they disappeared up the lane. "Maybe," he said softly, "that's the secret. Don't fight every storm. Just wait for the parade."

BENDING THE ARC

**"The arc of the moral universe is long,
but it bends toward justice."**

Martin Luther King, Jr.

Jonathan Hendrix, one of the youngest U.S. Attorneys General in history, knows that bending the arc won't happen on its own, help is needed. He is determined to curb runaway civil jury awards that are threatening to destabilize the economy.

Graduating law school, Steve Shane is a top wall street prospect. Shunning the big firms, he sets up his own practice and six years later has developed a solid reputation as a commercial litigator.

Hendrix recruits Shane to create *LawForce*, a government-supported, legal SWAT team to be deployed in key cases where an inequality of counsel threatens bad verdicts. Their first case – *Green Action Coalition v. Wildcat Oil & Gas*.

A medium sized oil and gas company, Wildcat is plagued by an apparently random series of environmental accidents. Not accidents according to the Green Action Coalition, a leader in the new era of aggressive environmental litigation, but evidence of a pattern of negligence. The damages sought by the GAC have the potential to destroy Wildcat. Acting for the GAC is a high-powered team of legal eagles from the blue-chip firm of Todd Ives Tillington, led by senior partner Andrew Tillington III. Wildcat appears hopelessly outclassed . . . then Shane is retained.

Shane and *LawForce* discover they are in for more than just a tough legal battle as they negotiate the twists and turns of the case to its explosive courtroom finale.